COGNITION

COGNITION

Jacques St-Malo

Ballista Press
2019

Cognition

Ballista Press

ISBN: 978-0-578441-07-8 (hardcover)
ISBN: 978-0-578446-29-5 (paperback)

Books > Mystery, Thriller &
Suspense > Thrillers > Technothrillers

Books > Mystery, Thriller & Suspense > Thrillers &
Suspense > Technothrillers

Books > Science Fiction & Fantasy > Science Fiction > Genetic Engineering

10 9 8 7 6 5 4 3 2

CONTENTS

Part Three: Will

PART ONE:
SENTIENCE

DESPAIR

> And when she could no longer hide him, she took for him an ark of bulrushes, and daubed it with slime and with pitch, and put the child therein; and she laid it in the flags by the river's brink.
>
> —EXODUS 2:3

The arrival of dawn brought no hope, nor did it herald any manner of reprieve. It merely bathed the desert sands in the deceptively soft, pinkish hue that had once led a Mycenaean poet to coin the world's first cliché. Beyond the vast windowpane, terraced gardens and a long fountain framed by flowerbeds stretched away towards a grove of palm trees. Behind it, the minarets of a mosque peeked over the palace walls, while in the distance a few lights dotted those portions of the valley that remained in the grip of twilight. The only movement on the grounds below was the sluggish gait of a gardener preparing for his daily chores. The scene, sleepy and restful, belied a world already falling to pieces over the horizon.

The town had so far managed to remain one of the rare corners of the world where palaces were still used as residences. But every institution that falls into disuse must perforce have one last instance, and this happened to be the place and time when monarchy, after centuries of decline, would finally become extinct.

It would not be without bloodshed.

A woman in her mid-twenties stood motionless in front of the window, holding a sleeping infant in her arms. Her eyes were lost in the distance, her stare desolate; her features haggard, sad, exquisite. The morning light poured into the room and through her nightgown, outlining a figure that would have aroused envy in women, desire in men, and disbelief in anyone who had ever given birth. She held the baby in a gentle, desperate embrace, as if she had found the child lifeless in its crib.

A soft knock came on the doorframe behind her.

"Your highness?"

Slowly, as if emerging from a trance, Anwaar turned around to face the maidservant she had summoned. "What news?" she asked.

"The eastern defenses have fallen," said the girl, barely a year younger than her mistress.

Strong, polished and resourceful—one of the few women in the realm with both a college education and full combat training—Nadia Karahan was the daughter of a Turkish woman who had served in the royal household and died young. She had lived in the royal family's shadow for longer than she could remember and had served the princess since the age of sixteen, first in Anwaar's retinue and then in her security detail, before becoming the newborn's nanny, a task undertaken of her own accord and with evident pleasure.

Anwaar once more let her gaze drift out the window. "So soon," she whispered. "They will be here before evening. And the King? Any chance of a truce?"

"None," said Nadia. "As Prince Nessim always says—I mean used to—oh, I'm so sorry…" She brought a hand to her brow and flushed deeply.

Her mistress ignored the gaffe and remained deep in thought, making up her mind. It hardly mattered whether her father-in-law capitulated or stubbornly fought to the death—that much had been clear since the war had begun. She turned back towards the girl, this time with fierce determination. "I have lost my husband," she said, "but I have no intention of losing my son."

"Of course not, but surely they wouldn't—"

"Yes they would!" snapped Anwaar. "It's him they are after, don't you see? They will kill him, or worse, unless we prevent it. Unless *you* help me..." Here she stopped, studying the young woman who stood deferentially before her, scrutinizing her expression, her lips, the blinking of her eyes, trying to find even the slightest hint of disloyalty, fully certain that she wouldn't. She had known the girl from childhood, and now that Anwaar's fairy-tale life had turned to dust Nadia was the closest thing she had to a friend.

"Your highness, I would give my life to protect him! You know that I can never bear children. To me he is like—"

Anwaar raised a hand in an instinctive gesture to stop the sentence from ending. For an instant she looked hurt, her eyes stinging with jealous tears held back by the will to appear dignified. Nadia was her son's only hope. Smart and handsome, she spoke fluent English and held a dual nationality, a critical asset in times of war: where others would be stopped, a Turkish passport would slip through. Anwaar's mind was made up. She placed a hand under the infant's head and carefully lowered him into the maid's arms. Stepping back deliberately, her fists clenched tightly and something snapped deep inside her like a broken spring. Still, she held firm.

"Listen, Nadia, listen carefully. Have you checked the bank account that I opened online in your name?"

The girl nodded once. "My wages were deposited punctually as you said."

"Yes, I wouldn't count on that after today. Anyway, it is domiciled so that no one can link it to me or to the royal purse. No one can touch it but you; no one but me knows that it even exists. Do you understand?" The young woman's eyes began to register fear. "Now," Anwaar continued, "I have made a deposit of a few million, in British currency. It's all I could gather, so you must make it last."

Nadia had heard the word *million* uttered often enough around the palace, but never in connection with her personal finances. She swallowed hard as she tried to grasp what was happening.

"A man called Jafar will pick you up in twenty minutes by the west entrance. You have seen him before and will recognize his face. He is trustworthy and owes me a favor—the life of his father, no less. He believes you had a child out of wedlock and will escort you to the northern border, posing as your husband. Once across you will fly alone to London."

She moved to a nearby desk and picked up a data chip, which she handed to Nadia. "I pulled some strings to obtain a birth record: you have officially given birth to a son and no one will question you. Neither Jafar nor anyone must be told that the child you carry is mine. Get up—get up!" Anwaar commanded, her voice rising from whisper to bark upon seeing Nadia fall to her knees, eyes wide with fright, her head shaking in helpless denial. At her mistress' insistence she rose, using only the strength in her legs to stand up, so as not to disturb the precious burden she carried. "When things settle down," said Anwaar, "I will join you. In the meantime, you must stay in England with my cousin Dhuka—you remember Dhuka, yes? She has been forewarned of your arrival. A young woman and her child, I told her; a friend of mine in exile. You must act the part and let them treat you as a guest."

"But," the maid entreated, "why don't we *all* leave?"

"You know why."

She did indeed. Anwaar was traceable. She bore an identity beacon just like everyone in the royal family, newborns excepted. If she had it removed, it would emit a warning. Besides, no princess could remain anonymous for long. But if Anwaar stayed behind, everyone would assume mother and child to be together. She must have them believe that, for his sake. Nadia knew that arguing was pointless, but still she tried, out of fear and out of the vanishing hope that an overlooked option might present itself.

"What if things don't settle down?" she protested. "What if they—if you are...?" She dared not complete the thought, but Anwaar was a step ahead, having worried about little else for days.

"If I am killed, you are to leave Dhuka's house and disappear—bring up the child as your own and never return here." Another person might have added *please,* but learning to entreat hadn't been part of Anwaar's upbringing. Instead, her eyes lost focus as she looked through Nadia into empty space. "I swear they will never capture me alive," she said defiantly. The young woman began objecting again but was cut short. "Leave now. Go!"

Trembling, Nadia back-stepped, hesitated and finally retreated. Anwaar made sure that she had left, walked across the room and quietly locked the door. Only then did she allow her mind to dissolve. Collapsing onto her bed, she dug her fingernails into the covers and, in one final act of sanity, managed to bury her face in a pillow as the first scream erupted from her lungs.

***

Not far from the main palace a young girl cowered against the wall of a mess hall. Shelling rocked the building to its foundation and a cloud of dust spewed out of a crack where the wall met the ceiling, coating the table and benches below with fine powder. The windows at the far end of the room lay in pieces on the floor. Still the structure held, and that explosion proved to be the last. Cautiously, Fatima removed the fingers she had been using to stop her ears, which rang with the high-pitched tinnitus familiar to veterans returning from the front. It seemed to come from inside her head and made her dizzy. Though she knew not how long it might last, she realized that her eardrums were intact, for she distinctly heard cries coming from a nearby courtyard. The wailing came not only from the women, but from men too. At thirteen she didn't understand the complexities of civil war, but if grown men were crying in terror it could only mean that the world was coming to an end.

She looked about her. Huddled nearby was Hamidah, the portly soft-spoken woman who was her surrogate mother. Further along the wall crouched two security guards from the royal staff, guns drawn. She knew them both well. The youngest she secretly admired: strong and dashing, his stern bearing concealed a generous heart and a witty sense of humor, which had often drawn a laugh—and a blush—from her. More than once she had felt a pang of jealousy when she caught him flirting with Nadia. The other guard she thoroughly disliked. An older woman would have recognized the sleazy, lewd stereotype, but Fatima merely knew that she didn't like the way he looked at her when no one was watching.

Like Nadia before her, Fatima had begun her training early under state tutelage. But while Nadia had been the upshot of happenstance, her clone was the product of choice, a decision by the royal family to beget themselves another Nadia. The two were sisters in name only. Hamidah had borne only Fatima—and this out of duty, although a maternal bond inevitably developed, which hadn't been discouraged. Nadia was the template and role model, but like other children born and bred for state purposes, she and Fatima had been raised apart. If her life had been austere and her childhood short, her lot was still meant to have been better than that of the average child in the kingdom.

But it was not to be. Fidgeting nervously, her fingers came into contact with the bracelet on her left wrist, a lovely bangle of sapphires and diamonds inlaid in platinum given to her by princess

Anwaar. Nadia had chosen it, Fatima knew, because Nadia could naturally tell what the girl would like. It was little things like that, more than their shared features, which made them alike. A thought lit up in her mind.

"Maybe Nadia will come," she whispered to Hamidah. "She will protect us."

The woman shook her head sadly. "She's gone. No, not dead," she clarified when Fatima's jaw dropped, "just gone—left this morning."

It is said that a little knowledge is a dangerous thing, and that is exactly what Fatima had been given. Her heart grew cold. For Nadia to forsake them—or the royal family—was beyond imagining. Hamidah must have misunderstood. Of course, people everywhere had been running away for days, but that was a cowardly act, one that Nadia couldn't possibly ... or could she?

Doubt began to fester in Fatima's mind as the yelling outside moved away from her vicinity and towards another part of the complex. Bursts of gunfire were heard, muffled by the concrete walls. The guards' bet had paid off as the building in which they hid was overlooked for the more attractive target of the central palace block. This meant they could sneak out through the back door of the compound. At a signal from the men, Hamidah stood up. She took Fatima by the hand and they all advanced towards the door that led to the kitchen. They scurried past ovens and counters, careful to avoid banging against any surface that might give them away. The older guard peeked out at the rear court: the coast was clear, so they made a dash for it. It was only thirty meters to the edge of the enclosure; they nearly made it.

The outer gate was closed, and although it took a mere five seconds to push back the bolt and slide the heavy door open, that was long enough for them to be spotted. The first to go down was the younger man, who held the rear. A burst of bullets hit the pavement a few feet to his right and traced an arc up into the gate, which rang out loudly with the impacts. Too late he turned to face their aggressors, and the rounds cut clean through his chest. Fatima, looking back, saw him fall without a sound before being nearly dragged off her feet by Hamidah's tug on her arm. Fatima couldn't believe how fast the plump woman could run.

The only exit route lay across the street, where two alleyways branched off, lined with storefronts and small buildings that might offer shelter. As they reached the far sidewalk the sound of sharp pelting reached her ears and Fatima saw a row of holes appear in the wall in front of her, showering plaster on the sidewalk. She kept running and began rounding the corner behind which the guard had disappeared. Then Hamidah's hand went limp in hers. Fatima stopped to look at the woman, who took a couple of inertial steps in the direction she'd been following, teetered for an instant, and crashed face-first onto the pavement. Her nose broke from the fall but she did not complain. Her eyes kept staring at the ground as a trickle of blood oozed from her half-open mouth.

"No! Noooooooooo!" Fatima shook her head vigorously, as if to dispel the stark reality she was witnessing. She stood there until an arm thrown around her waist lifted her into the air and carried her away from the spot.

"Let go! Put me down!" she yelled, to no avail.

They reached the front door of a private residence, unlocked and empty, obviously abandoned in a hurry. The guard dropped the girl and pulled her in behind him. "Now shut up," he said curtly, "or they will come and kill us."

Fatima quieted down, too overcome by shock to put up further protest. He led the way to the living quarters, which had a partial view of the administrative compound from which they had escaped, and of the palace walls further off. Entering what appeared to be the master bedroom he picked a chair and placed it in a spot safely away from the window but close enough to allow peering out while seated. He motioned Fatima to a nearby settee and pondered their situation. Those who had shot his colleague and Hamidah were unlikely to give pursuit for the time being. But the raid on the city raged unabated. An explosion sounded in the distance and smoke rose over the palace. That's it, he thought: there's no one left to defend. The man wasn't particularly bright, and the implications of this insight took a while to seep through his mind. By and by his eyes came to rest upon the uniform he wore and he sprang to his feet with renewed alarm. To be caught dressed like that meant certain death. Civilian clothes, he thought, there had to be clothes somewhere. "Stay here," he barked, and dashed into the dressing room to rummage through the owner's wardrobe. The first doors held women's dresses; he cursed aloud but was luckier on the second try.

Fatima sat with her knees curled up to her chin, shivering in the warm air, the realization dawning on her that she was friendless, homeless, and alone in an empty house with the person she distrusted most in the world. Why hadn't he been shot instead of Hamidah? And why had Nadia abandoned them all? Stunned beyond the point of tears, her eyes slowly took on the wild stare that betrays an imploding psyche.

The guard held out a shirt before him. The fit would be close enough. He then fetched a pair of trousers. Their owner had been overweight but it was nothing a belt wouldn't fix. Besides, he didn't want to appear too well dressed, for humble attire was held to be a virtue among the revolutionaries. He stripped to his underwear and held the trousers low, preparing to put his right leg in. That was the moment Fatima chose to bolt. She was able to tiptoe as far as the bedroom door without making a sound, but the bright daylight that poured through the window cast a shadow of her shape in his line of sight. He was upon her in an instant, pushing her brusquely back into the room. She tottered and tripped against the edge of the bed to fall heavily on the mattress.

"Do you want to die?" he demanded, eyes ablaze.

Fatima looked at him spitefully. "I don't care," she said, and tried to scurry away again. This time he grabbed her with both arms and hurled her back onto the bed, climbing on her and pinning her wrists to the cushions. "Are you out of your mind!?" he cried.

Indeed, at this point, she nearly was; but she needed one last shove to push her over the edge. This was readily provided, for as the man looked at her angry, pretty face and felt the tips of her budding breasts press through her gown against his chest, a familiar stirring awoke in him, and with it his second insight of the day. To be sure, his life was in grave danger, but with his master dead and the country in chaos, he no longer answered to anyone. Reaching down, he tore viciously at her garments. Fatima let out a scream, which was greeted by a crushing blow to the side of her head that left her dazed.

She was brought back by a different pain and the sight of the unthinkable being done to her. His hand covered her mouth, but her will to resist had drained away and she could only stare in horror at his devilish eyes, in which the usual slimy look was magnified a hundredfold in reptilian satisfaction. Nausea welled up in her as the man grunted loudly, the rhythm of his pleasure matching the cadence of her whimpers.

Suddenly his face disappeared in a flash of red that splashed warmly against her face. Fatima barely registered this new assault on her senses, but the resumed ringing in her ears told her a shot had been fired. The body fell forwards, the disgusting remains of the man's features landing on the crown of her head. She used what was left of her strength to squirm out from under the filth, barely in time for the contents of her stomach to burst forth onto the bedspread. When she looked up again someone had rolled the body off the bed and two militiawomen stood looking at her, assault weapons in hand and heads covered with black scarves. Freedom fighters, they called themselves. All guerrillas do.

"See for yourself the ways of apostasy," lectured the senior woman. "That's what they do to children." She left the room and returned with a damp towel and some clothes, which she handed to Fatima, who wiped herself off like an automaton, devoid of emotion.

"You are safe now," said the woman. "What is your name?"

"Fatima," was the numb reply, for the girl had drifted off to a faraway place from which she would never fully return.

"Come, then, Fatima. We will take care of you. Your wounds will heal and you shall learn the true way."

Fatima limped out after them. Over time, as foretold, her body healed. The injuries to her mind never would; but learn she did, and never had their leaders seen such an ardent pupil.

BIAS

> You have to think hard, in order to appreciate the geological scale… Imagine a plate spinning about six times around the whole world with a speed not much exceeding the rate at which our fingernails grow.
>
> —RICHARD FORTEY, *The Earth*

Baffled by the present and daunted by the future, it is to the past that we turn for answers, or at least for such comfort as can be drawn from smug contrasts with our forebears. Armed with the condescending wisdom of hindsight we survey bygone ages as if from a vantage, relieved to find their plainer beliefs, baser passions and crueler horrors easier to understand than today's ambiguity. But when applying new knowledge to old mysteries, a hunger for certainty makes us forget that our growing acumen is but a half-open eyelid in what has proved to be the longest of awakenings; that mankind's effort to improve its purchase on reality has followed an uphill course plagued by false summits. We plant the flag of conquerors on every hillock, letting the faint glow of our discoveries blind us to the darkness of our route. We succumb to hasty verdicts, much like medieval scholars spurned the belief that the Milky Way's origin could be traced to Hera's breast, only to have their devout cosmogonies dismissed in turn by industrial-age philosophers, and so on, in an endless process of revision and debunking, as if the fate of every society that ever laid claim to an ultimate truth were to be remembered more for its inherited delusions than for its hard-won insights.

Of all our rash judgments, few are as stubborn as our sense of change and permanence. It has long been known, if rarely emphasized enough, that a living being's view of reality reflects not just the creature's size and brain complexity, but its longevity as well.

If humans lived as mayflies do, for less than a day, then we would have no concept of winter, starlight, or dawn. If the moon happened to grace the sky during our fleeting lifetime, it might be called a disc or a shard, depending on the phase we happened to witness; but never crescent or waning, which imply the ephemeral. The leaves of trees would appear as timeless as the rocks on the ground and much of what people call the flow of the world would seem to stand still.

With a lifespan of decades, not hours, we still fall prey to our temporal horizon. When we gaze upon the sun as it disappears behind a cloud, we perceive only the transience of the vapor, never the aging of the furnace behind it. We are numb to the fluid nature of terrain, and build cities in the shadow of active volcanoes, in the middle of floodplains or astride crumbling fault lines. And when at some point in the past we first turned our attention to our kind, we readily discerned the change in human knowledge and beliefs, but failed to perceive the slower shift in inborn intellect, which we presumed to be a constant of history, as the palpable genius of the ancient Greeks appeared to attest.

But history spans only five thousand years, while hominids have walked the earth for millions. Long before the wheel and plough were invented, there was a time when self-awareness was truly budding on the planet; when every question ever answered had yet to be posed; when an unusually awake primate for the first time ever pondered its consciousness, only to be struck with the dizzying rush of loneliness that follows such musings. Time and time again this occurred in isolation, felt only by outliers of the species, until it became frequent enough to be shared by enough people that words were found for that state of mind and came to regard it as a permanent trait of humanity, as if self-awareness had always been around. And much as the rise and ebb of the tide was rightly attributed to heavenly bodies that were wrongly thought to be ageless, so was the fickleness of human behavior found to be driven by an underlying nature that was itself deemed immutable. But change it had; and change it would again; except that, for once, the change would not go unsung.

***

While the fall of the last monarch's regime was most lamented by his subjects, its ramifications extended far from the Middle East. The first took place in the eastern reaches of the Celebes Sea, a part of the world where islands number in the thousands.

From afar, this particular landmass seemed uninhabited; topped by a squat, long-extinct volcano and hugged by dense tropical foliage, its irregular coastline suggested little more than hidden coves and secluded beaches. Only when seen from above did it become apparent that halfway along the southern shore a tongue of sea protruded inland to form a lagoon, the far end of which bore unmistakable traces of civilization. Too large for a private villa, it might have been mistaken for a luxury resort. But while the scattered bungalows did play the part of hotel rooms and the large pavilion most definitely stood in for a restaurant, the similarities ended there. What looked like a conference complex actually housed a clinic, linked to a small but sophisticated research center. A state-of-the-art marina, a landing port, a modern power plant, a richly supplied warehouse and self-sufficient IT infrastructure, all added up to a high-tech community in the middle of paradise.

In a way, the facility was managed like a spa; in another, it was run like a medical laboratory, albeit one where researchers were conspicuously scarce. Most of the staff, locals from surrounding islands, had been hired as employees for administrative, technical and menial jobs, earning handsome wages in exchange for their discretion, devotion and diligence. Others, including a few medical doctors and the odd nurse or two, at first Chinese but later mostly Indonesian, worked under contracts that lasted from six months to a year—never long enough for them to learn the exact nature of the work they helped to carry out, which was ostensibly nothing but in-vitro fertilization procedures. That was how most people from certain circles chose to conceive anyway, and medical centers the world over competed to offer clients better deals and better odds at securing desired traits for their offspring.

In many countries, including China, the United States and most of Europe, the industry was heavily regulated. But local authorities had turned a blind eye to this remote clinic in exchange for contributions to various government programs, and the occasional inspection ensured that nothing 'indecent' took place, as it had on other islands leased to private parties. More thorough audits might have questioned the existence of lab animals in a facility meant for people; but their presence was justified as the best way to test innovative procedures approved for humans but the effectiveness of which was not guaranteed. The animals received proper care, which was good enough for the authorities as long as the kickbacks kept flowing.

Presiding over this establishment was a man called Xin Pei Cao, who looked like an oriental sage of yore—an affable, soft-mannered person with small twinkling eyes framed by copious wrinkles and a flowing white mustache that merged into a long beard. His origins were unknown to all around him; his aims understood only by Jianguo Zhang, the head physician and only permanent researcher in his staff, for whom Cao was a beacon of light in a world of darkness and repression. For several years they had lived undisturbed on the isle, first to set up the center and carry out their initial research, then to host and treat a steady stream of patients. But the hardliners now in office had proved to be nothing but trouble, so when Cao received the message from Jakarta he was worried but not surprised. He had been finishing breakfast with his guests—a young couple—when the warning came. It was brief: *They are onto you. Word has it they caved in to pressure from China. The cabinet is holding a closed-door meeting to decide on a course of action, but the military have been required. This link will soon be compromised, so you will receive nothing further from me.*

He sat back and took a deep breath. The bit about China troubled him more than the rest. It meant they had found out that Zhang was working with him, which the government could neither ignore nor forgive. The one remaining question was how much time, if any, they had left. Cao looked over his shoulder across the ocean. Nothing in the air seemed to warn of trouble ahead. There were literally no clouds on the horizon, and the morning promised to be glorious. He quickly made up his mind. Casually slipping the message back into the folds of his silky robe, he turned to the prospective parents. "There has been a development," he said. "Normally you would stay for another few days until we were sure that implantation has taken place. But someone has blown the whistle on me, so we must decamp at once."

The couple looked at each other but voiced no protest; it was a possibility they had foreseen. Throughout history people have gone to great lengths to satisfy deep-seated hopes, and the wish to have a child has led many to take risks compared to which this snag was a trifle. Infertility at the time had been largely resolved among the well-off, except in the rare instances when a woman's womb rejected an embryo. Even then, options were available that could often fix the problem. But for people of slender means fertility treatments were prohibitive, and the meager savings that might have otherwise secured critical traits for a child were instead spent on desperate attempts to conceive, with no guarantee of success. It was to such a group that this couple belonged, as had done all of Cao's visitors over the last year. Screened and for their worthiness as parents-to-be, they had also been selected for their willingness to overstep legal boundaries in exchange for the privilege of enjoying what most people took for granted.

Not much earlier Cao had hosted a different set of people, paying clients who had forked over huge amounts of money from which he had financed his venture. Ironically, what they had received in exchange for their contributions was far less than what he had bestowed on later customers such as the couple that now sat anxiously before him. "As far as you are concerned," he said, "nothing has changed. Your account has been credited with the sum I promised, which will give you a head start. Forget you were ever here, or that you ever heard of this place. As agreed, if anyone asks you must say you spent the whole time in Bali, on vacation. I had planned for you to fly back there, but this hitch forces our hand, so please go back to your room and be ready to leave in thirty minutes."

After the couple left the table Cao walked as quickly as his age allowed to the main building and apprised Zhang of the situation.

"This source of yours," Zhang asked, "are you sure he's trustworthy?"

"Yes, he risked his life by contacting me. You must leave at once. Use our toy and take the guests with you."

"You go", replied the other. "I can buy us time."

"That's insane! Do you have any idea what will happen to you if you are captured—if you are sent to Beijing?"

Zhang looked at him squarely. "The same that would happen to you, I suppose."

Cao dismissed the suggestion. "Nonsense, we can both leave. How quickly can you destroy the files?"

"At the touch of a button. But that's the easy part; the physical evidence could take all day."

"We don't have all day."

"And the live cultures? I must dispose of them."

"I can do that myself."

"There's also the equipment. We have to load it into—"

"Jianguo, listen, you have a life ahead of you; I don't. My work in this world is done. I'm proud of what I've accomplished, but it's over."

Zhang stepped forth to hold his teacher by the shoulders. "I have no family they can threaten, and all I can give them is recipes, which take time to implement. But if you are captured our whole effort will be wasted. Everything we've achieved—the lives of those children."

For the first time Cao was inclined to agree. Only he knew the names of the patients. In his original distrust of everyone, the old man had insisted on it, not foreseeing the implications. He muttered something under his breath and made a vain gesture of frustration.

"Leave with the patient," said Zhang. "I will load the equipment into the helicopter and follow shortly after."

"And the files—your research?"

"It's all in my head. If we get another chance I can rebuild it from scratch."

They both knew there would be no other chance. Still, Cao was forced to acquiesce. "How long will you be?" he asked.

"Two hours; maybe one."

Cao shook his head. Flying out was conspicuous, and to have Jianguo captured would be disastrous. But he couldn't wait any longer.

"Make sure you get rid of anything that might compromise the children—genetic profiles, tissue samples, whatever. Leave the hardware behind."

And so they parted.

Cao wore a headset that received live feed from the security camera above the research center. He saw the sunlight creep slowly up the mountain and over the village, but there was no unusual activity. It must have been an hour later that he caught sight of a van leaving the main complex and heading towards the landing port. He couldn't quite make out the details, but several boxes were being unloaded and transferred to a waiting helicopter. *Hurry*, he muttered under his breath.

Then he caught sight of something else: a small vessel entering the lagoon—a patrol boat, rapidly approaching shore. Cao bit his knuckles as the boat swung around in front of the marina, coming to rest against the mooring. Several men jumped out and trotted along the wharf. From their gait, Cao knew them to be armed.

The helicopter lifted off the platform, hovered in mid-air for a second, and plowed through the air away from the island. Already Cao knew it was too late. As it banked away over the jungle and towards the horizon, a streaking plume of vapor appeared over the hills and wound towards the aircraft at an astonishing speed. Upon contact both objects dissolved into an orange ball of flame.

"Jianguo!" he winced audibly, oblivious of the pilot beside him.

He slowly took off his viewer and looked over his shoulder at the passengers. The craft was a recreational vehicle, but not half as cramped as he had feared. The couple looked nervous, but bore it in silence. Cao glanced at the navigation display: they were slipping out of the jurisdiction of their pursuers, apparently undetected. The waters at the depth they were cruising were calm, and within a few hours they would reach their destination.

BLUNDER

Historical eras are never recognizable when they come into being; they can only be seen in hindsight.

—SUSAN WISE BAUER, *The History of the Renaissance World*

When germline manipulation first came of age it was greeted with uneven levels of enthusiasm across the globe. In reactionary climates and wherever fundamentalism held sway it was branded as anathema, while in countries that followed the moralizing precepts of the West it floundered under the waves of political correctness. But where legislation obeyed neither dogma nor pluralism it was seen as a chance to improve the local gene pool and jump ahead of other nations. Pursued with vigor, germinal-choice technology met at first with mixed results. Improved health (the first goal of state-sponsored engineering) proved to be relatively straightforward to achieve. The manifestations of brainpower, in contrast, turned out to be more elusive. This came as no surprise, since proof had always abounded that shared genes didn't lead to shared destiny: fingerprint ridges (structures far simpler than brain circuitry) had long been known to be unique even among monozygotic twins, which often failed to share blunt traits like schizophrenia or sexual preference. The likeness of clones was even less reliable, as separate gestations in different wombs led to greater divergence than natural twinning, while a myriad other factors that impinge on behavior proved impossible to control. Different environments, themselves the product of unlike histories, led supposedly identical children to different fates. Individuals born from early attempts to resurrect successful lives tended either to purposely avoid those occupations at which their former selves had excelled, or else became frustrated by the high standards set by their earlier incarnations. By definition, groundbreaking actions or ideas happen only once, and the key role played by serendipity became evident when intended replicas of historical figures dashed everyone's hopes under new settings. The vagaries of individual achievement, it soon became clear, held greater mysteries than a test tube could unravel.

Still, not all efforts went to waste, and mental abilities did evolve on average, granting pioneering countries an advantage until the rest of the world caught on to the trend, which of course was only the beginning. On its heels would follow sweeping changes of far broader consequence, as the early waves of disease screening and corrective changes slowly gave way to elective germline enhancement, where whole clusters of genes were inserted to bring about desirable features—aesthetic or functional—that chance might fail to produce. Involving merely the use of genes that had proved their worth historically, early dabblings paved the way for the design of altogether new molecules. And just as pacemakers and organ implants had done before, artificial chromosomes soon found their way into people's bodies … and into their brains.

There was a fair amount of doomsaying, but the world failed to become the dystopian nightmare that luddites had envisioned, for the temptation to equate genes with merit was curbed by a wealth of exceptions—every family had its failures, and seldom were the causes inborn. As had occurred with the earlier social experiment of formal education, germline engineering was soon made widely available to push civilization onward. But like schooling, its cost was high, its quality inconsistent and its prime varieties affordable only by those who could afford everything else. It would have been the perfect excuse for social discord, had people ever needed one. But unlike earlier rifts of social fabric, this one could be mended neither by reform nor by revolt, for the new privilege of being was more unassailable than the old advantage of possessing. The stage had been set for inequity on a scale without precedent and for the twilight of classical mankind, brought about not by its failure as a species, but by its very success.

***

Dragon motifs and all, the office décor managed to be opulent without being gaudy. At the head of a small conference table sat an irate man in his mid-sixties: Rear Admiral Feng couldn't believe his ears.

"What do you mean, disappeared? That's unacceptable. The Indonesians must be hiding something. Let's go through it again—slowly, this time. I want to know every detail."

Commodore Wei was visibly embarrassed, as if he had been personally responsible for the botched operation, which he hadn't even ordered, much less conducted. The admiral's words seemed to imply as much, and his unforgiving style had great effect on subordinates. There were others in the room besides him and Feng, but Wei would receive little sympathy—much less any help—from them. They were his close colleagues, which in a bureaucratic, competitive, populous China meant they were also his fiercest rivals.

"The raid," said Wei, "began at noon on Friday, exactly as foreseen by our local sources. Patrol boats had been surveying from a distance for 24 hours; no one was seen to leave, either by sea or by air. Reliable intelligence says that Cao should have been on the island, as well as Zhang. A dozen people—support staff—were found on the premises. They had seen Cao early that morning."

"What happened next?"

"At 11:02, a cruiser was stationed near the harbor's entrance, and an assault vehicle put eight men ashore. When they approached the complex a helicopter took off from the pad. They tried to contact it but it wouldn't acknowledge, so they shot it down. The pieces fell into the ocean, in full view of a patrol cruiser. Only one body was recovered from the wreckage: Zhang's."

"I presume the facilities were searched?"

Wei nodded. "Other people came ashore, including our informant. Not only the buildings, but the whole island was combed. Dogs were brought in and taken into the jungle and across the beaches, but didn't find him. They drove the search party back to Cao's house and just stood barking there. The house sits at the end of an overwater pontoon, and as I said, no boat was seen leaving the island, so unless he jumped into the sea Cao cannot have escaped."

"What about the lab?"

"All electronic evidence had been erased, samples disposed of, animals missing. They had obviously been forewarned."

Feng thumped the table with his fists in anger. "Leaks everywhere! They should have followed Zhang, not gunned him down. What of the detainees?"

"A technician, a nurse, two cooks, a gardener and a cleaning crew of four. They were questioned, but only confirmed what we already knew. Not surprisingly, the staff was rotated every few months. The nurse, however, recalled two Chinese medical assistants who stayed a bit longer. They left a month ago."

"Set up a hunt for them."

"Yes, sir."

Feng turned to another of his officers. "What have you found out about Zhang's activities in India?"

"He visited Bombay two years ago. We confirmed that he was seen in the company of Professor Saran—Saranja—"

"Sarangarajan," volunteered Feng, pronouncing the name perfectly and with ill-hidden condescension.

"Right," said his subordinate, silently cursing Indians in general for their long names and Admiral Feng for his language skills.

A knock was heard on the door and an adjutant poked his head in. The only female in the room—Commander Lin Mei Hsieh, who was apparently expecting some news—rose and went to the door. When she returned she looked pointedly at the admiral.

"I think we have the answer," she said.

As Feng looked up at her, his brow lost its furrows. At thirty, Commander Hsieh was a woman of steel, but also a woman of style, a fact that did not go unnoticed by Feng. Had he been a decade younger, he would have tried to have his way with her. But Feng had made his peace with such urges years earlier, so he contented himself with simply having her around. In so doing he had gradually come to realize that Hsieh was perhaps the ablest person in his staff, which only increased his self-satisfaction, as he believed that the establishment would one day give him credit for discovering her.

"We need a visual for this," she said to Feng, handing him a memory chip. He inserted it into a slot next to his seat and handed Hsieh a video controller. The wall on the far side of the room lit up and they all recognized a satellite image of the island.

"This is a daylight image of the scene. The dots highlighted by arrows are Indonesian cruisers. As you can see there are four altogether, including the one approaching to drop the squad on shore. Now, look at this patch of ocean to the north of the landmass. Nothing, right? But here's the same scene, in a different wavelength." She pressed a button and the image reappeared, colored in gradations of red, orange, yellow, green, and blue.

"Look at the water around the island. You'll see the same dots as in the previous image, now colored in bright orange. Those are the military boats. But look at the patch of sea again. What do you see?"

A pale green spot was barely visible against the vast expanse of blue. The imprint appeared to extend about a hundred meters back towards the island before vanishing. "It may not look very impressive," she said, "but images just like this one have appeared for decades in every satellite-tracking primer. If I'm not mistaken, it is the trail of a commercial submersible like those used by smugglers everywhere."

Commodore Wei paled visibly, while Feng cursed under his breath. Hsieh continued. "They are easy to detect by sonar, but only if you care to look for them. If they had mounted a proper military offensive it wouldn't have slipped by, but they trusted the coastguard and placed their faith on clear skies. In open water such crafts can rely on a simple compass and depth gauge to chart a rough course. Ocean currents lead to drift, but after two hours Cao could have switched to GPS without anyone being the wiser."

She flipped through more images. "These pictures were taken subsequently over the next seven hours. The submersible was due north at around 15 knots. The last one shows the vehicle above the surface—you can plainly see the orange dot—docked on another island, no longer in Indonesia but in the nearby Philippines. Since we didn't know this was happening we have only routine satellite images, but a picture taken 30 minutes later shows something missing near the dock: a seaplane. Our staff will confirm if it flew to Manila, but if it did, then anyone on board could have mingled with the crowd and disappeared into the city. Cao is unlikely to have left any trace."

Admiral Feng let out a grunt of annoyance as his thrill at seeing the mystery solved gave way to the shame of feeling cheated.

"Commodore Wei, you will redouble your efforts to scour for evidence left by Cao. And make sure that we hear of anything the Indonesians find out."

"Yes, sir." Wei appeared to expect further instructions.

"Well, get on with it!" snapped Feng. "You're all dismissed. Commander Hsieh, stay behind for a minute."

Hsieh felt confident. Feng wasn't known for dispensing praise, even in private, but perhaps he would make an exception.

"I am assigning you full-time to this task," he said when the others had departed. "I expect it to be a long venture, so have opened a new section for it, code-named Seagull. You take over our base of operations in Wuhan."

His words, while not strictly a commendation, were in a way more than that. Hsieh assented with a nod that bore only the slightest hint of gratitude. The new center at Wuhan hosted China's least visible military activities. Anything having to do with biological warfare and genetic enhancement—or whatever went wrong with it—was run from there, although for security reasons it was physically separate from the laboratories themselves, which were deep in the central mountains.

"Tell me," Feng went on, "how much do you know about Cao Xin Pei?"

"He's an enemy of the state. Isn't that enough?"

"No," snapped Feng. "Your new job requires you to know a lot more than that. What have you read about his activities, and about Zhang's involvement? Be frank. I know you're smarter than you try to appear."

His overt compliment held a concealed insult as well, so she wasn't sure how to react. Smart? Very well, she would give him smart. "A few months ago," she began, "intelligence was gathered to the effect that Zhang Jianguo, away on extended leave, has in fact been working for Cao Xin Pei for a couple of years. It was easy to conclude that he was using classified material to conduct further research in violation of the Milan protocol. Three weeks ago, these suspicions were confirmed by information leaked out in connection with King Masoud Al Faisal's deposition and subsequent execution. Cao sold a restricted sequence to Crown Prince Nessim, in defiance of a strict government directive."

"Correct. And what sequence was that?"

"Presumably, the Beta complement of the so-called Prometheus module."

"Ah," smiled Feng, "the Prometheus module. The Americans have a romantic name for everything." He paused and stepped over to a lacquered cabinet, from which he fetched a fancy thermos flask. Pouring out a cup of jasmine-ginger tea, he brought it halfway up to his lips, hesitated, extended it towards Hsieh and upon her polite refusal began sipping gently.

"Now," he continued, resuming his place at the head of the table, "what have you heard about this Indian researcher?"

"Prahbu Sarangarajan," said Hsieh, pronouncing the name effortlessly, "grew up in Mumbai. For over a decade he was the creative force behind Agarwal Biotech's effort on cognitive genetics. When the program was cancelled following the signing of the Milan treaty, he resigned and accepted a faculty position, working on sleep disorders. Then, on the day that Cao's operation was discovered, he boarded a flight to Paris and hasn't been heard of since."

"Good. What else?" Feng prodded.

Hsieh's smug expression slowly melted away as she shook her head. She had obviously missed something.

"Doesn't it strike you as odd," Feng asked rhetorically, "that Zhang paid a visit to Sarangarajan *after* Prince Nessim's visit to Indonesia? Why would he risk travel and exposure, unless he was missing some key information to complete whatever he was doing? Sarangarajan," he continued, in the patronizing tone that he usually adopted towards his staff whenever he wasn't scolding them, "wasn't just the lead researcher in India's cognitive genetics program. He was the person who first implemented the Beta complement in animals—in mice, specifically."

"The version that was lethal in primates?"

"Precisely."

"Sir, do you believe that Zhang developed a viable Beta cluster?"

"Just a hypothesis."

"That would leave us with one issue. The two complements were incompatible—even in frogs, I believe. Sarangarajan was working on a workaround when the Milan protocol brought all research to a halt, which would explain Zhang's visit. But if he really developed a viable

Beta, triggering Al Faisal's generosity, Zhang would have naturally wanted to take the next step—or Cao would, at any rate. Do you think that the women treated after the prince's wife—?"

"That will be your job to find out. Whether Zhang got what he needed from the Indian or didn't, he appears to have been playing with a full deck for the last year or so—Alpha *plus* Beta."

Hsieh turned to look out the window, her mind reeling from the implications of Feng's statement. Daylight was fading and snow had begun to fall softly on the streets of Beijing. It wasn't Cao at all they were after. He just happened to be the gatekeeper.

KEN

> We like to think of genes as information quanta, whose proteins serve specific functions. However, many genes regulate the expression of other genes, which regulate developmental pathways, which are also regulated by environmental factors, which are detected by yet other bodily systems unlike those in any machine.
>
> —RANDOLPH NESSE, *This Will Change Everything*

The doctors' offices were in a separate wing of the hospital, sparing visitors from the stressful asepsis of the surgery, inpatient and ER building. The furnishings were on the cozy side for a medical facility, and much welcomed by the twosome in the waiting room. Soft lighting allowed them to look out of a large window at the Golden Gate Bridge, which appeared hushed and stately in the gloaming. They were not kept long before being ushered in to a warm greeting from preimplantation specialist Gwendolyn Barker.

"Dr. Barker, nice to meet you," said Brad Jensen.

"Please, call me Gwen." She turned to Jensen's wife. "And you must be Athina. How *are* you? Please have a seat."

Years of practice had sharpened Barker's skill at judging people, and one look at the Jensens confirmed what she had surmised from their file. Of course, she couldn't tell in advance whether Athina would be an easy patient or not, but as *clients* the couple would be perfect. He had a finance degree and worked as an auditor; she was a software engineer. They would have no difficulty understanding the choices they faced, weighing the tradeoffs involved and making an informed decision. In short, it was a fair assumption that unless they subscribed to some radical ideology—in which case they wouldn't have made this appointment—they would be reasonable. She silently thanked her colleague for referring them to her.

"So," she grinned broadly, "I understand you will be starting a family?"

"That's right," said Athina, smiling back before exchanging a sheepish glance with her husband.

"Boy or girl?"

"Girl," they said in unison. Athina giggled. "We've decided to call her Cassiopeia."

"As in the constellation?" asked Barker, for nothing else came to mind.

"After the goddess," explained Athina, "the mother of Andromeda in Greek mythology."

The physician blushed. "Of course... Well, that's a great choice. Now, since we all have had different exposure to germline technology and trait selection, my first responsibility as a doctor, before we even start discussing your preferences, is to ensure that everyone is on the same page. Perhaps—"

"Oh yes," interrupted Brad, "I forgot to mention it in the form. We've done some reading: *Responsible Choices in Parenthood* and *Shaping Your Baby's Future*—besides a bunch of stuff we found online."

"Very good. In general, I would caution against what is said in web exchanges, but those books are from reliable authors." The doctor turned to Athina. "Did you read them too?"

"We both did."

"Great, that will make things easier. Normally we recommend prospective parents to attend our counseling seminars. That means five evening sessions. I will leave it up to you, since you no doubt are able to go through the tutorials on your own. But it's important to go over some of the more, uh, technical details together. Feel free to interrupt and ask questions, okay?" Two eager nods signaled their readiness.

"Good. As far as the procedure is concerned, the first thing we do is take a blood sample from each parent and screen the chromosomes for several hundred known disorders caused by the presence or absence of certain genes, and for any traits that you might be particularly interested in passing on to, or holding back from, your offspring. The screening of deleterious genes is done for free as per national health norms, while optional trait testing is done for a fee of 10 dollars per single-gene trait, and various fee levels for multiple-gene traits—you will receive a full list. A note is made of the genes found in the blood samples, for use at a later stage in the process. Then we get to work on the embryo production. There are two commercially-available procedures to engineer embryos based entirely on parent chromosomes, and a third one to add desirable traits not present in either parent's genome.

"The traditional method extracts around 20 eggs from the mother's ovaries and injects them with sperm from the father. With current technology around 80% of those eggs develop into viable embryos, which are allowed to grow to the eight-cell stage. One cell is extracted from each of the embryos and cloned. The cloned cells are used to screen for any genetic disorders that we might find in your blood samples. If a harmful gene is found, then either the embryo is discarded in favor of another, or—for disorders that allow it—an additional gene is inserted to cancel the effect of the original."

"What if," asked Athina, "both our parents went through a similar procedure—I mean, if our own genomes have already been screened?"

"Well, in that case the chances of finding a deleterious gene are very low. But we still do it, because although single-gene disorders were all identified long ago, new diseases linked to particular gene *combinations* have been identified, so the screening that your parents went through was not as exhaustive as today's. Anyway, this procedure is known as Standard PGD, which stands for Preimplantation Genetic Diagnosis and is covered by every medical plan in the country. But since you have both been pre-filtered for disorders, we can go one step further and screen for traits that are not harmful, strictly speaking, but merely undesirable to you. Some traits like skin color, hair texture, the shape of fingers—even height, to some extent—are influenced by relatively simple gene combinations, which can be tested at the embryo level. If you feel strongly about something, we can do the screening. This is called Optional PGD, since there's a limit to the number of traits we can eliminate through the traditional procedure, because as I said, only 20 eggs are extracted, so if you're too picky, none of the embryos will fit the bill. Are you with me so far?"

"Yes," said Athina, as Brad nodded confidently.

"We then have another, more sophisticated, PGD procedure, which in principle removes the upper bound on the number of traits that can be screened—time and money being the only restrictions."

"You mean the Weissman technique?" asked Athina.

"Right. The procedure wasn't around when you and I were born, but it amounts to inducing in vitro meiosis in non-sexual cells—bone, muscle, skin, or blood cells—don't worry, it's only a needle-sized incision. Now meiosis, as you probably know, is the process by which our reproductive organs produce gametes, or sperm and ova. These cells differ from those in the rest of our body (what we call somatic cells) in that they have only half the usual number of chromosomes—23 instead of 46. What Weissman discovered was a reliable way to induce cells from other body tissues to undergo meiosis. This is trickier than it seems, because cells from most tissues are already specialized for a role, so a large number of genes in them are inactive. Weissman's team developed a way to reactivate the genes, so a virtually unlimited amount of 'artificial' egg cells can be obtained from a small tissue sample, instead of the 20 to 30 mature eggs that are normally extracted from the ovaries. The rest of the process is the same: sperm is used to fertilize these manufactured eggs, and the resulting embryos are cloned and tested. Nowadays we can test for as many traits as you want—in theory, at least, because the costs can skyrocket."

"That's something I meant to ask," said Brad. "How do the costs add up? I assumed they'd be proportional to the number of traits tested."

"No. Suppose you want to test for 20 traits that you want your baby to have. An embryo is selected at random from the sample, cloned, and tested for the first trait. If it is present, then another cell cloned from the same embryo is tested for the second trait, and so on. But if a desired trait isn't present, then we must start all over again with a different embryo until we find one with all 20 traits. In the simplest scenario, where the 20 traits you select are determined by a single gene and have a fifty-percent chance of showing up in an embryo, finding an embryo with all 20 traits is like getting 20 heads in a row in a coin toss. At 10 dollars per tested embryo, you could spend millions and still not get what you want."

Brad sighed. "We bought our apartment on a mortgage, but we've only saved about a hundred thousand."

"That's more than enough for most purposes," said Barker reassuringly. "Our patients on average spend only half as much. You see, it's only the hard-to-have traits that drive up the cost, but for unwanted traits the odds are in your favor, since we're likely to find an embryo with none of the negative traits, especially since we'll be working with two genetic complements—yours and Athina's. Believe me, most people can only dream of investing that kind of money on their child, and I can assure you: not only will you be able to keep the baddies at bay, but you will be able to add some enhancement modules—maybe not 20, but certainly two or three.

"This brings me to the third procedure I mentioned earlier. Once PGD is carried out and you have selected an embryo, you have the choice of adding extra traits by means of an auxiliary chromosome. This allows you to add traits that aren't present in either of your genomes. This extrasome is inserted into the embryo before any cell division takes place, because if we waited until the 8-cell stage we'd have to perform 8 microinjections, increasing the risk of damaging the embryo. This means a decision must be made regarding which genes to include in the extra chromosome. We have several hundred gene modules in our catalog that have been thoroughly tested and are popular with customers—I mean patients—affecting anything from metabolism to breast shape, from muscle development to aerobic endurance.

"But before we get into the details, I want to make sure that you understand that in germline engineering there are no guarantees. Even for standard disease screening there's always a chance of something going wrong, and the hospital will insist that you sign very long forms. You can greatly increase the likelihood of getting what you want, but it will never be one hundred percent except for what are known as Mendelian traits, like eye color and such."

"And if we both are extrasomic?" asked Athina.

"It doesn't make much difference. Auxiliary chromosomes are designed to be replaced by newer versions. They have a built-in safety mechanism so they are discarded during meiosis. If you became pregnant through sexual intercourse, the extrasomes would be absent from your sperm and ova, so they wouldn't pass on to the child."

"I understand that facial traits," said Brad, "can be determined with relative accuracy."

Barker nodded. "Questions always come up about three things: lifespan, facial traits, and mental attributes. Regarding longevity, the answer is fairly straightforward: we are kept alive by a host of different mechanisms that act at the level of cells, organs, or the body as a whole. The presence of certain genes reduces the risk of developing some age-related diseases, so if a person has many of those genes, then their overall life expectancy will increase. Next we have so-called guardian genes, which prevent mutations in the regulator genes. Our catalog lists all known ones, which can be inserted in the auxiliary chromosome if they are not present in the embryo."

"Aren't they part of the standard procedure?"

"No. Standard PGD only screens for harmful genes, not for nice-to-haves. Sadly there aren't as many disease-fighting genes as you might think. That's an area where biotech companies keep experimenting, because the payoff is substantial. Several modules in our index have been on the market for less than two years."

"You mean designer genes?"

"Right. They are part of what makes us 'superhuman' compared to earlier generations, and our children 'superhuman' compared to us." Barker drew quotes in the air every time she said the word. "We may never get used to dying, but we are sure getting used to dying older."

"An easy habit to acquire," agreed Athina.

"We also know which genes hold sway over facial traits, and if you want your daughter to look like either of you, we could achieve it to a large extent, though not exactly—unless of course we simply cloned one of you, which federal laws forbid. As for designer faces I'm afraid the number of genes involved in morphology is too large to predict what a particular combination will produce. Also, remember that genes are largely expressed through their effect on each other, which means that physical differences between people—and even between species—often have to do with regulatory mechanisms and the interaction between genes, rather than with the proteins that make up the body."

"But I thought," protested Athina, "that you could predict the effect of a gene without having to build it."

"Only partially. Computers are of course an invaluable tool, allowing for example to determine the protein configuration that results from a given sequence of base pairs, *if and when* the sequence actually codes for a protein. This allows genes to be edited at lightning speed, discarding variants that produce unwanted foldings before working with live samples. Computers also allow us to work with the virtual proteins themselves, to see how they would interact with various biological elements, including other proteins. And they allow us to visualize the way one gene activates other genes, either alone or in concert. It's all quite amazing, but what computers *cannot* do is simulate the growth of an entire animal based on virtual proteins. We cannot predict an adult face from a particular complement of genes, and even if we try to copy someone's features there are genes for non-facial traits that have facial side-effects. You could insert the core facial-morphology module of a woman into a male embryo to get a child that looks like his mother, but their faces wouldn't be identical, which is probably a good thing. Secondary male characteristics triggered by the Y chromosome affect hormone production, bone structure, hair growth, and skin texture in ways that would never show up in a girl."

"And mental attributes?" asked Brad.

"Those are more complicated. At least faces are replicable in principle, even if not always in practice. But roughly one third of our genes have some effect on our brains, so neither all the money nor all the medical expertise in the world could replicate someone's brain while leaving the rest of the genome intact—not only would you destroy the embryo in the process, but with current technology we wouldn't live long enough to see the job done."

"So, what *can* we choose?" There was concern in Athina's voice.

"Oh, plenty! Just remember that for mental attributes all you can determine is propensity. Bear in mind that an average neuron makes about a thousand connections to other cells and receives many more. With about one hundred billion neurons in a person's brain, that gives about one hundred trillion connections. There's no way a few thousand genes can specify that much detail.

"You will have access to an online database that describes all gene modules that can be uploaded into the auxiliary chromosome. Next to each module's description is a table with success-rate benchmarks, including the likelihood of producing a particular trait, depending on which other modules you implement and on the genes present in the embryo's natural chromosomes, in other words the parents' genes—which is another reason to start by analyzing each of your own genomes."

"But," said Brad warily, "the number of possible combinations is—"

"Astronomical, yes. You will be using software to simulate scenarios that reflect your choices."

"What about enhancements?" asked Athina.

"Neural modules are all taken from the existing human genome. Yes, children on average are smarter than thirty years ago, but nothing you wouldn't find in the normal population. There's a worldwide ban on such research, under an international treaty."

"How's that?"

"Well, it began years ago, when people first figured out which portion of the human genome is absent in our ape relatives, and which of those genes are expressed in the brain."

"The Sapiens cluster?"

"Yes, though it's not a compact module like the ones used in extrasomes, but a scattered constellation of genes. Anyway, the process of finding out how each interacts with the rest of the genome was painfully slow, because you can't go around deleting genes from human embryos just to see what mental deficit the child has. But experimenting on primates was poorly regulated, so competing teams decided to tackle the problem from the other end, by gradually inserting genes from the Sapiens module into chimpanzee embryos. The whole thing was kept under wraps and things went well at first, but then someone screwed up by inserting many genes at once."

"Oh God!" Athina covered her mouth as the doctor's words sank in.

"Yes, well, that was the end of the program."

DURESS

> And the truth is that as a man's real power grows and his knowledge widens, ever the way he can follow grows narrower, until at last he chooses nothing but does only and wholly what he *must do*...
>
> —URSULA K. LE GUIN, *A Wizard of Earthsea*

Fog still hung over the karst islets of Ha Long Bay, but the first ray of sunlight had already pierced the cover. Xin Pei Cao sat alone on the second-floor terrace of a small waterfront abode. Dressed in plain but comfortable slacks and jacket, he carefully pondered the tray on which a Japanese breakfast had been served.

In a lacquered wooden bowl, tart pickled plums lay on a bed of white rice, sprinkled with dry seaweed, sesame seeds and a lump of wasabi paste. To one side, the spout of a terracotta teapot vented a thin trail of steam; five slices of raw tuna, arranged in a floral pattern, sat on a glazed-earthenware plate next to a tiny dish of soy sauce.

This house, a full-time cook, a part-time maid, a cat, and a few trinkets were all that remained of Cao's former enterprise. He gazed at the ocean and smiled, at peace with himself. What was done was done; he'd had his chance, his triumphs, his say. He'd left his mark on the world, and whether he was ever given credit for it or not was irrelevant: the sense of accomplishment was complete. He lifted the teapot and poured the green tea tenderly over the rice and pickled fruit. He then stirred the ingredients with a pair of chopsticks.

From the roof of a four-story building half a block down the street, a sniper took aim at his head.

Cao heard what sounded like a pebble striking against a wall, and lifted his gaze towards the sound, in time to see an object fall from a rooftop and clatter on the pavement below. He gazed at it with curiosity. A rifle? His gaze darted to the roof of the building, where the body of a man lay inert, arms dangling over the edge. Cao dropped the chopsticks and hurried inside. He crossed the hallway, reached the stairhead and looking down through the banisters saw the terrified cook on the ground floor, held at gunpoint by an unknown man. At the same time someone else pressed another gun to his head.

"What do you want?" he asked in Vietnamese.

The man next to him replied in Mandarin. "You should thank us for saving your life. The Indonesians want you dead but Beijing has other plans. Now move!" he barked, prodding Cao with his weapon.

The cook was gagged and tied to an indoor railing while Cao was led in handcuffs to a car that had silently rolled up the street. He was shoved into the back seat between his captors. The senior officer, wearing no sign of rank but apparently a marshal, began going through Cao's jacket. He found a set of keys, which he gave to his partner, then kept frisking. Reaching the chest he stopped, looked at Cao and tore open the old man's shirt to reveal a rectangular fist-sized object held by a thin chain that prevented Cao's head from slipping through.

"What's this?" barked the man.

Cao said nothing. The man turned the object around; a green indicator lit the front of the device.

"Undo it."

Cao shook his head.

With a quick jerk the man snapped the strand. The device let out a high-pitched squeal and fell silent. It was heavy; the indicator was now red.

"What is it?" the marshal insisted. Cao replied with a patronizing smile and the man slapped him. Cao's head tilted under the blow. When he righted it he whispered "eight, nine, ten."

In sudden horror, the marshal reached frantically for the door handle. The blast took off his head, tore through Cao and the other men, blew away the windows and ripped the doors off their hinges—all in one thousandth of a second.

***

Commander Hsieh's boots thumped on the concrete floor as she walked down a poorly lit corridor that smelled like a dungeon. The lieutenant leading the way had the darkest of reputations within Beijing's military. Brutal sadist that he was, he knew when to be unctuous and, well aware that Hsieh was under Admiral Feng's wing he was busy trying to impress her with the work he'd done. "We got his name through our Thai sources. We knew he would eventually contact his family in Chengdu. We have been questioning him since yesterday."

"I hope you haven't overdone it, because I need him to talk."

"Oh, he's lucid alright. But he's told us everything he knows."

"We'll see," said Hsieh.

They stopped next to a thick steel door. A guard opened to let them in. They were in a square chamber, twelve feet to the side, in the middle of which stood a chair, bolted to the floor. Cuffed to it, hands behind his back, sat a naked man drenched in sweat. One eye was swollen shut and fresh blood glistened on the seat between his legs. Traces of vomit had been carelessly wiped off the floor. A headband was fastened to his head like a crown of thorns. The man looked at the newcomers and quickly dropped his head.

Good, thought Hsieh on seeing his shame at being exposed before her. It meant his mind was still working.

At a desk sat a military doctor in a white coat (she wondered why they bothered with the coats) behind a monitor displaying the prisoner's brain activity. At a sign from Hsieh the lieutenant grabbed the man's chin and made him look up.

"All right," she began, crossing her arms three feet from the shivering captive. "Let's go over it again, I hope for the last time, but that depends on your co-operation. Don't hold anything back and don't stop to think about your answers. How many years did you work on the island?"

"T—two," came the labored reply.

"And you worked there as what?"

"A technician."

"What did Cao tell you about his business?"

"Said he helped people who c-couldn't have…he said it was a f—fertility clinic."

"You have a medical degree; you know fertility clinics. Did this look like one?"

"Y—yes." The man was breathing rapidly, fearing the torment would resume. Hsieh glanced at the man behind the monitor, who nodded once. The prisoner was speaking the truth.

"Did you see the people he treated?"

"Yes, young couples."

"Indonesian? Chinese? American?"

"All over. B-blond, black, oriental."

"Rich or poor?"

The man looked up uncomprehendingly.

"Did they look wealthy? Did they travel in style? Did Cao treat them deferentially?"

"Some, yes. One looked like an Arab."

"You said some were Chinese. Did you hear them talk? How did they speak?"

"Seemed ed—educated."

"What did they say to you?"

"I never really … I never sp—spoke…." The answer died on his lips. The man had stopped shivering and his eyes were glazing over.

"You mean you didn't have conversations with them?" she barked.

"Eh? No … no." The prisoner was drifting off.

"Wake him up," Hsieh ordered, "quickly!"

The man's face was doused with ice-cold water and he snapped back to attention with a series of gasps.

"Now," continued Hsieh, "how many couples came to the island during that time?"

"I—I don't know ... I really don't."

The lieutenant made as if preparing to strike and the prisoner cringed, but Hsieh glanced at the technician, who nodded as before. The blow was withheld.

"Make a guess," she said. "More than twenty?"

"Yes—yes."

"More than thirty?"

The man looked like a panic-stricken dog.

"N-no," he said.

"Very well," said Hsieh, adding mentally. Between twenty and thirty over the first year meant around fifty for the duration. "How long did each couple stay in the island?"

"About a week at a t-t-time."

That made sense. One week per patient with a window week in between, or twenty-five patients per year. Satisfied, she looked up and exited the room, followed by the lieutenant. "Make sure he lives," she said. "Throw him in a warm cell; feed him; let him recover."

"For how long?"

Hsieh shrugged.

CURIOSITY

We are all fragments of darkness groping for the sun.

—WILL DURANT, *The Story of Civilization*

It was one of those homes few people ever get to visit, let alone inhabit. From the nearest road all that could be glimpsed of the estate was a dense coppice of ancient poplars and a well-groomed hedge that hid a solid core of stone. The wall, built long before invisible barriers were devised to keep intruders at bay, enclosed over a thousand acres of private Devon lowlands, mostly wooded country except for a vast stretch of open meadow, perhaps once dotted with grazing sheep, that extended from the house to the river Exe, from which floating barges had the best view of the property.

The fields sloped up gently from the riverbank to a flat, emerald stretch of lawn larger than a standard polo field. Behind it stood Exebridge Hall, framed on either side by dark forest, bearing silent witness to the return of an age when wealth and power once again derived from lineage. A long, sinuous driveway, laid with gravel in the days of horse-drawn carriages, offered visitors a measured approach to the house. The effect was most dramatic in autumn, when passing vehicles blew aside the dry leaves in long ripples like the wake of a speedboat.

Not merely a large house but a national treasure, the building dated back to the eighteenth century and was dripping with history: any piece of furniture would have made a fine museum exhibit; paintings from the walls of the grand staircase would have fetched more on the auction block than the average person could earn in a lifetime. Royalty had once frequented the dining room, and the library held among its twenty thousand volumes some of the most prized collectibles in existence: a Shakespeare First Folio; a thirteenth-century Iliad from the library of Jean, Duc de Berry; a fragment from a Gutenberg Bible. Just as photography had once replaced painting as a means of depicting people and landscapes, so had e-text displaced print as the standard incarnation of readable type, but neither paintings nor books had disappeared from the market, having instead come to be sought as artifacts. Because where technology had evolved, human taste for luxury had not. Wool and cotton had never given way to the synthetic bodysuits once envisioned by futurists; historic homes had never ceased to be coveted by the moneyed elite over high-rise city housing. As for books, people referring to one usually meant a flexible e-paper tome, holding more works in memory than anyone could hope to read. And for the first time in history, people who owned no books weren't necessarily ill-read. But the tactile experience of holding a paper codex led people to seek books for the sheer pleasure that electronics could not provide.

The library was a two-tiered affair, designed for both comfort and elegance. Its layout was asymmetrical; several recesses branched out at random from a central vestibule where a dozen glass-covered exhibits displayed the collection's most appealing items. Side rooms held a couple of card tables, a large sitting area with a well-stocked bar and a grand piano, an exquisite desk and an antique chess table, its borders carved in arabesques inlaid with precious stones. Loungers of soft burgundy leather sat in various nooks. Up a corner spiraled a narrow staircase leading to the second level, itself as large as the ground floor but for the open space that was encircled by an ironwork balustrade. This floor housed seven thousand tomes, a detailed model of a three-masted schooner, two manuscript displays, a balcony's worth of African sculptures, and several armchairs. Curled in one of them was a fourteen-year-old boy, absorbed in a profusely illustrated edition of Anne Desclos's erotica masterpiece, *The Story of O.*

On the floor beside him lay another handsome book, a first edition of Stoker's *Dracula*, bound in black Moroccan goatskin with gothic flourishes of gilt tooling. Ethan had read it long before, but kept the book at hand in case someone walked in unexpectedly. The creaking staircase would give him time enough to slide the steamy tale into the bookshelf and pick up the vampire story.

He felt at home in this cozy retreat, where he had spent most of that month. The rest of the house was either too imposing for him to enjoy, or off-limits for someone who, after all, was only the housekeeper's son. The hired help enjoyed a fair amount of leeway around the household, and if Ethan couldn't exactly wander about Exebridge at will, he wasn't confined to the kitchen and stables either, as might have been the case a century earlier, but was allowed to roam through the ground floor and to have his meals in the small dining room next to the pantry, indulging in the same delicacies on which the family dined. When he was on holiday from boarding school he had a room to himself. For this privilege he was outwardly grateful, yet as he slumbered late into the morning swaddled in the soft goose duvet that his mother had procured, he sometimes felt a twinge of bitterness about the fact that, however comfortable the bed, it was still in the servants' quarters.

Few jobs, he reflected, rubbed in the truth of one's rank as thoroughly as that of domestic servant. At night when sleep was hard to come by, Ethan resolved never to work in another person's household, even if paid, like Nadia, more than most doctors. He sensed something demeaning, and increasingly so as servants aged, about one person having to spend their life tending to another's leisure. He thought he would rather be a factory worker in a faceless corporation, spared the gaze of those to whose wealth he contributed. But these were idle ruminations, for Taylor had shown nothing but kindness towards him. In fact, it had been the master himself who had first invited him to the book trove.

"Mr. Taylor, this is my son," Nadia Karajan had introduced him proudly the previous summer, Ethan's first at Exebridge Hall. Taylor noticed the young fellow's reserve and his firm handshake. Ethan had an elegant nose, deep eyes, and thick, black eyebrows that nearly touched each another. His skin was a shade darker than his mother's, with a healthy copper tan and an athletic build that was beginning to show through his shirt. It was clear that Ethan would grow to be a handsome man, and Taylor wondered if the boy's genes were 'designer'. How much could a woman like Nadia afford? Standard screening, most likely. No cosmetics. Besides, Nadia was comely enough to account for the boy's looks on the basis of natural heredity.

One afternoon Ethan was in a quiet spot of the garden next to a fish pond, where he would often sit to play games, speak with friends, or surf the virtual world until sunset, when the bugs or the cold drove him indoors. Taylor, out for a stroll, caught a sidelong glimpse of the boy sitting on the grass, engrossed with something he held in his hands. Ethan did not sense his approach and Taylor came to rest a few feet behind him. The boy had laid his headset aside on the lawn but was as oblivious to his surroundings as if playing a video game. His fingers were fiddling with a bizarre object made of wire and string. Memories of childhood wire-puzzles brought a smile to Taylor's face, and he felt the wish to try this one out.

Amusement turned to irritation when he saw Ethan grasp the main body of the contraption in one hand and apply pressure with his thumb to one of the wires, bending it at a right angle. Taylor felt like voicing a loud objection, but checked himself in time to see the boy gently lift the object until his eyes were level with the newly bent segment, studying it like an artist examining a creation. Then his hands went to work again, this time on a loose string, one end of which was attached to a wooden ball. He tied the other end to the hooked tip of the more convoluted wire section. Taylor now stepped, almost apologetically, into Ethan's field of vision.

"Oh ... Hello, Mr. Taylor." The boy instinctively lowered his hands as if to conceal the puzzle, but realizing that Taylor had probably already taken a good look, Ethan managed to erase from his face all but the subtlest hint of being taken aback.

He pointed at the pond. "A big one died this morning."

Taylor smiled and shrugged. "It happens. The large ones are older." He indicated the object in the boy's hands. "Nearly done?"

Ethan turned his eyes towards the puzzle. It was easier to let his gaze rest on it than on Taylor. "Almost there," he answered.

Taylor nodded. "Mind if I give it a try when you're done shaping it?"

Ethan bounced the wire nervously against the palm of his hand. "This one's rather diff—I mean of course, not at all. I didn't know you liked puzzles."

"I didn't know you built them. Who taught you?"

The boy considered the question. "Um … no one, really. There's a club of sorts—on the web. We challenge each other."

"Do you win?"

"I have, yes."

"Friends of yours? Young people?"

"No—not friends, really…. We don't talk much, just exchange tips. I suppose some are my age. Who knows?"

"Who knows, indeed," Taylor agreed, reminded of the dangers of virtual-world anonymity. "Here, walk with me to the house. I have some puzzles you might like."

Many would have envied this chance to spend time chatting with the famous tycoon, but Ethan, undertook it more out of a sense of duty than out of enthusiasm. He knew the man mostly through hearsay—from the staff, from friends at school, and from his mother, who referred to her employer more as a mythical figure than as a person. It made him queasy to think that she might be secretly attracted to Taylor, the sixty-year-old billionaire and womanizer, whose current love interest had once been proclaimed the embodiment of the perfect female shape. Was it true, his schoolmates would taunt, that Patricia Lindqvist had natural breasts that jutted out of her chest like those of virtual women? Was it true that despite that, he cheated on her?

"Sod off", he would answer, but for all he knew Taylor probably did sleep around, and yes, his girlfriend's body was a sight to behold. But Ethan's patience with Taylor's overtures would pay off in the end, though to what extent he couldn't have guessed that afternoon when Ethan was awarded his first glimpse of the famous Exebridge library. He would later recall that Taylor had walked towards a corner table and picked up a black object, which he handed to him saying "Careful with the vertices: they're sharp." It was a heavy, smooth, perfectly polished black tetrahedron.

"Nice," said Ethan. "Is it obsidian?" he asked, motioning to return it to its owner.

"No, no," said Taylor, and pushed the object back at him. "Look closely. Here, let me aim the lamp at it."

Ethan inspected it carefully under the light, turning it over and around a few times. All faces appeared identical, except perhaps—yes, that was it: what appeared to be scratches on the surface were in fact ruler-straight hairline fractures. Some turned at right angles; others formed a closed square; yet another seemed to extend halfway into and adjacent face of the pyramid. Ethan's eyes grew wide as he realized that it could be taken apart.

"It isn't really stone, you see," volunteered Taylor. "It's completely synthetic. That's why the pieces fit so snugly together. Most materials expand and contract with heat, humidity, what have you, so a puzzle can get stuck in damp weather. Centuries ago people began carving these in wood." He picked up another object from the shelf and held it in Ethan's view. "Not quite the same effect, eh?"

Ethan tried to dislodge a piece by pressing and tugging at it in several ways, to no avail. "How is it done?" he asked.

Taylor smiled. "That's for *you* to figure out."

He walked away from Ethan. "I will leave you to it. When you're done you can try your hand at those." He pointed at a nearby bookcase that held over two dozen mechanical puzzles of all shapes and sizes.

Ethan hesitated. "Are you sure it's okay? I mean, my mother says I shouldn't be—"

"I'll tell her you can come here whenever you want. And I will let Patricia know, too, though she rarely comes here. I will impose just one condition: nothing you find here leaves the library. Fair enough?"

Ethan nodded. "Yes sir, thank you." That was the first genuine smile he had seen on Ethan's face, Taylor thought as he left.

Ethan soon managed to disassemble the tetrahedron and put it back together. Later that evening he added the final touches to the wire puzzle and published its design. He made a gift of the original model to Taylor, who never managed to work it out, though in all fairness he didn't try very hard. Ethan had also taken stock of the library proper, and some of the wonders it housed. It wasn't the amount of information that kept him returning, but its selectiveness. He could, after all, slip on his viewer and access a thousand books for each one that sat on the shelves at Exebridge. But the deluge of rubbish in the virtual world was annoying, even with the best roadmap, whereas in the library every item was a jewel.

There was a section on horror stories and gothic novels, each of them a pleasure to read, to touch and to smell (he found that the scent of paper added significantly to the reading experience). He discovered that some stories he had always assumed to have been conceived for video were in fact meant to be read. Ethan had heard that before the world was interconnected English had been less ubiquitous, its usage different from country to country, its style often arcane; but he had never imagined that spelling and language had changed so much, and was astonished at being nearly unable to decipher an early edition of Chaucer. Other interesting things he learned about the past were that cars had once run on fossil fuel like that used by aircraft, and that *foie gras* was already a delicacy when liver tissue wasn't grown on farms like fruit, but was culled from the carcasses of geese force-fed and slaughtered for the purpose.

But he chiefly found reassurance, for the content of the books he read matched the text of online versions. This was important for someone who belonged to a generation raised entirely on virtual information. He welcomed these old books (some of them worm-eaten and fragile) as hard evidence, as talismans that linked the present with distant times. He wondered which might be the oldest item in Taylor's collection. Not a book, as it turned out, but a single, half-torn illuminated page, it nonetheless had a glass box to its own, and depicted what appeared to be a king and a holy person—a saint, perhaps?—engaged in verbal exchange. The two figures were almost childish, their stance oddly rigid, their hands held before them in an awkward but obviously pious gesture. Ethan stared long at the colors (blue, red and gold were predominant) and the painstaking attention to minutiæ on the scribe's part. He couldn't decipher the text, but a sign inside the box read: *De Civitate Dei,* circa 900 AD, one of two surviving fragments. Ethan marveled at the stained, uneven surface of the page, the origin of which he couldn't guess but appeared more resilient than paper.

He perused the shelves methodically, reading the first page of every book before deciding whether to skip or devour it. As the end of his two-month holiday drew near, he had only gone through eleven volumes and was beginning to lose hope of making any real progress.

He looked down at the viewer he had placed on the table. It had to be one of mankind's greatest inventions: a key to the world now taken so much for granted that people sometimes reacted to damage to their headsets as to a sudden loss of hearing. Ethan wondered if people in the past had ever felt life to be dull, growing up far from information, hardly knowing what happened beyond their hometowns. How did they learn about the world, about other places, about other times? How did they ever meet people with similar interests? Surely they couldn't have spent their lives traveling.

His eyes fell back on the engraved page of the book he was holding. Ethan had never seen drawings so explicit yet so elegant. Was this how people learned about sex before the internet? He imagined family dens stashed with erotic prints, but dismissed the notion as absurd. Perhaps, he mused, children spied on grownups engaging in the act, but he shuddered with disgust at the idea of eavesdropping on his mother. He struggled to picture a world where people lived in unconnected groups, with no one to answer their questions but neighbors and family. No wonder they hoarded books: it must have been like storing food for an endless winter.

Ethan heard the voices long before the young men reached the library. He recognized the bass drone of Julian, Taylor's son, who was beginning to sound more like his father every day. In an eyeblink Ethan was reading *Dracula.* He heard two others—Julian's friends, he guessed—both unknown to him. "This had better be good," said one impatiently. "Play has resumed. What if our turn comes up?"

"No worries," reassured Julian. "With Mike as bowler we can show up tomorrow and miss nothing." The other boy laughed.

Ethan closed the book and placed a foot on the floor to get out of the armchair. Taylor's children hadn't been in Exebridge during Ethan's first summer there, having spent the holidays in France with their mother. But he knew that Julian didn't like him around when he had company, and resented his father for being overly permissive with Ethan. He would sometimes pester the boy in Taylor's absence. Julian was sixteen years old to Ethan's fourteen, and stood half a head above Ethan, so there was no issue of rivalry. But young Taylor wouldn't let Ethan go without a snide quip about his person to draw a laugh from his friends.

"Okay, where is it?" said one of Julian's pals.

"Let me close the door, first." Ethan heard Julian walk to the entrance of the library, pull the double-doors shut and turn the key in the lock. He froze. It would now be doubly embarrassing to reveal his presence. Matters were decided while he hesitated: Julian walked to the large desk and pulled out something from a drawer. "Who wants to go first?"

"Let Jason try. He won't get far."

"Haw, haw," said a voice Ethan assumed to be Jason's.

Ethan wondered what purpose a racing heart could have in a situation where the best strategy was obviously to keep as still as possible.

"Headset goes on like regular eyewear," explained Julian. "It's live video feed. There are two parts to the test—the first is spatial exploration: shapes and forms; avoiding traps that keep changing as you move about; doors leading nowhere. Are you there yet?"

"Shhh, I'm trying to focus, here. Bloody hell! You said there were no time limits."

"I said speed didn't count. But you can't take forever."

Time passed. Julian and the third boy chatted in whispers as Jason struggled. Ethan heard only bits and pieces of their conversation and the occasional imprecation from Jason. The others sniggered and discussed football.

"Uh, oh ... Third wrong answer. I've been kicked out."

Guffaws. "Record time, Jason—record *low* time. No, no, do the second part! Come on, you need both parts for a score. Hey, I didn't do well on the first one either, if it's any consolation. The second is easier: you get to play detective. It's all about insight—no mazes."

Ethan's pulse fell back to normal. It was unlikely they would head upstairs, and in any case he figured that his best option would be to pretend he had fallen asleep and not heard anything, so he let *Dracula* fall open on his chest, pressed his chin to the cover and shut his eyes. But no sooner had he done so when he was startled by another burst of mirth.

"Let me see," said Julian. "Yup, 20 on the first part and 15 on the second—certified twerp."

"I'd like to see *you* try," Jason rejoined.

"But seriously, Julian," said the third boy, "what do the scores mean?"

"No idea."

"Didn't your father tell you?"

"I don't think he knows either. But not a word about this—it would tick him off."

"You said it's broadcasted from the cloud?"

"Isn't everything?"

"So if you play again—"

"The puzzles change."

"It feels like a video game. How can it measure intelligence?"

"What else would it be measuring, your sexual vigor?"

"No, but—two numbers and that's it?"

"Maybe it's just one aspect of intellect."

"Yes, like how to find your way out of a tricky cupboard."

"All right Hamish, your turn," said Julian to his other friend.

"So you can laugh at my expense? No, I'm heading back out. Jason, you are wicketkeeper."

Julian had no wish to be left alone, so the door was duly unlocked and they left the library noisily. Ethan waited for a minute after the voices faded before walking down the stairs. He went to the library entrance, stepped out into the passage and listened, went back in and up to a window: the three young men, dressed in full cricket garb, were strolling away across the lawn.

He went over to the antique desk and opened the middle drawer; it held several trinkets but nothing like what he sought. He then tried a side drawer. There it was: a small black device with an attached headset but no glove controls or keyboard; only a power switch, a thumb joystick and what looked like a selector or trigger button. Near one of the top corners, the characters α,β were neatly inscribed in red. No brand, no label, no power cable. Holding it gingerly he held one last argument with himself. Julian had made it clear that nobody was meant to use the gadget. Then again, Mr. Taylor was out of town and his son was in a ball game…

Ethan sat at the desk, slipped on the headset and flipped the power switch.

***

Red color flashed briefly at his third failed attempt, then an azure background reappeared, showing his scores: 113 and 30. He recalled Julian declaring the second part to be easier, but Ethan had found exactly the opposite. Maybe if he gave it another try.

It wasn't clear to him what alerted him to the presence of someone else in the room. Perhaps a faint scent, or a sound that didn't belong in the hushed atmosphere. Whatever it was, it flooded his mind with incongruous emotions: thrill, panic, anticipation, and impending doom. He felt the palms of his hands grow cold, his cheeks burn, and his confidence evaporate as the memories of every blunder he had ever made piled up before him. Slowly, he reached up and removed the visor, knowing exactly what would greet his eyes: silky black hair, crimson lips, dimpled cheeks, and transfixing indigo eyes belonging to Valerie Taylor, Bruce's fifteen-year-old, staring at him nonchalantly.

"Hullo," she said.

To a boy on the verge of manhood all females—especially his elders—are unfathomable. But for one just awoken to the natural pangs of self-doubt (and the not-so-natural ones of social disadvantage), the sight of a stylish young woman of flawless poise and beauty is completely overwhelming. Ethan heard himself mumble the beginning of a sentence, his tongue as useful as a piece of sausage in his mouth. When he saw that she was smiling he managed to string some words together. "I'm sorry. I couldn't help it." He placed the controller and visor back in the drawer, certain that she could see his hand shake, and hating himself for it.

Valerie drew nearer and raised a single, perfect eyebrow. Help what?" she asked, and Ethan realized that maybe she hadn't known to whom the device belonged.

"Uh ... it's just that—well, Julian and his friends were playing with that gadget and—" That's it, he thought as the answer left his lips, expose Julian and let *him* do the explaining if word got to their father. "It looked like fun, so I decided to give it a try..."

"Oh," said Valerie, unflappable. "I won't say a word."

His soul teetered on the brink of something, but what that something was he couldn't tell. Was there a hint of complicity in her tone?

"Thank you," he said abruptly, "I must be going now." He made for the door in haste. "Good day, Miss Taylor."

He regretted it the second he left the room. Gripped by self-reproach he walked out of the house like a zombie, the image of Valerie's face branded in his mind. At eighteen he might have forced himself to retrace his steps; at twenty-five he would have stormed her like the hordes of Genghis Khan. But Ethan was fourteen, and his parting words rang madly in his head, sounding increasingly silly with every reprise. *I must be going now.* Going where? Where was he off to in such a hurry?

The only suggestion that his flustered brain seemed to offer was to run down to the river and dive in headfirst. With any luck he would drown.

INTELLECT

> The lawyer, with his trained discontinuous mind, insists on placing individuals firmly in this species or that. He does not allow for the possibility that an individual might lie halfway between two species.
>
> —RICHARD DAWKINS, *The Devil's Chaplain*

Like a vision from faerie legend, two white horses wove their way through the forest, hooves pummeling the damp, moss-covered ground, flinging a spray of divots behind them. The young women, one a platinum blonde, the other's hair raven-black, rode like Valkyries on their steeds, crouching on their saddles to avoid low branches. Their attire (white cotton shirts, beige riding breeches) added a modern touch to the dreamlike tableau. Upon reaching a sunny clearing they slowed down to a lazy trot. The blonde dismounted daintily while her companion, her mount still moving, leaned forward, allowing her arms to carry the full weight of her body; she leapt from the stirrups, shot her legs backwards until they came together above the mare's rump, then pivoted left and down for a gymnast's touchdown. "What do you think, Natasha?" she asked, stepping forward. The ground was covered with soft, wild grass. Along the further edge of the clearing a small brook trickled.

"It's like a Jane Austen story."

"You'd need a dress and a flower garland," said Valerie. "Trousers are too risqué for the period."

"And *you* should be more romantic."

"Who says I'm not? I fully agree that a single man in the possession of a good fortune must be in want of a wife."

"That's not romantic," Natasha laughed, "that's bookish!"

"Hey, wasn't I the one who suggested this lover's setting?"

"Yes," admitted Natasha, surveying the landscape. "The perfect spot for a picnic, and then..." She bit a forefinger and smiled.

Valerie shook her head, grinning. "What's your plan?"

"Oh, I'll show up with a basket after the game and ask Kyle over."

"And bring him straight here? He'll be all sweaty."

"Uh-huh," said her friend lusciously.

"Feeling tartish, are we? Just do me a favor and don't fall in love with him."

"Promise," giggled Natasha.

"All right, let's go back."

They retraced their path at a lazy pace, allowing the horses to stop and nibble at weeds. Natasha swayed in her saddle, enjoying the scenery, her ringlets nearly white in the sunlight. "Did all women wear dresses?" she asked.

"In Austen's day? I'm sure they did; long flowing dresses."

"Must have been awkward riding—though I wouldn't mind. Sometimes I think I would have enjoyed living in those days. Ever fancy that sort of thing?"

"Sometimes, but I envision armored knights and drawbridges."

"Too dirty for me," said Natasha.

Valerie laughed. "Then you wouldn't have enjoyed the eighteen-hundreds."

Natasha seemed taken aback. "Why not?"

"Because by your standards most people were dirty back then. And they died young."

"Puh-*leeze*!"

"It's true. Genes were mixed at random. Some people were too fat or too thin, too short or too tall; went bald or lost their teeth; girls grew hair on their legs and had to wax it off."

"Girls like us would have been princesses," said Natasha gaily.

"Girls like us didn't exist. Back then you had a pretty face and bad teeth, or a firm bottom and sagging breasts."

"Like poor people."

"Right," said Valerie, averting her gaze.

Children of the wealthy are always class-conscious, but it had never bothered Valerie much until she was eleven and became financially literate. While shopping in London against her mother's advice (Valerie liked picking clothes off the rack instead of having them tailored) she had overheard two attendants chatting. One of their colleagues had been offered a job elsewhere as floor manager, for a salary which from their tone Valerie understood to be rather good. But glancing at the price tag on the vicuña bomber jacket she had chosen, she realized that the manager would be earning the equivalent of two jackets a month. Valerie knew that people were paid to work, but had never given a thought to the amounts they received.

In the stories she read there were rich people and poor people. Oliver Twist was the poorest she remembered, and at the other end were kings and queens who lived in palaces. She had visited Blenheim and Windsor and, but for some obvious trappings, neither had struck her as much grander than Exebridge. If anything they were drafty and ill-equipped.

It was clear that the shop attendants were not starving, nor were they dressed in Dickensian rags. But they just as obviously didn't live in a house like Exebridge. Valerie had always assumed that store clerks lived in the small houses around Belgravia and Knightsbridge—close to their workplace—but now she wasn't sure. Suddenly aware of how little she knew about real estate, she still doubted that a paycheck worth two jackets per month would pay for rent on Belgrave Square. The more she thought about it, the less sense it made.

On the way home she browsed for information on wages and salary levels. Tons of facts, most of them useless—legislation, political debates, percentage increases, and endless diatribes on the issue of taxes—led her only to conclude that wages rose and fell over time, inevitably to someone's chagrin. But more probing revealed some numbers.

Are British doctors overpaid? The article had some tables that compared earnings in the medical profession since the year 2020. British physicians, the author concluded, were only slightly better off than they had been at that time. Valerie had seen the family doctor twice in recent years, for food poisoning and for a broken rib from being thrown off a horse. Well dressed and well mannered, the avuncular man appeared to be at ease in Exebridge. Surely he must earn more than the article suggested.

British CEOs, said another report, earned figures that when translated into vicuña knitwear amounted to between 50 and 300 garments per month. That was more sensible. Was her father a CEO? She ran a query on Bruce Taylor and was greeted by an avalanche of entries. She narrowed down the search by requesting the word "wealth", and there were far more links than she expected, but one caught her eye: *Britain's 100 Wealthiest Individuals.*

It wasn't that her father was the third richest man in the country that sent her mind reeling, but the sheer immensity of the gap between any figures she had read about in connection with people's income and what her father was said to be worth. A lifetime of earnings at the highest executive level would build only a small fraction of her father's fortune. Surprise led to disbelief, then quickly to pride, then to self-conscious embarrassment, and eventually to a vague sense of dread, a feeling to which Valerie would grow used over time but never fully shake off.

They reached the cricket field and secured the horses. Natasha spotted Kyle and waved at him. He blew her a kiss, which she returned with shut eyes and pouting lips. Several heads turned at the exchange, and a tall boy with hazel eyes fixed his gaze on Valerie until she noticed him, then brought two fingers to his forehead in a friendly salute. Valerie returned a half-smile and raised her arm noncommittally.

"He's hot for you," said Natasha suggestively. "Perhaps you should have a picnic, too?"

"I've told you he's not my type."

"Sometimes I wonder what your type is. You're such a put-off."

Your father's cute, Valerie said to herself, and was shocked by the thought. It had been only a couple of years since she had felt any interest in the opposite sex, but from the start the objects of her attraction were older men, and Natasha's father, at forty-four, she found particularly handsome. As if Natasha might read her mind, she turned her gaze back to the field. Not a single boy on the lawn had plain looks, but she couldn't picture herself spending more than a few minutes with any of them. She contemplated with horror the prospect that she might never be attracted to anyone her age—the exception being a crush she could scarcely avow to herself, let alone to Natasha, who presently said, “I’d better hurry up and shower. Mind if I drop by the kitchen to fetch some goodies?”

“Help yourself. But, I thought you didn’t mind the sweat?”

“I don’t mind *his* sweat.”

Valerie watched Natasha saunter towards the house, then sat on the lawn to watch the game. A gawky boy who wasn’t playing walked over and sat down next to her. “Enough horseback for a day?” he inquired.

Tony Steinberg was welcome company, for he made her feel neither threatened nor fawned upon. He was also the only friend that Valerie shared with her brother.

“Not enough for Natasha, though. She’ll be back for the horses.”

“And for Kyle, I suppose.”

“Of course.”

“I wonder what she sees in him. I’d go for Jason, myself.”

Valerie’s chuckle was heartfelt. “Does he know you’re gay?”

“No, and don’t go telling on me.”

“Julian knows, so it’s only a matter of time.”

“He won’t say a thing. Most of them aren’t ready—you know boys; it makes them feel awkward. Give them a couple of years.”

She didn’t know boys, but was curious. “Have you found someone?”

“You mean a gay someone? No. We are a dying breed, you know, with improved pregnancy controls and the rest—a hundred thousand births per year, worldwide.”

“Don’t dramatize. You’ll find your match.”

He nodded, unconvinced. “Could take forever, though.”

“Come on,” laughed Valerie, “you’re only fifteen. Have you tried online?”

Tony shook his head. “Dirty old men, that’s what you get. I want someone my age, and smart.” He lay back on the lawn and closed his eyes.

Valerie looked at the grass between her boots. Tony wouldn’t be so glum if he could see older men through her eyes. It would indeed be hard to find someone young and smart enough. Could that be her problem, too?

Tony was the only youngster Valerie looked up to, intellectually. They had met when Valerie switched schools for the second time, after that Sunday morning when her parents, still living together, had a row over her. She had overheard them from the parlor's anteroom and, knowing they would change subject the instant she showed up, paused at the sill.

"Ah, but you didn't listen to me!" her mother was scolding, visibly hurt. "All you cared about were your ambitions. Julian wasn't enough. You had to go ahead and fix her up like a guinea pig—my baby!"

"Now that isn't fair," said Taylor, "I didn't trick you into anything. You agreed—"

"I agreed because I loved you! And it makes me feel sick—sick!"

"Odette, please! She has a head start on future generations."

"But the module was untested. Even now it's not allowed."

"Of course it was tested. In China they—"

"They use their children like lab rats. And I let you drag me to that island so they could get their filthy hands on me!" Odette was on the verge of tears, not because she actually believed the logic of her accusation, but because she and Bruce had developed differences on so many fronts that it was clear their marriage was over. Hearing Julian approach behind her, Valerie walked in and wrapped an arm around her mother's shoulder.

"Don't get upset, *maman*. Many people give their children enhancements. Besides, I'm fine, see?" Julian surveyed everyone quizzically and took his place while a maid brought in some fresh tea.

Odette cupped her daughter's cheeks with both hands. "Oh, of course you are fine, *ma chérie*, my sunshine. Everyone in Marne will drop dead at the sight of you."

Valerie glanced at her father, who nodded gravely.

"If you still want to," he said, "you can move to France in August."

In spite of Odette's misgivings Valerie had never given her parents cause for concern. She was a sweet child and a loving daughter, if a bit reserved and, as her teenage years rolled in, increasingly skeptical about everything and everyone. Like Julian she had skipped a year in elementary school and later transferred to one of Britain's finest institutions, which placed great demands on its students. But unlike Julian, who quickly became a model student in this new competitive environment, Valerie began coasting and had recently become disruptive. Not long before the breakfast episode, the school had contacted Odette with a polite request to discuss Valerie's development.

Both parents had attended.

"I've had several chats with her," the headmistress began, stating the case tactfully. "We try not to jump to conclusions based on a teacher's opinion or the results of a test. But in twenty years of practice I have only twice heard of a child with such extreme aptitudes, and had never met one myself until now." She made a dramatic pause, anticipating a barrage of questions, but Taylor merely smiled patronizingly while Odette hardly paid attention to her, looking instead at her husband with venom, which he pointedly ignored.

Disappointed, the headmistress cleared her throat. "Anyway," she continued with the same cautious professionalism, "I would like to share with you one of our sessions with her, to illustrate the point." The hologram showed her engaged in a friendly conversation with Valerie. Taylor crossed his arms with faint annoyance, resolving to speak with the board and have Valerie's sessions erased. It should be easy, since Taylor was a major endowment source for the school.

"Let's try something else," the woman was saying in the playback. "Imagine an island with only two sorts of inhabitants—*knights* who always tell the truth and *knaves* who always lie. Now suppose two people from this island come (let's call them John and Peter) up to you and John says 'Peter and I are both knaves', while Peter says 'John is a knave'. What would this tell you about John and Peter: are they both knights, both knaves, one of each, or is it impossible to tell?"

When she finished stating the question, she leaned back and prepared to rephrase it, but was interrupted by Valerie, who said, matter-of-factly: "Well, Peter's telling the truth and John is lying, so John must be a knave and Peter a knight."

"I beg your pardon?" the headmistress was taken aback.

Taylor, as the scene played out, felt something similar. He had heard the riddle before and knew he would need to follow a deductive process just to validate the answer.

"Can you take me through your reasoning?" the woman asked Valerie.

"I'm not sure what you mean." This was Valerie's first hint of uncertainty. "John and Peter both said the other was lying, so they can't both be telling the truth—or both lying—which means only one person is speaking the truth, and that must be Peter, because John said they were both liars."

"Y—yes, that's right."

The headmistress interrupted the video. "At Valerie's age a child's mental development is measured, among other things, by their ability to handle so-called quaternary cognitive relations. Those allow us to see, for instance, that two-thirds is more than three-fifths. But even among adults only some can process quinary relations—of which the knights-and-knaves problem is an example—and even then it is typically accomplished by breaking down the problem into chunks of lower complexity. Valerie not only processes quinary relations at an unusual age; she does so without procedural decomposition. To her it is like being asked to group objects by color or by size: a mechanical task, not one that involves effort."

Taylor's lips formed another little smile. Odette, however, wasn't amused. "You said Valerie was having problems in class. From what I saw, the problem is boredom, so why—"

"Precisely," nodded the headmistress. "We're not talking about learning issues or adjustment problems, which can be easily tackled. You see, Valerie may never be happy in a school environment, in the normal sense of the word."

Odette shut her eyes and pressed her fingers to her temples. "I knew it," she said, the barb aimed at her husband. Taylor placed a hand on her arm, which she quickly pulled out of his reach.

"Now surely," he said, "it can't be that bad. We've been through this before. Why not move Valerie ahead another year?"

"*Mais je te dis que non!*" cried Odette. "She has few enough friends as it is."

"My dear, please, Valerie has plenty of friends. She has Natasha, and Betty, and—and—"

"You can't even name a third, and they are both older than Valerie. She cannot be placed even further away from her age group."

"Now really, Odette—"

"I apologize to you both," interrupted the headmistress. "It isn't my role or my place to take sides here, but your wife does have a point. Even if Valerie were placed further ahead, in a year or two she would be in the same predicament. It isn't the level of instruction that needs adjusting but the pace. Imagine minds as engines, each with different horsepower; schools are not highways but more like city streets, where speed is controlled by stoplights, forcing everyone to move at the same pace. Quick learners must constantly wait for the rest."

"Well then," said Taylor impatiently, "we should find a school that runs like a highway."

"I'm afraid no school in Britain fits the bill. Variable-pace instruction isn't a new concept, but it runs against education policy, which insists on dictating what children are taught, and when."

"And elsewhere?" asked Taylor.

"Well, there *is* a school in France ..."

It was Taylor's turn to scowl as Odette raised an eyebrow to say under her breath: "*Ça ne m'étonne pas.*" Because rich or poor, sharp or obtuse, people rarely let a chance slip by to wax parochial.

It all led to the breakfast discussion, and it was Odette who prevailed in the end—one of the few battles she would successfully wage against her husband, if a crucial one. Valerie didn't make the decision any easier for her parents, being initially opposed to the move, then supportive of it when her father said he'd prefer her to stay, and at last indifferent to either course of action, all within the space of five minutes. They eventually agreed that Valerie would move to her mother's estate in Champagne, a half hour's drive from Champs-Sur-Marne, spending the school year in France and the summers in Devon. There was to be no study program, no timed exams, no boring assignments with deadlines; only a list of topics, a calendar, a tutor and the chance to learn as much as she pleased.

When they were left alone Julian spread jam on his toast and spoke in a perfect imitation of their father. "Really Valerie, you give them too much grief. Why can't you get your act together?"

"Julian, shut up! Everyone goes to school but no one said they're supposed to like it."

"Do you know Tony Steinberg goes to Marne? He was younger than you when he joined."

When Julian's friends gathered in Exebridge days later, he made a point of introducing Tony to her. With the tactlessness that only teenagers can muster, he led Tony to where she sat and pointed as if to an object. "This is the one who's being sent to Marne. She thinks she's smart."

"Hullo," said Tony.

Julian, prey to the universal glee of teasing a younger sibling, said: "Give her one of your tests."

"Sure," said Tony. "What's your address?"

Valerie, her mind filled with murderous thoughts, had no wish to play along, but Julian spelled out her account.

"There," said Tony. "It is last year's. *Bien facile pour un élève de Marne.*"

After smoldering for a while, Valerie went to her bedroom and put on her headset. The left half of her visual field showed the quiz and the right a space for answers. There were four sections of six items each. She picked up a pointer and jotted the numbers one through twenty-four in the air.

The first six were verbal analogies, in order of difficulty: "TENOR is to ALTO as CELLO is to ____?" Valerie wrote VIOLA.

"PRINCIPIA is to OPTICKS as ELEMENTA is to ____?"

It took some online work for her to find the reference to Newton and Euclid. OPTICA, she wrote.

The analogies were followed by associations: "PRIMATE IMITATE ______?" That was easy: APE.

But others were less so: "GARMENT BARNACLE MAGMA ______?" When she hit upon the word MANTLE, Valerie began to be pleased with herself.

The second half of the test was more abstract:

Seeing how the first figure transformed into the second, Valerie applied the same logic to the third figure and drew the answer:

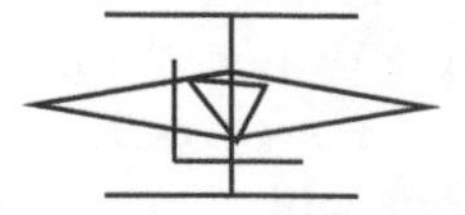

The next item took longer. It asked for the fourth element in a sequence of dot patterns.

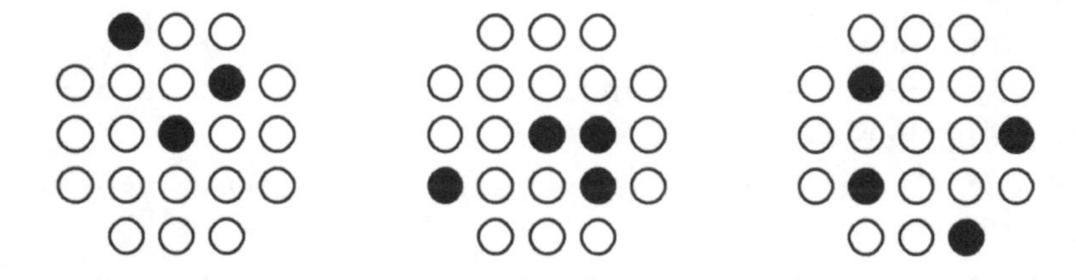

She tried rotations, reflections, and foldings without success. Perhaps the dots were supposed to move independently. In her mind she assigned letters to each dot, and hit on the solution:

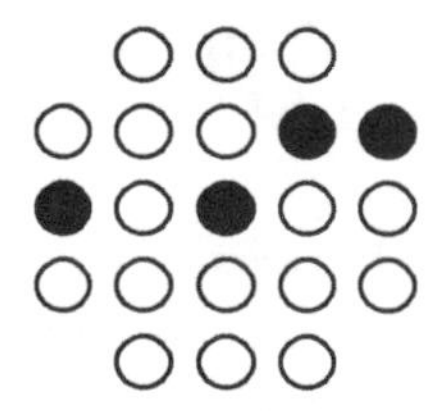

The items varied widely, but in the end it was a simple number sequence that stumped her: 1, 2, 7, 20, 61, __? For an hour Valerie added, subtracted and multiplied, to no avail. After spending more on that item than on the rest of the quiz her patience ran out, because she knew that Tony might leave before she got a chance to make light of his challenge.

Julian and his friends were nowhere to be found. With the staff's help she tracked them to the woods, where they had been chasing a hare with her father's prize hounds. Valerie heard the barking before the group came into view. The boys stood around the base of an old tree, where one dog dug furiously into a burrow, goaded by Julian's yells, while another hound panted nearby, intermittently licking a bloody front paw. At Valerie's approach it stood up and took a few steps in her direction, limping visibly.

"Boy, are you going to get it," she admonished, jumping off her mount.

Julian looked at his sister with annoyance. "He'll be fine. The leg's not broken."

"Leave the beast alone. Is it a squirrel?"

"Get lost Valerie, you sound just like mom."

Ignoring him, she handed Tony her headset. "All but one," she said.

Tony put the visor on. "Not bad: eighteen out of twenty. Number five is wrong, and the answer to the last one is 182."

"Hey Julian," he declared. "Better keep an eye on this sister of yours."

She mistook the source of his flattery and disguised her discomfort with a question. "How many did *you* get right?"

Tony's eyes twinkled. "All of them." Then he grinned and added: "after a couple of days."

A high-pitched squeal announced the dogs had found their mark. Valerie turned away in disgust and rode back, having made a new friend and earned the grudging respect of her brother, who would never again speak lightly of her abilities. Tony sought her out now and then, at length becoming her only male confidant. As for Julian, what might have become bitter sibling rivalry was forestalled by Valerie's gender and their disparate interests. Where he aimed to compete she would concede, and her interests soon took her far from the arena in which Julian meant to prove his worth.

She glanced at Tony, dozing in the sun. He looked contented, his earlier despondency gone. Valerie was struck by the ease with which he managed to be friends with the boys and with her at the same time. When alone with Valerie, he was full of philosophy and gossip; with his male friends he was witty and boisterous. She wondered what he was like at home.

Valerie gazed at the players, most of whom she knew well, studying their expressions as the balance of the game tipped for or against them. Their looks made it clear that they took the play seriously. She had listened to their talk, heard their enthusiastic sharing of trivia about every team sport known to man. Their erudition hinted at hundreds of hours spent watching games, filling their heads with facts that would be irrelevant a decade later. How many movies could she watch, how many books could she read, in the time it had taken Julian and his friends to master the finer nuances of their favorite sport? She spotted a large ant on a dead leaf close to her foot, and suddenly felt certain that an hour spent watching this insect would yield greater insight on life than a week watching sports. But she had grown suspicious of anything that smacked of self-evident truth. Perhaps she was missing something.

She looked at Tony. "Why do you like cricket?"

"I don't," he replied. "Do you?"

Valerie was stunned. "I don't believe I like anything that involves tossing a ball around," she said.

"Nor do I."

"Then why do you play?"

"Um, let's see ... Do you like deafening music?"

"No, but—"

"Then why are you so keen on clubs and parties?"

Valerie shrugged. "I like the scene, the company."

"Well there you go." He hadn't even opened his eyes.

She looked at the field again. "What about them? Do they play just to socialize?"

"No, it's also a proving ground—a rehearsal."

"For what?"

"For power games later in life. Without something to contend for, they'd feel unmoored. People are compelled to establish a pecking order when there isn't one."

"And when there is?"

"Then they feel compelled to challenge it. The behavior has outlived its purpose, but we're stuck with it."

She reflected for a moment. "What will you do after Marne?"

"Cognitive science, most likely."

"Sounds like you're decided."

"Not quite, but if I am to devote years to something, then it had better address the big questions, like why reality is the way it is, or why we perceive it to be so. And I see only two roads leading there:

to study reality or to study perception. The study of reality is old, and to make any progress you must trudge up a steep mathematical hill. I don't think have the stomach for that. And you?"

"I don't know. I agree about big questions, but I have yet to decide what those are."

"Then your problem is worse than mine!"

"I think it's fair," said Valerie, "to ask whether life is something we should do something *with*, or is more like watching a movie, whose purpose lies in the experience itself."

"But why seek a purpose at all? Most discussions I've read suggest that life is what you make of it, whether you decide to save the world or collect toenail clippings."

"Discussions fail because they start with life in the abstract and ask for its purpose, which is like discussing the color of light without specifying *which* light. It makes more sense to start with a life that clearly has purpose, and work from there."

"Which life would that be?"

"My mother has a lapdog bred for companionship, a purpose it fulfills to the letter. Or take the fish in our trout farm, also alive for a purpose."

"A grim one, I'd say."

"Yet one which proves that life can have purpose."

"A purpose external to the life in question, which won't satisfy most people; they want a purpose that doesn't rely on third parties."

"That may be a mistake. A musical note has clear purpose, but only within a given context. To ignore the context is to invite the conclusion that a note's purpose is merely to sound. By the same token, why shouldn't the role of awareness transcend the individual brain, and involve the symphony around it?"

"That's an interesting question. But I would still choose the life I know, even without a purpose, over a dog's life, even with a purpose."

"As would I. Now ask yourself what makes your life preferable to a dog's, even one as pampered as my mother's."

"Oh, I don't know, the life of a dog seems … limited. I'd rather be wheelchair-bound with my wits intact than a healthy dog without them."

"And if your choice were between living in your mind, even if occasionally struck by depression, or living in Kyle's mind over there, always happy?"

Tony rewarded her with a rare laugh. "I would choose mine, thank you very much."

"Yes, I thought you might. Could it be that, rather than valuing life per se, what we value is awareness, and the greater the awareness the greater the value we place on it? Look, we even treat animals differently based on how conscious we believe them to be."

"But, isn't awareness one of those things we become fond of only after the fact?"

"I contend the opposite. People sacrifice pleasure for enlightenment; curiosity kills the cat. Even religion has Adam and Eve trade blissful ignorance for self-aware suffering."

"And it's supposed to have been wrong, a mistake—a sin!"

"The question I struggle with is whether Adam and Eve, having tasted the fruit and the penalty, would really want to trade back."

As Tony chewed on the statement, Julian walked up from behind them with Jason and Hamish. "Off your bum, you bum," Hamish prodded Tony with the tip of his shoe.

Tony followed them to the field and Valerie's attention returned to her mud-encrusted boots. It was time to clean up, so she struck a path towards the house.

DRIVE

> The motives of mankind are plainer than the motions they produce.
>
> —R.D. BLACKMORE, *Lorna Doone*

The luster of youth had somewhat faded from the woman's countenance. Now a commodore, Lin Mei Hsieh had never married, and her knack at alienating men through condescension had long been part of corridor gossip within the Chinese military. Admiral Feng knew her softer side, but made no effort to divulge it, for he was still a strong man in the administration and, in no hurry to retire, planned to live out the rest of his life in his current post, playing the cards that suited him.

Early that morning Hsieh had requested an urgent meeting.

"One of our devices," she said, "detected a high score, in Britain."

Feng's eyebrows rose. "You mean a high Beta."

Hsieh nodded. "You will recall that we assigned someone to work at Taylor Labs. Well, their chief developer, a man called Ramsay, lent a device to Bruce Taylor, who appears to have tested it on himself, his family and, judging by the number of logins recorded, on others as well."

"Are we, uh—?" Feng waved his hands vaguely.

"We are covered. The device was developed outside the purview of Code Seagull, so our exposure risk is nil."

The testing program had been Hsieh's idea, and a hard sell on Feng, who favored a covert search for more obvious signs bound to surface sooner or later. Hsieh, in turn, had always been skeptical of Feng's approach. What if there *were* no obvious signs? What if the children appeared normal in every way? In that case, Feng assured her, all their worries would have been over nothing.

But Hsieh knew better than to take his glibness at face value, for if anyone had gone out on a limb to secure their funding, it was Feng. China's supremacy depended not only on the operation's success, but on its remaining unknown to the rest of the world.

"Do we know to whom the score belongs?" asked Feng.

"No. We will try to procure DNA samples—strands of hair—from all family members under the age of seventeen, including nephews and nieces. Unfortunately his house is busy: he has regular visitors."

"Could he have tried the test at his office, or elsewhere?"

Hsieh shook her head. "The devices store the GPS location of every use. Both high scores came from his home in England."

"Both?"

"There was a high Alpha as well."

"But not—"

"No, not from to the same user."

They both knew how disappointing this was.

"How many scores were logged altogether?"

"The device was on his property for ten days, with eight scores logged during that time. The first is probably his own, because he told Ramsay that he used it himself. There was another low score a day later, and a high Alpha, then five over the week, including the high Beta."

"Family members?"

"We don't know. Drones have captured a steady stream of guests; most are in the relevant age bracket. Either way they must be close to the family. We will set up a long-term watch."

"This could take years."

Hsieh already felt they had been at this for an eternity. "It took the U.S. ten years to find Bin Laden," she said, "and everyone knew who he was."

"He also knew he was being hunted," said Feng. "But go ahead. We shall see which approach produces the first results, yours or mine. By the way," he enquired, "how are the, ah, students doing?"

"Developing as hoped."

Feng smiled. "Can we get them interested in programming?"

"Some are already quite good at it. Why?"

"This device you are using is … rather crude, isn't it?"

"We had our best engineers—"

"Our best, none of which carry the Alpha complement, so they don't know what they're trying to measure: they score low marks on their own test."

Hsieh tried to guess what Feng was hinting at. He had backed her proposal to design the test, even though it was certain to draw international attention. He had also expressed doubts that it would help them to discover a child with the Beta or, even better, with the full module. But his old-school tracking methods had produced no results either. Could this mean a change of heart?

"We could use the Alphas to improve the test. Is that what you are thinking?"

"Not to improve it," Feng replied, "but to build another from scratch. Your device hasn't borne fruit because its purpose is transparent. Cao must have warned his patients to steer their children away from tests. We need to build something attractive for teenagers; something they will pay to use. Our Alpha students are older. Have them seduce their peers, whomever and wherever they are. If we can't ferret them out, let's invite them to show themselves."

***

Bruce Taylor's generation was the second in his family to call Exebridge home. The duke of something or other who had first built the house would have turned in his grave at the thought of a commoner's surname being attached to the title deed of such an estate. As for the fact that the commoner's father was an American, it would have made the poor duke jump out of the grave altogether. But in this narrow sense at least, society had accomplished one of the aims of the revolutionaries of old, namely for wealth and power to devolve away from the old patrician classes of the world and into the hands of a broader group, which quickly competed with itself and became indistinguishable from the first.

Among the elite, Stuarts had given way to Smiths, Sirs to Misters, and family names were no longer of help for guessing social standing. But the foundations of inequity remained intact, since the primal urges that have always led humans to seek ascendancy over their kind run deeper than the ebb and flow of social tide. But for as long as people failed to grasp this simple truth they applauded the power of pigheaded toil and lucky foresight to make moguls out of yokels, and found comfort in the belief that social imbalance was only pernicious if it derived from things other than skill, which was seen as a fair gauge of merit, much like swordsmanship had been regarded as a fair measure of worth in the days when disputes were settled by duels.

Bruce's grandfather, a native of Oregon, had diversified from chemicals to software when quantum computers first hit the market, riding the greatest wave of wealth accrual since the advent of the internet. The new technology transformed the financial sector, an event that his eldest son had brilliantly exploited. But it was the grandson who had led the family business into the life sciences, and by the time he turned sixty, Bruce had witnessed change on a scale never imagined by his visionary grandfather, who had belonged to the last generation to think of progress as something that took place outside people's bodies.

Up until then, technology had steered an unerring course aimed at pampering, rather than improving, human constitution. Fire had been tamed and houses had been built to keep the delicate human frame warm and dry, not to make it sturdier. Antibiotics had fought infection in lieu of the body's natural defenses, and for several centuries people became less resistant to disease, as life's natural weeding process was curbed by chemical intervention. All that, however, had been forgotten by Bruce's day, when the word on everyone's lips, whether in praise or anger, was the increasing perfection of man.

Not far south of Bristol, where Taylor Laboratories sprawled across the countryside, a visit from the Chairman led to a flurry of preparations, which is why Taylor preferred to appear unannounced. His craft lit gently on a platform in the field, its thrusters flaming blue for a loud couple of seconds before shutting down with a sigh. When he stepped down several people had already walked onto the grounds, like ants emerging from their hill. An open vehicle glided up to Taylor, and he recognized his COO Bill Stavins sitting next to the driver. Disappointed, he squinted at the figures on foot. Where was Greg? As the car came to a stop he spotted the young man emerging from the complex. Taylor waved and Greg Ramsay, wearing sneakers as always, broke into a jog.

"Bruce!" said Stavins, beaming genially as he shook Taylor's hand, "has it been two months already?"

"Let's pick Greg up," said Taylor, climbing in. "How's the family?"

"Never better; growing quickly."

"Not in number, I hope."

"Goodness, no. But Samantha is in high school now, worrying about boys, and Billy is twelve and starting to develop that teenage attitude..."

"I know exactly what you mean," said Taylor. "Hullo, Greg. Hop in."

"Morning, Mr. Taylor."

He pointed at the young man's chin. "Is that the new fashion?"

Ramsay had a patch of fuzz next to his Adam's apple. "Didn't get it quite right, did I?" he asked, rubbing his throat with his knuckles.

Taylor grinned. "How are things coming along?"

"Synthesis is complete. None of the lemurs show signs of senescence. The data is solid enough to claim a 15% increase in lifespan before visible aging."

"Splendid," said Taylor. "You can give me the tour later. Bill, I'm telling you this chap will one day make us immortal."

Stavins grimaced good-naturedly. "I'll pass, thank you very much. By the way, should I convene a meeting?"

"Yes. But only with Design for starters—and Legal, we need Richard, too."

"He's in London, but will join virtually."

The meeting room held six people, plus a convincing hologram of the company's Chief Legal Counsel. "Let's begin with the lawsuit," said Taylor. "Richard, will you bring us up to speed?"

The lawyer consulted a document lying before him, invisible to the rest. "Last week," he began, "FullerTech filed suit claiming, under U.S. law, a patent infringement by our Cora line of blood-vessel stimulants, specifically C-5 and C-7, used in beef. They argue—"

"Which is nonsense," thundered a middle-aged man from across the table. "Our sequences increase shelf life by 20%, for loin and for rump. Theirs won't get them halfway there."

"Which is probably what tempted them," said the Chief Counsel, "to file suit in the first place. But to your point, Mike, their claim revolves around the synthesis process, not the products. They say that sequencing requires five-step Brent catalysis, which is FullerTech proprietary."

"Only partially," said the other gruffly, though with less self-assurance. "We use Brent only to build the templates, and then switch to our protocols. We could circumvent Brent entirely, except it wouldn't make sense. The first step of the process is public anyway. We've used it before and they never complained."

An image flashed across Taylor's mind of a row of limbless, anencephalic cows hanging from a beam, their motionless hulks supported by harnesses, feeding tubes protruding from their bodies while electric current kept muscle tone at the optimal level. He had seen his first cattle farm when he was eight. "Disgusting," his grandmother had said when he described it. "When I was a girl we ate meat that had been grazing in the fields—that's what people still do in Africa, you know—not these mutant steaks." Bruce had stared wide-eyed as he imagined the old woman chasing a cow with a fork and knife. "How come we eat farm meat?" he had asked, and his father had explained that beef tasted no better from being allowed to run wild, that farm tissue helped to curb disease and eliminated the need for grazing land, and that it prevented having to slaughter sentient animals. Grandma had remained unimpressed. "I will have some spaghetti, please," she had said, winking at her grandson.

Taylor smiled at the recollection. "Very well," he said, "let's do two things. First, we need to know exactly what 'partially' means in this context. Michael, I want a full protocol detail, with schematics, delivered to Richard's office by Monday. Then local counsel can determine how valid Fuller's case is."

"No problem," said the man.

"Now, this alternate process—is it tested?"

Michael turned to the woman beside him for confirmation. "Absolutely," she said. "But the route we have chosen is ten percent cheaper."

"Well, hopefully cheap won't become dear. Can we implement the other option if it comes to that?"

"Yes," she said, "it's doable."

Taylor nodded. "Let's make sure we're ready just in case. Richard, please keep us apprised of developments in America, and Bill, you call the shots, since you'll be the one briefing the Board." More nods went around the table and Taylor looked at his Legal Counsel. "Anything else you need from us? Very well, then thank you." The lawyer appeared to place a hand on the table, and vanished.

"Now," Taylor proceeded, "let's move on to Zenith. Bill, I only took a quick look at the report you sent me, so if you don't mind..."

Stavins knew Taylor well enough to know that he never gave a cursory glance at anything and had probably read the report through and through. But since he wanted to hear it live, Stavins cleared his throat and turned to a staff member. "Is it loaded?"

The wall on the far end of the room lit up and Stavins took Taylor through the presentation. "The clusters were engineered to be sold as a single module, to emphasize their intended synergy. But we make it explicit that each can be activated alone—the trigger molecules can be injected separately. Since the impact is developmental, parents must decide within the one-to-three-year age window, so the choice will be theirs, not the child's. The key selling point is the clinical-trial data: communications will enrich the visuals with interview quotes, but so far we've highlighted that the full module adds an average of eight years to the prime stage of a person's life."

Taylor was pleased. This development would further strengthen their role in the pursuit of mankind's oldest dream. Aging had long been known to be related to glycation, telomere length, and various types of oxidation. At first Taylor Labs had introduced modifications to maintain lifelong production of telomerase, preserving the length of chromosome ends, which in turn allowed cells to keep dividing like a child's. An early challenge was to prevent cancerous growths, but once that obstacle was surmounted, the Labs' products had increased the average lifespan by 5% in animal carriers, and clinical trials now proved there were no side effects. The first patents would soon expire, but Taylor had wasted no time exploring new lines of research.

Much to his chagrin, a major competitor (a leader in diabetes medicine) had beaten him to germline tweaks that slowed down impairment due to glycation, or food sugars binding to proteins, which damaged connective tissue to cause inflammation. So Taylor had focused instead on unraveling the intricacies of oxidation, a long-misunderstood gamut of processes that damaged tissues but protected against disease. Free radicals—highly reactive molecules that led to cell aging—had also been found to signal repair networks, and research in Bristol had led to discover the relative harm and benefit of each type of radical, allowing to develop DNA clusters of huge promise.

It was essential to keep everything hushed until patents were secured and developments reached completion, but the module would sell for around five thousand, most of if going to clinics and middlemen, but leaving over one thousand in profit for Taylor Laboratories. It was an option that would-be parents wouldn't pass by: the benefits were too obvious; the risks too small. And if twenty or thirty million people worldwide purchased the module... Taylor presently found that he envied the young, much as his elders had envied him. At sixty he was far stronger than his father had ever been, and not from exercising. He wondered what would happen next, but the generation gap loomed ominous like never before.

The young were supposed to improve on the old, if only through better preparation, which was fine as long as people only competed in their age group. But lately that assumption no longer held true. Bruce thought of his offspring. How would they fare against the five-year-olds from the trial group? He hoped the question was rhetorical; that wealth would hold them aloft. After all, the empire had already been built; the hen laid a golden egg every morning and all his children needed to do was keep the foxes at bay.

Still, empire-building and stewardship called for different skills, and the balance between ambition and temperance was not to be taken for granted when relaying a torch. Bruce had exercised painstaking caution with his son and was proud of the outcome. Courageous, pragmatic, politically astute, Julian possessed all the traits of the leader he was meant to be. No child his age or older, Taylor felt certain, could boast a complement of genes to match Julian's.

His approach to parenthood had been that of a conservative investor, albeit one with deep pockets. All bases covered, Julian had been given every advantage available at the time of his conception, and Taylor had what kings of old could only dream of: a made-to-measure heir. Odette had played a passive role in this, accepting Taylor's judgment regarding the genetic constitution of their son, to the point where her contribution to Julian's makeup was less than twenty-five percent rather than the usual half. Taylor had bet ten million on Julian, and even that was a small sum compared to what he had subsequently invested in Valerie.

Emboldened by the fruit of his first procreative enterprise, Taylor had come to believe that he could risk more on the second. A snag was that his wife had put her foot down and demanded that Bruce honor an earlier agreement, not only for their second-born to be a girl, but for Odette to have a say in the matter of the baby's genes. A long discussion ensued. In the end, Bruce adopted the sly approach of letting Odette carry the day on every particular except one: in exchange for their daughter to have all technically-feasible attributes that her mother desired, a neural-development innovation would be included in the package. As certain things could be purchased in Asia that were banned in the West, this required Odette to travel to Indonesia for the implantation procedure. Taylor was careful not to mention the cost of the module, but if anyone was able to hide a nine-figure expense, he could. Taylor was certain that events would prove him wise in his decision. Odette, on the other hand, had always suspected that they would live to regret it.

They were, of course, both right.

QUALM

The happy childhood is hardly worth your while.

—FRANK MCCOURT, *Angela's Ashes*

If blissful youth can be dismissed so offhandedly, it is only because the bittersweet experience of adulthood, whatever its rewards, cannot but feel like a letdown in comparison. Indeed, Ethan would always look back on his early years with nostalgia. His first memories were less of incidents than of sensations: the sweet taste of apple sauce, the image of toys afloat in bathwater, the delicate touch of soap bubbles on his fingertips, the feeling of new grass beneath his feet.

For Nadia was fond of parks, and often took him there. Extensive lawns and lush fronds had a restful effect on her mind, perhaps because they were so different from the arid landscapes of her youth, the memory of which reminded her that, deep down, she would always live in fear. In London, with its generous supply of greenery, Ethan promptly discovered the magic of playgrounds, where wood or steel playsets offered more ways for him to explore his growing sense of balance than any virtual game would provide. And in spite of the loneliness brought on by exile and single motherhood, Nadia had been cautious about making friends during their first years in England, which meant that Ethan had played mostly on his own.

One overcast afternoon towards the end of his fifth summer, when the park had fewer children than usual, Ethan was enjoying the wind in his face and giddy moments of freefall as he hurtled back and forth on his favorite swing, the leftmost of a set with long chains that traced a great arc through the air. He had recently learned to propel himself and was gaining momentum when the most peculiar feeling came over him. He would have been at a loss to describe it, but it crept upon him like encroaching darkness, making him feel that something was amiss with the world. The outline of shapes, of trees and their leaves, acquired unusual vividness, as if a veil had been lifted from his eyes to throw colors into starker relief. With it came a sensation like that of having forgotten something but being unable to remember what. It was a sense of loss, an urgent tug on his heart that demanded something with mute insistence. He tried shutting his eyes to make it go away, but this made it worse, filling his head with vertigo, as if he had stepped off a ledge into a precipice.

He came to a sudden halt from a jerk of one of the chains as he passed close to the ground. The abrupt stop made him slip off the swing and tumble face down in the dirt. Stunned but unhurt, he lifted his head to see another boy, perhaps a year older, holding on spitefully to the swing with both hands. Indignant, his pride hurt, Ethan stood up and rushed back to wrest the swing seat back. "Hey!" he cried, "I'm not done yet." The boy glared at him, tugged quickly at the seat and pushed it forward again viciously, slamming the edge against Ethan's face. He felt a sharp blow on his lip and tottered back. The hand that he brought to his mouth felt something wet, and a drop of blood slid between his fingers. Ethan turned frightened in Nadia's direction, but she was already on the spot. She grabbed the young aggressor by the ear, twisting it strongly enough to wring a yelp from the brat. "That was *very* wrong of you. Don't ever do it again." The boy began whimpering, and with a final yank Nadia sent him squealing away, then bent tenderly over Ethan, pulled a paper tissue from her purse and applied it to his lip. "There, you'll be all right. It won't swell if we let it bleed a little."

Ethan was wondering whether to cry or put on a brave face when he saw a man striding towards them, face crimson with anger and chin concealed by a blond, partly-grown stubble. He sported ragged cotton denims, a backwards-facing baseball cap, a sleeveless shirt, and an ornate tattoo on his upper right arm. Ethan saw in his eyes the same stare of the boy who had attacked him. "You fuckin' bitch!" the man shouted as he drew nearer, "I'll teach you to lay a hand on me lad." Ethan's eyes opened wide in panic, then in surprise as Nadia rose a bit and casually lifted the hem of her dress up to her waist, exposing her thigh to the approaching man while she kept her eyes on Ethan. Why her mother might want to reveal her leg was completely beyond the child's imagination, but if her intent was to distract the man then it wasn't working, for he was now upon them. Nadia suddenly righted herself, and in a blur of motion shot her exposed leg into the air at a near vertical angle, slamming the heel into the man's nose as her other foot dug into the ground, acting as anchor and lever. A muffled pop was heard and the man's feet briefly lost contact with the ground. He fell back on the hard soil, where he covered his nose and began to groan, rolling from side to side in pain. Ethan was still in shock when Nadia picked him up and away from the scene as fast as she could.

Back home, still catching her breath, she sat in an armchair and held Ethan close to her for a long time, lost in thought. When she finally spoke, her voice was reassuring. "Looks like we're going to have to avoid that park for a while, aren't we?" She ran a hand through Ethan's hair and held his chin. "Let me see that lip. See? I told you it would be fine."

Ethan had shed exactly one tear from each eye. He scratched the itchy trails they had left on his cheeks.

"Mummy?"

"Yes, dear?"

"Will I be able to do that when I grow up?"

"Do what?"

"You know ... when you kicked the man."

"Ah."

"Will I?" he insisted. "I've tried the exercises that you do in the morning, but I can't. Are they only for women?" There was genuine concern in his voice, as if he had just learned that the male half of the species was handicapped.

Nadia looked at him tenderly. "It isn't something you're born with. It takes practice—long and hard practice."

"Can I learn?"

"Um, I suppose you c—" Her eyes lit up suddenly. "You know, that's not a bad idea; not a bad idea at all," she said, squishing him. And so it was settled.

Having acquired some proficiency in self-defense, Ethan daydreamed of using his skills to rescue a schoolgirl from the hands of ruffians. But since he got along well with classmates, and rather awkwardly with the girls that struck his fancy, his schooldays were less epic than his daydreams. As it happened, the only person that he ever rescued from abuse was a younger boy, which landed him in more trouble than he could have anticipated, although it did earn him the kiss of a fair maiden in the end.

But that was still years ahead. Martial arts provided a sense of purpose and discipline, bolstered his confidence, and cast Nadia in a different light in his eyes, revealing a side of her that he had rarely glimpsed before, but which would surface increasingly often.

Most children give little thought to their mother's child-rearing or to how far it strays from the norm, but Ethan would remember Nadia's as being full of contradictions: strict and uncompromising at times and unusually permissive at others, unlike what he glimpsed in other parents. Her only rule, so easy to follow that it became a habit, was never to post pictures of himself online, and to use only his first name. But Nadia never asked him to make his bed, pick up his clothes, or do the dishes; she never yelled at him nor expected his assistance in household chores. And yet when it came to his own accomplishments, while she readily celebrated his successes, she challenged his rare failures with the words: "If I can do it, so can you," making them sound as a simple statement of fact, which made them sting more.

During Ethan's early years Nadia had devoted her full time to the child. On occasion she would take Ethan downtown, but in general she felt threatened by crowds, and while she would eventually gain confidence and in time began socializing, her life was initially reclusive. While Ethan slept, she cooked, watched television, or read. While he was awake they played games, and she taught him to read. This was a watershed event, because words led to stories of faraway places and distant times, of wonders and strange happenings. And the stories led to questions, and Nadia had enough foresight not to feed him the canned answers that she had received as a child, which she saw as insidious bedfellows of dogma that stunted the mind under the pretense of guiding it. And Ethan was less surprised by her knowing so much than by her not knowing everything.

This prompted him to seek information on his own, and although Nadia shielded him while she could, Ethan soon discovered that facts abounded online. At the age of six he saw a globe in a shop with names written all over. He begged her to buy the globe and spent a week poring over it until he had mastered every detail. He then quizzed Nadia, asking her which was largest—New Zealand, Madagascar, or Ireland—and laughed when she got them in the wrong order, and Nadia laughed with him.

The inevitable question soon came: "Where were you born?" he asked one afternoon as she was folding laundry.

Nadia had rehearsed the reply, but was still taken by surprise and Ethan was looking at her when she finally said, "in Ankara, the capital of Turkey."

That much was true.

"Are we Turkish?"

By now she was on her guard. "I am Turkish and also British. You are British, but can choose to become Turkish if you want, when you turn eighteen."

"Was I born in London?"

"No, in Ankara." That's what some fake records said, though it hardly mattered, for his British papers were real enough. The lie, however, left her throat as dry as it had the first time.

"Why don't we speak Turkish, then?"

Because I hardly remember, she thought. "Because we live in England, not Turkey." She tried to sound casual.

Ethan asked her to say several things in Turkish, and she obliged.

"I want to learn," he declared.

"Why? You will have few people to practice with. If you want to learn a language, then why not learn Spanish or Chinese?"

"No!" cried Ethan in a rare fit of willfulness, "I want to learn Turkish."

"All right, then, have it your way." And from then on she forced herself to address him in Turkish. It felt odd at first, but she soon realized that his young mind picked up the words as fast as she could remember them. She downloaded some books for him. He never really mastered the language, but their conversations became a mish-mash of tongues. When walking together in a crowd, they enjoyed, like many immigrants before them, having a private form of communication.

She knew there was more to Ethan than met the eye, but Nadia had never been let in on what to expect, so she fretted constantly over him. When Ethan failed to talk unusually early, she was more relieved than disappointed. She never reasoned that even sequoias are unimpressive as saplings, and the fact was lost on her, having no point of comparison, that he had learned to read without effort. Reassured by the apparent normalcy of his progress she started to encourage it, and with some trepidation she began to allow Ethan to hang out with schoolmates, on condition that they play indoors. As a result, he developed an early taste for video games, but his attempts to get Nadia to share his enthusiasm were greeted with gentle frowns. "I used to play a lot at your age," she said, "until I realized that the games are all the same."

"No, they're not," Ethan protested.

"They are too—all point and shoot."

"This is an adventure game. You follow clues to discover things."

"You should try chess instead." Surely something like chess would bring any unusual skills to light.

"What's that?" he asked.

She helped him to download an online version. "You can play against the program," she explained, "but it's more fun if you play with a person. Let me show you," and she went through the rules with him. Ethan made the obvious mistakes, which she pointed out. He found his minor pieces gobbled up, and in a few minutes Nadia had cornered his king. They played another round and Ethan did better, grasping the essence of the space in which the different pieces could move. Nadia was kind, but relentless, and she didn't offer as much help as the first time, so Ethan's defenses eventually collapsed.

Ethan pursed his mouth as he surveyed his defeat. Nadia looked at him and smiled. At least there was nothing unnatural about his performance. Had they persevered, they would both have learned something, but that was the last time they played chess together, because not long afterwards Ethan took to a very different art form.

Nadia had rented a series of furnished flats for them to live in, which made it easy to decamp in a hurry, if needs be. She had come to feel safe in the city's anonymity, but stuck to the habit of changing residence every few years, not wishing to become well known in any neighborhood. This was hard on Ethan's budding friendships, but she was adamant. Their third move took them to a modern condo with a small study that had an electric piano—a well-built instrument with a weighted keyboard and proper sound.

"Look, mum, I bet it's just like Clive's!" he exclaimed, referring to a schoolmate who often sat at the piano before music class and played short classical pieces to which Ethan listened attentively.

Ethan began pounding on the keys, randomly at first and then methodically, delighting in the high and low notes, the octave pattern, the difference between half and whole tones, and becoming so absorbed in the task of noise-making that he stopped only when Nadia begged him for a respite. The next day he was at it again, and Nadia began thinking of sending the thing away when she discovered a pair of headphones in a drawer. After that she heard only the soft pattering of Ethan's fingertips on the keys.

Two months later Ethan came to her in a flurry of excitement and declared that he had learned to play 'one of Clive's pieces'. She followed him to the piano, where he proceeded to demonstrate.

She had only heard the melody a handful of times and didn't know its name, but the tune was unmistakable: Beethoven's *Für Elise*, note for note.

Nadia burst into clapping. "Ethan, that's beautiful!" There was pride in her face, and something else, which Ethan didn't recognize but made him feel good all over. He took up her offer of piano lessons and (like most beginners) he hated sheet music at first, but gradually came to appreciate the help it provided, especially once he realized (unlike most beginners) that he could hear the music in his head as he read the score. Nadia was dazzled by his growing skill in something so far removed from her experience, and eventually became curious as to his intentions. When he turned thirteen she asked him if he planned to play professionally, and was surprised by the finality of his answer.

"No. There are three kinds of musical talent, and I only have the second kind."

"Good heavens! What do you mean by three kinds?"

Ethan explained. "The first is a talent for following music—for recognizing styles, humming a melody, knowing when someone sings in tune. Not everyone has it."

Like a palate for wine, Nadia thought, but kept this to herself. "And the second?" she asked.

"It's the skill to play music, to interpret it. It goes beyond appreciation."

"Beyond app—" Nadia cast a suspicious look at him. "Did Clive fill your head with these ideas?"

"No, but I believe I'm right."

"I see. What about the third level?"

"That's the ability to create music. I don't have it."

"Have you tried?"

"Many times. I don't have it," he repeated categorically.

"You could still be a famous pianist," she said, although fame was the last thing she wished for him.

Ethan shook his head. "I don't like performing."

It was true that audiences made Ethan uncomfortable. Whenever he felt watched, he fumbled, in contrast with Clive, who was a show-off. And he hated the thought of endless practice, which he knew was expected of pianists. Ethan had listened to recordings of his favorite pieces by several virtuosi. They all had an individual style, and he learned the meaning of interpretation. But while he liked some better than others, there were those among which he would have been hard pressed to choose. Why would he drive himself mad practicing a sonata only to have someone else's version judged superior?

But while Ethan's pastimes were meant to entertain no one but himself, and his achievements sought to win no praise but his mother's, they eventually attracted attention elsewhere.

In the forgotten past of man's ancestry, the family may have been the strongest shaper of juvenile minds. But in modern cultures its influence has lost ground to that peculiar social institution known collectively as 'school'. For Ethan it would be a patchwork of events, now memorable, now commonplace: exams, horseplay, friendships struck or lost, moments of pride or self-conscious embarrassment, and always, underneath it all, a pervasive sense of tedium. Because the formal education of children has always been second only to the justice system in its inability to keep up with the times; and British schools, where venerable practices such as caning the backside of students survived until the dawn of the twenty-first century, had never been at the forefront of a field notoriously resilient to progress.

Not that anyone was willing to admit it—in fact, education in Ethan's day was regarded as nothing short of revolutionary, riding as it did in the wake of two reforms, neither of which, unfortunately, was visionary in nature. The first—a belated reaction to the rise of the internet—had involved a shift in emphasis from the retention of facts to their unearthing. The bits of information from which learning is built, so hard to come by only a century before, had almost overnight become available to everyone who cared to look, and in such surplus that the ability to sift through an ocean of data had become a critical skill.

The second reform was also remedial: an attempt to address the rising gullibility of people in a society where specialization had increased to the point where blatant ignorance was no longer the exclusive province of the uneducated. The blame was laid on the cursory, watered-down exposure of adolescents to an excessive number of disciplines, which was claimed to impede the development of genuine understanding: the greater the collective knowledge of mankind, the more pitiful the share held by individuals. Ethan's school, a rather good one at the time (aside from the few that only the right connections—which Nadia lacked—could procure) boasted novel approaches to instruction, but in fact still suffered from glaring shortcomings that would have made Victorian pedagogues nod their heads in recognition, to wit: universal prescriptions involving sequenced courses to be marched through in lockstep, fixed-length academic cycles, consensus-based study programs with obsolete curricula based on centralized management philosophies, and teaching methods that held individual ability in complete disregard, followed by tests that measured little else.

Until the age of ten Ethan endured boredom stoically, idling the hours away doodling, playing with imaginary friends, building wire puzzles, and being occasionally scolded for it. Then his school adopted the use of standard universal schoolbooks in class. These e-books consisted of pages of electronic paper attached to a processor-laden spine that made them look like octavo-size printed books, except that they displayed only sanctioned material. This frustrated Ethan at first, until he chanced upon a loophole in the system: the books granted students access not only to the texts used in class, but to anything deemed legitimate aid, including the school library. Ethan was thus able to treat himself to *The Lord of the Rings*, *The Three Musketeers*, *The Wind in the Willows*, and a wide range of adventure and fantasy novels.

He then made friends with Jeremy Hastings, a boy who kept largely to himself and was a frequent target of derision for his chubby figure and the prominent display of something that Ethan had never seen among his peers: prescription glasses. When Jeremy, who was usually alert and on top of things, hesitated a second too long to answer a simple question from a teacher, Ethan realized that he wasn't the only one reading unorthodox literature, so he approached the boy during recess.

"What do you read in class?"

"Huh?"

"You've been using your textbook for something other than coursework. I do it all the time; I just finished the Foundation trilogy."

"Ah, yes," said Jeremy, suddenly more responsive. "Science fiction: I don't have time for that. I've only read Orwell because he's on the list."

"What list?"

"Of the best 100 books, of course; you can't read just anything. You've got to have a plan."

Ethan had the sudden feeling of being lectured. "I read what I enjoy," he said defensively.

"Only the more reason to stick to the list, or you won't know if something is good until after you've read it. You could spend all your life reading and miss all the good stuff."

Ethan had just gone through his first summer at Exebridge, so he got the point, even if he found Jeremy to be rather dogmatic. "Where did you find the list?" he asked.

"It's online, of course; but my father gave it to me. He teaches literature at Oxford." Ethan felt relieved, as a reason for Jeremy's erudition seemed to present itself. "There are many lists," Jeremy went on, "but this is the most authoritative. There's another with the top 100 musical pieces of all time. I can send them to you, if you want."

Authoritative. Ethan masticated the word. But he took the boy's offer and, armed with these quaint roadmaps, proceeded to tackle universal culture.

The journey proved long and arduous, but a lot more fun than he had first imagined. The world of music was quicker to explore, for listening was easier than reading. He discovered not only new pieces by his favorite composers, but also treasures to which he would have never been drawn on his own, like Satie's Gymnopédies or Vaughan Williams' Lark Ascending. His piano teacher had told Ethan that he shared the surname of a famous conductor, so he listened to some old recordings and mentioned them to Jeremy, who gave him a supercilious "Oh yes, Karajan is overrated". He also discovered Franz Liszt, whose Second Hungarian Rhapsody he silently vowed to learn one day. As for literature, having tried a couple of books from Jeremy's list and found them indigestible, he went back to his schoolmate for guidance. "No, no, no," Jeremy laughed, "don't start with Proust. Read Twain or Poe instead; or Victor Hugo."

Ethan had read *A Connecticut Yankee*, for the Arthurian content, so he followed Jeremy's advice and read *Huckleberry Finn*, which he loved. He then turned to Poe, which he liked even better—especially *The Mask of the Red Death*—and from then on he was hooked, even though years later he would argue that Lovecraft's *The Rats in the Walls* or Blackwood's *The Willows,* neither of them on Jeremy's list, were better than Poe's stories. From this he drew another lesson: never to blindly trust the opinion of others. He also learned the value of lists, of rankings, and of expert opinion in the labyrinth of life; he learned about good taste, bad taste, and snobbery, and learned that some books work their magic through the power of the stories they tell, while others mesmerize through the strength of the telling. And he slowly came to see what many a critic spends a lifetime without suspecting: that style, the storyteller's most formidable weapon, should always play second fiddle to clarity, which in turn should be slave to precision.

Ethan completed his coursework at home, and in class, while teachers spoke or students took turns at answering questions, he would look up only when his turn came along—twice on average per period—and return to his reading. Eventually, word of this habit got around.

Briefcase in hand, a mild-mannered man greeted the school's principal. "Morning, Sarah," he said. "You were looking for me?"

Ms. Perkins looked up. She tried to maintain a solemn style with all school personnel, but with Wilson she couldn't help it and her lips curled up. "Come in, Geoffrey. I'm reviewing Ethan Karajan's case. You have his results?"

"Ah, yes, yes, Karajan," said Wilson, consulting his notes. "Let's see: friendly chap, full of curiosity—quite cultured, I must say. He may be the most interesting subject I've tested."

"Student, Geoffrey; these are children, not subjects; we are not in a hospital. Now, what did you find so interesting?"

"Well, his overall score is fairly high—in the top 0.1% of the general population, which is more than enough for advanced placement, though I've seen higher ones. I concur that he could skip a grade or two, but I wouldn't call it abnormal—after all, fifty thousand Britons would score at least higher. On the other hand, his spatial ability..."

"What about it?"

"It's hard to explain without an example." Fishing into his briefcase, Wilson produced several pieces of wood and others made of plastic. The former looked like building blocks, while the latter, resembling Tetris-game shapes, he proceeded to line up on the desk.

"Our battery includes a puzzle that involves arranging nine

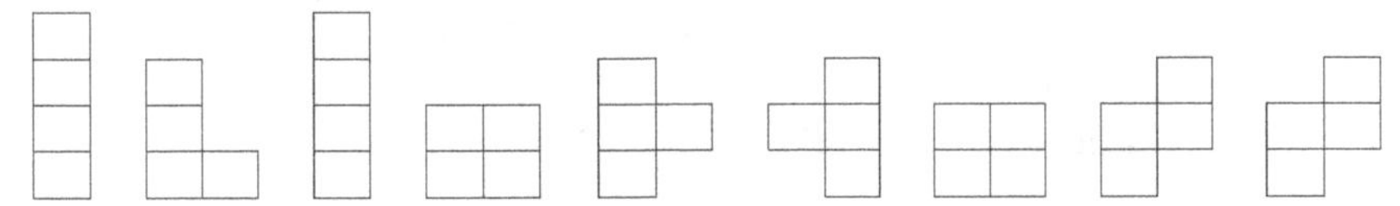

shapes, called tetrominoes, into a 6 × 6 square. It took Ethan a minute to come up with this solution." Wilson carefully put the pieces together to illustrate:

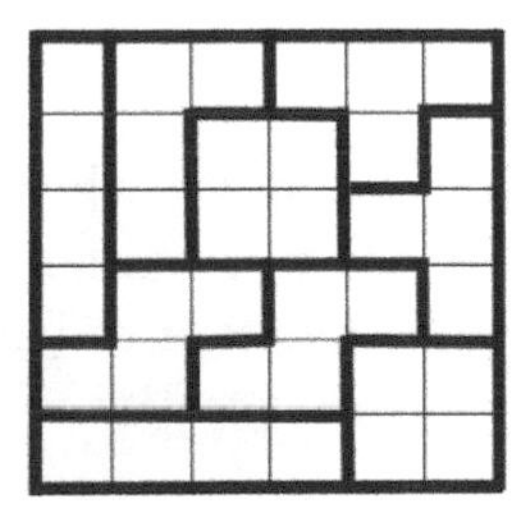

"That in itself doesn't mean much—I've seen some do it faster. But something about the way he approached the task made me challenge him further. The boy kept looking at me as if to make sure that I wasn't pulling his leg, so I gave him this other puzzle to try—just for fun, since it's not part of the battery." Wilson called her attention to the wooden blocks. "The aim in this case is to assemble a cube. It's called Hara's Diabolical Cube, after its designer."

"I can see why."

"The only known solutions, aside from Hara's, were found by computer. Ethan solved it the time it took me to complete a phone call."

"He could have looked it up online."

"I was watching; my office has glass walls."

"Are you saying he has some sort of savant syndrome—like people who count cards at blackjack or draw cityscapes from memory?"

"No, this is different, something I've never seen before."

The note to Nadia asked her to meet with Ms. Perkins, who informed her, in a rehearsed speech coated with euphemisms, that Ethan had started behaving irresponsibly in school, paying scant attention, and had been caught—of all imaginable perversions—*reading* in class.

This was the last thing that Nadia expected to hear. "Reading what?" she asked.

"I believe it was *Les Misérables,*" said the principal, with dramatic emphasis.

"Oh," Nadia sounded relieved. "Well, I haven't read it, but I understand it's nothing to be ashamed of."

"No, of course not, it is required reading for the upper forms. But Ethan is in sixth year."

"Have his marks dropped?"

"No—well, at least not to the point where it would be cause for concern. What his teachers are worried about is that he might be bored. We have been debating whether to have him skip a grade."

"I see. Well, I shall have a talk with him, and if he agrees, you have my permission. I suppose you think it is advisable, or you wouldn't be talking to me, yes?"

"We were not certain at first. You see, all sorts of children attend this school. Many have traits that have been selected by their parents, and if there's any genetic predisposition towards accelerated learning, then we allow parents to point it out so that we can prepare. In Ethan's case, you didn't mention any genetic intervention, but unusually smart children are naturally born now and then. I wanted to make sure that his behavior was in fact due to boredom, so we had him do some tests."

Nadia's tone became icy. "Ethan didn't mention that. What sort of tests?"

"They are games, really, questions and puzzles, followed by a chat with a trained professional."

"But no medical procedures?"

"Heavens, no! That would be against school policy. We respect student privacy and would have asked for your consent if that were the case."

"Which I appreciate."

"Yes, well, anyway, the tests validate our findings, so with your permission and Ethan's, he will be placed in eighth year next term. He skipped third, did he not?"

"Yes. Why do you ask?"

"Oh, I was just wondering if you knew that his spatial perception skills are unusually high—I mean off the charts. He has a special gift that might be worth exploring. If you agree—"

Nadia shook her head. "No more tests."

"But—"

"I'm very sorry. This is as far as I want it to go. Please."

Ms. Perkins immediately softened. "I understand," she said. "I'm a mother, too. All we want is for our children to lead happy, normal lives. Old Geoffrey will be disappointed, but a child's welfare always comes first."

Nadia forced a smile. "Thank you."

"Very well, then. Just give me a call when you've talked to Ethan, would you?"

Nadia's hand felt clammy when the principal shook it, and she correctly guessed that Nadia was nervous. But Ms. Perkins would have never imagined that the same soft hand was ready to drive a pair of scissors through her throat if she probed any further into Ethan's constitution.

PERSPECTIVE

> The power of instruction is seldom of much efficacy, except in those happy dispositions where it is almost superfluous.
>
> —EDWARD GIBBON, *The Decline and Fall of the Roman Empire*

Sitting in the garden with her eyes shut, Valerie could have sworn she could tell whether she was in France or in England just from the scent of the country air. Her mother's château was a modest abode next to Exebridge (Taylor's prenuptial agreement had seen to that). But ten acres and five bedrooms were space enough for her mother and a steady parade of suitors, whose visits extended anywhere from hours to months.

At dinner that evening sat Odette, doing most of the talking, her daughter, doing most of the listening, her eighty-year-old father, who usually did neither, and Alain, a well-known French actor and Odette's current fling, whose grandiloquent interjections aimed to charm and sometimes succeeded, at least with the object of his affections.

"I heard," said Odette to her daughter, "that Julian is planning to study economics."

"He may change his mind; he still has two years left," said Valerie with complete lack of interest. No one but Julian himself could be the source of this information, and she felt annoyed by her mother's choice of words. Why couldn't she just say *Julian said*?

Her mother persisted. "Have you given any thought to your plans?"

Alain looked up expectantly; Valerie's grandfather remained bent over his soup.

"I *have* studied economics, among other things."

Alain looked back down at his plate, while Odette's father smiled at his half-raised spoon. Valerie, from her own perspective, was merely stating a fact, but Odette awarded her daughter a stern look. "There's no need to be rude. I'm only trying to make conversation. Why is it always so hard to hold one with you?"

"It's not. I just wish conversations were not about me, that's all."

"We were talking about something else a minute ago and you still weren't interested."

"You mean I was silent. So is Grandfather." The old man emptied a spoonful with a barely audible slurp.

"That's not a fair comparison, Valerie!" Odette's complaint was made more poignant by the French pronunciation of her daughter's name, with its guttural *r* and last-syllable stress. "You are young and growing; at your age I was *full* of talk. With your intelligence, my darling, you should be hungry to learn. Instead all we get from you are monosyllables. Is this how you behave with your friends?"

Valerie raised her glass to her lips and shrugged. "Mostly, yes, except if engaged in meaningful conversation."

"And what conversation would that be, *mademoiselle mépris*?"

"The Great Conversation, of course."

"Excuse me?"

"I think," interjected Alain, "she means philosophical discourse."

"Oh, for the love of God," exclaimed Odette. "Do you really expect us to sit here discussing metaphysics?"

"Is that what you think I want? To debate inanely like people who argue over politics, looking at everything from their narrow stance and pontificating on topics they barely understand? You want to know the questions I have? I'd like to know the purpose of life and why it feels the way it does; I'd like to know why we have a sense of humor and why we fall in love. I'd like to know if our will is truly free, why there is such a thing as time, and why anything exists at all. Of *course* I think about my plans—study choices and the rest—but nobody can be sure of making the right choices unless they can look into the future and see themselves on their deathbed examining the life they have led, which by definition is impossible!"

Valerie paused for breath.

"*Le diable m'emporte!*" exclaimed her grandfather, his eyes merry with appreciation. All heads turned at the first words the old man had uttered all evening. Odette looked at him with concern and threw reproving glances sidelong at her daughter. But grandpa was merely chuckling. "Engaging in the Great Conversation," he said to Valerie, "is like speaking with people from a distant star: to answer questions posed by long-dead people, in the hope that unborn generations will answer your own. It's a lonely pursuit, *ma petite*. But take a walk with me after dinner, and I'll let you in on a secret."

They ambled down the garden path in the fading light, two generations apart, each the other's favorite person in the world. He was the only grandparent she remembered, for Bruce Taylor had been born late in his parents' life, a pattern he had chosen to follow in turn, as do those for whom children are more of an afterthought than a dream fulfilled. As for Odette's mother, she had died from a blood clot shortly before Valerie's birth.

Her closeness to her grandfather went back to when Valerie was three, and even then he recognized in the toddler an unusual glint of awareness, a gentle sense of wonder that went hand-in-hand with intolerance for the commonplace. The girl could be tender and harsh, often in the same sentence, but he was in her eyes the only person who would never disappoint, if only because he seemed to know what made her tick.

One afternoon in her not-so-distant childhood, when Valerie sat moping in a corner because her parents were busy entertaining and all the children were playing together, which had kept her from going on horseback (she was too young to ride alone), her grandfather had caught sight of her and suggested a stroll, with the promise to show her something special. He took her to a sunny spot near the conservatory where a large spider had spun its web. "Now look," he said, producing a small jar from his coat pocket. Inside was an angry hornet. Valerie's eyes grew wide. He unscrewed the lid, approached the web, and with a supple jerk flung the tiny prisoner against the sticky threads. The wasp buzzed and struggled, entangling itself further. The spider was upon it in an instant, wrapping its victim in silk as if whipping up cream. After a minute the arachnid, having readied its next meal, retired back to the center of the web.

Valerie for once became as loquacious as her mother. "Did you see?" she said eagerly, and went on to describe in great detail what they had just witnessed together.

Her grandfather then delivered a second surprise. From a different pocket he produced another jar. This wasp was a shiny beast with a long, black abdomen and a small white mark between its wings. "What do you think will happen?"

Valerie stared at the insect. It appeared to be smaller than the previous wasp.

"The same?"

The old man grinned broadly. "Watch," he said.

Employing the same maneuver, he dropped the wasp onto the net. It didn't become entangled, but righted itself up and proceeded to walk across the web as if at home. The spider, which had lain motionless, took off hurriedly in the opposite direction, left the web and scampered down a branch. Valerie couldn't believe her eyes: the previous lesson had just been turned on its head. She turned to look at her grandfather with the tender gaze of astonishment that Odette always pined for but was never able to produce in her child. "What happened?" she asked.

"This wasp is called an ichneumon, and it *hunts* spiders."

Valerie would recall that as her best afternoon in months. Now, as she walked with her grandfather over a decade later through the same garden, she felt a pang of melancholy at the thought that he wouldn't be around forever. "What did you want to tell me?" she asked.

"It isn't really a secret. I just didn't want to discuss it with Alain there and your mother lecturing."

"Right," said Valerie. She held Alain in reasonably good esteem, but her concept of him was influenced by her father, whose rarefied social standing made him look down on individuals that drew sighs from the masses, so that he viewed movie stars with the disdain that some reserve for circus performers: as interesting but quaint individuals deserving more pity than admiration.

"When I was your age," said her grandfather, "I had little interest in old people. It seemed to me that they shared the earth with us almost like another species. Their conversation bored me, because their wisdom drew from anecdotes that felt out of place or out of touch. They made noises when they ate, and they even smelled funny… Do I smell funny to you?"

She gave the question some thought. "I would recognize your scent, but I don't know how you used to smell when you were young."

The old man nodded. "We lack a shared frame of reference. Maybe that's what makes eighty so hard to explain to sixteen. But there was a philosopher who said that there is knowledge by acquaintance and knowledge by description. My knowledge of old age is of the former sort, while yours can only be of the latter—a poor substitute, all things considered, because when it comes to life all comparisons fall short. But maybe you can picture how your perspective will change if you consider something that has a clear beginning and an end. Take a summer vacation: just as it seems at first to stretch infinitely before you, only to later leave you wondering where it all went, so it is with life. In the end we are like sea creatures allowed just a brief peek above the surface. The time we are allotted seems unfairly short for the immensity we must survey, and at my age it feels like you've hardly begun to get your bearings when the current starts pulling you back under. But wouldn't you say that a summer well spent feels better than a summer wasted?"

"Yes, except," protested Valerie, "that people can learn from previous summers, but life seems to demand getting it right the first time. How can people do that, luck aside?"

"Well, there's tons of advice on how to live one's life—all of it rotten. And although I wish I could offer you something better, the task is beyond my powers. At best I can tell you what life is not: life isn't a reward, a punishment, a test, or a competition, even if it sometimes feels like all of those things.

"When I was your age—here I go again—discussing the meaning of existence usually involved discussing religion and God, concepts that have lost so much currency that they are no longer given a fair hearing outside of mosques and America's Bible Belt. Atheism is now the fashion, but people love extremes in faithlessness every bit as much as in faith, and when philosophy jettisoned God it threw out the proverbial baby with the bathwater, because the concept of God is quite useful as a synonym of totality."

"Why?"

"Because it shows the dangers of explanations that fit the individual viewpoint. You know those nested Russian dolls?"

"Matryoshkas."

He smiled. "If one doll tried to account for its hollow structure, it might conclude that hollowness is needed to fit a smaller doll inside it. In a way, this is trivially true, but the individual doll's viewpoint misses the visual impact of the series. Only the full array reveals its æsthetic purpose. In the same vein, tackling an existential question without addressing totality just pushes the question sideways, leading to another question. The real meaning of totality probably involves how its parts relate to one another, rather than just the structure, or behavior, of the parts in isolation."

"But, how would totality, which is by definition entirely self-referential, make sense of itself?"

"Perhaps you'll tell me one day, but the answer is likely to be beautiful, because nature's workings are always more wondrous than humans assume them to be. Anyway, I digress. Do you recall when I read Jules Verne to you as a child?"

Valerie smiled. "Voyage to the Center of the Earth!"

"And the passage you liked best—remember that?"

"When they find the old marking by Saknüssem?"

"Right. Do you know why it's the climax of the story? Because it's often exciting to walk in the footsteps of fable and legend; for whatever reason, communing with a fellow awareness brings great thrill. And since so much joy comes from shared experiences, it helps to have counterparts who are still alive. So look for them, Valerie, if not at home, then elsewhere."

PRIDE

> But what [my father] had to offer I didn't want—and what I wanted he didn't have to offer.
>
> —PHILIP ROTH, *Portnoy's Complaint*

Ethan and Valerie had already met thrice. The first was little more than an introduction, mediated by Bruce Taylor. Visual creature that he was, Ethan had taken in the sight of her like a drowning man draws air into his lungs, but he was too focused on the setting to do anything but proffer a polite handshake and a gauche how-do you-do. Valerie, much at ease but scarcely interested in meeting the housekeeper's son, had planned to reply in kind by holding his hand perfunctorily, as her brother had done. She had once been introduced to the head gardener's daughter and remembered the girl's callused palms, sadly incongruent with the man's claim that his daughter was too dainty to toil beside him.

But on this occasion the fleeting contact flooded her with the strangest sense of well-being, drawing her attention to his features and making her fingers linger in his grasp. The sophisticated woman that she would later grow up to be would have relished the sensation. But Ethan withdrew his hand and that was the end of the episode.

Their second encounter was when she caught Ethan in the library with the device left by Julian and his friends. After Ethan's flustered departure she had walked over to the desk and retrieved the gadget from the drawer. She knew it well, for she had tried her hand at it, encouraged by her father. She put on the viewer and activated the power switch. Ethan's score was displayed, and it was almost the opposite of her own, which had been 120 on the second part and rather low on the first. This struck her as odd, but she returned the device to its place.

In their third interaction Ethan played an unwitting part. After a day in town, Valerie had returned to Exebridge alone, knowing that Julian and her father were still to arrive. Upon entering the house she was surprised to hear the faint sound of an orchestra playing somewhere. She was inclined to head directly upstairs, but knew that if guests had arrived she would be expected to make an appearance, so she paused in the main vestibule. The sound most definitely came from the ground floor somewhere off to her left, perhaps from the library. Walking in that direction she recognized the orchestral chords from Chopin's first piano concerto. The playback was from the end of the first movement, and as her mind followed the music she instinctively anticipated the piano passage that would follow. When it did, she froze in her steps, halfway across a sitting room known as the 'blue' salon.

The piano was distinctly louder than the orchestra, as if two different sound systems were playing at different volumes. Aside from a few guests, she couldn't recall anyone ever playing the grand piano, a magnificent old Bössendorfer. But someone was now clearly at the keyboard. She crossed the carpet to the library door, expecting to find a small gathering. Instead, sitting alone with his back to her was the housekeeper's son. A cylindrical speaker, no larger than a phone and placed next to the sheet-music rack, strained to reproduce a minus-one rendition of the concerto, while Ethan played the solo part. He was lost in the music, mouth slightly ajar, fingers alternately gliding over the keys and bearing on them with the weight of his shoulders, fixing Valerie to the doorsill.

The first movement ended with the usual flourish, and Valerie felt the vague urge to clap, but Ethan hadn't seen her and she wished to keep it that way, so she watched him embark on the romanze. His demeanor relaxed, his lips came together, his gaze softened, and he began to caress the keyboard slowly, lovingly.

The playing was enthralling enough for Valerie, but with the help of Chopin she felt herself descending into a quiet trance. Soon, all she perceived was the melody. Then an unwelcome noise intruded upon her aural bliss—that of Julian's unceremonious arrival, followed by her father's. The sound managed to register on Ethan's consciousness, too, and he quit playing in the middle of a beat. His hand darted to the speaker, turning it off. Valerie underwent a frustrating physical sensation that she was too inexperienced to recognize. Turning on her heels before he could leave the bench, she went to greet the newcomers, knowing that Ethan would take the hallway to its further end, from where he could sneak through a concealed pantry into the kitchen.

Interesting as these episodes were, they paled when compared to the fourth. Valerie was returning from an afternoon ride along the riverbank when her dreamy state of mind was alerted to the sound of voices coming from the far end of the fish pond, one of them loud and plaintive:

"Stop it!" it entreated. "Give it back. Come on, give it back!"

Valerie urged her mount around a bend in the path and came into view of the scene as it played out.

The boy being bullied was Jimmy, who would one day grow to be youngest Governor of the Bank of England, in whose ear ladies would whisper "Oh, James!" as in a tacky old movie.

But he was eleven at the time, and two teenagers—Alex and Philip—distant relatives of Valerie's, were having fun at his expense, tossing around a remote control which he was much distressed to recover. When he approached one boy, the object would fly over his head to the accomplice, bringing him slowly to tears. In frustration he lunged at one his teasers. Alex dodged the charge and Jimmy fell headlong on the grass.

Emerging from behind the flowerbeds, Ethan was taller than Jimmy, but to all appearances hardly a match for the others. "Haven't you had enough already?" he said.

"Who the fuck is this?" asked Alex.

"The stable boy or something," said Philip.

"I don't recall asking his opinion." Alex tossed the remote into the bushes and approached Ethan. Jimmy ran to fetch the remote, retrieved a model yacht from the pond's edge, and made himself scarce.

Ethan started to walk away but Alex blocked his path, and Ethan was too busy gauging him up to notice Philip sneak up from behind. His shirt was yanked and a foot behind his heels made him trip backwards.

"Hey!" yelled Valerie, digging her heels into the mare's flanks.

In the seconds it took the horse to trot around the pond, several things happened.

Ethan spun like a cat and stopped his fall by striking the young man's stomach. Philip fell over but didn't let go of the shirt, so Ethan tumbled on him and landed a punch on the boy's mouth, knocking a tooth in. This loosened the grip on his collar, but Alex now grabbed him by the scruff and waist-band, and tossed him aside like a sack of cement. He landed on the footpath, his ribcage grating against the stones. Alex moved in to kick him where he lay.

"Stop it, everyone!" Valerie cried, now on foot.

Ethan rolled away and blocked the kick. Still on the ground, he slammed his instep into the other's groin. Alex collapsed and retched dryly, unable to let out the shriek that his lips were trying to produce.

Ethan held his aching side and, seeing his shirt ruined, peeled it off to inspect his ribs.

"Son of a bitch!" wailed Philip, blood dripping between the fingers he held over his mouth as he ran towards the house. Alex limped after him.

Years later, Valerie would still go pink in the face at the memory of what she did next. Walking up to Ethan, she held his face in her hands and pressed her lips to his. Her hands moved to his chest and around the back to his nape, where she held fast, kissing him fiercely. Then, just as suddenly, she disengaged, ran to her horse, jumped on the saddle and galloped away as if pursued by the devil, leaving Ethan alone and flummoxed to ponder the wondrous feeling of being alive.

***

The injured boys were long gone by the time Taylor returned home, but he had already been forced to make some unpleasant calls to aggrieved parents. This, more than the incident itself, was what infuriated him. Philip, the boy with the marred dentition, wasn't just anyone, but the son of a cabinet minister and brother-in-law twice removed. As for the other, his father was Taylor's chief equipment supplier, so Taylor held the upper hand in the relationship. Still, a swollen testicle was no laughing matter (or if it was, Taylor wouldn't say so openly). He had promised to inquire into the matter at once and, if the aggressor was found at fault, to press charges. But Taylor was quick to offer his confidence, for he suspected that Ethan wasn't the sort to pick a fight unprovoked, that this wouldn't be the case. Even so, he was sure that the boy would apologize for the injuries, or else Taylor would see him off the premises.

Taylor hated being caught off guard almost as much as he hated losing face. He also hated apologizing, and he now scolded himself for having been so permissive with Nadia's son. Before speaking with Nadia, however, he had to speak with his children and hear their version of the story.

"How did it happen?" he asked.

"Philip and Alex," said Julian, "were walking by the pond when Ethan yelled at them, and when they replied in sort, Ethan attacked them."

"That's a lie," said Valerie. "You weren't even there. It was self-defense. Alex provoked him and Philip started the fight."

"She's just saying that because she has a thing for Ethan. I've seen the way she looks at him."

"Damn you, Julian," she said.

"Nonsense," said Taylor. "Valerie wouldn't give such a boy a second thought. But that's beside the point: are you sure of what you just told me?"

Valerie nodded, stung. *Such a boy?*

"Well, since Ethan was provoked, then there's nothing to be done. I will let everyone know that Valerie is a witness, and I doubt we'll have to worry about this any further. Fair enough?"

Valerie smiled weakly.

"Which doesn't mean Ethan is blameless," Taylor went on. "He was unnecessarily rough and should apologize."

Valerie's smile vanished. "What!? Your sense of justice is absurd."

"I beg your pardon?"

"Imagine two men in a brawl: one pulls out a gun and shoots the other, and is sent to jail just because the first was unarmed."

"As he should. What's wrong with that?"

"What if the victim is twice the size of the shooter, and the larger man has the other grabbed by the neck—"

"Then he should call for help, but it still doesn't justify—"

"And is making him suck his willy."

"Valerie!" said Taylor, flabbergasted. Julian giggled despite himself.

"Would he still be to blame?"

"If the other man was unarmed, it would still be murder. I don't see your point."

"That figures," said Valerie, rolling her eyes.

Taylor lost his patience. "Valerie, what have I told you about that attitude of yours? I will not have it; do you hear me?"

"But don't you see? That was just an example. Life is full of instances where the strong humiliate the weak and get away with it simply because the weak can only defend themselves by drastic means, which are deemed unacceptable."

"Humiliation and murder are very different things. Violence isn't the solution: there's other ways, higher instances."

"I suppose rape victims should also appeal to a higher instance, but in the meantime relax and enjoy it."

"All right, Valerie, that's enough. You've had your say. I will speak with Nadia, Ethan will apologize for the injuries and we'll forget about the whole thing." His tone was final, and he turned away dismissively.

Valerie stormed out of the room, slamming the door behind her.

Nadia was expecting to be summoned and appeared promptly before Taylor. She wore a deadpan that only made her look more stylish, which did little to set Taylor at ease. He had rehearsed several ways to broach the subject with her, and her demeanor made him wish to adopt a roundabout approach. But having weighed this option for a moment, he decided that professional directness would work better.

"I trust that you know why I called you," he began.

"Yes, sir, and I apologize for the trouble I've caused. Ethan will be spending his vacations elsewhere from now on." She said it softly and without the least strain in her intonation, and Taylor couldn't help but admire the fact that Nadia could be smoother than he was—and from a position of disadvantage, too.

"The trouble *you've* caused? Don't be so hard on yourself. You know what they say—boys will be boys." By this he meant Ethan, but Nadia assumed he was referring to the aggressors. "Yes, sir," she said, and Taylor saw that he had managed to bring out a trace of a smile in her face, which stroked his ego in a pleasant spot.

"Given the seriousness of the injuries, I feared we might have a problem on our hands, but Valerie told us what happened, and I think that a simple apology will get Ethan off the hook."

"Oh," she said, her smile evaporating. "In that case I will be glad to—"

"I didn't mean *you*, woman," said Taylor with a laugh that came out a bit forced. "I meant Ethan."

Nadia's face turned ashen, but she handled herself impeccably. "I'm afraid that's impossible, sir. I have sent Ethan away with some friends."

"Why? That was wrong of you. He's old enough to face up to his own actions."

"My fault, again. If there's anything *I* can do, I will be more than happy to oblige, but I want to keep him out of this."

"Keep him out? But he's the one who start—" Taylor caught himself barely in time. "Now, Nadia, let's not blow things out of proportion. It isn't right that you should cover for him—or healthy, either. I know it must be hard for Ethan without a father and all, but children shouldn't grow up thinking they can do whatever they want. It's time Ethan learned his place."

"Believe me, Mr. Taylor, if I showed him his place, your displeasure would only increase."

Taylor wasn't sure what she meant by that, but he didn't like the self-righteous tone in which it had been spoken. He was a man of strong convictions, which his success and status had only served to boost, and one of them was the firm belief that he was endowed with wisdom nothing short of Solomonic. But as with every person whose sense of fairness derives more from habit than perspicuity, he was better equipped to pass judgment than to judge, so he adopted a stiff tone that he had often used when delivering ultimatums to bigger fish than Nadia, and which had never failed to bend them to his will.

"I cannot allow that sort of attitude around here," he said, and was immediately struck by a sense of *déjà vu*, which he brushed aside like an unwelcome burp. "I am willing to be reasonable, but I expect the same from everyone else, so if Ethan doesn't offer some form of apology, then I'm afraid that your contract here will be forfeited."

Such were the clumsy words that brought an end to Ethan's eventful summers at Exebridge Hall, and left Taylor staring helplessly at Nadia's elegant behind as it disappeared without a word down the hallway, not to be seen again.

Later that evening Taylor tried to speak with his daughter, but she refused to emerge from her room. When he returned from a business meeting the next day, she was gone. "Mom was here this morning," explained Julian, with feigned detachment. "Valerie called her. They've both gone back to France."

Taylor was in an ugly mood for several days after that, as he reflected on the dubious privilege of having a daughter who could afford to leave the country on a tantrum.

EASE

People sup together, play together, travel together, but they do not think together.

—Allan Bloom, *The Closing of the American Mind*

Anchored in a sheltered cove several years later, three yachts sat tight in the gentle swells. During their tour of the Sea of Cortez the passengers had settled into a pleasant routine of late breakfast followed by sightseeing, sunbathing, cocktails, water sports, and early dinner, hosted by a different person each evening, which provided the perfect excuse for the owners to show off their vessels. Taylor's cruiser, two-hundred and fifty feet long, was only the second largest, so he made every effort to outshine his peers in terms of cuisine, if only to prove that his chef was the best. And to judge from Orson Haggart's contented look, he had clearly succeeded, so he sat back proudly to sip his port while the staff cleared the dishes. The ladies had adjourned indoors for a game of bridge with the previous evening's hosts, leaving Taylor, Haggart and a trio of youngsters at the table. The teenagers, bored and lethargic, slouched in their chairs gazing emptily at the sea.

"Eddie, I hear you're starting college next month," said Taylor pleasantly, addressing Haggart's eldest son, a brawny, stylish young man who sported a plum-colored shirt—unbuttoned—and a mane of golden curls matted with seawater.

"Off to Princeton," declared the boy, as if resigned to the inevitable.

"Splendid choice. What major?"

"Business, with the eventual goal of law school."

"A lawyer! God help us all," Taylor grinned at Haggart. "Julian has just completed his freshman year at Yale."

Julian and Eddie exchanged lukewarm glances.

"And you, Valerie?" asked Haggart.

"Oh, I decided to stay in Europe," she answered with polite detachment.

Taylor made up for his daughter's condescending modesty: "She's in her second year at Cambridge."

"Well, well, I thought that you were—uh, that Julian was—"

"Older, yes," said Taylor, familiar with such perplexity, and he listed the milestones of his daughter's scholastic prowess in an offhanded way that embarrassed Valerie as much as it made Julian wish to stick a finger down his throat. Eddie glanced at Valerie, enraptured.

"Wonderful," said Haggart, impressed in the cavalier way shown by those who go through life as if presiding over it. "What is your concentration?"

Here we go again, thought Valerie. "Philosophy," she said.

"Aha! Kant and Hegel, I imagine. Or is it Milgram and Rawls?"

"Any of them would be the archaeology of the subject," she said, smiling only with her lips, and Taylor again felt the urge to clarify. "I tried to talk her into something a bit more practical, to no avail."

Valerie rose to the challenge. "My father would like me to learn a trade—in case I need to earn a living, I suppose," she added looking at Eddie, who grinned on cue.

Taylor scowled. "Very funny, Valerie. I just want you to be able to hold your own when you sit on the Board of Directors, where the best philosophy credentials will be of less help than a major in nursing."

"Since when is nursing an unworthy pursuit?" asked Valerie. "Oh, I see, you mean professions not aimed at making money. Or perhaps you mean girlish occupations—well, rest assured, philosophy isn't one."

"No," said Julian, seeing a chance to give some back. "It's for geeks who argue all day over bad coffee, only to conclude that reality doesn't exist—unless it's oriental philosophy, in which case reality exists but you don't."

This drew a laugh from everyone, Valerie included.

"Hmm," Haggart droned on, sensing the moment was ripe to show some depth. "Well, here's a conundrum for you. Two young men drive home drunk after a party and send their cars into a spin: one hits a tree and receives a fine; the other a pedestrian, and gets ten years in jail. Why should punishment for identical behavior be determined by fortuitous outcome? Philosophy won't give you a straight answer."

They all smiled in agreement, except Valerie, who said, "Maybe not, but common sense might. Take Russian roulette. The penalty for bad luck is a bullet in the head. And while odds of one in six are bad enough to prevent most people from playing, some will try it now and then. Drunk driving is also a game of odds—as is driving in general—so penalties must be high enough to dissuade an acceptably high fraction of people from engaging in behaviors that an uncomfortably high number of people deem unacceptable. It's a conundrum merely because people—legislators in particular—insist on drafting penalties in terms of what people deserve or don't. But life isn't like that. You can't outlaw chance."

No one spoke, and Haggart had lost his smile from keeping up with Valerie.

"Hey guys," attempted Taylor for the third time, "why don't you show Eddie the new game room?"

That seemed to work, for it brought Julian to his feet. "Mind if I borrow your wave-runner while the sun's up?" he asked.

"Enjoy," said Eddie.

Taylor wasn't thrilled by the idea. His yacht had no such toys for a reason. Julian had inherited his thrill-seeking nature, but what the father allowed in himself he tried to prevent in his son. Still, eager to see the younger generation leave the table, he said nothing. Valerie turned to Eddie. "I'll show you around," she suggested, which was all the prompting the young man needed…

***

"…And this is my cabin," she said, having bypassed all quarters except those on the way to her room. An awkwardly excited Eddie hoped the bulge in his shorts would behave. To his surprise Valerie bolted the door shut as soon as they were inside.

"Natasha says you're good in bed," she declared point-blank.

"Huh? Well, I—I guess I—" But Valerie had already removed her top, relieving him from having to think any further.

Not long afterwards, around the time when he began wondering if heaven might indeed be a place on earth, Valerie concluded that Natasha was easier to please than she had assumed.

***

"You can leave the bottle here," Taylor instructed the butler, who understood the hint to make himself scarce and readily vanished below decks.

Haggart leaned back and clasped his hands behind his neck. "Ah, to be young again," he said dreamily.

"I'm trying to teach them that life must be navigated—not understood. I get mixed results, as you saw. Last year I gave them a million each to test their investing skills, instructing my banker to do whatever they said without consulting me, as long as it was legal."

"Interesting. How did they manage?"

"Julian quickly found a way to turn the million into two, then made a silly bet and lost sixty percent, so now he's back to where he started minus two hundred. He'll be wiser next time. I shudder to think what Valerie's done with her share—given it to Greenpeace for all I know."

Haggart chuckled. "Consider yourself lucky. Eddie would have spent it all in a week."

"So", said Taylor, "tell me about this deal of yours."

Haggart waved a hand towards the coast. "Here in Mexico," he said, "many large companies are still family-run, and Segufarma is no exception. The founder's sons have proved amenable; the business is worth at least twice their asking price."

"That's a bold assertion. The industry's collapsing."

"Just hear me out. Segufarma offers group and individual health plans, and owns a major share in the country's top hospital chain."

"Still," interrupted Taylor, "health insurance? You know that in Asia extrasomics are self-selecting out of the system, so insurers find themselves with an increasingly risky portfolio, driving premiums through the roof and leading even more of the healthy to drop out.

It's a death spiral. Besides, don't forget that Mexican laws forbid genetic screening of applicants."

"Yes, but Mexico hasn't yet fallen prey to our brand of health reform, so a legal loophole allows the sale of coverage that excludes explicitly listed ailments—as many as you want—as long as applicants aren't tested. By pulling out of group coverage and focusing on individual insurance, we could attract the growing number of U.S. extrasomics who are tired of subsidizing everyone else. Inverse self-selection would generate solid profits. Actuarial calculations show the marginal savings for each disease that you exclude from a plan. You can then share those savings with the people you cover. It's a textbook no-brainer."

"Hey," said Taylor, "you're the insurance buff; I expect you've done the numbers. But to prevent others from joining the bandwagon, you'd have to know in advance which diseases are likely to… Ah, I see."

"Exactly," said Haggart, greeting Taylor's insight by raising his glass in a silent toast before downing its contents and reaching for a refill.

"Speaking of health reform," he said upon regaining the apex of comfort, "have you heard that Senator Reynolds proposed banning all gene modules purchased from foreign makers?"

"Bah," Taylor brushed some crumbs off the table with a significant sweep of his hand, "I have dual citizenship and the controlling share of the company. Nothing prevents me from spinning off the U.S. affiliate into a local entity to comply with the law while remaining in charge. Besides, it's probably just Reynolds' knee-jerk reaction to the latest rhetoric from this idiot—what's his name?"

"Wade?"

"Right, Wade—another damned populist."

Haggart snorted. "Yeah, I thought we were done with those."

"Done!? America has a long history of populism."

"Since Trump?"

"Tradition gives precedence to Jackson."

"Ah, but those were not just populists; they were also pragmatists. They appealed to nostalgia, to American grassroots and enterprise. They embodied the establishment, even if they denied it in their day.

They were family men—or tried to be—and acted on sentiments held by much of the electorate. Wade feeds his own notions to the crowd. He reminds me of a twentieth-century messianic ideologue, which is far more dangerous."

"You think?"

"Ideologues believe in absolutes, in retribution, in judgment day. They are too comfortable with death, if not their own then that of others. Besides, candidates should feel *for* the masses, not with them."

"Don't you think it's all just bluff? Wade knows that nothing carries an election like a good dose of vitriol."

"Vitriol should target the failings of the political class, not of the people."

Taylor chuckled. "You and I are hardly 'the people'."

"No, we're the latest butt of popular discontent. In Jackson's day prejudice targeted ethnic origin; in Trump's day it was passport origin; now it's chromosome origin."

"Well, you can't blame politicians for pandering to resentment any more than you can blame used-car dealers for selling lemons. It comes with the trade."

Haggart smiled wanly. "What is surprising is that voters buy the same lemon every time, always ready to believe that whatever is missing from their lives must be somebody's fault."

"That's tribalism at work. People blame outsiders for their problems, and when that recourse is exhausted and unfairness has only worsened, they turn on each other. You can always count on the rabble backing whoever cries injustice. It's virtually won a seat in the senate for Wade."

"Don't you think that's just the start?"

"Oh, I don't know. It takes serious backing to run for president, and Wade's more of a street-corner preacher. If García gets re-elected this year, then Wade may stand a chance, because the vice president is weak and there's no one better in the pipeline. But if Reynolds wins, then Wade will be running against an incumbent, in which case all bets are off."

"Even if García wins, Wade and Reynolds can both run again next time."

"One bridge at a time, my friend."

"And in the meantime?"

"Get cozy with García while throwing my full weight on Reynolds."

"You think he's a winner?"

"I said throw my full weight *on* Reynolds, not behind him."

Haggart roared with delight and raised his glass for another toast. "Here's to throwing weight around."

"Amen."

HARDSHIP

> I asked so little from life, and even that it denied me ... like alms refused not from unkindness, but from reluctance to undo one's coat for the handout.
>
> —FERNANDO PESSOA, *The Book of Disquiet*

Moneyed scorn notwithstanding, voter disaffection is neither fated nor capricious, but must be sown. For the pain of unfairness is no abstract social malaise, but something concretely felt by individuals, and if the world seemed prosperous through the lens of show business, the eyes of the average person alive at the time beheld a rather different scene. In an age when the greatest challenge posed by someone's evening might be to tackle an overlong wine menu, over two billion people eked out an existence on a budget that wouldn't have covered the price of one beer. And half of those souls, people able to laugh and weep and wonder at the warmth of the sun on their faces, who had perhaps at some point harbored dreams and ambitions, survived on a diet that the likes of Haggart and Taylor would have deemed cruel if forced on a dog.

That such conditions were endured by so many for so long is remarkable, but those caught in the grip of starvation, their bodies weakened by hunger, their spirits crushed by hardship, their attention absorbed by the task of making it through the day, possessed neither the time nor the energy to devise a means of escaping their fate. That task befell the social stratum of the 'merely' underprivileged, who had known quelled hunger, clean shirts, a soft bed and a shower; who had seen enough moments of respite to look upon their lot and realize that they deserved better. It was in their midst that bitterness rankled as the simplest hopes of youth were dashed by reality. And it was in their company that America's poor were to be found.

In earlier centuries they might have remained unaware of what they missed. Unable to read, to travel, to consort with the rarely seen well-to-do, they could only imagine what a life of plenty might entail. It had taken the odd place like Paris or St. Petersburg, where ostentation rubbed shoulders with squalor, to sow the seeds of insurgency. But technology had erased any cushioning distance and everyone now had access to a virtual world awash with images of luxury that seemed to be everywhere, yet ever beyond reach. For virtual wine had no taste, virtual tubs didn't offer much of a soak, and vividly-rendered images of nubile creatures in every beckoning posture imaginable had become so ubiquitous that the unlikelihood of ever stroking so much as a lock of their hair was enough to drive the male half of the underclass completely insane.

As a child Connor Dashaw would have hardly been called a misfit. His bane, in fact, was to be normal in every sense. When he was too young to remember much he lived with his parents in a dingy trailer park, but his first memories were of a place in the outskirts of Chicago—hardly a fancy abode, but a step above the cramped quarters of the mobile home. Its interiors were decked with chipboard furniture, shoddy wallpaper and posters better suited to a sporting goods store than to a residence. The vinyl siding, once painted light blue, had turned a dull, peeling gray by the time his family moved in, and the small front yard was more often than not taken over by the family car. Still, it was home.

His mother was the sort person to whom the phrase *sort of person* best applies, easier to describe as a type than as an individual. The world had seen myriads like her—people who make up the bulk of humankind, leaving an imprint only through the weight of their numbers, and giving purpose to horoscopes, tabloids and soap operas.

Life was something that happened to Amanda as it happens to a mushroom in the woods, and while the workings of existence were opaque and inscrutable to her, this only made life appear simpler in her eyes. Wiser minds than hers, she reasoned, had come and gone, and whatever issues they had been unable to agree upon were clearly beyond her power to settle, so she never gave thinking a try and judged the world by other people's standards, believing them of course to be entirely her own. Questions she had few, and as for answers, they were offered right and left in such profusion that she felt she could simply choose among them as she might choose between cereal brands, never imagining that to sift through the prejudiced views of others might require even greater skill than weighing matters for herself. Her every conviction could trace its origin to an emotional response elicited by someone's opinion, and early on she fell into the universal habit of trusting those towards whom she felt more empathy. Her religious beliefs were her mother's. She hated the memory of her father, a staunch Republican, so she invariably voted Democrat. She didn't believe in UFOs because she had once overheard—at an impressionable young age—a dear uncle speak condescendingly of those who did, so she laughed heartily at stories of alien abductions even while quoting the gossip columns as gospel truth. She lived her life by the advice she found in self-help literature, and subscribed to shallow, mass-market interpretations of oriental philosophy, falling prey to the mystic appeal of the exotic in the sincere belief that a few minutes spent ruminating on a higher purpose could somehow redeem a lifetime of petty jealousies, empty prattle, and selfish desires. Her face was as dull as her character, and she did little to make up for either. Other women of scant means might have spent carefully on a few well-chosen wardrobe items, sacrificing variety for a small measure of grace. But Amanda took her cues on fashion from movie stars who do their utmost to dress shabbily off camera, so she favored a liberal assortment of cheap sweatshirts, jeans, flip-flops, and other unflattering garments—a shame, really, for as her husband often said, she had great thighs.

Ronald Dashaw, Connor's father, was a rough mid-western man who had left rural life for a factory job, progressing from graveyard shift to line supervision until the assembly plant that put bread on his table was unexpectedly shut down. By then he was married and had Stacey and the younger Connor to support, so he couldn't wait for something better to knock on his door and became a customer-service clerk in a busy shopping mall. If the pay was inadequate, at least Ron was promoted to Manager. Then disaster struck.

People had begun to leave as the evening wore on, and some early-bird shops were already closing for the day. It was Saturday and Ron's assistant, who usually handled the afternoon shift, was on leave. Ron instructed the new clerk to begin the accounting process that must be completed before they all left for home. He glanced up and saw only a woman waiting. A male customer had walked in before and taken a slip from the take-a-turn dispenser, but he had walked back out after a few minutes. Ron pressed a button and called out: "Fifty-four?" A screen on the wall beeped and flashed the number. The waiting customer glanced up, looked at her paper slip and said nothing, so Ron pressed again and called out: "Fifty-five?" The woman rose, walked over to the counter and smiled. "I'd like some information regarding your winter specials." He got to work on the request.

Ten seconds into the transaction the customer who had picked a turn before the woman walked in and approached the counter.

"Excuse me," he said, handing Ron a paper slip. "My turn is fifty-four."

Ron nodded. "I'll be with you as soon as I'm done with this customer."

"But I was here before," he protested.

It had been a long day and Ron was tired; the last thing he needed was a whiner. "I called your number and you were not here, so I'm serving the next person in line."

The man didn't budge. "I was just outside," he said irately. "When my number appeared on the screen, I walked in. I've been waiting for 20 minutes and was here before the lady. What about your colleague?" The man referred to the new clerk, who was busy studying a screen.

"I'm sorry," said Ron. "She's taking care of something else."

The customer exploded. "So what's the point of having people take turns if you're going to serve whomever you want?"

Ron had heard enough. "Well," he said curtly, "I guess you will just have to wait."

The man tossed his ticket on the counter, turned his back on them and left. Ron felt a vague sense of relief; by morning he had put the affair behind him. Then on Monday he received a message from his boss, asking him to the main office downtown.

Ron had been personally hired by the General Manager and greeted him warmly. "Hey Carl," he said. "What's up?"

The reply was less than enthusiastic. "Have a seat, Ron."

He sensed that something was amiss, but had no clue as to the source of the other's embarrassment.

Carl hesitated. "I—I don't know how else to say this. I've been asked to let you go."

Ron was thunderstruck. "Asked by whom?"

"Mr. Farrell."

The company owner was known as much for his haughtiness as for openly flaunting his extrasomy. Ron had met him only twice.

"B—but why? I've met all my objectives. You know that I—"

"Yes Ron, I know and I told him so. I've told him several times before. This has nothing to do with it."

"With what, then?"

"He mentioned … an incident on Friday evening. With a customer."

"That asshole?" gasped Ron.

"Ron—"

"No, let me explain. This guy comes in like he owns the place and accuses me of skipping his turn when he wasn't even in the—"

"That asshole," said Carl, "is Farrell's son-in-law."

Months passed without Ron finding another job. He took to heavy drinking and spent the evenings yelling at Amanda and watching television. Connor reacted to his father's dismissal with stoicism. He found part-time employment in a supermarket and spent little time at home. His sister Stacey took it harder. She had been promised a car for her high-school graduation if she kept her grades up, which she had. The car never materialized, and though her grades were good enough for admission, they were not high enough to earn her a scholarship, so her college aspirations were thwarted. She spent days alone in her room, increasingly quiet and withdrawn, her outings with friends dwindling to the point where she only went out with a girl she had recently met. This proved to be a turning point, for she started spending less time at home and returning after midnight. It began once, maybe twice a week. Ron was usually too drunk to notice when she tiptoed in, so it was

Amanda who first took her to task. "Where do you think you're going?" she asked. "Does this look like a hotel to you?"

Stacey replied with rolling eyes and lame excuses. She then grew insolent. "I can move out if you like," she said, defiantly.

"And live without free room and board?" rebutted her mother. "I don't think so." But Stacey's threat had the desired effect and she was spared further rebukes for a month.

Their next confrontation took place before Ron, who was snoring on the couch when Stacey arrived. Her mother had waited downstairs on purpose in order to be there when she returned. "Look at you!" she scolded. "Where did you get those clothes? Ron, look at that watch. Ron, wake up!"

"Huh? What? Oh, please ..."

"Will you look at her?" she pleaded. "That watch *has* to be stolen, I swear to God."

"Come on, Amanda, it's probably fake—besides, it looks nice."

His wife was incensed. "Is that all you have to say? And the handbag? I suppose that's fake, too? I've seen those online. At least a thousand—that's what they're worth."

Ron hiccupped. "Fine, lez talk about it tomorrow, okay?"

Stacey wasn't around the following day and Ron forgot his intended lecture. Still, the seed of doubt had been planted, so he began paying attention to Stacey's habits. He looked at her eyes and arms for telltale signs of substance abuse, finding none. He tried in vain to recall if Stacey had lost or gained weight in the last few months, and tried to convince himself that perhaps she had really landed a rich boyfriend. She was pretty and smart, so why wouldn't she? One evening when his wife was out, he overheard Stacey talking on the phone in her room.

"Yes, of course I was paid," she said. "The usual." Her tone was flat, tired, businesslike. "Can't you wait till tomorrow? Okay, okay, no need to yell. Meet me in the park."

Ron heard her walk over to her closet to put her shoes on. As she picked up her purse he hid in his bedroom until Stacey stepped out. He looked at his watch. It was nearly nine o'clock. The night was overcast but not cold. *Meet me in the park*. There was only one park within walking distance, and at this hour it was probably full of miscreants, mostly drug dealers. Ron heard her walk down the stairs and on an impulse he walked to his closet, stood on his toes and pulled out a revolver from the top shelf. He tucked it into the pocket of a coat fetched from a chair, went downstairs and stepped outside. The street was empty. He shut the door noiselessly and peered to his right. His daughter's receding shape was rounding the corner fifty yards away.

It was indeed the place he'd imagined, poorly lit outside the main paths, yet far from empty. He could vaguely discern small groups of riffraff engaged in illicit transactions. He kept far enough to avoid being seen, which given the shadows was close enough for him to hear the heels of her shoes striking the pavement. She strode with assurance, as if she knew the place, past a young couple too busy fondling each other to notice, and a heavy-set man who extended a noxious vial towards Stacey with an implicit offer. She then veered onto an unpaved trail. There, next to a bench between two large trees, stood a young man.

Ron hesitated, then struck diagonally across a patch of grass and dirt that was darker than the trail. He couldn't see where he stepped, but the ground was damp and clear of leaves, so his sneakers made no sound. He came to a standstill behind a tree not thirty feet from his daughter and peered intently into the murk, but couldn't recognize the man. Stacey had fetched something from her purse and was handing it over. From the way the man examined it, Ron knew it to be cash. The memory of a childhood friend of his who had become a drug dealer flashed briefly through his mind.

"That all?" The man's tone was gruff and unceremonious.

"He wanted a straight trick," protested Stacey. "I couldn't ask for—"

"Well, then you should have *offered* him more."

"Come on, it's so … gross."

"You never complained before. Is he paying you in other ways? That's a nice watch you're wearing."

"N—no, of course not," she said, but instinctively covered one wrist with the other. The man slapped Stacey across the cheek, unemotionally, like someone might reprimand a misbehaved dog. "Don't you *ever* go behind my back again," he threatened. Ron's blood turned to ice. Stacey let out a soft whimper and he was thrown back eighteen years to the old trailer home, his two-year-old holding onto his extended fingers with chubby hands, laughing merrily. *Thank you, Lord, for this gift of a child.*

He began shaking in the dark.

"If some john wants to get kinky," the man ranted on, "you just charge him double, you understand? Eh? Look at me when I'm talking."

Ron stepped forward but wasn't immediately recognized. The man heard the footsteps that Ron no longer tried to conceal and Stacey, following his gaze, stared uncomprehendingly until Ron was upon them. She then brought a hand to her mouth in horror and stepped back as if trying to vanish behind the trees. Without pause, Ron pulled the gun from his pocket and fired a round into the surprised man's forehead.

The concussion echoed in the quiet evening, and ill-defined human shapes scurried away into the surrounding gloom. Stacey's hand was still covering her mouth as Ron turned to her. Not enough time had passed for him to build any expectation regarding Stacey's reaction, but never in a million years could he have guessed how she would thank him. Taking two steps towards her father, she pounded his chest with angry hands. "How *could* you! See what you've done," she cried indignantly, pointing at the lifeless body.

At a loss, Ron tried to hug her. "It's okay, baby," he said. "He won't bother you again."

She pulled away. "What am I supposed to do now? How will I support myself—and Connor? Don't look at me like that—of *course* I give him money. At least *someone* does."

Ron's heart imploded. At the wail of approaching sirens Stacey threw her arms up in exasperation and scampered away, leaving her father standing dumbfounded. Ron let the gun drop; it landed on the path with a soft thud.

Connor didn't hear about the incident until the following day, when uniformed officers paid a visit. Ron had been arrested on the scene and had readily confessed, refusing his right to a phone call. The police wanted to question Stacey but she was nowhere to be found. The trial was brief. The victim had been unarmed, so the prosecution was tough on Ron. His lawyer advised him to plead guilty to second-degree murder. The pimp's long rap sheet, Ron's clean record and Stacey's part in the affair, led the judge—a father of three—to be 'lenient' and give Ron twelve years, to serve no less than eight. Amanda could only bawl and wring her hands as he was led away.

Connor's spirit wasn't crushed overnight, but crumbled slowly like a boxer's strength, pummeled by disappointment upon humiliation. His father's downfall had been the last straw, but only because it came on top of his own failures. The years in which he had shown promise in sports had come and gone, but his dreams had never hinged on that. He had most often envisioned himself as a corporate executive in a suitably hazy industry. Dutifully following his father's advice, he had always tried to excel in his schoolwork and had in fact done rather well, but the schools he had attended were regarded as a mere step above no schooling at all, and he lacked any rare endowment such as inner-city miracles are built upon.

The truth about his limitations crept upon him surreptitiously, like an ulcer forming in the back of his mind to fester slowly over time. For years he pushed it back, fueling the hopes of his childhood with the small victories that life grudgingly conceded, believing that one day he would find his true calling, come into his own, succeed at something—at anything. But as the canker grew from nagging doubt to overwhelming conviction it ate away at his soul like a nest of maggots until there was nothing left but the darkest certainty that he belonged to the forgotten ranks of mankind. Of course he'd read stories of unassuming people who had risen out of obscurity to triumph against all odds. But the very mention of odds meant that the vast majority would not succeed, and despite his unremarkable talents Connor was still shrewd enough to realize that if the media focused so much on stories of success it was precisely because they were so rare. He was caught in that awful middle ground where a man finds himself to be merely bright enough to realize that his gifts are unexceptional, unfortunate enough to come into the world a child with ambitions but no means to fulfill them, and when his dreams were one by one laid bare as unrealistic, he woke up one day to the knowledge that he had no dreams left at all.

What he eventually came to feel, in his heart of hearts, was that whichever road he chose in life was irrelevant, because every path led down a gully of mediocrity that he increasingly felt had been allotted to him from birth. If he joined the corporate world, he would always remain a clerk; if he ever appeared on television, it would be in a talk-show audience to clap on cue; if he ever drove an expensive car it would be as a chauffeur, and if he ever went to war he would be one of those nameless soldiers who are felled by the first shower of bullets as backdrop to some hero's deeds. It was plain to him that he was destined to be a lance-bearer, a menial worker, a sideline character. And he didn't care that most humans led that sort of life, for this was *his* one chance at existence, and the very idea that he might turn out to be less than a footnote in history, that he would never experience half the things he saw every day in the media, and that the lifestyle portrayed everywhere as a normal, God-given right would be forever closed to him, all chiseled away at his morale with relentless persistence, reducing in the end to rubble what no isolated setback could have destroyed.

Although Connor perceived it as the grayest of mornings, the sun was shining brightly on the day that he decided to end his life. He wore a jacket as he left home into the mild air, his eyes glazed over and his mind distracted. But he didn't shuffle along hesitantly like someone drowning in self-pity and secretly longing to be rescued, for his resolve wasn't the anguished cry for help of teenage suicide, nor was it the wish for respite that the terminally ill may seek. It was the profound disillusion that a sensitive soul undergoes when, aware that life could be an ocean of wellness with islands of grief, it encounters the opposite. It never crossed Connor's mind that suicide can run in families, and that his grandfather's hushed death might be a sign that his own thoughts were unhealthy. Melancholy blotted out all explanation with blind rage against his shortcomings; because he couldn't find it in his heart to blame his parents and he felt too ashamed to blame God. Since the source of his pain seemed to be his very existence, he walked down the street with the grim determination to enter the nearest station and dive in front of an approaching train, wondering only whether he would have the courage when the moment came. He had six blocks to walk, and his route struck diagonally across a large open square. There, words that he had often heard from his father reached his ears, now spoken with far greater aplomb.

"The extrasomic aren't satisfied with being healthier than the rest of us. Now they want to exclude us from society so they can control the world!"

Connor glanced to his right in the voice's direction, and saw a blond, thin man standing on a dais usually taken over by amateur showmen seeking to coax donations from bystanders. The man was surrounded by a good three hundred people, and bore no resemblance to Connor's father. Still, the words managed to break through the armor of misery that enveloped his mind.

"The best schools and the best jobs are meant for them," the man blustered on. "And where does that leave you and me? It used to be that anyone with enough courage and determination could work hard and rise in this country. Everyone had a fair chance. It was called the American Dream. Now it is a club, and the cover fee is an outrage."

Connor slowed down. He felt no change of heart—yet. As things stood, his besieged mind could offer but a sliver of attention to the world around him, and for the time being that sliver was taken over by what he heard.

"The President spoke last week about the fairness of our school system. Well, I say fairness my ass. We all know that to get into college you must pass certain tests. And we all know that only children from certain schools pass the tests in the first place. But which schools are those? Not those in this neighborhood; not those you and I attended. No, they are the schools for children whose parents have purchased trim bodies and natural suntans. These children, no brighter than many who now stand before me, are groomed for success. The top colleges in our nation might just as well have a sign saying *Non-Extrasomics Needn't Apply*. We are heading the way of China, my friends, mark my words. My father, God rest his soul, still remembered the days when Asians flocked here to learn our ways. Can you imagine that today?"

Connor stood transfixed. None but his father—certainly not a stranger in the street with a crowd around him—had ever spoken like that to him, and there was no question in his mind that the words were meant for no ears but his own. They were the words of a prophet. The diatribe continued for some minutes; then people close to the rostrum began throwing questions at the speaker, who answered with either smiling assurance or righteous invective, as befitted each concern. He filled the open square with his presence, which seemed larger than life. Around him, barely visible through the crowd, was a ring of bodyguards.

A young woman, barely twenty, slipped into Connor's field of view, though beyond the edge of his numb awareness.

"Hi," she said.

Connor failed to make eye contact.

"We want to make a real difference in America," she said. "We are fighting to end injustice. Will you help us make a difference?" She carried a book in her arm and a campaign pin on her jacket.

Slowly, his eyes roved towards the voice. He realized that its source was female, smiling, and cute, roughly in that order. Used to being dealt with in curt tones by unappealing individuals, this was a new experience for him. He had never been the target of personalized marketing, and lacked the insight to guess that his age, clothes, engrossed stare, and world-weary look all fit a profile.

He acknowledged her presence with a couple of blinks, and she stepped forward. "I'm Alix," she said extending a hand, which he took mechanically. The touch of her warm fingers came as a shock. "Connor," he blurted out.

"Hello, Connor. Would you like to meet Mr. Wade? We are looking for people like you to join our movement." Unbeknownst to her, Connor already had.

He didn't meet Aamon Wade until the next week at his Chicago campaign office. Security was tight, which Connor would soon recognize as the norm. When asked to step through a scanner gate and leave his jacket in the waiting room, he felt not insulted but awed at being led into the company of greatness. Even before stepping into the same room as Wade, Connor already felt that admiration that from the beginning of time has moved those seeking leadership to lay their lives at the feet of those who offer it. And even before Wade put a large, reassuring hand on his shoulder and stole what was left of his pride with a hearty, made-just-for-you speech, Connor was more than ready to follow his newfound to the ends of the world.

Wade had been briefed about his modest abilities and promptly put them to good use. Connor was given the task of gathering information that would fuel the candidate's provocative speeches. Initially this involved raking the cinders of his life for examples of all that was wrong with society and with the government's tolerance of privileges that increasingly accrued to the extrasomic. Soon Wade began calling him Connor, my man, which made him feel all warm inside.

Staffed in the campaign pollster's team he slowly but steadily came back to life. He learned about public opinion and the electoral process, about the media and its perverse twisting of facts for the sake of sensationalism or hidden agendas, about Congress and its corrupt inbreeding. He learned of the role of proselytism in opening people's eyes to the truth, and of the evils of the two-party system, where pussyfooting Democrats let the people down through socialist demagoguery, while Republicans did nothing but foster crony capitalism. He learned what it meant to be an independent candidate, to be true to one's convictions, and to never read a speech, but to preach with courage and pizzazz. He learned who was on their side, who could be converted, and who was a lost cause. Most of all he came to realize that the awful feeling of being denied every means to move ahead in the world, of having every door to prosperity shut in his face, was shared by many people. It was the hallmark of modern injustice and, moreover, had a clear cause. Crafty and insidious, the small segment of the population to which, following Wade's lead, he would soon refer jeeringly as the 'cosmeticized', was quietly spreading its influence across the globe. And if anyone could prevent that from happening it was Aamon Wade, so when the candidate was elected U.S. Senator for Illinois later that year, Connor spent a whole week celebrating.

PART TWO: ATTITUDE

WONDER

All that has been learned about evolution in general and mental process in particular suggests that the brain is a machine assembled not to understand itself, but to survive.

—EDWARD O. WILSON, *Consilience*

In the end it was neither fears nor desires of her own that drove Nadia away from Britain, but Ethan's wish to see more of the world. In their conversations she had always downplayed travel and never taken him farther than Scotland. Much against her instincts she had let him join school trips to France and Italy; but Ethan had grown restless over time and, if not for Nadia's rein on his expenditures he would have boarded a train to head out as far as a rail pass would take him.

Ethan brought up the subject not long after they left Exebridge, and in an unguarded moment she told him they would move to America if he gained admission to one of its top schools. This shut him up for a few years, until he surprised her with an acceptance from Columbia University, which exhausted her store of excuses. The thought of remaining alone in London never crossed her mind.

Even for a fortunate student, it is at most a teacher or two that make all the difference. Ethan's switch from engineering to physics was at least partly due to an information-systems course he took with one of those quirky, ebullient professors who go off on digressions that add richness to dry subjects.

"Information is cheap these days," he said, "but it wasn't always so. People once wrote on clay tablets that were carefully guarded like the precious items they were. And before writing came along, the only place to store information was in people's heads, so when a wise person died it was more than the loss of a loved one. Today we preserve information by uploading it to the cloud, letting others take care of its safekeeping. Access has become so simple that sorting through data is more of a challenge than storing it. We shall discuss web-search algorithms later on, but the phrase 'information overload' is more than a useful idiom.

"Now, if a lifetime of learning fills you with dread, then remember it isn't a new prospect. Medieval monks did it, and even in those days people asked themselves what was really worth learning. But the question has become more pressing with a growing ocean of data that forces us to be ever more selective. Early attempts to prioritize led to drafting compendia like the Bible, which was long held to contain the answers to who we are, where we come from, and what our purpose in life might be. I won't pronounce myself on the veracity of ancient teachings, but supposing that the origin, fate, and purpose of the universe could indeed be described in plain English, how many words should it take to do so? A paper-printed Bible has roughly a thousand pages. But, why a thousand? Why not a billion, so that no one could ever read the explanation—or just five lines, perhaps in the form of a limerick? If a fairy offered to share the answer to that question, but said it would take five thousand of your lifetimes to spell out in its shortest form, would you be disappointed or would you think the fairy was wrong? And if the answer fit in a hundred-page book you could read on the subway, shouldn't *that* also be disappointing? In *The Hitchhiker's Guide to the Galaxy*, a computer built to answer 'the ultimate question of life, the universe, and everything' spends ages calculating, only to spew out the number 42!

"If this sounds like a case of damned if you do and damned if you don't, then let me show you not a book or a sentence, but a simple rule—and no, it doesn't answer anyone's ultimate question, but it's interesting alright. The rule sends any number x to its square plus a constant, or $x^2 + c$, starting with $x = 0$. The next value is c, which then becomes $c^2 + c$, then $(c^2 + c)^2 + c$, and so on. If the rule is applied indefinitely, then the values either grow so much that the computer overflows, or else stay within finite bounds forever. It isn't hard to see that if its absolute value ever exceeds 2, then the sequence is guaranteed to blow up. But the fun begins when c is a complex number, of the form $a + ib$, where i is the imaginary square root of -1. Some fellow called Mandelbrot once had the idea, while studying another problem, of coloring each screen pixel according to how quickly the sequence blew up. Some of you may have already seen a close-up of the Mandelbrot set, but it is worth revisiting.*

"No matter how much you zoom into a portion of this set, the twists and curlicues never become simpler; instead they spawn and multiply indefinitely, always keeping some resemblance to their larger versions but never repeating identically. Now consider this: if such a simple rule can produce infinite variation, then how surprising can it be that the more elaborate rules of nature generate the richness we see around us? Some people claim the universe to be nothing *but* information, and believe the simplest description of its complexity is the universe itself—much like the fairy's first offer. But as the Mandelbrot set shows, the existence of infinite complexity doesn't imply that the *rules* for it must also be infinite, or even too long to jot down on paper."

Some students would have renounced all questioning for good after such examples, but on Ethan they worked like a spur in the ribs. The next three years went by like a breeze, and at twenty-one, perhaps from an unconscious urge to break free from Nadia, he moved—this time on his own—to California, where he joined the graduate physics program at Caltech. After soggy Britain and the seesaw climate of Brooklyn (which he had learned not so much to enjoy as to endure) he wrongly assumed, like so many before him, that summers in Pasadena would be like those in New York, only hotter. The amount of sunlight made him giddy at first, but he soon got himself a mountain bike and began riding farther and farther from campus, feeling his energy increase by the week. Early into his second year, his housemates talked him into driving to Las Vegas for fall break, and he was quickly enthralled by the arid landscape they traversed. The canyons, the Joshua trees, and the sand dunes beckoned to him with mysterious strength. He remembered the East

---

* See this book's cover.

Coast autumn foliage spectacle, which he had thought at the time to be sublime; it seemed tame in comparison.

They stopped for lunch along the Mojave Freeway, and while his friends quickly headed for the air-conditioned diner, Ethan walked slowly across the parking lot, taking in the scenery. The sun glare was merciless; the heat brutally dry. A scorching wind blew through his shirt as he turned to the desert, spreading his arms wide and allowing his body to be stroked by the furnace, feeling unusually alive, like he belonged there. Ethan would later drive alone to that spot when he felt restless, to stand idly amid the intensity of the landscape, letting it seep through his pores.

***

"Do you think there's a limit to how much we can understand?" asked Mark Wiggins, his housemate, one evening over a helping of pasta and ragout sauce.

"You and I, or humans in general?"

"In general. I was tutoring an undergrad this morning and this guy just didn't get it. I thought it was my fault, because when I don't understand something it is often because I'm looking at it from the wrong angle, like that picture of a young woman which on a double-take appears to be an old hag. If you don't see both images but someone points out that the woman's chin is the old hag's nose, then it suddenly pops into view, right? But with this student it was like he didn't see and never would."

Ethan grinned. "What were you trying to explain?"

"The old Monty Hall puzzle, where you have three doors, one of which hides a prize, and you must choose at random. After being shown that there's nothing behind one of the doors you didn't choose, you are then asked if you want to change your original choice."

"Yeah, you should always switch."

"Exactly. Many people don't get it at first, or the puzzle wouldn't have been worth televising. But ask them to imagine one thousand doors instead of three, and tell them that the 998 empty ones will be opened before they are allowed to switch, and they will immediately see the advantage of switching. But this student couldn't see why something I did to the other doors *after* his initial choice could affect the accuracy of that choice. I don't think he was pulling my leg; he was honest about his inability to understand, like when someone insists that tic-tac-toe games can be won even after you show them it's impossible. But this is Caltech. If you picked out people from the street at random, you might find most of them easily fooled by such problems."

"How does that lead to your question about limits to understanding?"

"Well, if people's trouble were just with game-show puzzles, then it wouldn't matter. But there are issues that have to do with the application of justice, with government or economic policy, which voters can't understand but which have broad repercussions. Perhaps it happens to everyone, at some level. We take for granted that anything that is explainable should be understandable by humans, and yet what we study at school is full of explanations that only a small fraction of mankind would understand. So why shouldn't there be explanations that *nobody* could understand?"

"There must be," agreed Ethan. "But why worry? Our reptilian ancestors could understand even less, and yet here we are."

"I worry because people will confess without embarrassment that they aren't good at math, chemistry or economics, just like someone confessing to poor bowling skills. But tell them they shouldn't decide important political matters and they will call you all sorts of names, because they feel their grasp of vital things is as good as the next person's."

"Maybe," offered Ethan, "they see abstract reasoning like knowledge of Latin, the lack of which doesn't prevent making sense of the world."

"That's the problem. Take a dog that associates its dish with eating. At first glance it seems to have understood that plates are food receptacles. Then you see the dog, grown hungry, scratching at its empty dish, and you realize that the animal hasn't understood the concept at all, but instead thinks of the plate as a spot where food sometimes appears. Replace it with a bowl made of plastic rather than steel and the dog will ignore it. Something like that may be at work when people believe that understanding how the universe works is just another form of knowledge, like how a vacuum cleaner is put together, or that explanations are all like showing how the earth revolves around the sun: counterintuitive but easily understood. But what if our deepest questions are not only impossible to answer by us, but such that if given the answer we couldn't make sense of it or even recognize it as being an answer? What if we are all just dogs pawing at our food dishes?"

"Maybe we are."

"Shall we give it a try?"

"How?" asked Ethan.

"Explain to me, in plain English, the toughest thing you can imagine, and see if I get it. Take your thesis research, for example."

"Umm … let's not go there."

"Why not?"

"Because one of the lessons—maybe *the* lesson—of physics is that some things can only be explained in mathematical terms."

"How many abstruse concepts does your research hinge on?"

"Just one, actually."

"Then either I fail to understand it, in which case my fears are well founded, or I succeed, in which case they are overblown."

"Let's see … have you read the story *Flatland*?"

"The sci-fi novel? Sure."

"You'll recall that its creatures are stuck in a two-dimensional plane and can't imagine a third dimension, until a sphere barges in and demonstrates."

"Right."

"Well, at some point in the story an even simpler space is discussed: a one-dimensional universe called Lineland. Not much time is spent on it because simplicity makes for boring plots. But Lineland leads to a more important insight than Flatland, because the reduction of two dimensions to one isn't merely a step further; it isn't just a matter of geometrical tightening, but creates a conceptual prison of sorts, where existence has a definite order and the notion of distance is inseparable from that of 'behind' and 'ahead of', because distance and order are one and the same thing."

"Sure."

"And if we were to tell a Lineland inhabitant that a pair of objects can have separate existence without lying either ahead of or behind the other, we'd be laughed at, because in their view the only way for two points in space to lie neither ahead nor behind each other is for them to coincide. Right?"

Mark nodded.

"That's how we perceive time. We are used to one event happening before, after, or during another. But we cannot imagine—we cannot even logically conceptualize or express in words—another alternative."

"Things that exist outside time?"

"No, that's the Lineland trap. If you asked a Linelander to picture an object different from another, but neither ahead nor behind it, they would think you mean an object outside space—a concept, not an object. In the same way, I don't mean a conceptual or frozen or 'imagined' event, but one that isn't bound to *linear* time."

"Uh-oh, I can feel understanding fly out the window. Wouldn't causality break down? How can a clock tick if time itself doesn't know in which direction to flow?"

"That's because you think of clocks as mechanisms, which by construction are embedded in one-dimensional time. Causality should be thought of more as an explanatory relationship, like ±1 relates to the square root of 1. The operation explains the dual sign, but it makes no sense to say the operation 'precedes' the roots. A mechanistic view of the universe is misleading because it presupposes that causality fits that paradigm. It's like trying to explain a knot to a Linelander using only words from a linear universe."

"But, theories involving higher dimensions have been around for ages."

"Not where the dimension extended is time, except for some odd cases that involve symmetries which make time as good as linear."

"How do you prevent closed time loops from changing the past?"

"Loops are only an issue if you picture two-dimensional time as a handful of spaghettis, which is equivalent to extrapolating linear time to a multitude of itself. But think of a two-dimensional sheet that never intersects itself and the problem goes away."

"Two dimensions? Why not three?"

"No, exactly two."

"And how does time *pass* at all then, if not one moment after another?"

"Now we come to the mathematical concept."

"I thought that was it—the dimension thing."

"No, that was a preamble. It is essential for the time surface to be non-orientable…"

Ethan would remember this exchange when informing his advisor that he planned to leave academia for the corporate world. The market for science graduates had seen a slump that season and many students were extending their stay in school, doing more research to increase their chances in the next hiring uptick. Others had decided to look for work in industry, finance or consulting.

"All I can say is you've done well here," said his mentor. "But career guarantees are as fictional in science as elsewhere, so if you set your mind on other pursuits, you'll be neither the first nor the last to do so, and I wish you every success. I can't speak from personal experience, so must use my brother as example. When we were both in our twenties, seeing that academia didn't offer the lifestyle he wanted, he joined a bank. For whatever it's worth, he's the smartest person I know, but that was never the issue. It was rather that creativity, which serves entrepreneurs well, is rarely encouraged within company ranks. It is reliability they applaud, and nothing cripples original thought like having to work to a drumbeat, so my brother came to feel like a seagull recruited into a rafter of turkeys, where performance is measured in strides and flight is forbidden unless you first prove you can run. Strong fliers being clumsy on foot, he was repeatedly found wanting, which made him bitter. So make sure you look before you leap."

Ethan gave it some thought, but one morning as he saw the professors walking around campus, their hair unkempt and their attires unbecoming, something in him rebelled against the prospect of joining their ranks.

ROUSING

We can well imagine creatures with *fewer* cognitive faculties than we have ... so why should there not be creatures with *more* cognitive faculties than we have?

—STEVEN PINKER, *How the Mind Works*

It could have happened anywhere, but in retrospect perhaps it was fitting for metropolitan Russia—rather than, say, rural Tennessee—to be the first witness. A beautiful tsarist building with pastel-colored façade, opulent stucco pediments and statue-decked cornices had somehow managed to become a private club, among the most exclusive in St. Petersburg. Its food, savored by oligarchs and mobsters alike, was superb. Spring had arrived and the front garden was in full bloom when some guests emerged and made for the street. One of them held sway over the rest. Tipsy and in a foul mood, Vassily Kholodov walked briskly down the walkway, engaged in a churlish tirade that was stoically endured by an underling.

Kholodov, a media mogul whose fame rested as much on his financial success as on his volatile character, was displeased at having failed to force an agreement on another businessman of high standing in Russia's entertainment industry, who had remained in the dining room. As he walked he made vague threats of how he wouldn't allow things to stand as they were, of how so-and-so would regret his obstinacy, and so on. Forty years old but with genes selected for athleticism, he was innately agile and muscular, but spent as much time cultivating his body as he did nurturing his business. Upon reaching his car, which stood blocking the driveway, two members of his security detail kept an eye on pedestrians while he boarded. The black sedan then steered onto the street, tailed by a chase car. It was a routine maneuver for Kholodov's driver, who had gone through the motions hundreds of times: back out onto street; engage autopilot. Perhaps this had bred overconfidence, for a few seconds later a screeching of tires was followed by the characteristic report of colliding metal frames.

The first to react were the chase-car guards. One jumped out and trotted over to check on Kholodov while his colleagues dashed with self-important concern towards the vehicle that had struck Kholodov's. An arm went inside a jacket, stopping short of drawing a weapon when it became obvious that there were several onlookers.

The driver of the blue car stepped out—middle-aged, slightly overweight and clearly no threat to anyone. "I'm very sorry. Is everyone all right?" he asked. No one noticed a young woman—no older than twenty—emerge quietly from the passenger's side. Under other circumstances her looks would have certainly drawn stares.

Kholodov had been jolted by the impact, and that was enough for his short fuse to ignite. Instead of waiting for the guards to handle things, he burst forth and accosted the apologetic driver with fury. "You idiot!" he yelled. "Why don't you watch where you're going?" He stepped menacingly towards the man as he spoke, while the guards exchanged glances, wondering whether to intervene.

"My insurance will pay for the damages," said the other.

"Does it look like I give a shit about your money?" Kholodov exclaimed, eyes flaring with contempt. He slapped the dented trunk of his expensive vehicle. "See what you've done!"

"Well," the other shrugged, "that's all I can offer." It was a nervous shrug, just as there are nervous laughs, but Kholodov took further offense. Springing forward, he took the man by the coat lapels and shoved him back violently, making land on his backside.

That was when bystanders saw the young woman, who had approached just before things got physical. She seemed to reach out towards Kholodov, never actually touching him, but the man's stare suddenly went blank. He stood erect for a second before toppling to the ground like a falling tree, his face hitting the pavement with a dull thud, eyes unblinking. Some moments passed before it dawned on everyone that he was dead.

The other man had regained his feet. "Let's go, papa," said the girl, taking him by the elbow.

This brought the guards out of their stupor. "You're not going anywhere," said one, and guns were pointed at the man and his daughter.

She turned her gaze on them—a gaze that a pedestrian would later struggle to describe. 'Unearthly', he said, which was not very helpful but quickly caught on. The ground didn't shake; there was no clap of thunder, no blinding light, no sudden wind or portent of nature—only the sudden sensation, for everyone around, of hearts skipping a beat, much like a person feels who has nearly stepped in front of a speeding truck. It was the second time in less than a minute that they were visited by this discomfort. A moment of eerie silence gave way to the sound of two guns clattering on the ground, followed by the bodies of their wielders. Everyone else, including Kholodov's driver, who was unarmed, backed away, caught by an irresistible urge to hide. Father and daughter climbed into their car, the girl now behind the wheel, and drove off.

The first person to collect his wits about him and call the police was the club doorman. Patrol cars were on the scene within minutes. Several witnesses had phones with them, but no one had thought of recording the scene or the fugitive's plates—nor did they even recall if it had any. As a matter of procedure a search went out for a blue car of a rather common make, presumably with a dented hood and fender. Attention quickly turned to the unusual circumstances of the case, namely the identity of the victims, the fact that they were armed while the fugitives were not, and everyone's assurance that the only contact between the deceased and the alleged perpetrators had been Kholodov's initial aggression.

Reporters then arrived and the story began spreading. Bewildered and unclear witness testimony provided fuel for distortions, fabrications, exaggerations, and conjectures galore. Had Kholodov been involved with local mafia? Had he finally got what was coming to him? Had the eyewitnesses been paid to lie? Even the businessman with whom Kholodov had been dining saw his reputation tarnished. But what sensationalists relished most was the inexplicable fact that three grown men—two of them armed and trained—had been felled without violence by what appeared to be little more than a teenage girl.

A month later someone reported an abandoned house in the city outskirts. In its carport was a vehicle matching witness descriptions. As it turned out, both house and vehicle belonged to a family who kept to themselves and went by the not unusual name of Soloviev. No one knew of their whereabouts, but the furor surrounding Kholodov's death had by then abated somewhat, and this new finding only drew interest in the distant quarters of China's Central Military Commission, where an obscure but influential officer was the only person to come close to the truth of what had happened that day in St. Petersburg.

Lin Mei Hsieh, now a middle-aged woman, had spent half her life pursuing ghosts. Admiral Feng had recently passed away, and with him her remaining hopes for further advancement. Commodore Hsieh carried enough clout of her own to avoid being pushed aside, but the classified nature of her role made it hard for her to flaunt her skills, and among those who knew what she had been entrusted with, an increasing number were defecting to the faction which believed that wild goose chases were a waste of the people's money. Fortunately for her career, the President was not among them.

***

A warm summer drizzle fell over the streets of Wuhan as the car wound its way through easy traffic and made it onto the long bridge at an unhurried pace. At greater leisure, the Yangtze River, dark and muddy, flowed beneath. It was long past sundown but the streets were still fairly busy. Gathering speed to leave sixty meters between his car and the one behind, the man rolled down the passenger window, picked up a device from the seat beside him, pressed a button on its side and prepared to toss it. The timing was good for the airwaves to be saturated with transmissions.

He had rehearsed the throw a dozen times with objects chosen to weigh as much as this one, hurling the first in broad daylight to make sure it would clear the railing, then practicing at night. One. Two. Three. Out the window it sailed, down fifteen stories and into the depths of the river with barely a splash. The car sped on, reached the opposite bank, stopped for a light, and made a left turn. The man checked the rearview mirror. No tail was in sight. Touching his shirt pocket, he felt the thin shape of the memory chip he had placed there as a precaution, hoping it wouldn't be needed.

He drove on past blocks of high-rise buildings, then exited the road and headed for a residential complex, parked the car and took the lift to the seventh floor. The hall was well lit; the door to his apartment locked. He reached out for the keypad next to the knob and, out of habit, let his gaze fall on the doorjamb. The trick was centuries old but effective: a hair-thin piece of string held against the frame to be caught by the shutting door, easily dislodged by the slightest intrusion.

It wasn't there.

In his sinking heart, disappointment overtook fear. Everything had taken place so smoothly that he had begun to think he would get away with it. He paused to weigh his options. If they were onto him, running back to the car would be pointless. He must play the part to the end. With a tired sigh, he reached inside his jacket, pulled out a gun, tensed his muscles, pressed the entry code with his left hand, and kicked the door open. His first shot claimed a victim, but there were three men lying in wait, so he didn't get to fire twice.

One officer stepped over his body, kicked the gun away from a still-twitching hand and went through the jacket pockets. A phone was retrieved and handed to his superior, together with a wallet, the contents of which were promptly examined.

"Nothing here."

The officer redoubled his efforts, eventually reaching the shirt. He produced the memory chip, inserted it into a pad slot and studied its contents. He nodded and surrendered the device, saying "got him."

His superior was less triumphant. "It's him alright, but we don't know if he had a chance to send the information. This," he pointed to the chip, "is too clumsy. I wouldn't have carried such evidence around."

"Maybe he wasn't expecting us," said the officer. "He had no access to the data before this morning, and we've had him bugged since Friday. All signals from his apartment, his office, his car, his phone, were clean—no encryptions."

The senior officer looked again at the body, then at their fallen colleague. At length he nodded. "Right, let's inform Commodore Hsieh."

By then the screen at the bottom of the Yangtze River had long since flashed the words *Transmission Complete* for none but the catfish to see, and had melted upon itself to be washed away by the current.

***

General Henry Lasker stepped away from his desk and looked out the window. The city of Washington sprawled before him and beyond it the rest of the world. Global population had been stable for decades, but ten billion was still a huge number. As a child, Lasker had often tried to visualize large numbers in a step-by-step fashion. He pictured the number 1,000 as an array of half-inch cubes, arranged to form a larger one, ten units to the edge. That was something he could hold in his hand. He then imagined using a thousand of such cubes to form a larger one, half as large as his desk. That was a million. By imagining ten such large cubes side by side, he could even go one step beyond, to ten million. But after that it became fuzzy. He knew that one cubic meter of fine sand would contain about 10 billion particles, but it was impossible to picture the whole without losing sight of the grains. Ten billion lives going on at once...

He was hardly one to heed accounts of the supernatural or the paranormal, but large numbers held a particular fascination for him because they acted like a probability booster: the next-to-impossible could become commonplace when life's vicissitudes were allowed to play upon a large enough group of people. In his youth he had read about Neville Ebin, a seventeen-year-old from Bermuda who died when knocked off his moped by a taxi in 1974. A year later the young man's brother Erskine, who had by then turned seventeen, was riding the now-repaired moped on the same street, when he was struck and killed by the same taxi, driven by the same driver and carrying the same passenger. There was also the case of twins Loretta and Lorraine Szymanski, who happened to attend school in Pittsburgh and were surprised to meet another set of twins of the same age and in the same class, also called Loretta and Lorraine Szymanski, but in no way related to the first pair.

The magic of large numbers worked in more sinister ways, too. Lasker knew that every minute, by sheer statistics alone, someone in the world was being murdered, two people were taking their own lives and a dozen young women were being raped. If such apparently extreme occurrences took place so often, he reflected, then to what ends of darkness might human behavior be driven over a decade or two? He viewed the world with the same distrust and fascination that an ancient seafarer might have felt towards the ocean: a place where horrid dangers lay hidden just beneath the surface, their threat enhanced by murk and mystery. Lasker envisioned himself as a dragon-slayer of sorts, which in an age of biological warfare wasn't too farfetched. Military intelligence meant to him a lot more than preventing wars or winning them. He felt entrusted with the safekeeping of mankind from unknown evils, wherever they might arise, which in recent times had increasingly appeared to be the Far East. The feeling presently came upon him that he was growing old for his job, and just as he began to indulge in self-pity a knock on the door announced the appearance of a spirited man of thirty-five in gala uniform—Lieutenant Colonel Vance Havelock, Head of the Advanced Bioweapons Unit.

"General, sir?" Havelock's tone was half-annoyed, half-apologetic, as if being caught in dress uniform was something to be ashamed of. "You said it was—"

"Urgent, yes. It always is, at my age. Who knows," he added blithely, studying the colonel, "if I'll croak before relaying some critical news."

Yes, Havelock would not disappoint. "Have a seat, Vance," he said. The officer appeared to hesitate; he was in no mood for a chat and his superior was still on his feet. But Havelock knew that Lasker wasn't one to be hurried, so he capitulated by dropping into the nearest chair. Lasker handed him a pad and talked as Havelock's eyes skimmed the screen.

"We received this through Homeland Security. The informant was killed. It's a major breakthrough in Code Seagull."

"Code Seagull? I'm afraid I don't—"

"You wouldn't. It was before your time and has been dormant for years. I've given you clearance for the files, but the short of it is this: we long suspected that, despite the international ban, the Chinese never suspended their cognitive genetics program. Now, the—"

"Sir, forgive the interruption, but if history has taught us anything, it is that prohibitions are only enacted when everyone's already doing whatever is being forbidden."

"Well, if it were up to me, that fucking bill would have been killed before it got to Congress, but you know how it is with the Ethics Committee: they will do anything to undermine our competitive edge. All we can do now is try and catch up. Anyway, about fourteen years ago the Chinese announced that they were ending their research on the Prometheus module. This was just after India reported success with the human version of the Alpha complement."

Havelock nodded. "I heard about that. Some mishap led to the Indian program being terminated."

"The government program was, but a privately funded effort carried on for another year. That's when the lobbyists exploded on the scene, arguing that only the very rich could afford such procedures. A few dozen implantations had already been carried out. Then their President gave in to international pressure and that was the end of the story in India. The Chinese were expected to support the ban, but they stalled. A year later and without explanation, they agreed and the Milan protocol was enacted. Now Vance, why do you think they waited a year?"

"Trying to catch up, perhaps?"

"Not a bad guess. Sure enough, a year after the treaty was signed we gathered that they'd managed to render the Beta complement."

"In humans?"

Lasker assented, and Havelock let out a long whistle.

"Of course they denied it. Then we heard of another development: an effort of some sort had been initiated, under the code name Seagull. We knew nothing about it except that it was connected with the research program that the Chinese had supposedly abandoned. We assumed that it was merely a covert extension of the same shit, but it was buried so deep that we couldn't confirm it. It's apparently being run by Commodore Lin Mei Hsieh."

"Tough cookie."

"Yeah."

"But, if they had the Beta and India had already come up with the other piece, didn't they have all they needed?"

"No. It seems the Beta module that China developed was incompatible with its complement—as developed by the Indian team. The combination was lethal in anything neurologically more complex than a flatworm."

"So they had reason to keep on working," said Havelock. He pointed at the pad: "But if this is accurate, then they haven't reached their goal. So what the—"

"Something else must have happened fourteen years ago. Something they didn't expect."

"You said someone was killed?"

"A former navy officer—name was Huang."

Havelock looked up. "Charlie Huang? I knew him."

Lasker nodded gravely. "Outstanding man, from what I hear."

Havelock settled back into the chair and turned his attention to the message. "The original Chinese follows the English text," said Lasker. "The translators are good, but I'll let you be the judge." Havelock was silent for a couple of minutes, then threw Lasker a quizzical look.

"I don't understand," he began cautiously. "It's evident that Huang finally hit upon whatever the Chinese were trying to cover up. I'll have to read the whole thing, but they appear willing to risk anything short of war to prevent us from accessing even this bit of information. What is odd it is that they seem to be hunting for something—something outside China."

"Right, let me fill you in. Code Seagull isn't the name of a research program; it's the name of a manhunt. Now, a couple of things are clear. The first is that they are working under the assumption that it may be a long search—which makes me believe it's not a person they are after, but an organization or group of people—and they don't want us to find it first. Our task, of course, is to make sure that we do. We have a name and a place to get us started."

Havelock laid the notepad down on Lasker's desk and slowly placed his hands on his knees. "Looks like we have our work cut out for us, but as you said, it could take a while."

Lasker nodded. "Years, maybe, which is more time than I have. And which is why I've decided—with General McGrath's agreement, of course—to put you in charge the Special Projects Division as of next month." This meant he was being unofficially designated as Lasker's successor. Havelock tried to react with cool dignity. "Yes, sir. Thank you."

He hesitated.

"Something else on your mind?" asked Lasker.

"Well, sir, you said a couple of things were clear. We discussed the first. What's the second?"

"Oh, just that whatever it is they're after, it has them scared shitless. Now, go and enjoy your dinner." And Havelock was dismissed with a friendly nod.

MALICE

The belief in a supernatural source of evil is not necessary; men alone are quite capable of every wickedness.

—JOSEPH CONRAD, *Under Western Eyes*

Throughout history, people seized with the urge to redress old grievances have resorted to violence. Above all sources of resentment, the occupation of one's homeland reigns supreme, and in the Middle East, where land is scarce and grudges are sanctioned by deities, this has led to no end of trouble. In those days, as today, most people believed in an afterlife. The meaning of the word *belief,* however, was far removed from that which we currently associate with our insights regarding the universe and death. It wasn't the result of a long and mentally arduous process, beginning in childhood and lasting well into middle age, marked by a shift from gullibility through skepticism to the hard-earned conviction that a broader, more complex reality lies beyond what we call existence. Thought had yet to reach the point where it allowed such insights to be gleaned except in terms rather vague and abstract, which failed to provide comfort to those seeking immediate relief from the dread of oblivion.

Most animals—awake, no doubt, if not fully self-aware—perceive their mortality only in the face of pressing danger. Threats overcome, they slip back into ignorance of the fact that they will one day cease to exist. But humans were never so fortunate. Self-awareness brought with it an understanding of death that transcended instinct. It sprang from a mental grasp, however tenuous, of the infinite; from the painful recognition that the domain of the infinite does not extend to life on earth, and that the event feared most is the only one sure to happen. Understandably, people lent ready ears to claims that the pointlessness of life and the finality of death were both illusory. Viewing the world in terms either mechanistic or magical, depending on what they sought to explain, they juggled the two in their minds, and congratulated themselves on their ability to keep them in separate mental buckets, like fire and gunpowder. And when it came to death, existence, and origins, it seemed to most people that a choice was being forced upon them between a stance of almost cynical disbelief and one of faith-based acceptance, with its call for unquestioning trust. The first viewpoint led to the disquieting image of an uncaring universe, ticking away like a giant piece of clockwork, devoid of sense or purpose. It suggested the nightmarish vision of waking up in the middle of a long flight to find the cockpit unmanned. Not surprisingly, many people embraced the second stance.

Now, faith shouldn't have been a problem. People had always believed all sorts of things on no grounds at all, usually with few consequences to lament. There were those who believed that if they walked under a propped-up ladder something bad would befall them (and sometimes they were right). There were those who believed that aliens had once visited the earth, and delighted in the fact that it was impossible to prove them wrong. Few people bickered over such beliefs, for their ultimate veracity bore little weight on general peace of mind. But even in the simplest superstitions the seeds of trouble had been sown, because ingrained in most beliefs lay the conviction that the objects of faith demanded certain behaviors of man. A ladder might demand merely that it not be walked under, but the spirit of a volcano might require a periodic sacrifice to appease its fury, and a more complex deity could insist on a host of rituals to be performed with life-disrupting regularity. The practice of worship was born, and it was only a matter of time before someone declared that it was in their god's best interest that other deities be spurned. Once a link between virtue and faith was established, religion became a prime outlet for xenophobia, as even in primitive societies the practice was well established of jeering at the gods of rival clans and desecrating their temples. But it was in the Middle East, where tribes had long squabbled over dusty settlements and windswept lands, that the worship of jealous deities found its most pernicious expression, to the world's sorrow.

It fell to the tribe of Israel to first claim the exclusive favor of a one true god. But, unlike faiths that would follow, Judaism didn't foster the widespread conversion of others, so its practitioners would remain in the eyes of the world a people linked by ties of blood as well as of belief—a perception which, more than once, would cost them dearly. Next arose Christianity, which introduced the ambiguous concept of a god-prophet, a potentially embarrassing reversion to polytheism from which it was rescued by the even more awkward doctrine of the Trinity. It also distinguished itself by officially encouraging religious persecution, which it carried to atrocious extremes, much to its later regret. Finally came Islam, by many standards the least contrived, least ambiguous of the great monotheistic traditions; but also, when followed to the letter, the most meddlesome in people's daily lives, with its surfeit of strictures regarding prayer, dress, sexual conduct, facial hair, drinking, eating, and reliance on sacred texts—much like the orthodox forms of Jewish belief that Islamists viewed with revulsion.

The Qur'an, penned in the seventh century, was understandably mute on the topic of germline manipulation. Compared with other faiths, mainstream Islam had shown remarkable tolerance to science, and many within the ummah welcomed the advent of genetic engineering as long as its practice followed the Prophet's admonition of causing 'neither harm nor reciprocating injury'. But while some nations encouraged geneticists to keep up with global trends, others denounced it categorically, issuing fatwas that declared the mere existence of genetically tailored children to be an abomination in the eyes of God. The practical observance of these injunctions, needless to say, was colored by self-interest.

The great monotheistic systems had all seen their day in the sun. Born in an atavistic, brutal world, all had at some point sanctioned violence. But society's attitude towards aggression had evolved over the centuries. In the days when Judaism was a vanguard belief, physical force was part of everyday life, to be met with violence in kind. Centuries later, in the heyday of Christianity, Judaism had mellowed substantially, and its flock was so dispersed across the world that clashes between it and other faiths had mostly become instances of Jews being harassed. Violence was less ubiquitous in domestic life, but was still the essence of war (itself deemed honorable) which meant that carnage had a legitimate place in virtuous living. Unprovoked aggression, including invasion and slaughter, was a lawful means to exert superiority, and often had religious overtones. Christians were proud to collect the heads of Moors on their lances, and Moors were only too happy to return the favor. But with the decline of the Ottomans, the Christian cause lost its urgency, and successive schisms led, despite inquisitorial purges, to the gradual softening of Christian belief.

Not that the world had renounced violence. Although practiced with more hypocrisy than pride, warmongering and xenophobia were still very much in fashion. No longer daring to use religion as an excuse, many did fine without it. But Islam, the youngest of the great western faiths, had yet to come full circle in its maturation. It was still on the rise as its sister beliefs were ebbing; its militancy was closer to the surface and likelier to show intolerance, especially towards those at the hands of which it had previously suffered. It thus gained notoriety with outbursts of violence in a world where aggression was no longer deemed moral, where religious leaders often joined voices to condemn acts of war. Its repudiation of other beliefs was no different from that followed by older faiths in earlier times. But by the new standards, religious war was as out of place as a fistfight in a courtroom; ideology being no longer the issue, fighting was simply bad form. And Islamic leadership seemed anarchic. There was no supreme authority but the Qur'an, but there were plenty of imams, who could preach death to the infidel, in allusion not only to Jews, Christians, and unbelievers in general, but also to Muslims who chose to ignore the intransigent tenets that had given Islam a bad name among bigots of other persuasions. The truth was that the faith of Mohammed, like others before it, was caught in the throes of internal dissent, and its greatest struggles were being waged within its ranks.

***

Where the ancients measured time by reigns and kings, the lives of modern nations are reckoned in presidential terms, and it was election year again in the United States. The meeting was eagerly anticipated, and a smaller town would have been abuzz with excitement for weeks. But the nation's capital was unimpressed by historic encounters, and had often hosted gatherings of far greater moment. This was, after all, a mere party affair, albeit one the opposition had reason to be proud of.

Dan Reynolds' platform for candidacy was stronger this time around, hinging on a foreign-relations maneuver that some were already calling a masterstroke, even as others dismissed it as garden-variety demagoguery. On the face of it, it was little more than one more attempt to solve a centuries-old conflict. But it was the first time that a candidate openly endorsed the mainstream views of Muslim nations against the claims of Israel over its neighbors—not some vague declaration of goodwill, but an explicit statement to be reaffirmed after Lebanon's president gave a speech that evening. The text had been cleared beforehand with Senator Reynolds, who had in turn slipped a copy of his intended reply to the Lebanese aides. In it, Reynolds promised to allow any means, force included, to make Israel comply with a list of demands that President Karam had put together on behalf of its neighbors. The demands were such as Israel would never meet without coercion, and were therefore a blow to its hegemony and national pride. Reynolds had secured Russia's tacit support in the matter, while Karam had obtained China's vow not to intervene, in exchange for a pledge to turn a blind eye to the escalating conflict in Urumqi, which the Chinese were handling in their usual heavy-handed way.

The security at the reception was as tight as could be expected for any public event involving a presidential candidate and a foreign head of state. The Secret Service was in charge of logistics, and procedures were standard: food and drinks purchased and screened beforehand; dishes and silverware unpacked under their gaze; canapés prepared off-site in what could only be described as a military setting. Guests went through scanner arches and purses were peered into. As for the hired help, the process was more humiliating, though hardly unusual for such an occasion. Two scanning booths had been set up inside the back entrance, segregated by sex. All non-government personnel had to strip bare inside and wait for a ring-shaped device to slide down the walls, ruling out objects concealed on, or inside, their bodies. Only then could they slip into specially issued uniforms: white for kitchen staff; white and green for waiters.

A comely waitress emerged from one of the cabins, her thick eyebrows and large doe eyes distracting enough for any man, but intentionally so for the evening's guest of honor. She was known to the staff as Ameera. When the main party arrived she managed to stand second in line next to a huge fruit-punch bowl on the kitchen table, holding a tray with two glasses. The waiter preceding her was walking towards the swinging door, at the head of a long corridor leading to the banquet hall, when a busboy with an armful of silverware tripped into him, upsetting the tray and spilling glasses on the floor, where they shattered noisily. Startled gazes fell on the scene.

"Oh, I'm so sorry!" cried the busboy apologetically. He took the tray from the dumbfounded waiter and placed it on a cabinet top, where he proceeded to pick up the pieces before trying, somewhat clumsily, to wipe the tray clean. A girl from the kitchen grabbed a mop and a dustpan, and shook her head. "What were you thinking, Ehmet?"

"No damage done," said the aggrieved waiter, inspecting his uniform for stains. A Secret Service agent moved closer to the scene and monitored the cleanup with impatience. Ameera, in the meantime, had side-stepped the mess and disappeared behind the swinging door. Once alone in the corridor she bit on something inside her cheek. She bent forward and, parting her lips, let a clear stream of saliva dribble into one glass. She then repeated the operation on the second goblet and mixed the refreshments with a finger. Seconds later she appeared at the other end of the passage smiling like a summer morning, and made a beeline towards her target.

"Mr. President; Senator Reynolds," she beamed coyly, "would you care for some fruit punch?" The host offered his guest the first choice, and Karam reached for a glass, not without taking his time to smile back at the dimple-cheeked young woman. Reynolds took the other. Within the hour, both were well into their second drink. The event was a huge success and made all the headlines. Several people, predictably, were furious. Each in their own style, they reacted with venom.

"Son of a bitch," muttered President García, within earshot of no one but his chief of staff, who wondered whether he was supposed to acknowledge the remark.

"Bullshit!" cried Aamon Wade, for all to hear and the media to broadcast. "How dare he speak of friendship with Muslims? How many does he have on his team? Reynolds is a hypocrite."

"This is bad news," said a businessman over a glass of scotch in the best club of Shanghai.

"Relax," said his partner. "Reynolds is stepping on too many toes. He won't be president."

Shortly before midnight the catering staff slowly emerged onto a side street. The clumsy busboy now walked with feline grace down the sidewalk. He crossed a parking lot entrance, stopped to zip up his jacket, and continued down the block. Reaching a poorly lit bench he sat down. A minute later, a nondescript car pulled over with the passenger window rolled down. Inside, the waitress Ameera was at the wheel. The man saw her, stood up, walked to the car and hopped in.

Several blocks away the woman fetched a phone from the door bucket.

"It's Fatima," she said curtly. "On our way back to New York." A pause. "Understood," she acknowledged, and hung up. She dropped the phone beside her and smiled at the man, who grinned back. Stopping at an intersection, she lowered her left hand as if to pull the phone back out, then motioned with her head over the man's shoulder and with sudden urgency asked, "Is that a police car?"

The man's head turned in alarm. "Where?" Fatima reached over towards him, a loud buzz was heard and her accomplice slumped over. She pressed the accelerator and drove off. Two days later the man's body was found in a dumpster, fingertips abraded and face disfigured.

Upon his return to Lebanon, President Karam had already developed a fever. He was treated for flu-like symptoms and felt better for two days. Then he relapsed. Blood tests revealed no infection, but he was put on a standard course of antibiotics and taken to the hospital. A week passed before his behavior became erratic, by which point it was too late. In mounting panic, hospital took a spinal-fluid sample that finally revealed the truth, which was hidden from the media. In a desperate attempt to save his life he was put into induced coma, but died within days.

***

Fatima stepped from the train onto the busy platform of the rail-to-air terminal. Businesslike, she scanned for a Flight Departures sign. The exit she sought was at the far end of the hall. As she began walking an impersonal voice announced the airtrain's departure, and its carriages moved on. She pushed through the crowd unobtrusively, allowing hurried passengers to overtake her and slow-pokes to fall behind. She stared ahead and avoided eye contact—an easy task in New York. But as she reached the middle of the platform, a woman who had spotted her from afar suddenly did the unthinkable and called out to her.

"Nadia!" she cried cheerily.

The word coursed like a spasm through Fatima's body, and it took every ounce of her prodigious self-control to avoid acknowledging the greeting. She walked on, aware that unless she made an obvious escape their paths would cross.

The other, however, refused to be ignored. "Don't you recognize me? My word, do you look young! How have you kept in such form?"

Used to split-second decisions, Fatima decided to gamble. Her face broke into the same radiant smile she had worn the previous evening. "You must be mistaking me for my sister," she said, extending a hand "I'm Ameera."

The woman returned the handshake and hesitated. She had never heard Nadia mention a sister, and this girl's voice, though identical to Nadia's, had a strange accent. But the face was unmistakable, and the age difference... They *had* to be sisters. "Ameera," she repeated, "it's so nice to meet you. I'm Wendy, Ethan's piano teacher."

"Delighted," said Fatima. "Did you just fly in?"

"Yes, I'm staying for a week in the city with my daughter—on vacation. Only yesterday I was thinking of surprising Nadia if we had some free time. Why, her son must be a grown man by now! Does she still live in Brooklyn?"

"Oh, yes," said Fatima with perfect composure, her mind racing furiously. "But she moved across the street. What address do you have for her?" she asked solicitously.

The woman fetched a phone from her purse and after a few clicks presented the screen to Fatima. "Here: is that still the one?"

Fatima glanced at the street name and number, noting the odd spelling of the Turkish surname, which explained why her online searches had always drawn blanks. She added 20 to the street number and said, "The new address is 257." She had to prevent the woman from contacting Nadia. She could pretend that she was also on the way to town and offer Wendy a lift. She could easily dispatch the woman. But the arrival of another train took matters out of her hands.

"Here's my ride," said Wendy, and pulled her luggage to the train doors. "It was nice meeting you."

"Listen," said Fatima, "Nadia is out of town for the weekend, but I will ask her to call you on Monday."

"Will you? That's a dear," said Wendy, waving as the doors pulled shut.

Instead of proceeding to departures Fatima retraced her steps, found a quiet spot and placed a call.

"No," she said in Arabic, "I haven't been compromised, but I have news. The son of Prince Nessim may be alive. Because Nadia Karahan is living here and has a son—a grown son. No, I cannot bear children and neither can she; it must be the child she took—he goes by the name of Ethan. No," she lied, "but I will find out. I can handle it myself," she protested. Then her eyes became stone cold. "Yes, I understand. I will call you as soon as I know." She looked at the phone, turned it around, removed the battery, and threw it in a trash bin. As she walked out of the terminal she disposed of what was left and crushed the memory chip with her heel. She then headed for Ground Transportation.

GRUDGE

> And there are secret stories that remain hidden in the shadows of memory like living organisms; that send out roots, tentacles, grow appendages and parasites, and in time become the stuff of nightmares.
>
> —ISABEL ALLENDE, *Cuentos de Eva Luna*

Ethan hadn't seen Nadia for months and was almost as eager to call on her as she was to have him visit. But something was wrong. He hadn't felt it when he planned the trip, nor as he flew over. It hit him when he landed, like it had years before, in London when Nadia had fought off the stranger in the park. He stopped at the airport restroom, wondering what to do. He called Nadia and was relieved when she answered. "I have to buy some things," she said, "but will see you at home." He thought of telling her to head straight there, but the feeling intensified. He then considered asking her to come pick him up, but it didn't help either. "Okay, he said," and hung up, feeling miserable.

The driveway was free, but he parked the rental on the street, so as not to use her space. He grabbed a knapsack from the passenger seat, hopped out and, using his key, let himself in.

An unfamiliar, elusive scent greeted him. He walked towards the staircase, but thirst made him change his mind, so he walked past the dining room and headed for the kitchen. Opening the refrigerator, he saw Nadia's fresh lemonade, leaves of spearmint and pieces of rind blended in. Ethan drank a large glass and left it in the sink. The odor struck him again in the foyer—a strange, sweet perfume. Then, on the threshold of the living room, the awful feeling paralyzed him. It worsened when he thought of taking another step, and also when he considered retreating. It was like having a leash on his brain, rooting him to the spot. Three full seconds he stood there, until the sensation relented and allowed him to step forth.

The room came fully into view and a grin began forming on his face when suddenly every hair on his nape bristled in alarm. This visual rendering of his mother was a decade too young.

Besides, she would never dress in clothes so visibly Middle Eastern. But what really threw Ethan off was the look she threw at him—haughty, condescending, sardonic, vaguely amused by the effect it produced, as if sizing him up—the gaze of a woman eyeing a man like no mother should ever look at her son. Ethan felt nauseous. What was this apparition? Where was Nadia?

Sound came from her lips: a short sentence, the language utterly alien.

"I beg your pardon?" he asked.

"I said," repeated the woman with a pronounced English twang that dispelled all similarity with his mother, "that you must be Hassan."

For a moment Ethan felt relieved. This was obviously a mix-up, which would no doubt soon be set straight. He put on a weak smile.

"No, I'm Ethan, Nadia's son. I thought she was out. Is she upstairs?" Years later he would still wonder if he had ever really entertained the possibility that the woman was a guest. Her rejoinder cleared all remaining doubt.

"A Jewish name, the cunning bitch..." She rose from her seat and took a step in his direction, stopping three feet from him, her left hand hidden in the folds of the tunic while the right hung at her side, making no attempt to greet him. Her eyes glowered, and this time there was no mistaking the contempt that came across.

Ethan grew pale. Like a mugger's victim whose mind refuses to believe what is happening, he grasped for alternatives to the increasingly obvious fact that he was facing an intruder. "Excuse me!" he gasped. "Who are you?"

The woman smirked. "Who am I? Who are *you* is what you should be asking—you don't even know your real name. I suppose you don't know who your father was, either, or where you came from. She has lied to you all these years."

Ethan felt the palms of his hands begin to sweat and his mouth dry up. The woman's insulting tone diminished her credibility in his eyes, yet part of him wished that she would go on talking, so that he could later confront Nadia with what this look-alike seemed so keen to share. The rest of him wanted to strangle her, so he made a conscious choice to disengage. "Listen," he said between clenched teeth, "I don't know who you are or why you are so upset, but I'm sure we can work it out when my mother gets back. In the meantime, I will ask you to please—"

"Your mother? Your mother died soon after you were born. Nadia stole you from her arms." The woman's venom was as remarkable as her self-control, which made Ethan wince, for it again reminded him of Nadia. "She ran away with you, leaving us all behind to die. She betrayed her country and her faith."

Clearly the woman was insane. "What faith?" he asked. "And how could she betray it by running away?"

"Not by fleeing. By taking you with her. You don't belong to her."

"I don't belong to anyone."

"Oh, but you do. You are too valuable to give away."

Give me a fucking break, said his face, his unease shooting through the roof.

"I see." Her tone was patronizing again. "Even that she hid from you..."

Through the sheer window curtains a car appeared, swerving into the driveway.

"Good," said Ethan. "Now we'll get this straightened out." He turned his back on her and made for the entrance hall, a mistake that he would relive in his nightmares. The woman's appearance had deceived him: for all the disgusting differences that he perceived between her and Nadia, he still refused to recognize the threat behind her verbal taunts. He heard a hurried step behind him, and the jolt hit him like a sledgehammer. There was an instant of blinding pain and the lights went out inside his head.

The woman put the stunner away and pulled out a deadlier weapon. She stood next to Ethan's body and faced the living-room door at an angle that would keep her hidden. She released the safety catch and waited.

Nadia pulled two bags of groceries from the passenger seat and walked briskly up the porch steps. She crossed the foyer and headed for the kitchen. "Ethan!" she called, espying his knapsack on the floor. She emptied the bags' contents on the counter. Her task completed, she hollered again, "I'm home!" and turned around to search for Ethan. Halfway through the motion, her muscles tensed with an unwholesome mix of shock, pity, and terror. Standing across the kitchen, a gun leveled at her face, was her younger self.

"F—Fatima?" The word left her lips like a sigh.

Nadia heard herself reply in Arabic, "That girl died long ago."

The young woman's eyes indeed had a ghoulish air about them.

Nadia had always feared that someone would come after her, and had prepared by covering her tracks, living in isolation, taking every precaution she had ever been taught, plus some of her own device. Only when Ethan had come of age and they were both settled in New York had she begun to relax, allowing herself to believe that if no one had found her out by then, perhaps no one ever would. The one person she hadn't counted on was Fatima. Of all the people they could use against her, this was the cruelest choice. Her voice choked with emotion. "I imagine … that you've been through a lot."

"Do you?" The words were a drawn-out sneer. "You stole the baby and fled like a coward, leaving us all to rot."

"You had Hamidah—"

"She was killed the day you abandoned us."

Nadia's eyes welled up with tears. "I am sorry."

"Don't pretend. She meant nothing to you."

"That's unfair."

"Unfair? I was thirteen years old. Do you remember my thirteenth birthday? I do. Your mistress gave me this." Fatima shook her left wrist, around which sparkled a strand of diamonds set in platinum. "First I wore it to remember you. Now I wear it to remember your betrayal."

"My *betrayal*?" Nadia echoed helplessly.

"You took what wasn't yours. You are an infidel and a traitor. Your very life is an insult to God."

Nadia felt a cramp in her stomach. "Oh dear," she whispered in horror, "what have they done to you?"

"They saved me from a life of slavery."

The surreal portrait was complete. Bereft of arguments, Nadia could only gape at her alternate self, for whom the full scope of existence had been a long scream in the dark. *There but for the grace of God...* What grace, what God?

Unexpected movement caught her eye: Ethan, like a shadow behind Fatima. Nadia forced herself to keep looking at her clone, but her training was rusty and Fatima saw the hesitation in her gaze. Her head spun round, gun still pointed at Nadia, who lunged even as Ethan took the last step to slam his fist into the woman's temple.

Fatima could have easily stopped either attack, but not both. She instinctively raised her left hand to ward off the blow while squeezing the trigger with her right, so the bullet, aimed at Nadia's heart, burst through her liver instead. The shot rang like a clap of thunder in the enclosed space. Having failed to deflect Ethan's blow, Fatima fell unconscious on the floor, with Nadia nearly on top of her. Ethan looked at them in shock.

"Ethan. Ethan!" Nadia's voice roused him from stupor. She was lying on her side. A black, red-framed stain slowly spread over her blouse. He dropped to his knees and reached out to her. "Don't move. I will—"

"No," she interrupted, her heaving voice so stern that Ethan felt like a child again. "Do as I say: bring my phone; not yours—mine."

"But—"

"Now!"

Still dazed by the electric jolt, Ethan rose and walked around the kitchen island to fetch her phone while Nadia turned her attention to Fatima. Stifling a cry, she propped herself on one elbow and inspected the woman's face. Ethan's blow had left a mark on the girl's upper cheek and temple. She fetched the gun that had fallen next to her and leveled it at the very same spot. She pulled the trigger just as Ethan was returning. The bullet, a hollow point, obliterated her features. Ethan jumped in the air with a yell. "Why?! What—"

"Later," she said between labored breaths. "Give me the phone."

Ethan handed it to her, flummoxed.

"Now, go to the front door. Open and shut it loudly."

Ethan stared uncomprehendingly. She waved him away and dialed as he left the kitchen.

"I've killed an intruder." She spoke in short bursts. "I'm hurt. Yes, alone." The front door was heard slamming. "My son has arrived. Please hurry." She hung up just as the operator was asking her to stay on the line.

With Ethan back at her side, Nadia reached for the chain around her neck, which bore a huge diamond pendant. She had worn it for as long as he could remember. She tugged until the clasp faced forwards. "Unlock it," she said.

He unfastened the chain with trembling hands. "Now," she instructed, "put it in her pocket."

Ethan looked at the corpse beside them. "Who is she? Why is this happening?"

Nadia shook her head. "Later," she repeated, grimacing with pain. "Do as I say."

He obliged, averting his eyes from the blood and the brains on the floor. Only two minutes had passed, but Nadia felt herself fading. She forced herself to speak again, voicing the words between gasps for air. "When they arrive ... tell them you found us ... like this ... and that you never ... saw her face. Don't tell them ... about the necklace. Let them find..."

Ethan realized that she had purposely disfigured the woman. "Is it true?" he asked. "Did you take me from my mother?"

Nadia's eyes did not open, but she managed a hoarse whisper. "No. She ord–she begged me ... to take you before she died."

Nadia's breaths became shallower, but it was their sudden absence that brought him out of his reverie.

"Mum? Mommy!" he cried like a child lost in a crowd.

The police found him bent over her body, convulsed with tears. He wept partly for his loss and for the answers she had taken with her. But mostly he wept for the quiet old age that she would never get to enjoy. He couldn't have known that Nadia's life had exceeded all her childhood expectations, and that she would have lived it all over again had she been given the chance.

CONJECTURE

We have arranged a global civilization in which most crucial elements profoundly depend on science and technology. We have also arranged things so that almost no one understands science and technology.

—CARL SAGAN, *The Demon-Haunted World*

Somewhere in the National Security Branch of the FBI, Emilio Balderas stepped into a meeting room. He recognized his boss (Executive Assistant Director Eric Ressler) and Larissa Kane, whose long-worded role (Associate Director of Central Intelligence for Military Support) had been on and off the CIA's organization chart at various points in time. The two other people were unknown to him.

"This is Dr. Vijay Bhasin," said Ressler, "from the Centers for Disease Control." Balderas began approaching the man, but stopped as Ressler kept speaking. "You know Larissa, of course. And this is Sammy Akkad, from Mossad." Balderas nodded at Akkad, who returned the silent acknowledgment.

Kane addressed the Israeli. "Shall we begin?"

The man shifted in his chair. "Four days ago," he began, "following the death of President Karam, our Lebanese sources shared a disturbing piece of information. The official version of Karam's death is apparently false. The cause was indeed encephalitis, but not from any virus. He died of rabies."

"Then why hush it up?" interrupted Balderas.

"Well," said Akkad, almost with reluctance, "he was never in contact with animals—wild or domestic—in the weeks before the symptoms appeared. But according to the medical team in Beirut, the time of infection coincides with his trip to the United States."

"Screw the team in Beirut!" Ressler burst out. "Do we have any proof, is what I'd like to know." Kane raised a placating hand and Akkad flushed out his embarrassment by clearing his throat. "During his illness Karam underwent two spinal taps. We were able to secure a sample."

"That's when Mossad contacted us," added Kane, "and why I in turn contacted Dr. Bhasin. Doctor, if you please?"

"Right... I've examined the sample, and two facts are certain: it belongs to Karam and it has the rabies antigen."

"The antigen, yes. What about the virus?" asked Ressler.

"We have isolated it and are mapping it against known specimens," explained Bhasin.

"Why map it? Is it rabies or not?"

"Yes, beyond doubt. But we found something else: abundant bacterial sheaths of a kind that, uh, lead me to conclude that, uh..." He shot a glance at Kane.

"Go on," she said.

"The virus," Bhasin said contritely, as if guilty of blasphemy, "appears to have been a phage."

No one reacted. "Meaning?" asked Balderas.

"A segment of viral DNA that infects bacteria and reproduces by inserting itself in the bacterial chromosome without disrupting the surrounding cell. When the right conditions are met, like certain chemicals or radiation, the phage is excised from the chromosome and viral replication begins."

Balderas was flabbergasted. "Is that sort of thing common?"

"Oh, yes, phages are plentiful in seawater, for example."

"Then what's the problem?"

"We don't know of any rabies-related phage in nature."

"Are you saying this thing was engineered?"

"That would be my conclusion."

Ressler shot a glance at Kane. "Christ," he muttered. Akkad began nodding to himself, as Balderas insisted: "How do such things exist?"

"A more pertinent question," said Kane, "and the reason we went to the trouble of flying Sammy over from Tel Aviv, is whether we are dealing with a bioweapon."

"That's possible," said Bhasin, "but we'd have to know what vector was used to transmit the phage. You see, the rabies virus is fragile. It becomes inactive if exposed to the air for long and can only be transmitted through bites or other intrusive means. For inflicting damage on a large scale, something like the flu would be far more efficient—you could concoct a deadly strain and let it spread."

"Why rabies, then?" asked Kane.

"Not for a terrorist attack, but for assassination. Even the worst strain of flu, anthrax or whatever, doesn't guarantee that infection will lead to death. The only known virus that is always lethal is rabies. If you want to dispatch a single victim, there's no better choice."

"And how would it be delivered?"

"As I said, by means of bacteria of some sort. I can think of several—but you must understand, this is mere speculation."

"Don't worry," interjected Ressler, "we're not the Nobel committee."

"Yes, uh, well. Take a harmless but resistant bacillus—one that can stand exposure to air or stomach acid, making it easy to deliver. Then insert the phage in its DNA and modify it to be triggered by a specific genetic makeup."

"Specific in what sense?"

"Some viruses kill birds but not humans; there are lab viruses that target, say, prostate cancer cells but not others; they are used in hospitals everywhere. If you know enough about someone's DNA, you can design a virus to kill that person and that person alone."

"What about," asked Akkad, "one to kill only people of a certain ethnicity?"

"Like Jews but not Arabs?"

Akkad nodded.

"No. We can thank interbreeding for that. There are markers shared to a greater extent by some ethnic groups, which is useful for administering targeted medication. But if someone aimed a virus at Israelis, they'd end up infecting most of the Middle East, not to mention a good number of Americans, Europeans, even some Asians. It's fortunate that viral ethnic cleansing is too messy to be practical. But engineering something to kill a specific person—that's doable."

They stared at one another in oppressive silence until Ressler spoke again. "Emilio, will you please share your findings with everyone?"

Balderas, like the others in the room, had been digesting the news just received, and his demeanor during the exchange had slowly assumed that of a man for whom the purpose of a recently completed task has at last become clear.

"We have," he said, "reviewed the details of Karam's visit to Washington. He never veered off plan. A security detail saw him to the hotel the evening he arrived. On the second day he visited the White House, then attended a gala hosted by the National Institute for Near East Policy at the Kennedy Center, where Senator Reynolds was invited to speak. On the third day he visited the American-Lebanese Chamber of Commerce. From there he went back to the airport."

"And in which of those places," asked Bhasin, "did he eat or drink?"

"In all of them," said Balderas. "But the Hay-Adams receives so many heads of state that it's practically run by the Secret Service. The weakest links were the two soirées."

"And Karam's entourage?" asked Ressler. "Could it have been an inside job?"

"They have access to him every day at home," said Kane. "Why wait for an international trip—not to mention the risks involved?"

"To blame it on us?" suggested Balderas.

"Or on us," rejoined Akkad.

"Which they haven't," Kane pointed out. "They have the perfect excuse, but have studiously avoided it."

"Why?" said Ressler.

"Perhaps they have an inkling—or more than that—as to the culprit."

"Care to point any fingers?"

"I think that's exactly what the perpetrators are betting on. If Israel hadn't received this piece of intelligence, or had decided to keep it to themselves, or if the Lebanese had blamed someone, the repercussions would have been ugly. I'd say we were lucky."

"Who benefits from his death?"

"Take your pick," said Kane. "Even the current administration stands to profit, since Reynolds is an opposition candidate."

Ressler grimaced. "Let's not go there."

"There's also Wade," said Balderas. "Reynolds' loss is his gain, and they're declared enemies."

"Israel isn't exactly in mourning, either," added Akkad.

Ressler didn't like the turn the conversation was taking, so he kicked the ball forward. "Did Karam have Lebanese enemies in the U.S.?"

"None openly so," said Kane.

"And if we regard all these scenarios as unlikely, what are we left with?"

"Several radical groups," Kane replied, "hate the idea of any harmony between the U.S. and the Muslim mainstream."

"What if," suggested Balderas, "it was neither the U.S. nor Israel they wanted to embarrass, but Reynolds?"

"To make him lose? Then why not target Reynolds, since murder was clearly on the table?"

"Maybe that wouldn't provide a good reason for the finger-pointing you mentioned."

"It's farfetched," said Kane, "but it does add up."

Ressler's frustration had reached a tipping point. "All right," he said. "I enjoy speculating as much as the next person, but we need more facts to make headway. Sammy, we appreciate the heads-up, we really do. Emilio, please look into the logistics surrounding the two venues that Karam visited in D.C. And Larissa, I trust you will keep us abreast of any development overseas, yes? Good. Thank you all for coming." And so concluded their first meeting.

***

Ethan had no trouble adhering to Nadia's injunction to feign ignorance regarding her killer's appearance. His recurring nightmares were reminder enough. The investigators valued the necklace found in Fatima's pocket at roughly the price of a fancy car, and upon failing to find it listed as stolen, Ethan's testimony was taken at face value and the murder was written off under the technical term of assault with the intent to steal, in other words a botched robbery. Despite the perpetrator's sex, it was hardly the most bizarre incident on record with the Brooklyn Police Department that season.

Getting rid of the nightmares was another matter. Ethan briefly attended the counseling sessions that the case officer recommended, but only for as long as it took to cancel the rent contract on the house and get rid of the few possessions that Nadia had left behind. As soon as he could, Ethan flew back to California and was glad to be back among his schoolfellows, although even there he felt unable to share his grief openly, for fear of inadvertently letting it slip that he had spoken with the attacker. As the initial shock gave way to sadness, he had the sensation of being gradually engulfed by a fog that made every joke ring hollow and prevented the music he had always enjoyed from rekindling the daydreams it used to trigger. He forgot, without even realizing it, all his plans to look for a job. On the other hand, the lack of explanations for the attack and for the hellish look-alike of whom he would always call his mother spared him from imagining that he might be on anyone's hit list. This, plus a standard regimen of antidepressants, prevented him from falling apart. His thesis work had been all but complete before the incident, so he managed to graduate with the gentle encouragement of his advisor, who had heard the news in stunned silence and shown Ethan a degree of warmth unusual in a man known more for his flights of fancy than for his displays of affection. Ethan's housemates, whose research would take another year to complete, did their best to cheer him up. He then received, as next of kin, a notification from Nadia's bank in his inbox.

Ethan had never enquired about her finances, but had assumed that like single mothers everywhere, she had never been able to afford a house. But the infamous diamond's worth paled against the investments to her name, the worth of which would buy a nice apartment with a view to the bay (no mean feat in San Francisco). He wondered why Nadia hadn't made such a purchase herself, and recalled the day when he'd told her about his Caltech scholarship. She had beamed with pride, declaring that she had always assumed a doctoral program to be more expensive than college. "I suppose you can use the money when you marry."

He had laughed at the time, failing to grasp the meaning of her words. Now that he thought about it, she had never scrimped on clothes—hers or Ethan's. They had always eaten daintily and his schools hadn't been cheap. In fact, he couldn't recall ever doubting her readiness to spend on whatever he asked of her, except—

"I'm out of here," he announced the next morning.

"Got an offer?" asked Mark Wiggins, encouragingly.

Ethan shook his head. "I just need some time off, to get my thoughts together."

"But, where will you go?"

"West. Other than that, I have no idea."

"Across the Pacific? Are you—I mean—is everything all right?"

"Yeah, I'm fine. Just going on a walkabout."

Fittingly, he first landed in Australia. He had briefly considered China, but when looking up flight options to Beijing he felt a sudden pang of the old vertigo from that fatal day in Brooklyn, and nearly abandoned his travel plans. It cast the sensation, which he dubbed the *strangeness*, in a new light, and made him wonder if it might be a premonition—a warning against boarding a doomed flight or something like that. He found the idea repellent, but it was reinforced when he randomly chose a different option by clicking on a banner ad of the travel webpage, which redirected him to ticket promotions for Sydney, upon which the strangeness immediately disappeared. He made a mental note to keep an eye for news of plane crashes on his travel date, specifically on flights to China, and felt a mix of relief and disappointment when there were none.

Travel, like fairy tales or new languages, wields a formative power that wanes quickly with age, weighing old tourists down with cultural ballast wherever they go. But the travels of youth imprint on a person's character like foster parents on a fledgling's mind, and Australia's north coast would be etched on Ethan's mind as a place of healing. From desert to jungle, it held for him all the magic of the unspoiled, the warm, the gigantic. And when his roaming led him south, he wondered if in truth he might not be even fonder of the cooler, humid landscape of western Tasmania, which would remind him of England but for the alien—if lovely—vegetation. It was also around that time that he weaned himself off his medication, which was running low anyway.

He then headed to India, where for the better part of three months he explored the alleys of Kolkata, the deserts of Rajasthan and the foothills of the Himalaya. In due course he found the courage to board a flight to London, where he revisited his earliest memories and shed healthy tears. He spent the rest of the year train-hopping, like generations of young travelers had done before him. And like many of them, he found himself slowly drawn to Greece, which held special significance for its closeness to Turkey. Would he dare to go across?

After a week, feeling that he was as ready as he would ever be, he flew to Istanbul, a sight to astonish anyone, although the real shock came from realizing that Nadia's Turkish, which he had always taken for native, had been less fluent than her English. He didn't know what to make of this, but it made him feel forlorn amid the crowds and the bustle of a people whose language he understood but somehow didn't share. Where, if anywhere, did he belong? He suddenly missed California.

Time to head back.

MORALISM

> The difficult task of knowing another soul is not for young gentlemen whose consciousness is chiefly made up of their own wishes.
>
> —GEORGE ELIOT, *Middlemarch*

Not that Valerie failed to derive enjoyment from the act, or she wouldn't have kept the relationship going for long. But as fair shares go, postcoital afterglow is one of those things that life dishes out unevenly, and she was usually the one to turn around and fall asleep. In another era Eddie might have lit a cigarette. Absent that archaic option, he resorted to an even older one: chitchat.

"Val?"

"Hmmm."

"You'll be done with your doctorate soon."

"Uh-huh."

"So, what are your plans?"

"Keep going."

"More school!?"

"Uh-huh." But Valerie made the mistake of tilting her head and he could see her eyelids ajar, so she gave in. "You're also nearly done. Won't you practice law?"

"Sure, just not in school."

"Philosophy is an academic discipline; not-in-school is hardly an option."

"Yes, I guess so."

He hesitated. "Is it really about things like logic and aesthetics, or is it more like…?"

"More like Julian would describe it?"

His sheepish grin made Valerie laugh.

"Discussions," she admitted, "do tend to be open-ended, but analysis can be fruitful even if inconclusive."

"How?"

"In the same way that blind alleys can be revealing even if the exit remains hidden. The most interesting insights poke holes in concepts that are bandied about as obvious, but which have merely gained credence from repeated use."

"Like good and evil?"

"Those catchall notions are wellsprings of debate. Evil has been described as a supernatural force, as an illusion, as pathology and as extreme selfishness. It cannot be all four. But which, if any, is it?"

"Why not say that evil is as evil does, and let the matter rest?"

"That assumes the victim's viewpoint, when it has more to do with the perpetrator's. Philosophy addresses the issue in two ways. The first fixes the doer and varies the deed, starting with a pair of actions that feel unmistakably wrong and right, and gradually tweaking them until they become hard to tell apart. Imagined scenarios involve trolleys and fat men, and they conclude that a hallmark of evil is instrumentality, or the deliberate infliction of harm as the means to an end. But I like the other slant better, which fixes the deed and varies the doer. Imagine a mother and child enjoying a morning in the sun when they are surprised by strangers. Two of them keep the mother at bay while a third grabs the child and proceeds to tear it apart, limb from limb, encouraged by its screams and the mother's—a true story, by the way."

"Well if that's not evil, then I don't know what is."

"The mother and child are gazelles; the strangers are lions."

"Oh… That's different," Ed protested, even as his expression acknowledged the hit.

"Yes, but why? The lions could be securing a meal, in which case the harm would be a consequence of the benefit sought. But cats play with their food, and enjoy a victim's attempts to flee. That shows deliberate intent, and pleasure from harming."

"I still find it hard to call it evil. Cats have no choice regarding their behavior. Their digestive systems can only process meat, so they would perish if they didn't kill. As for playing with their victims, maybe evolution has programmed it into their nature."

"Right. This brings us to a quandary: either there's something about evil that sits comfortably across the entire spectrum of consciousness and much of the animal kingdom, or—"

"I'll pick door number two, wherever it leads."

"Or there's something about the existence of alternatives, the mere knowledge of which renders an innocent act despicable. And then there's context. Think of an infant's need for constant attention from its mother. In the absence of alternatives, its selfishness is healthy. But the same attitude in a capable adult seems perverse. What varies is an acquaintance with options not involving reliance on one's mother. Infant awareness perceives only its own pain: it is selfish in a primal way. But adults develop a sense of fairness and realize that some actions undermine it. (No moral judgment, so far.) It's what a mind *makes* of such knowledge that gives it moral connotation. Conscious interactions are rarely simple, so judging their fairness depends on many things, but where rectitude looks at context, evil judges only by the end of the stick it happens to hold—a stance consistent with nothing but itself."

"Oh, I don't know. I mean, you play white if you happen to hold white, but if you hold black then you *must* play black."

"Are you sure? Just because life is so often a struggle, that doesn't mean it's a tournament. Picture an island with a single fruit tree and two monkey troops, one of which has staked a claim to the tree. Although there's food enough for all, its owners only share it in exchange for services from the other troop, such as access to its females. What would you say to that?"

"I'd say that resources in human society tend to be built rather than found. If people can't own the fruits of their labor, then why make any effort? Communism has been tried before, with dire results."

"I'm not saying the market economy wants fixing. It's human nature that does."

"That's absurd!"

"What is—the want or the fixing?"

"Both! Yes, there are innate troublemakers. But of our broadly-shared traits, is there any that is broken?"

"I'd say. When someone whose birth has placed at a huge advantage over others devotes their life to increasing that gap and regards fellow travelers as rivals—"

"Whoa! Should anyone born to privilege turn down every chance of self-improvement?"

"Only if you define self-improvement as emulating the rutting moose or the strutting peacock. And out of choice, too, not necessity."

"Gosh, Valerie, you sound as if life had treated you poorly. Why fight a tide that flows in your favor?"

"Because the point I'm trying to make is that only those who have been grossly shortchanged may be forgiven for believing life is mostly about themselves and only incidentally about others. But to think it from a position of power is unforgivable."

"I fail to see what's wrong with getting ahead if the means are legal."

"Laws are beside the point. Owning slaves was perfectly licit not long ago."

"Arrgh," protested Eddie, having managed to get them both all worked up, "why do you resort to such dramatic illustrations?"

"Because they happen to illustrate; because getting ahead needs others to be gotten ahead of; because it is like saying, I know we're both lost in the woods, but while you were trying to figure the way out I was busy bagging all the berries I could find, and now that you're hungry you must do my bidding if you don't want to starve. Not that you weren't working, too—I could see you sweating beside me—but you weren't paying attention and I beat you to the resources."

"Come on!" cried young Haggart, seeing his moral code exposed as one befitting fowls and quadrupeds. "That would be an indictment of virtually everyone we know, including your family and mine. Who are we to admire, then—the vagrant, the saint? I always assumed that we saw eye to eye in certain matters, Valerie; that…" His voice faltered. "That we had something going between us," he blurted out at last.

"Of *course* we have something going between us," laughed Valerie, trying to defuse the tension. "It's called sex, and yes, I've enjoyed it too. But don't get romantic on me, will you? It spoils the mood."

"But, but," said Eddie, color draining from his face, "don't you ever long for something different—to settle down, move on?"

"Move on?" she asked playfully. "You're leaving me already?" But Haggart saw that the prospect didn't pain her overmuch, which was more than he could bear. "No!" he protested forcefully. "I meant move on *with* me."

Valerie's countenance changed at once, and it embarrassed him to read in her eyes the dismay that comes from unwittingly stepping on a small creature. "Oh, Eddie, no—no, no, no…"

***

Incarceration can put even the strongest marriage to the test, and the Dashaws' was far from idyllic to begin with, so it didn't take long for Amanda to abandon her husband to his fate. As her initial sympathy gave way to self-pity, Ron's grit degenerated to resentment, and Amanda's weekly visits to the state penitentiary became sporadic, guilt-ridden spats, the content of which was so familiar to custodians that they paid no heed to the ill-disguised recriminations, halfhearted apologies and awkward silences of a love that, on its deathbed, wonders how it ever came to be. Hardly a year had gone by when Amanda filed for divorce. Left to herself—for Stacey had stayed away and Connor had promptly decamped—she found solace in the arms of an old high-school flame, eager to play commiserating confidant and to take her in when their house was repossessed.

Connor had expected his lot to improve with Wade in the Senate, especially after his former manager Graciano Yglesias was appointed Wade's scheduler. But he soon found that congressional teams need fewer helping hands than campaigners. The new chief of staff, an outsider called Evander Garfield, informed Connor that there was unfortunately no place for him in the office, given its new requirements, available budget, and so on. Connor found work in a fast-food chain in Evanston, from where he was recruited after a year, and for twice the pay, as a busboy in an upscale restaurant not far from the Magnificent Mile. His eloquence eventually caught the attention of the maître d'hôtel, who promoted him to full waiter, a position he held contentedly until he realized that it might well mark the end of the line in his professional growth. He had by then purchased a car and was renting a studio where he could receive company without shame, but it was a far cry from the life he had once imagined for himself.

Connor remained his sister's only link to their family. They met a few times a year, whenever he failed to hear from Stacey and grew worried for her sake. He had a key to her downtown apartment, but always felt edgy when he let himself in, fearing he might run into one of her customers. (She never brought them home, but then she never discussed her professional arrangements with her brother.) More often than not he found Stacey dozing on the couch, and this was no exception, but when he let the door shut loudly she failed to stir.

"Hey, it's me," he said. It was mid-morning but the blackout was drawn and the room was dark; a large screen displayed a shifting wallpaper. Stacey was fully dressed and had clearly lain there all night. He let sunshine flood the room, picked up the remote from the floor and turned the screen off. "Stacey?" Still nothing. He reached out to her face: she was warm but unresponsive. Connor looked around. On the countertop between kitchen and sitting room lay the detritus of whatever she had been snorting the night before.

He knelt on the floor and shook her by the shoulders. "Stacey, wake up. Wake up, dammit!"

She let out a weak cough, which built up to a noisy, uncontrolled fit. Her eyes opened in alarm; she pushed Connor aside, rolled onto the floor and went on coughing on hands and knees. When the spasms subsided she looked up at him miserably, staggered to her feet and rushed to the bathroom. Connor heard her spit into the washbasin. She returned with some pills, drew a glass of water to swallow them, and dragged herself back to the couch; leaning back she pressed her hands to her temples, eyes shut tight as a tear drew a trail of mascara down her cheek. "Put out the lights, will you?" Connor obliged, bringing the sunlight down to a thin line on the carpet. Stacey opened her eyes and Connor found it hard to believe that, despite everything, she still looked pretty.

He sat down beside her. "You know," he declared, staring at the floor, "it's only a matter of time before you overdose".

She didn't reply. "There's this rehab program," he volunteered, "where they use, believe it or not, a drug cocktail to wean you off the others."

Stacey shook her head. "Can't afford it."

He vouchsafed her an incredulous look. "I'll pay."

"I don't mean the treatment. I just can't afford to live differently."

"You mean the jewels, the car—the dope, for Christ's sake?"

"All of it!" she shrieked. "I do … what I do, so I can afford this place, the Mercedes, the lifestyle."

"And that?" He pointed at the countertop. "Is that to forget the price you pay?"

She was silent and Connor regretted his bluntness. "Besides," he protested, "I get along fine on a fraction of what you make."

"Well, I guess we're just—different."

"I can teach you."

"To live poorly?"

He swallowed. "It's not that bad."

"And what I do isn't as bad as it's made up to be. Only problem is youth doesn't last forever."

"Another reason to switch."

She tried changing the subject. "Any change coming your way?"

He shrugged. "I'd like to go back to politics."

"Again? That's dangerous."

Look who's talking. He held his tongue, but she wasn't fooled.

"Especially," she said, "when you think you have some injustice to redress."

Fire lit his eyes. "Are you happy with your lot?"

"Of course not! Life can be horrible, but blaming others won't help."

"So, let them be merry while the rest of us rot—is that what you're saying?"

"Who's them, Connor? There *is* no them."

The pity in her eyes incensed him further. "Since when are you a sociologist?"

"I'm just your sister. And bad people do exist, but they're individuals, not groups."

"Enemies band together."

"You mean terrorists."

"And undeclared foes."

"Connor, I hope you know the danger of imagined conspiracies."

"If you're worried that I'll be wasting my time—"

"No! The danger is they give rise to real ones. The Nazis imagined a Jewish conspiracy, so they formed a real one against the Jews."

He looked at Stacey in vexed confusion. "And how are we supposed to know who can be trusted if we don't know who can't?"

"If it's a recipe you want, then beware of those who gain from another's loss. They're the worst kind, even in my line of business."

"God, Stacey!" Connor lashed out. "Have you no self-respect? You spend your life trading—you sell your—"

"I sell something I don't value much for something I do, so the deal is fair. And those who call on me have no better use for their money, so nobody loses."

"That bastard abused you!"

"No one does, now."

They sat quietly together, each lost in their variant of hell, until Connor stood up to go. "You should visit dad," he said.

"I don't want to talk about it." She emphasized the point by walking over to the kitchen to wipe up the evidence that was lying around.

"He's all alone in there. He doesn't blame you, if that is what's holding you back."

Stacey clenched her fists around the rag as she held it under the faucet. *That's what the drugs are for, to drown the remorse and the shame and the helplessness.* But for some reason it was easier to keep up the act of umbrage.

"Don't you have any work to do?" she asked accusingly.

"It's Monday."

"Huh?"

"The restaurant's closed."

"Then do something else."

"He misses you."

"Just leave!" she yelled.

Long after he'd gone she sat in the same spot on the floor, weeping softly into the kitchen rag.

WORRY

Old age is the most unexpected of all things that happen to a man.

—LEON TROTSKY, *Diary in Exile*

It was a fine spring afternoon when Bruce Taylor learned he was dying. The sun shone through the windows of his New York penthouse and fell on the dust that hung in the stillness of his study, motes glistening as they followed their random paths through space. He looked at the rug beneath his feet. He had often seen the sunlight on the study floor, but now it seemed surreal, as can happen to people upon learning that life is to be shorter than expected. A dark rage had begun to well up within him, but he was still firmly in the stage of denial.

Across from him sat Dr. Oliver Green, bald save for some wisps on the back of his head, wearing an expression of sympathy that befitted the vague discomfiture of knowing that he was older than his patient would ever live to be. Now virtually retired, he had been the family doctor since before Taylor's children were born, and Taylor had flown him in from London for this consultation. He needed to hear Green's opinion regarding the latest test results received from the uppity doctors at the Sloan Kettering Institute. "It makes no sense," he said. "I have none of the genes associated with the disease."

"You don't," Green agreed, "but genetics is only one factor; there's also radiation and chemical triggers."

"But," argued Taylor as if negotiating a difficult equity placement, "ninety-five percent of cancers are curable. No one dies of it these days."

Green let out a raspy cough. "Five percent is still a lot, although admittedly this particular type of leukemia has a prevalence of one in a million. It's what we call an orphan disease, which means that—"

"I know what it means," Taylor interrupted gruffly. Twice in the past he had turned down requests to fund ailments of that sort. His tone then softened, humbled by his predicament. "I just … can't believe they won't come up with reasonable alternatives. How could this be stage-four already? I went to the hospital as soon as I felt ill."

"It tends to be asymptomatic in the early stages. Didn't you feel fatigued at times? Night sweats, perhaps?"

Taylor looked out the window. "I suppose I did. Nothing serious, though—certainly nothing that yelled *cancer* at me."

Green studied Taylor, his wealthiest patient by far, thinking that when it came to sickness they were all very much alike. "It doesn't mean you shouldn't get treated," he said. "There *are* options, you know. When you and I were young it was chemotherapy, but there are much better tools, now."

"How long would it buy me, roughly?"

The doctor hedged. "I'm not an oncologist, you know."

"Come on, Oliver, you owe me better than that."

The doctor coughed again. "Two to three years with checkpoint inhibitors, versus five or six months if you do nothing."

Taylor pondered the answer. Looking about him he felt that the furniture, the soft leather scent pervading the room, the muffled sounds of the city outside the window, all had acquired a different tinge. At his age he had had plenty of occasions to think about death, but had never guessed it would come to him in this guise. Two or three years; so much unfinished business.

He knew that Julian was far too young to step into his shoes. It made him shudder to think of how naïve the boy was. What to do? Bill Stavins was a first-rate executive, but far too ambitious to be entrusted with a stewardship role. Perhaps if he offered Bill a greater share in the holding company, something linked to its long-term success... He cursed himself for not having devoted enough time to a proper governance plan, but at least that was something he could still put together. His head began to throb. *Two or three years...* He had never been sentimental, but all of a sudden he felt terribly lonely. He thanked Dr. Green, who was glad to get away. Taylor saw him to the door and returned to his study, where he sank into an armchair, wondering how he would tell his children, what to do with Patricia and, what was most important, how to prevent the Labs from collapsing after he was gone.

A practical man to the hilt, he laid out his priorities in the order they had always held in his eyes: first, his business; second, his family; and third, whatever else gave him pleasure. The first person to be neglected was therefore his trophy girlfriend, who had shared his life for over a decade and was for all practical purposes his wife. He never meant to be rid of Patricia, but she was hardly the motherly type to be content with nursing an ailing old man from whom she had received no sign of commitment. She complained about his shortening temper and his new obsession with work, and this led to even greater neglect on his part and a near infidelity on hers, at which point Taylor sent her packing, ostensibly with enough money to rebuild her life, but in fact heartbroken. Even Valerie, who had never shown much warmth towards Patricia, was moved to pay her a visit and lend a shoulder to cry on.

***

Candidate interviews for associate positions with Blake & Whitney were concluding in the west coast. Junior Partner Paul Langdon and Head of Staffing Raymond Kluber were comparing notes for the day. Hundreds of applications from Berkeley, Stanford, and other top schools had been winnowed down to 85 résumés, mostly from MBA programs. Only 20 would receive offers that season.

"What did you think of the last one?" asked Kluber.

"He will be a ... turndown. Yes, a definite turndown. I've applied the same scenario with everyone today."

"Your insurance case?"

"Yeah; this guy was too cocky. When asked how the client might turn profits around he immediately said it was a pricing issue. He spent the summer with the folks at Quadrum, who happened to be losing money, so in his mind every problem is price-related."

Kluber dragged the candidate's icon to the rejection heap. "Didn't shine with me either; wouldn't stop talking. Some people think that if they just rattle on, you won't see through them... Okay, one more and we're done."

Langdon turned to his notebook. "Karajan," he said. "Very young, brilliant academics, no business experience."

"Reminds me of Grünewald, from last year."

"That was a good hire. Want me to have the first go?"

"Sure, I can finish my write-ups."

"See you in thirty, then." Langdon left his colleague and headed for the interview room, where a striking, dark-eyed young man rose to greet him. "Ethan Karajan."

"Paul Langdon. Thanks for waiting. Do you live in the area? Ah, I love San Francisco. All right, let's see. It's been a year since you graduated. Not in a hurry to work?"

"I took a year off to travel before settling down."

"Not in Tibet?

"No. Why?"

"Oh, last year a candidate spent the summer in Tibet before joining our practice in L.A. But what attracts you to consulting? Bored with physics?"

"No, but I don't see myself in it indefinitely. I suppose I'm more of a people person than I thought."

Langdon smiled. "Grew up in Britain, eh? I couldn't tell at first, except a sister of mine—but never mind. Suppose a company, a large, multiline insurance firm, calls you for help. The industry has grown but the company's profits have declined to the point where they're losing money. How would you tackle the problem?"

Ethan looked down at the table. A few seconds passed, then several more. Langdon was about to speak again when Ethan said, still looking down, "the revenues from customers—they're called premiums, right?"

"Right."

"And the costs—aside from things like rent and salaries—are proportional to the volume of customer claims?"

"Variable costs, yes."

Ethan looked up. "You said the industry was growing. What about the company's client portfolio?"

"Increasing as well, in line with the sector."

Ethan looked down again. More time went by and Langdon's mind wandered. He pictured Ethan on one of his teams. *So, Dr. Karajan, Herr Doktor Professor, never been exposed to corporate settings before, have you? Physics, eh? How about risk levels—ever heard of those?*

"The types of insurance offered by the company—what are they, exactly?"

The interviewer was shaken out of his reverie. "Uh, they run four business lines: automobile, healthcare, household, and commercial insurance, which covers property damage but mostly provides liability protection. The only thing they don't sell is life insurance."

"And," asked Ethan, "have all business lines seen a similar decline in profits?"

Langdon's eyes twinkled. "No, they haven't. Automobile and household are doing fine, in fact. Profits have grown. Unfortunately, they are offset by losses in the other two units."

"And the number of customers—"

"Has remained steady in all business units," said Langdon.

"How about risk assessment? Are the skills needed for each type of insurance the same all around?"

Langdon relished the question as if it had been his own. "You tell me. What do you think?"

Ethan pursed his lips. "I would say that automobile insurance is more about statistics, while insuring large manufacturing facilities probably requires a different type of skill. As for healthcare—"

"Hold on, finish that thought. What does it tell you about the client's issue?"

"Maybe they are assessing risk improperly in commercial insurance, or are spread out too thinly. Has competition changed recently?"

Langdon was beaming at this point. "It has increased considerably: lots of new players, most of them focused on a single type of insurance."

"Perhaps we could figure out if it makes sense to exit one or two business lines, and re-focus?" ventured Ethan.

"And how would you decide whether a given line is worth divesting, or improving?"

There was a long silence again; this time Langdon enjoyed it. At length Ethan resumed. "I would like to know how much of total business volume is accounted for by each business unit. Is the company particularly strong in some versus others, in terms of market-share or scale?"

"Yes, it is. Let's stop there." Langdon grabbed a bottle of water, his manner relaxed. "What can I tell you about the Firm? What would you like to know about us?"

***

"Eric," said Larissa Kane, "thank you for meeting me here."

Ressler had driven up to Langley, alone. The week had been hectic for both, so their small talk ended where it began. "Emilio's hunch proved correct," she said, "but that spells trouble."

"Emilio has an overactive imagination," rejoined Ressler. "But I'll give him credit if you do."

"A month ago, according to Mossad, the Lebanese got wind of a man called Ahmed Zamalek. He's linked to Omar, the eldest son of Ibrahim Al Faisal, who always wanted Karam dead. The trail ends at Cairo International, with Zamalek boarding a flight to JFK. His dossier is being transferred to you as we speak."

Ressler nodded, but his expression was far from satisfied. "Let me get this straight. A foreign head of state was killed, on U.S. soil, on orders from Al Faisal?!"

"That … seems to be the case." Kane wasn't proud of what she was saying, but had no choice. "And there's more: an unknown sum of money changed hands. The source was American."

"You mean it originated *in* America, or from an American national?"

"We don't know; hence this meeting."

Ressler scowled. "By the book, we must inform National Intelligence. Then McGrath will want to bring in Defense, and who knows where that will lead."

"Courtesy; professional duty—call it what you will: I wanted to brief you first."

Normally reluctant to relinquish control of an investigation, Kane on this occasion seemed almost glad to pass the buck. It lifted a weight off both their shoulders, and she rationalized the decision by telling herself that involving the top brass would speed things up.

She was wrong. It would take a year to hear back from Ressler, by which time the scene had changed. Whether the sudden absence of Middle Eastern allies had hurt Reynolds' power base or (as his detractors said) merely underscored the urgency of his rhetoric, the fact remains that he carried the election. The Director of National Intelligence was instructed by President García to pursue the inquiry into Karam's death as discretely as possible, to prevent a scandal from tarnishing the exiting administration. And while the Bureau wasted no time acting on Kane's lead, the sheer number of transactions that had occurred in the relevant timeframe made the task impracticable, because the guilty parties had carefully avoided blockchain exchanges.

In a private briefing before Reynolds took office, President García asked him to meet a certain officer from the Pentagon.

"Come in, Colonel Havelock," said Reynolds.

"Thank you, sir, for receiving me. I won't guess how busy you must be with the inauguration."

"Busy is putting it mildly. But I will say one thing: of all the intelligence the President has shared with me, I find yours to be the most intriguing, and not because it regards my person."

"I understand."

"Well maybe you do, but I'm perplexed. If there were any danger, shouldn't I be dead by now?"

"I'm afraid that's not how this virus behaves. It is lethal only for the intended victim. If you were infected that day, then your immune system would have cleared it, but a memory will remain. We know what the antibodies look like, and that's what we want to test. It's just a blood sample."

"Heck," said Reynolds, removing a cufflink, "if your theory is correct, then I will treat it as if the target had been me." He pressed the intercom. "Let the medic in. And," he added after releasing the button, "I trust you to find out who did this."

"That's the plan," said Havelock.

ETHOS

> We shall never know how much genius has been lost to the world by reason of the need to make a living.
>
> —CLIFTON FADIMAN, *The Lifetime Reading Plan*

Managing Partner Wayne Peikoff yelled at the team throughout the ride. The car was mostly guiding itself, which was just as well, for he hadn't asked if anyone else cared to drive, and repeatedly slammed his hand on the wheel with mercurial sarcasm aimed mostly at Project Manager Cliff Boyer, who rode shotgun while Ethan and an analyst kept low profiles in the back seat.

"That's not what the client asked for!" he ranted. "What about the market-size estimates? All you had to do was browse the web and pick a number here and there. But no, the only thing I asked for, you forgot." Ethan had in fact jotted down six requests from Peikoff; all but one of them included in the presentation they now took to the meeting. Boyer, pale with stress and lack of sleep, made halfhearted attempts to justify their approach. "This is based on the latest version of the model, which—"

"I don't give a shit about the model! We had to address their questions, build a solid case and build a few scenarios. Now we can't even do that. What are we going to say? Oops, we didn't look at market potential because we thought it wasn't important? Jesus fucking Christ…"

Peikoff lowered the window to gain admittance to their destination's parking. "Well, here we are. We'll just have to defend what we have and hope they don't kick us out for incompetence," and with that capstone to his pep talk he led them into the building. They were ushered into an executive dining room where a long table of white marble with dark leather inlays had been laid out for seven. Juice and soda were served and the CEO walked in with two executives. Ethan knew them well: in their presence Peikoff was all smiles and engaged in witty repartee, followed by name dropping, a joke or two, and overtures of friendship to the same vice president that he had previously ridiculed behind the man's back. The CEO mentioned the political climate and Peikoff disclosed the gist of a recent conversation with White House officials.

Salad was served, consisting of whole leaves of romaine lettuce onto which creamy dressing would be ladled by a waiter. Peikoff, enthused by the vividness of his own swagger, picked up a leaf by the stem with his fingers like a crudité and kept talking. His emphatic hand motions made the lettuce wiggle in the air while the waiter looked on helplessly, dressing dish in hand. Ethan wondered who would be the first person to laugh, but as he looked around the table he realized that everyone was engrossed by Peikoff's anecdote. He felt a growing sense of frustration, not so much at his boss for putting on such an act, but at everyone else for finding it anything but ridiculous.

Someone had thoughtfully laid pen and paper next to each place at the table, and Ethan took notes. 'Today's Chestnuts' he scrawled across the top of the page, followed by every business platitude uttered by Peikoff, who was a grandmaster of the hackneyed turn of phrase. Within the hour his list included a good dozen: keep in the loop, hit the ground running, win-win, the big picture, appearance is reality, bring up to speed, back of the envelope, low-hanging fruit, two heads think better than one, reinvent the wheel, the devil is in the details, and back to the drawing board. He was waiting for Peikoff's favorite: *ceteris paribus*, but when the perfect moment came his boss, incredibly, ignored the bait. Ethan was adding the words 'close, but no cigar' when the CEO presently interjected 'all other things equal', drawing a smile from Ethan that the client warmly returned, taking it for mutual understanding.

It was Boyer who had to shoulder the burden of taking them through the fruits of their effort, except for the few technical bits that Ethan was called to expound upon. The meeting went off without a hitch, because the team had taken all cues for their analysis from the same executives with whom they now sat. Once the CEO had expressed the required level of interest and a date had been set for the next progress review, Peikoff was in a relaxed mood, and as they drove back Ethan couldn't help speaking up. "It seems he liked it, after all," he declared, to no one in particular.

"Yes," agreed Peikoff, then "Pshaw! You mean because of what I said earlier? Do you think I owe my success to my well-placed friends?" (No, thought Ethan, you owe it to the business world's fondness for jerks.) "If I got this far it is because I'm always on my toes, ever on the lookout for what could go wrong and what we could do better. Clients know that I pledge myself body and soul to solving their problems. Perfection is meeting the standard," he said orotundly. "Right, Cliff?"

"That's right," nodded the manager, exhausted (and not without relief, Ethan could tell).

***

"Morning Lou," said Ressler, acknowledging Special Agent Louis Hayes, who, like Emilio Balderas, wore a self-satisfied grin on his face. "Well, what have you got?"

"A catering outfit," said Balderas. "It served canapés at the Near East Policy event."

"Please tell me you found a match."

"We did."

Someone else might have jumped out of his chair to high-five them, but Ressler just brought his hands together and pressed the knuckles to his mouth. Still, Balderas could see the lips quirking up. "Two of their staff," he resumed, "went AWOL the day after the gala, and haven't been heard of since. We asked for scans and one matches Ahmed Zamalek."

"Visually, you mean."

"More than that. We have cranials from the event and from immigration at JFK. Fake Egyptian passport, went by the name Ehmet."

"Ehmet, Ahmed… You'd think they had more imagination."

"Maybe they do: Ehmet is the Uyghur variant of Ahmed."

"I'm not following."

"Karam was criticized for turning his back on Urumqi to curry favor with China. The name may have been chosen on purpose."

"I see. Who owns the outfit?"

"Gourmet Delights. But guess since when?"

Ressler made a wry face. "And before?"

"A shell company. The deal was handled through law firms, so unless we involve the judiciary..."

Ressler had a peculiar tick in his left eye, the corner of which would twitch under stress. It might have interfered with field duties early in his career, but had somehow escaped attention and never hindered his progression. Balderas could see the tremor now.

"How did Zamalek get past the scanners?"

"He hadn't been flagged. Nor had the other."

"Yes, the other—are they connected?"

"They entered the U.S. hours apart, so we assume they are."

"You ran his picture through the files, yes?"

"*Her* picture," corrected Hayes. He clicked on his pad and handed it over. "No match. The catering staff knew her as Ameera."

Ressler studied the image. "Do me a favor, will you? Send this intel at once to Larissa Kane. She may help us identify the woman."

"Will do." Hayes took back the pad, folded it shut and prepared to rejoin the conversation. Ressler looked at him. "I meant *now*, Agent Hayes."

"Yes, of course." And as the red-faced agent busied himself with the task, Ressler turned back to Balderas. "Did Zamalek leave the country?"

"No departure record, at least under the name he used coming in."

"If they left by sea," Ressler continued, "there may be no scans. Have they been flagged?"

"Zamalek has. His file was shared by the CIA. We can add the woman's picture to the watch list."

"Do it, but no specifics until I brief the Director. We meet tomorrow."

"We are working to find out who sold the company. If the old and new owners are unacquainted, it will play in our favor."

"Tread carefully," cautioned Ressler. "We don't know where loyalties lie, and we can't bring Karam back, so we're looking at a game of patience. You know what I mean, Emilio."

Balderas nodded and the officers stood up.

"Hey," Ressler called out as they left. "Good work, you two."

***

The spring of his third year with Blake & Whitney was Ethan's first as Junior Manager. A new cohort of associates had joined the office the day before, but he had been working with a client and had missed the round of introductions. He knew nothing of the fall-season recruits except that one had been assigned the office next to his, which, from the tone of the comment, was held to be lucky for him.

Cassie Jensen, said the nameplate. Associates and managers shared offices two apiece, but when Ethan poked his head in that morning the space was empty. He knew the other occupant was away on duty, but the formerly vacant desk bore every sign of a consultant still waiting to be staffed: an uncluttered place, new supplies, and a notebook, left carelessly turned on. Ethan stepped closer to glance at the display, which showed the page of a novel: *The Shipping News*. Ethan recalled the author's thrifty prose, the dropped conjunctions, skipped pronouns, elided verbs; the best passages all nouns, adjectives, tidy, terse. He returned to his desk and was swallowed by the day's activities, which included a long meeting, lunch with his team, and data mining until late at night. When he left, the office next to his was dark.

The rookie was at her desk the next morning. When she didn't look up, Ethan took a good look and felt himself rubbernecking. He dropped his belongings on his desk, reflected for a moment, stepped back into the corridor and retraced his steps. "Hi," he said rapping on the doorframe and pointing a thumb at his office, "I'm Ethan, your neighbor."

"I'm Cassie." Her hand was soft and warm.

"Welcome to the Firm." For once, he wasn't just being polite. "Cassie," he repeated, "is that short for something?"

"The full name is Cassiopeia—but I never use it." The feigned downplaying concealed annoyance from repeating something too often.

"Wife of Cepheus."

She looked surprised.

"Just thinking out loud," he clarified. "With a last name like Jensen I hardly thought you were Greek, unless your mother—"

"No—I mean yes, she is. It's just that people usually say ... other things."

ALLURE

> She was one of those rare, even among already pretty, women that are born with a natural aura of sexuality: always in their lives it will be the relationship with men, it will be how men react, that matters.
>
> —JOHN FOWLES, *The Magus*

He tagged along only because Cassie had said she would be there. The lounge was cavernous but the setting lent it a college-bar atmosphere. The noisy crowd competed with a live band, which played rather well, even if Ethan didn't much care for the jazzy tunes that made up its repertoire. A few lucky patrons sat around tables close to the ensemble, while the rest crammed the place like so much cattle, making it hard to get a drink or hold a conversation. To Ethan's amazement, everyone seemed to love it.

Cassie had indeed shown up and was already the center of gravity of a small cluster of males, all doing their dapper best to be witty. Ethan joined them and strained to catch the gist of their conversation while sipping a martini that threatened to spill from the jostling of passers-by. Someone shared a joke; Ethan outdid him and drew a good laugh. Then they turned to current events and Ethan's mind began wandering. President Reynolds was derided for his latest mediatic *faux pas* and his inability to get the country out of recession; Aamon Wade was criticized for his rants against Reynolds, which were deemed on the mark but incendiary. Someone expressed hope that a certain governor would run too; another observed that, unlike Wade, this governor was far too dull to rally a sizeable majority behind him, yadda, yadda, yadda. Out of the corner of his eye Ethan studied Cassie while pretending to follow the nattering. With hardly a word, she held rule over the evening by mannerisms alone: a slight tilt of the head, a pouting of lips, hair expertly flicked over an ear, a furtive glance shot across the room and averted when roving eyes met hers. The talk turned to gossip about a lead vocalist whose disproportionate earnings had led the band to break up.

"Raking in thirty million a year," said Dominic Pyle, a junior partner. "Five times what her sisters get."

"It figures," agreed Cassie.

"Why?" asked Ethan. "Since when is nothing better than five million?"

"Peer-group dynamics," offered Pyle. "It's not absolute wealth that matters, but that relative to your social circle."

"Speak for yourself," laughed Ethan.

"I'm serious. Imagine you could earn as much as you wanted, on the one condition that all your acquaintances earned twice as much. Private jet? You've got it, but all your friends get a better one, and so on. Does that sound like heaven or hell?"

"Heaven!" exclaimed Ethan. "Hell!" Cassie cried out in unison. They exchanged self-conscious giggles and for an elusive instant caught in each other's eyes that magical first glint of mutual attraction. A second young woman joined the circle and Ethan was soon wedged in a discussion about company mergers. He tuned out of the exchange and began looking around. He swallowed the last of his martini. "Refill, anyone?" he said. No one took up his offer, so he made his way in the general direction of the bar, in no real hurry to reach it. Either the music had improved or the drink had made him less picky (the band was now pounding away an upbeat, dancy version of blues). Ethan gravitated towards the stage. As he reached it the music stopped and the pianist brushed past, headed for the restrooms. The sax player, a bodacious chocolate-skinned woman not much older than Ethan, looked at him and smiled coyly.

"Play any ragtime?" he inquired.

"You bet. Just wait till Ben gets back—unless you want to give it a shot," and she gestured at the bench. Before he knew it, under the double spell of gin and teasing, Ethan was sitting at the keyboard, pouring forth a dose of Scott Joplin. The band didn't miss a beat and were soon following his lead, egged on by Ethan's new fan. He finished the piece and was in the middle of a second when the piano man returned. "Well done," he said to a round of applause, "but I do need the job, so if you don't mind..." Ethan stood up. "Come back soon," said the girl, and they broke into another high-spirited air.

Dodging past the front tables he ran into Cassie, who had been watching him play with a twinkle in her eye. "What on earth—?" she began. But now that he was no longer part of the music Ethan again found it annoying, so he put an arm around her waist and said, "Why don't we go somewhere we can actually talk?"

He courted her with measured deliberateness, and Cassie felt herself falling for him gently, as if drifting into a cloud. She was drawn to Ethan's sense of humor, the breadth of his knowledge, and the way he used his tongue on her body. He had a way about him that evoked a gallant style of yore, and while she didn't find him pragmatic enough (more dreams than actions, was how she would have judged anyone else), this was something Cassie believed she could overlook.

Romances that blossom in tightly-knit workplaces soon become fishbowl affairs, and with the affections of a woman like Cassie at stake there was no dearth of contenders. Dominic Pyle, extrasomic like most of his colleagues, was trim, a bit on the wiry side but not unpleasant to look at, with light brown hair and eyes to complement a smile that was at its sincerest when laughing at others.

Those who like their heroes puppy-eyed and their villains ogrish would have been disappointed. Surefooted where Ethan wavered, astute where Ethan was profound, solicitous where Ethan was aloof, it isn't clear who would have made better dinner conversation. But there's no question that Pyle's business talk was better received at work. Adroit and eloquent, he navigated the world relying on an instinct for knowing, always and everywhere, how to flatter without being unctuous. He was the consummate professional when engaging clients in clever gab with the threefold purpose of displaying his wit, making them feel that he held their work in high esteem, and coming across as the poster child of reliability. Industrious to a fault, he did not mind toiling straight through the night, for he had no family to return to nor anything better to do than work, and made a point of always appearing terribly busy, if not with the task at hand then with whatever he would invent for himself. He always took calls during meetings, even if a client was present, and while he apologized every time (except to his juniors) he never seemed too upset about it, which was remarkable in someone who could display cold anger rather well. The truth was that being in such demand tickled his ego, and that a busy, stressful, workday made him feel alive, as it often does for people whose inner lives crawl with demons. He would say to a comrade-in-plight, as if confessing to an illness, "I have so much to do that I hardly know where to start," or "you think two projects are too much to handle and then you find yourself managing four." Such words conveyed less a state of exhaustion than an exalted sense of heroism.

On weekends, when not at work, he managed to get invited to gatherings where he could broaden his network, or trolled the nightclub scene, trying to score. He never entertained at home, and when dining alone ate straight from the package, for sitting down to a meal was for him not unlike sitting down for a bowel movement—an occasion for primitive satisfaction, yet hardly an event to look forward to. Not surprisingly, when he took his staff out to lunch he made quick business of it, and was known to have once ordered the same entrée for the whole team before anyone had a chance to speak up.

Those who have never witnessed firsthand such caricatures of behavior may be forgiven for doubting their realism, or for assuming they could inspire nothing but sniggers. But the firm's leaders regarded Pyle as a steadfast, committed and smart consultant, well deserving of election to the partnership. In the office hallway hung a framed statement of the firm's mission, claiming to foster a non-hierarchical culture and to hold corporate values in higher esteem than profits (a reliable sign that a company treasures the opposite). As for the firm's true role model, Dominic fit it to the letter. It was others like him who had led Blake & Whitney down the path followed by many professional services firms, to become a temple of greed. Rival in love he was, and if by some standards unworthy, he was one to be reckoned with, shamelessly hitting on Cassie when Ethan wasn't around. So when Pyle was transferred to New York, Ethan breathed easier.

For a while.

***

Valerie reached her father's New York apartment before sundown. She draped her coat over the back of an armchair and sat down, ignoring the view of Central Park as she tried to catch the gist of his phone conversation, which had been going on for a while. Even in his condition he played his part well. To Adam Schultz, Taylor came across as eloquent and imposing as ever. Only a loving ear like Valerie's could detect the tired, dispirited man behind the voice. Taylor blew a kiss at her and returned to the call.

"TensoChem's profits have dropped by 75% in three years. We can't even sell it without taking losses. Yes, exports to Asia have plummeted because they now get most of their products from India. Yes, Adam, I *know* they're commodities! But raw-material prices have dropped alongside—you said so yourself."

Valerie approached the massive desk where a report lay idle, detailing TensoChem's situation. Taylor had read it minutes before and tossed aside. The company manufactured chemicals for industrial processes in sectors as diverse as food, agriculture, textile, cosmetics, resins, and leather goods. It had been her great-grandfather's creation and source of wealth, inherited late in life by Bruce Taylor and his sister, neither of them involved in the business, which had been left to be run by a hired team until someone from the next generation came of age. Since Julian had never shown interest in that business and Valerie had never shown interest in business at all, it fell to their cousins to take over, and in no time they had run it into the ground. But as chairman, Bruce Taylor still held the largest share in the concern and deep inside felt that his nephews were siphoning cash away at the expense of profit reinvestments, but he was too ill to roll up his sleeves and find out. With one eye ever on the emptying sandglass, he was devoting all his remaining energy to buttressing Taylor Labs against every foreseeable contingency, so he had no time for TensoChem. But the impending demise of his family's original venture filled him with nostalgia and dark foreboding, fighting for his attention with his other losing battle. The company's creditors threatened to take over, and one of them, perhaps out of courtesy, but most likely in the hope for a last-minute cash injection, had met privately with Taylor to warn him. All he could do was complain to Schultz, his CEO, whom he suspected of sharing the narcissistic interests of his relatives.

Valerie flicked through the pages and fighting an instinctive distaste forced herself to study the balance sheet. She then followed several links through the document, from which she gleaned that revenues had indeed dropped sharply, not because of loss of volume, which had in fact remained constant, but due to a 30% drop in average prices in both domestic sales and exports. As a result, income was no longer enough to cover financial interests. Accounts payable were at an all-time high, and suppliers were beginning to withhold raw-material deliveries. This was putting pressure on production schedules, to the extent that over 50% of TensoChem's orders were delayed or only partly fulfilled. Some customers had drifted to the competition, and the sales team found itself devoting ever-increasing time to managing client expectations instead of satisfying them.

Valerie heard the conversation end and glanced at her father. He was lost in depressing thoughts, elbows propped up on the desk and forehead resting on the upturned palms of his hands. For the first time in her life she saw the age in him and felt a pang of tenderness. She walked around the desk and planted a light kiss on his head. Disease and its ineffectual treatment had thinned his hair considerably, so she could feel the warmth of his scalp through the strands of silver.

"Will you let me help?" she asked.

Taylor raised his eyes and smiled. "Just having you around is more help than you imagine."

Valerie pulled back and leaned against the desk. "What I meant," she said, reaching out for the pad and sliding it towards him, "is whether you will let me help with TensoChem."

Taylor's smile vanished for an instant, then reappeared, sadder. "I wish you could… But don't worry. This is nothing, really."

"I'm not worried. But *you* are. Let me handle this."

Taylor looked at her daughter. She had grown more beautiful than he had ever expected—and he knew his expectations had been unreasonable. If only she had shared more of his tastes, how much they could have done together. Her intelligence seemed so profound at times that it was scary. And to think she could be so unreasonable...

"And what exactly," he asked affectionately, "do you propose to do?"

"Give me five weeks. Let me analyze the business using any means I see fit. No questions and no peeping over my shoulder. I will need access to all information about the company data, without exception. You will keep Schultz in the dark about this, but lend me Jerry Springer full-time. He will hand me every piece of information that I ask for. You won't ask any questions from either of us. We will work out of my apartment."

Taylor's eyes widened with amusement. It was the first time he had ever crossed a business word with Valerie and he couldn't believe that it was she, not himself, who was the instigator. Taylor suddenly felt that he couldn't get enough of it.

"Jerry?" he asked. "The analyst?"

"Yes, the analyst; your Financial Planning Director if I'm not mistaken. You speak highly of him all the time, but ignore his advice."

"Do I?"

"Probably because he isn't outspoken enough, so instead you listen to Schultz."

"I've had enough of Adam."

"Do we have a deal?"

"Five weeks, eh?"

"On my own. Tell Schultz that you need Jerry to work on a confidential acquisition, and that you will steal him for a month. And one more thing. When I'm through, I will lead a meeting with Hidei Nomura to discuss our findings."

Taylor pulled a wry face. Nomura was the creditor who had approached him in confidence. "But Valerie," he complained weakly, "you aren't on the Board."

"I doubt he will refuse. We'll go together and I will speak on your behalf. He knows what you are going through, but he's in a tighter spot himself." Taylor chuckled for the first time in weeks. "That he certainly is," he agreed. If the business defaulted, Nomura would find himself holding bad assets, and last in a long line of creditors, to say nothing of the disgruntled suppliers. And unlike Taylor, Nomura didn't have an empire of larger companies to fall back on. Five weeks wouldn't make things any worse than they already were, and Nomura had given him three months anyway. In the old days, he would have fired Schultz, hired a turnaround manager and bought his nephews out. But his time had run out. He doubted that Valerie, despite her intellectual gifts, had anywhere near the business experience to pull the company out of the hole. But, if only for the pleasure of sharing with his daughter, for once, what he took to be one of the joys of life—wrangling with business ventures, whether they were booming or failing—he was willing to play along.

"Deal," he said, and couldn't refrain from extending a hand towards Valerie, who shook it ritually. He would be literally dead before changing his ways, she reflected.

UNEASE

> Could a congress of gorillas, gathered to plan the breeding of the supergorilla, plan a human being? Discard the line of development of mightier muscles, stronger and longer teeth, greater specialization to master their tropical environment?
>
> —GORDON R. DICKSON, *Dorsai!*

"Huan Liu, have a minute for an old friend?"

Few people used his Asian name. His mother had, but she'd been dead for years. And some of his Chinese friends just couldn't bring themselves to call him Bob with a straight face. But Bob he was to everyone else—either that or Dr. Liu—so it took him a full second to react. The words had an East Coast accent that bounced in his mind like a pinball down a ramp, lighting up old memories and ringing bells: graduate school, first day of spring semester, course on social structures. He turned around with a smile.

"Vance!"

They exchanged the same handshake as twenty years earlier, when designer faces were rare even in Stanford. Liu's former classmate was tall and strongly built, with piercing green eyes and flowing dark hair that was already turning silver. But the oversized, crooked nose was something no parent would have ordered. Neither of them was extrasomic.

"I'm Vance Havelock," he had said back then.

"Bob Liu."

Quizzical look. "I just heard Wei call you Huan."

"You speak Mandarin?"

"I lived in Beijing as a child. I'm not really fluent; I write it better than I speak."

"You mean Pinyin?"

"No, Hanzi characters—I wouldn't call myself a master, but I can read most texts."

"I'm impressed."

"I guess it's Huan, then?"

"Yes. I didn't see you last semester. What program are you in?"

"Sociology. I'm taking this for optional credit. You?"

"Biological Anthropology, elective for me as well. Where did you go for undergrad?"

"West Point."

Liu whistled softly. "And studying sociology... Are you leaving the military?"

"No, I plan to go back and join foreign intelligence."

"To spy on China?" Only the wink was missing.

"Well..."

They ended up close friends, and the following year shared a house on campus with two other students. Havelock was insatiably curious about the land of Liu's ancestors, seeming to know more about Chinese history than Liu did—recent history, that is, from the twentieth century debacle to the nation's consolidation as the world's leading economy. Vance was obsessive about current affairs and devoured whatever had any bearing on the state of the world. The relevance of events, he claimed, was inversely proportional to their antiquity. This never failed to spur Huan into passionate rebuttals: only by plumbing the depths of time, he countered, could one hope to understand people's behavior. Endless discussions ensued.

"Don't talk about the Ming like it was the dawn of mankind. There's plenty that came before."

"Yes, yes, I know: there's the Tang, the Han, the Zhou... But they are lost in the mists of time."

"Lost in the—" Huan would throw up his hands. "See? You sweep it under the rug like so much dust, dismissing two thousand years of culture, of warfare—of politics, your favorite topic!—two millennia as rich as the history of Rome from its foundation to the fall of Constantinople. You know why the Ming dynasty is regarded as ancient? Because the oldest artwork that can be legally taken out of China belongs to the Ming period, so Americans rarely see anything older outside a museum. The Xia dynasty, now there's an old period for you, a thousand years before the Zhou—around the time the Minoans began settling Crete."

His legal name was Huan Robert Liu, a gift he owed to a young mother's concern for the welfare of her only child in a country where most people would have unflinchingly spelled his first name with *J*.

He had been hired out of graduate school, on Havelock's advice, for a back-office job in the Defense Intelligence Agency, where the only traveling he did was virtual and the only enemy he faced were the long nights poring over conversations transcripts, attempting to find hints of un-American sentiment that might hide more sinister intent. Although the United States had by then shed its role of world policeman, it wasn't yet ready to relinquish its hegemony, which it had always felt threatened from several fronts: the bona fide menace of terrorism, the ever-present phantom of sedition, and the steady encroachment of foreign competition. It was the latter that had lain at the crux of the mutual mistrust between China and the U.S. for as long as anyone could remember, for the strained relations between the two countries dated back to the time when China had joined the failed bandwagon of communism, from which it had taken a hundred years to recover.

Liu had expected change in Havelock, but was still shocked by the sight. The colonel's bearing preserved a good measure of martial poise, yet his lithe frame had become stiff and drawn, and his face wore a troubled look. Only the unabated fierceness of his eyes triggered a real sense of recognition in Liu. You look like hell, he would have said when they were in school. But the candor of youth had given way to studied politeness. "You look worried."

Havelock took it in stride, rubbing his cheek. "Listen, do you have anything urgent to do after your lecture?"

"The Department invited me to dinner, but that's three hours away."

"Let me buy you a drink, then. I know a good joint two blocks from here."

It came as no surprise to Huan that the place Vance had in mind was dark and quiet, like an off-hours pub, ideal for private conversations. They settled into cozy chairs and ordered drinks.

"How's the family?" asked the colonel.

"Lucy is working full-time again, teaching. Bobby's in college in Texas—wants to be a doctor, who would have thought? And Amy just keeps on making us proud. She followed in her dad's footsteps to major in anthropology, got married and has a baby girl of her own. She lives in Vermont."

"And look at you: a professor at Yale."

"I can't complain."

"Always the optimist. Where I saw threats you found solutions. Maybe you're the one who should have stayed in Intelligence."

"I couldn't stand it, remember? I embarrassed you by resigning in my second year."

"Oh yes, you rejected the promotion you were offered."

Liu smiled wistfully. "Couldn't take the pressure."

"What you couldn't take was having a boss."

"Not everyone's born to be a soldier."

"You may not like command and control, but your upbeat outlook would have helped you to deal with ... stuff."

"Family issues?" Huan asked cautiously.

"No, Gloria and the kids are doing fine, thanks for asking."

Huan nodded. "I see. Health problems."

"No, no, no," Havelock was quick to correct. "I know I look like shit, but the doctor says it's only stress."

"You used to thrive on stress!"

"I was naïve about girls, too."

He suddenly switched to Mandarin. "It wasn't the fieldwork—sure, I risked my neck for years, but it was fun in retrospect. You know what gets to you in the end? Not talking to anyone—not to your wife, not to your mother, not to your doctor. We are social creatures; we need to share our fears, our triumphs. The last few years have been bad. We could use your help."

"We?" Liu's eyebrows jerked up. "Are you trying to recruit me?"

"All right, *I* could use your help, on a short-term basis. You could carry on as usual. You'd be an advisor, just an advisor, not ordered around."

"So you *are* trying to recruit me." Huan seemed irked and amused at the same time. "And you need an anthropologist, of all things?"

"That was settled long before your name came up."

"And how did it come up?"

“My suggestion, of course.”

“Of course. Should I thank you?”

Havelock held his gaze, then looked away. Liu studied him again: the wasted features, the haunted look, as if the man carried the burden of a terrible secret. They had met briefly during the last crisis, in which Havelock was involved to his neck. There were rumors of biological weapons…

“Suppose I agree. What next?”

“Well, let’s see, today’s Thursday. Can you extend your stay through the weekend?”

“And tell my wife I’m doing what?”

“We’ll come up with something.”

“Don’t I need clearance first—a background check, an investigation?”

“You’ve gone through it.”

“Twenty years ago.”

“No. Last week.”

The plane reached sixty thousand feet and pierced a southwest course to the New Mexico desert. Several squat structures were the only sign of life, but when they landed a vehicle emerged from the ground and approached the craft.

They walked down a bare tunnel. “The military has operated bases like this one since World War II,” explained Havelock. “Many things were developed here: nuclear weapons, spy aircraft, satellites, and all sorts of bio stuff. People thought we kept aliens from space, pickled in jars. They were wrong, of course—aliens don’t come from outer space.”

Liu stopped dead in his tracks, gooseflesh creeping up his neck.

Havelock had walked ahead, forcing him to catch up. “You can’t imagine the trouble I went through to get you access to this place, but I couldn’t have you thinking I was mad. Here we are.”

An airlock disengaged and they stepped into a laboratory fancy enough to make aliens in jars seem a distinct possibility. Technicians behind windows were engaged in various activities to which Havelock paid no attention. He handed Liu a pair of synthetic shoe covers and led him through a door where they stepped in a puddle of liquid (rodent-proofing, said Havelock) to a hatch opened with a fingerprint pad. The space behind was enclosed in a single-pour shell of concrete, devoid of drains or outlets, powered by batteries and equipped with its own air generator. It contained a wealth of equipment: screens, cameras, and several tanks with nests of harvest mice, twenty or so to a vat, all minding their business.

Liu breathed a sigh of relief.

The floor of the central tank was a grid, its orifices too narrow for even a mouse to squeeze through. An elaborate contraption stood to one side; Havelock reached out for a touch-screen and a panel lit up with a checkered pattern, two hundred cells across by as many down. A tray came into view, vertically aligned with their line of sight, with a honeycomb of light emitters matching the onscreen pattern. The tray was held above the tank by a robot arm. Havelock turned his attention to the console and turned a dial reading *Delay* to 2 seconds.

"Select cells by touching the screen, like this." Havelock demonstrated by running a finger over the screen, lighting up a row in the honeycomb.

Not quite convinced, Liu touched several more, then two or three near the edges. Finally he slid his hand diagonally across the middle, lighting fifty cells.

"The paraphernalia," Havelock explained, "is for McGrath. He won't fund anything that doesn't smell of gunpowder."

Liu winced. Mice scurried about and others stayed put. All seemed, if not jittery, then at least aware that something was happening.

"It singes their skin, that's all," said Havelock, and pressed *Fire*.

A long buzz rang out as lasers zapped through the tank's grid to light up the dark floor beneath, replicating the pattern selected. The mice kept motionless; not one was hurt. As the lights turned off they all resumed their activities.

"You could choose any pattern and they will avoid it. We have hours of video, but I didn't want you to take my word for it. And yet if I do this," Havelock set *Delay* down to zero, "they don't stand a chance." He quickly traced a line across the screen and a new series of beeps rang out. Two mice somersaulted with audible squeaks, stung but unharmed, as Havelock had said.

Liu shifted uncomfortably. "What should I make of it?"

"It took these guys years to figure that out," Havelock said, indicating the workers in the outer room as he ushered Liu towards the exit.

"What's so special about these mice?"

"They carry the Beta complement of the Prometheus module."

Liu frowned. "I thought it was unviable."

As they stepped through the toxic slick on their way out, he felt that he understood its purpose better. "What if they escape?"

"There's no plumbing or cabling going out, and that puddle would kill them in seconds. Failing that…" He rapped on a window and a technician looked up. "Is Mishka there?" The man pointed at a chair in a corner. On a cushion placed carelessly on the seat, a gray tomcat lay fast asleep.

Liu grinned weakly.

"The cat has no trouble catching them."

"Then why lock the place up like a vault?"

"I don't get paid to take risks."

"But—" Liu was unsure how to phrase his next question.

"The high tech, the lasers, the glass tanks: it all makes for good demos in controlled environments. But the real world has predators and disease, and this trait confers no evolutionary advantage. To get assortative mating, Indian researchers had to code a pheromone response to get the females interested."

Liu seemed perplexed. "Inbreeding?"

Havelock shook his head. "We wanted female Alpha carriers to mate with male Betas."

"Did it work?"

"No. The embryos won't come to term. Development crashes when the neural system starts to form. We're missing something."

They made their way back through the tunnel.

"If the cat has no problems—" Liu resumed.

"We've spent taxpayer money exploring all avenues. It's hard to sell animal abuse as a defense project."

"I'm sure it's been done before."

"You know what the difference was, all along? Cats have minds; lasers don't."

"What?" Liu almost laughed before realizing Havelock was serious.

"Not in the philosophical sense, but basic thoughts—as in, *shall I lick my paw?*—are fundamentally unpredictable. Machines, on the other hand, think algorithmically. We missed that for years because machines are so quick. Let a computer choose a firing sequence and the mice get zapped—they can only run so fast. But allow a few seconds between choice and firing, and they will all sit in safe spots, as if they knew the sequence beforehand."

They walked out of an elevator and into a meeting room. "I am surprised," said Liu, "that you knew what to test for."

"The Beta was meant to enhance foreknowledge; we just needed to find out how it would manifest itself. It took us five years to figure out that if the firing sequence is chosen by what is known as a pseudo-random number generator—which picks a string of digits from the computer's internal clock—then the mice avoid being zapped. But if the sequence is truly random, selected for example by the particle-decay of a lump of radioactive stuff, then they are hit. What do you make of that?"

Liu wasn't one to stare blankly into space if he could avoid it, but as they sat across from each other, that's exactly what he did. A sergeant brought coffee; Havelock poured an inordinate amount of sugar into his cup and said, "That will be all." The man withdrew and they sipped in silence.

"Radioactive decay," Liu said at length, "depends on quantum behavior, which is essentially unpredictable, like your cat's thoughts."

Havelock nodded. "And that explains why this trait is of little use against predators; why it has no evolutionary advantage and these mice tend to be out-reproduced by unmodified strains."

"Have you engineered it in other species?"

"All attempts have proved lethal in primates."

"What about cats?" Liu suggested.

Havelock grinned briefly, then shook his head gravely.

"Then why bring me here?"

"We haven't made it work, but have good reason to think someone else has—in humans."

"Someone … in China?"

"China has been hunting for them as well, for over twenty years."

"Twenty years!? And what do you think you can do at this point?"

"Find them before others do."

Liu brought a hand to his forehead, caught by a sudden urge to laugh. Havelock was dead serious so he kept himself in check. The colonel, however, didn't miss much. "What's so funny?" he asked.

"Oh, nothing—I mean—it's just that … twenty years, and I guess you don't even know who, or where—" He made some ineffectual gestures to explain himself.

"Difficult," said Havelock, "doesn't mean impossible."

"Fine. What else do you know?"

Havelock summarized what he had on Cao Xin Pei, Code Seagull, the Indian scientist Sarangarajan, and China's search for anyone bearing the Prometheus module.

"The few people who knew how to implement the full module in humans are dead. Barring new flashes of insight, our only option is to find a living carrier, though I sometimes think a dead one would do. Anyway, China is only a stakeholder—one of several—in the chase. And it is a chase, mind you: someone *will* take the prize."

O?INION

In a moral argument, we expect the successful rebuttal of our opponents' arguments to change our opponents' minds. Such a belief is analogous to believing that forcing a dog's tail to wag by moving it with your hand should make the dog happy.

—J. HAIDT, *The Emotional Dog and Its Rational Tail*

"What are you reading?" asked Cassie, dropping purse and keys on the console that framed the entrance hall of Ethan's apartment. She had arrived earlier than usual and caught him in a moment of self-indulgence.

Ethan set the beer bottle on the hardwood floor, laid the pad flat on his chest, and smiled.

"It's called *Tigana*."

"Fantasy! You have time for that?"

"Shouldn't I?"

She laughed. "Oaths and spells, phony high diction, fast women and throbbing manhoods? Life's too short. Not that I dislike romance, but *Sons and Lovers* is more my style."

"I can't blame you; the prose is flawless."

"And the characters. They're more believable than most people you meet on the street."

"Yes, characters who keep floundering because they don't know what they want from life, or how to hang on when they find it."

Cassie sat beside his legs on the sofa. "That's how people are: fascinating but complex, especially when it comes to relationships."

"Relationships would be simple if people didn't work so hard to spoil them."

"I can't picture you falling for a simple woman."

"I don't mean simple people, I mean simple relationships."

"Don't they go hand in hand?"

"Bollocks."

She dropped a kiss on Ethan's lips. "I love it when you go British on me."

He laughed. "I suppose that's a kinky term."

"My point," she went on, "is that fantasy lacks the context that teaches us about life."

"On the contrary: our species evolved in a world of battles, magical belief, egos quick to take offense, and people keen to prove themselves. Fantasy strips away the distracting veneer to reveal the world for what it is: a theater for animal nature. Battles may now be financial, kingdoms may now be companies and soldiers may be employees, but magical belief still prevails. People don't care how anything works as long as it does. Just this morning in a call I heard Pyle speak of Peikoff as of a demigod—the idiot."

Cassie stiffened, but Ethan was looking at the ceiling and didn't notice. "How is that magical?" she asked.

"Because others look up to an asshole just because he's the office head."

"Well, he's assertive."

"How's that an explanation?"

"It makes him effective as a leader."

Ethan shook his head. "Leadership is when the top dog of a sled team shows the way for the rest, but runs the same distance and eats the same food. Peikoff wants to ride *on* the sled; he wants to be pharaoh. He takes a perfectly good profession and spoils it by stepping on everyone. He speaks of devotion and commitment when he means frenzy and abandon. He overpromises in the sales pitch, then expects teams to over-deliver. The crunches we go through are all from self-imposed deadlines, and Peikoff never contributes until the day before the work is due, then rips presentations to pieces and tells everyone off because they won't read his mind."

"I see you had a tough day."

"Yeah. Cliff's resigning."

"Why? What happened?"

"He gave Doug a week off when his child was born. Not a month—or six, like they give fathers in Sweden—but five fucking days. And Peikoff, that proud mahatma of ours, scolded Cliff for allowing an associate time off mid-project."

"Okay, so Peikoff's a jerk, but that's life: those birds that sing outside the window every morning—their songs may be soothing, but to them it's pitched battle. Think how dull things would be, if plans didn't sometimes go wrong now and then."

"That's tripe. Would ice-cream be more exciting if you found the occasional turd in your scoop? Life can be thrilling enough without heartache."

"Then where would satisfaction come from?"

"There are many challenges that don't require anyone to lose. Why would people jog, otherwise? Most never expect to win a race."

"Maybe they jog to stay fit. Anyway, this isn't the marines and Cliff can quit if he wants."

"He just had a child, has a mortgage, earns one twentieth of what Peikoff receives, and works twice as hard. Even that would be okay if Peikoff would say 'thank you' instead of tossing around sarcasm and uninspiring mottos like 'perfection is meeting the standard'. And Pyle takes after his mentor, so beware of cozying up to him."

Cassie bristled. "I don't *cozy up* to anyone, and what does Dom have to do with it?"

"Since when is he 'Dom'?"

"That's not fair." She slid away from him.

(Cassie, Ethan might have said, it is jealousy that makes me lash out. You know I love you, but I have always been clumsy with women, and am sometimes assailed by an awful sensation that I haven't found words to describe but which scares me out of my wits. This new project you will start in New York—a place, by the way, about which I have mixed feelings—will put you within striking distance of Dominic. And he's devious, Cassie. He collects women like a ten-year-old collects spiders in a jar. What do you see in him? He will just as soon lick someone's balls as tear them off if it suits the occasion. He strives to be like Peikoff but lacks credibility. All his efforts are staged on the premise that life holds only two lots: that of winners and that of losers, and since he desperately wants to avoid losing he will sell, fuck, steal or charm his way into winning, or die in the attempt.)

(But Ethan, she could have answered, you do us all an injustice by denigrating the value of charm. Look at yourself with uncritical eyes and you will see someone who could be chairman of any board. You carry yourself about with a presence that is almost regal; why do you think I fell for you? I may be ambitious, calculating, perhaps a bit vain, but my feelings for you are true, and if you would only play the part that you are clearly built for, I would bear your children and we would achieve so much together... But you must be willing, Ethan, and I don't sense the fire in your blood. When I have you all to myself and look into your soul, all I see are shades of sorrow that belong neither here nor there. What have you done to warrant regret? You've never opened up enough to let me know. Yes, I see that Dominic would rather do well than do good, but his transparency makes me feel comfortable, in control, powerful.)

Then again, lovers are rarely so candid with each other—or indeed with themselves—so the exchange went rather differently:

"You never heard how Pyle was elected, did you?" asked Ethan.

"Yes, and I don't care." (She hadn't, and she did.)

"This client came to Peikoff, tearing his hair out because he wanted to acquire a company but the investment bankers had spent two months on the valuation and done a shitty job of it. With tender offers due shortly, Peikoff offered to redo the entire valuation in a week. Pyle was the manager who led the effort, and the only consultant who didn't resign or end up in the hospital."

"Well, good for him."

"Yeah, he's a regular hero."

"Can't you think of anything positive about him—about Peikoff, even? I challenge you to list three virtues of the firm's partners."

Ethan rolled his eyes. "I don't know… They are tireless, I'll grant you that—the corporate equivalent of ironman athletes."

"What else?"

"They are … eloquent. They are good on their feet and can deliver persuasive messages."

"That's two. One more to go."

"They are decisive. They don't waste time mulling things over."

"See? That wasn't so hard."

"But those are redeeming virtues!"

"Must we keep arguing?"

"I'm just stating the facts."

"You're stating your opinion. You have a right to it, but it's still just an opinion."

"And that's just bad logic. Opinions aren't something one has a right to. You may have a right to *express* an opinion, but you cannot help having one, and it can be wrong. As for Pyle, he's a cold-hearted pragmatist who has never felt an ounce of tenderness in his life. He sees people as either useful or useless, and is perfectly happy to pave his road to glory with corpses. He may be charming, but when he's had his way with you, he–"

"You know what?" Cassie burst out, jumping to her feet, "I don't need this. Not from you." She collected her belongings. "Enjoy your beer," she yelled as the door slammed behind her.

***

A mere instant by the political clock's reckoning, the Reynolds administration neared the end of its first term, and Larissa Kane neared retirement. Her face looked tired as she tore open the sachet to dump the sweetener in her coffee. "I know you called for patience Eric, but Jesus…"

"Following a money trail," said Ressler, "is easier said than done."

But the shine in his eyes suggested there was more than an update to share. "Lawrence, Garfield, Junior. Ring a bell?"

"Should it?" The mug tinkled softly as she stirred. "The only Garfield I know is Wade's campaign manager."

"Exactly."

Kane let the spoon drop. "You can't be serious."

"The law firm behind the caterers was run by Larry Garfield, Evander's brother."

"Was?"

"It shut down two years ago. Garfield–the attorney–retired at fifty and hasn't practiced since."

"Wealthy?"

"And then some. We can't subpoena his tax returns without blowing this open, but I know some folks at the IRS."

"Don't tell me he evaded."

"No, he was too careful. But here's the thing: after a steady income of under two million since who knows when, he suddenly made twenty-seven million during the last election."

"When Wade didn't run?"

"When Wade *decided* not to run. But he's running now, and isn't short of funding. Let me ask you, Larissa: if this were a foreign country, what would you do? What is your, um … considered opinion?"

"I'd be trying to get someone in," she replied. "I mean on the campaign team."

Ressler nodded. "Working on that."

***

"Scotch," said Havelock, "is meant to be sipped, not pondered."

Liu gazed stubbornly at the amber liquid. "I'm amazed you have any in here."

"It helps."

"I bet it does." He imbibed gently, deliberately, before posing his question. "What do all superheroes have in common?"

"I beg your pardon?"

"Superman; Wonder Woman; the X-Men—what do they all have in common?"

"Why, they … can do things others can't."

"Yes, of course, but their skills differ from one hero to the next. What they have in common is what they *cannot* do. They all have average intellects; their minds are normal in every way. They are duped by villains as easily as anyone, and share all too human concerns—perhaps that's what makes them so endearing. If the people you hunt are even remotely like you describe them, they won't behave like some whiz kid on steroids. This isn't Einstein we're talking about, but a different cognitive plateau. Did you watch Tarzan cartoons as a child?"

Havelock grunted, which Liu took as affirmation. "Long before becoming a children's movie, Tarzan was a serious attempt at adult fiction. Forget the unlikelihood of a child surviving ten minutes in the company of apes; the question is, how would Tarzan have behaved if he had looked just like another ape, with no physical challenges? The mental difference would at first be invisible. It would take a while for the super-ape to see that it was different, but by then it would also perceive the difficulty of communicating the difference. If it had the ability to learn human language, someone would still have to teach him. In the original story, the boy happens on some abandoned books and teaches himself to read—how convenient. But that assumes a civilization to leave books behind. If Tarzan had been the first ape with human intelligence, there wouldn't *be* any books for him to find."

"But," said Havelock, "even without language, could it not use its skills to attain leadership within the troop?"

"Yes, but would it? Imagine that some perverse trick had given you an ape's body at birth, to grow up in the jungle. Can you honestly tell me you would aspire to lead an ape troop?"

"Why not? I wouldn't know the diff—"

"Oh, but you would! That's the curse of intelligence: we notice before being able to solve. Think of what it takes to lead a troop: regular fights and shows of bravado, vigilance, grooming of others and by others. It takes practice to stay at the top. How much would you stand before becoming fed up with animal hierarchies? If nothing else, you'd be incredibly bored, tempted to avoid 'normal' frictions with the troop. You might assume an inconspicuous rank and use your brain to find food with less effort or to keep dry in downpours."

"And if threatened? A human can kill an ape with little risk to itself. Couldn't it learn about poisonous plants or how to build weapons?"

"Maybe, if in-group threats were a risk. Why?"

Havelock showed him a report describing a traffic incident in Russia. "This," said Havelock, "involved the slaying of armed men by an unarmed young woman. Let's call it a 'first contact'. The question is, can we stop it from escalating?"

"From the looks of it," said Liu, "I doubt it."

"You're saying we're fucked."

"No. If they were bent on harm or on dominance, we would have noticed already."

"But they operate above the law," protested Havelock. "Suppose an arrest were attempted. They might just kill the enforcer."

"Sure, but let me understand: you're afraid of their unwillingness to submit to the judgment of human society; you worry they might—and I emphasize *might*—deem their moral stance higher than ours. Don't you think that's to be expected? Would *you* submit to the judgment of apes?"

"We're not talking about apes!" Havelock rose and began pacing the room.

"No, it seems we're talking about pride."

Havelock ignored the remark.

"People," Liu went on, "have trouble explaining what they don't understand, so any attempt to explain a mind smarter than the explainer's is hopeless. But I have an analogy that I think is convincing."

Havelock stopped pacing. "An analogy for what?"

"For differences in intellect. The object of comparison must be sufficiently removed from intelligence to get the point across without being perceived as an insult. What works for me is driving skills, which only correlate with intelligence up to a threshold. This allows the analogy to be appreciated, because by people don't feel threatened by it."

"Why would they? Robotaxis are the norm these days."

"Exactly. So picture two equally smart people sharing a ride. Jack races cars for a living, and Jill is the textbook defensive driver. Jack is behind the wheel, doing eighty on a rainy two-lane road, and he's thinking, *another puddle, and a bit of understeer coming out of that turn; will need to change the tires soon. I wish Jill would be more talkative. Let's play some music. That car in front is planning something stupid; if I push it now he won't invade my space.*

"And what is Jill thinking all along? *Why is he going so fast? If we start skidding he won't have time to correct. Such reckless driving... Ouch, that car almost slammed into us! And Jack fiddling with the stereo. Please, God, make him slow down…*"

A smile of recognition grew on Havelock's face.

"You get the picture. To a lesser intellect, a higher one seems reckless, in need of taming, of being prevented from running the company, the country or whatever. Intelligence doesn't always breed followers: when differences become so pronounced that those at a disadvantage cannot keep up, a loss of trust occurs, in a direction opposite to what you'd expect: the followers are the ones who give up."

"Where does that leave us?"

Liu scratched his head. "If there's any chance of finding someone with the skills you've described, then you shouldn't try to profile the person like you would a criminal."

"What if China is doing precisely that?"

"Then I wouldn't want to be around if they succeed. But I think your odds will improve if you focus your attention on the hunters, not on their quarry. Repress your hunting instincts for once; be a scavenger."

Havelock returned to his seat. "You said that someone with higher intelligence—a unique member of its kind—would be limited by lack of peer interaction. What if it had peers?"

Liu took some time to answer. "I believe there's nothing you could do against a collective of such minds. You couldn't guess their intentions, much less their next move. And they certainly wouldn't engage in something as prosaic as running a business or a government, so don't look there."

"But if we got our hands on one, couldn't we—"

"No!" Liu barked as to a child with a finger in a wall socket. "You keep thinking of understandable skills, like those of a math prodigy who can be exploited to someone's advantage. These Prometheus children, you wouldn't know *what* you could make them do."

"And yet we must find out. You've seen what's going on," Havelock said, pointing his thumb at the biohazard vault behind them.

Liu nodded.

***

Dining mavens agreed that Elixir didn't serve the best fare in Chicago, but it was the trendiest restaurant in town and especially popular with the 'in' crowd, whose taste in food couldn't hold a candle to their need for each other's company. On Fridays it was impossible to book reservations, and the coveted room near the street showcased the nation's elite, imported and domestic. At a table for four sat a chatty threesome: Qiuyue Li, a ravishing broker from Hong Kong whose body blossomed out of a red dress that was snug in all the right places; Colin Sachs, a successful entrepreneur who kept trying, ineffectively, to keep his straw-colored hair from falling over his eyes; and Julian Taylor, known by name to many patrons, less for his exploits than for his family's wealth. They had just ordered drinks when a fourth diner made her entrance, drawing stares unusually round-eyed for such an overweening crowd. Even Qiuyue had to concede defeat to Miranda Vázquez as Julian rose to greet her, not out of sudden chivalry but so that everyone in the room would see that she came to dine with him.

Peck on the mouth, kiss on the cheek, handshake, loud slap on the back, and they all settled back in their chairs. Miranda ordered a glass of wine and Sachs resumed the conversation.

"Anyway," he said, "now that NM has a fourth level, most people will have to wait five days for new releases."

"Em-em?" asked Miranda.

"NM," corrected Julian. "New Music." He turned to Qiuyue. "How do you say that, again?"

"新的音樂," said Qiuyue, and sipped her cocktail. Julian nodded with mock importance while Miranda suppressed a giggle. "I won't even try," she said. "It's a music website, right?"

"I gather you don't have an account," Sachs rebuked kindly.

"Is it that good?"

"It's addictive," said Qiuyue.

"How?"

"It's hard to explain," said Sachs. "You'll have to judge for yourself."

"Can't people wait five days for a song?"

"No, people pay hundreds for a concert ticket, and this is only a dollar a week at the first level. Half the accounts belong to teens. It's like a new Facebook phenomenon."

"Lucrative?"

"They have a hundred million accounts and climbing. That's $400 million a month."

Eyebrows rose. "All profit?"

"They've signed deals with studios for a four-day exclusive to new recordings—five since yesterday—before a piece is released. The artist gets a guaranteed million and the studio another. Nine out of every ten of top hits last year were pre-released on NM."

"Who gets to judge?"

"Colin here was just invited—that's what we were discussing when you arrived."

"Wow! And what's with the levels?"

"The website," explained Sachs, "is structured like a skill game. But the better you get the more you pay—exactly the opposite of what you'd expect, but also the sooner you get to hear new releases. As of today, the coolest thing in town is to listen to the good stuff four days before everyone else. Or five, if you count non-subscribers."

"Can't someone make pirate versions?"

Julian shook his head. "It's tamperproof. You need a brainwave headset. Do you know the EEG-scanners used by quadruplegics, like that artist in Vermont who sculpted a Michelangelo while hooked to a ventilator?"

"I didn't know they used the same headsets," remarked Qiuyue.

"Well, not identical."

"I remember!" exclaimed Miranda. "They look like bicycle helmets. Don't the military use them?"

"Yes," said Julian, "in artillery. The Air Force also tried them out, but the device stops responding if you lose concentration, so you don't want to be flying on it. What I don't get," he added, turning to Sachs, "is why make it a game at all. They would earn a lot more by charging in geometric proportion to the lead days offered."

"They are in a sweet spot," said Sachs. "Delaying a release is straining on studios: you can't make it too easy on players without losing the exclusive. Mass media would outbid them."

"So," asked Miranda, "must you pay *and* play to get to the first level?"

"That's right," said Julian. "Level zero's a hookup. Then they charge a dollar and you can access Level 1 for a week. After that, it's up to your skills."

"And what does it take to reach Level 4?"

Julian shrugged. "I haven't got past two. You?"

Sachs shook his head. They looked at Qiuyue.

"Okay," she said, "three."

"See?" laughed Sachs. "See? That's why we get skewered by the press, you know—things like 'only the elite have access to music' and that sort of crap from populists like Wade."

The waiter arrived with the main courses; another helped to set up a foldaway tray. "You can always count on Wade for daft remarks," said Julian. "He's the sort to say that the way to get rid of inequality is to abolish it."

"China did that once," said Qiuyue, "and it didn't go well. But, is Wade going to run?"

"Hah," grunted Sachs, "don't get the Pope started on Luther."

"Never mind," said Qiuyue.

"No worries," Julian reassured her. "You see, the road to office is so thorny for candidates, that only those with a talent for running have any chance. But running isn't the same as holding office—no, the filet is for the lady," he indicated Miranda. "I'm having the fish."

"My apologies," said the waiter, and circled around.

"And," continued Julian, "if you weed out anyone who is bad at campaigning, that leaves only those who make lousy presidents. And Wade," he declared looking at Qiuyue, "is the worst ideologue and haranguer the world has seen since your Mao Zedong."

"There you go. Please enjoy your meal." Julian was glad the waiter had respected their conversation and not interrupted with explanations like *tonight's halibut is served with couscous and a touch of ginger, sprinkled with*—none of that nonsense. "

By the time desserts came they had veered away from politics, then back to the subject again.

"Why did he drop out of the run last time?" Miranda meant Wade, and applied a fork to her Chocolate Delirium.

"He likely knew he would lose," said Julian. "Reynolds was strong, and in our pocket, too," he winked at Miranda, happy to take credit for his father's puppeteering.

"Would you care for some coffee or tea?" asked the waiter.

"I'll have a macchiato," said Qiuyue. "A decaf espresso for me," said Miranda. "Regular black," was Julian's request, which Sachs seconded.

The waiter vanished. Sachs glanced at his watch. "Shucks, there's no time for coffee." He looked at Julian. "We'd better tell them."

"Tell us what?" Miranda's eyes roved from Julian to Qiuyue, who returned the questioning stare.

"I've got courtside tickets for the Bulls game," said Sachs. "It was meant to be a surprise, but we've spent longer than expected, so—"

Miranda clapped her hands. "Forget coffee!"

"Better get your coats then," said Julian. "I'll take care of this." The girls stood up eagerly. "Allow me," Sachs told Julian.

"Absolutely not. Ball game's your treat; dinner's mine." Julian took out his phone and settled the bill before Sachs could insist.

ANOMIE

> There are certain queer times and occasions in this strange mixed affair we call life when a man takes this whole universe for a vast practical joke, though the wit thereof he but dimly discerns, and more than suspects that the joke is at nobody's expense but his own.
>
> —HERMAN MELVILLE, *Moby Dick*

When at last it became clear that Wade would indeed run for President, Connor was no longer sure he cared. But the daily routine of waiting on the high and mighty had reinforced his convictions about social unfairness, and Wade—who had lost none of his verve—managed to draw new fire from the smoldering embers of Connor's heart.

One evening, as he brought drinks to a table, his motions were brought to a standstill by the arrival of a jaw-dropping creature of bronze skin and dark eyes, whose appearance made forks pause in midair. "Is that—?" he enquired of a colleague.

"Miranda Vazquez. You've seen her in lingerie pasted all over Chicago's public transport. The guy she's with is Julian Taylor. Ring a bell?"

"No."

"Taylor Labs?"

"Nah, he's too young."

"That's Taylor's son, of course."

So there it was, the impossible dream in the flesh: the swanky style, the supermodel girlfriends, the cavalier banter, all demanding his fawning ministrations. He hovered around the table, ashamed of his behavior but unable to fight it, trying to catch as much of their conversation—and of Miranda's profile—as possible while remaining solicitous, which wasn't difficult, for the quartet was used to boatloads of attention and didn't think twice about backtracking on their orders, requesting ingredient changes, asking for extra plates to share their entrées, and so on. They talked about politics, calling Wade a crass man and an idiot, as Connor expected they would, then discussed the music website that was so popular with teens but which Connor scorned because it smacked of Asian elitism. He reflected on the affluent diners he had served over the years, always eager to splurge on alcohol but tightfisted when tipping.

"Wade's followers," said the girl in red, the most acerbic of the lot, "think we're parasites, living off others' efforts. They have no idea what the competition is like. Here's evidence: where did you go to school? I know Colin went to Dartmouth."

"Yale," said Julian.

"Stanford," said Miranda. Connor nearly dropped the tray he was carrying.

"And I'm from MIT," the Asian girl concluded. "Wade ascribes success to credentials, and credentials to privilege. But education is a prerequisite, not a guarantee. Grant any degree to the average person and throw them into the pool; they'd have zero chance of swimming."

As Connor went to the kitchen to fetch the orders for another table, he pictured himself bringing coffee and accidentally spilling it down the girl's smug cleavage. The sous-chef arranged the plates amiably, but Connor felt a burning pulse in his temples. He looked at the staff around him. Did no one else feel betrayed?

Back in the dining room the head waiter greeted him with a smile. "It's your lucky day," he said, and indicated with his eyebrows the table of the hateful four, which Connor was shocked to see empty. Out the front window he caught a last glimpse of the red dress as it disappeared into a waiting vehicle. He pulled out the tab counter from his pocket and glanced at the settled account. It showed the largest tip he had ever seen.

He tried to shut out the world by taking refuge in the wine cellar.

The months that followed saw his old foe creep upon him like mold on a damp surface. First came a loss of interest in music, as the bond that links melody to pleasure slowly decoupled in his mind until every tune became nothing but another tinny noise, and he stopped turning on the sound system in his car. His appetite was next to vanish, and the first symptom he recognized. Finally, insomnia marked the onset of full-blown depression. He forced himself to bed at the usual hour, only to feel his body tense up instead of relaxing. He had been there before, but struggled to remember how he had managed to crawl out of the abyss.

The answer, when it materialized on the news, couldn't have been clearer. It was trivial to find out the address of Wade's campaign headquarters, and in less than an hour he had made himself presentable and walked up to the door and through the busy lobby. Getting past security would be harder. He wondered if anyone would remember him, or if there was anyone he would recognize.

"I'm here to see Graciano Yglesias," he told the uniformed receptionist, and received the reply he'd been hoping for: "Who should I announce?"

He was pulling out his ID when a friendly hand landed on his shoulder. "Look who's back!"

It was George Valenzuela, former errand boy. To judge from his deportment, he had been put in charge of something. "He's with me," Valenzuela told the receptionist, and Connor was soon wearing a visitor's badge to one of the top floors of a building that before the year was over would house a team of five hundred, all working for Wade.

Valenzuela pointed across the open-plan office. "There he is. Catch you later."

***

Peikoff's assistant was on the phone. "Wayne says to come over."

The associates on his team were proofreading the presentation, so Ethan went to Peikoff alone. He found him pacing his office, purple-faced, reading what Ethan had forwarded earlier.

"This is a piece of shit," he said, and tossed the pad on the desktop. The page flickered briefly but remained lit as Peikoff proceeded with his tirade. "You messed with the cost of capital. That changes everything; the project now looks barely viable."

"Yes," Ethan acknowledged, "and I adjusted the conclusions to reflect—"

"Two days ago the numbers were far better. The client expects a go-ahead."

Which you couldn't wait to share, did you? "The first coefficient was generic," he said. "This one is sector-specific, so more credible."

"Then you should have used it on Tuesday!"

"We didn't have a good source on Tuesday. Now we do."

"But why the hell did you change it?"

Ethan rolled a hand inside his pocket into a fist and took a deep breath. "Either the cost of capital is relevant or it isn't. If it is, then we want to be as precise as possible, and today's numbers are more accurate. If it isn't, then we might as well use a risk factor of one, in line with the market, and forget about accuracy. So which do you want?"

Peikoff's face darkened further. "Don't get smart with me. Look at this chart." He reached for the discarded presentation and flipped through the pages. "Here, we discussed this yesterday. The graph should be a curve, not a straight line."

"The line you drew on the whiteboard was—"

"Precisely! You gave it no further thought. You took my five-second doodle and threw it into the presentation. If you'd bothered to study the problem you would have seen that the relation is nonlinear, that the curve bends away from the *x*-axis as it moves further out. But you just wanted the whole thing to go away."

Because I hadn't slept for two days, which is something you can't complain of because you always retire when you're done barking.

But Peikoff wasn't finished. "You're wrong if you think cutting corners will take you anywhere. Where do you see yourself, ten years from now? Do you want to end up a librarian, a high-school teacher?"

Ethan's vision hazed over. "I'd be proud to be either," he blurted out, "but if I ever catch myself venting my frustrations on someone half my age and half my tenure, I will know my life was wasted."

There were legends of consultants fired more summarily. One had accepted a job offer from a rival firm and, under the pretext of protecting company information, Peikoff had seen him escorted out by security. Compared to that, Ethan's overnight termination was almost polite. He received three months of severance in return for a written resignation, which he was happy to provide. The office gossiped for a day or two and settled back into its hectic rhythm.

The first thing Ethan did was to board a flight for New York, where he showed up unannounced in Cassie's office.

"You're kidding, right?" she asked upon hearing the news.

"Look at it from the bright side: I can now take you on that trip to Rajasthan."

"Without a job…" She tried to smile but the result was unconvincing.

"I don't need to work for a while. Come on—you should take a break, too."

"Ethan, I'm in the middle of a project. You know how it is."

"I mean when the project is over."

"It's you I'm worried about. What will you do?"

"I don't know. I could study remotely; we could be together, even if you are transferred again."

"Ethan, that's really sweet, but—"

Her choice of words made his skin crawl, and it dawned on him that Cassie's surprise at his arrival had been tinged with embarrassment.

"But what?" he protested.

She dithered. "You can't take a sabbatical and expect the world to welcome you back like nothing happened."

"I'm young enough to start over."

"Start over!? Have you no ambition?"

Ethan gave her a troubled look. "To lord it over others, like some of the clowns in this place? Hell, no."

Cassie seemed offended by his reply. She ran her fingers through her hair, tossing it back over her shoulders. "You're starting to sound American."

"I am?"

"And you're acting impulsively. You need to think this over."

"Well, today's Thursday. Let's drive to the Adirondacks tomorrow and—"

"I can't." Cassie blushed. "I've … made commitments for the weekend."

Commitments. Ethan felt the urge to sit down. He let himself fall into one of the chairs opposite Cassie's desk, placed his right hand on his leg and covered it with his left. They were both cold. "Wh—what do you mean?" he asked, losing his composure.

Cassie's countenance had gone from fiery to pale. She walked to the door and shut it quietly. She then sat down on the chair next to his. Their knees almost touched.

"Ethan, I—" She stopped and looked around her, as if trying to gather courage from the furniture. "I meant to tell you next week when I flew to California, after the progress review. I know this is awful timing, with your leaving the firm and all…" She was on the verge of tears.

"Go on," croaked Ethan, doom written all over his face.

"I slept with Dom." Her confession was almost a whisper and she looked down at her lap as she spoke.

Ethan was silent. She looked up and their eyes met. "Just like that?" he asked.

"No, not *just* like that. It's only that I—that he…" She slowly shook her head. "I'm sorry I hurt you."

Ethan stood up, his stomach in knots. "Is he here, in the office?"

Cassie shook her head again and touched her fingers to a tear. He could see relief beneath her distress.

But Ethan was now aware of something else: a surge of the strangeness was washing over him. He thought of sitting down again, but that made it worse. The feeling subsided only when he thought of leaving.

Why had it passed him by on the flight to New York, or even on the day when Cassie had cheated? There had been a hint when he weighed the choice to fly over, but it had vanished the moment he made up his mind, as if the decision had been the right one. Why was the damned sensation so unhelpful?

Without a word and under Cassie's distraught gaze, Ethan inched his way to the door and slipped out. He walked to the reception under the effect of tunnel vision—hating himself, wanting out. As he passed the front desk the feeling returned; when he called an elevator it became overwhelming. The door opened but he felt unable to get in, and stood in place before the empty car until the doors shut again. He looked about as if searching for clues, at the ceiling, the floor, the elevator banks; all had the disturbing, surreal tinge. Behind the glass doors and the company logo, a group stood by the front desk with their backs to him, waiting to be ushered in. One of the firm's partners emerged from the far end to greet them; then an associate brushed past the group and walked onto the landing, where he stood next to Ethan and pressed the elevator key. The same car, which hadn't left the floor, announced itself with a chime and the consultant boarded. Ethan slowly turned to do the same, but not before one of the visitors in the lobby glanced over her shoulder and took a good look at him across the glass pane.

The strangeness suddenly gone, Ethan walked into the elevator and out of the building.

EXPERTISE

> The spread, both in width and depth, of the multifarious branches of knowledge during the last hundred odd years has confronted us with a queer dilemma. We feel clearly that we are only now beginning to acquire reliable material for welding together the sum total of all that is known into a whole; but, on the other hand, it has become next to impossible for a single mind to fully command more than a small specialized portion of it.
>
> —ERWIN SCHRÖDINGER, *What is Life?*

From a conference-room came the voice of Graciano Yglesias. Connor could see his silhouette through the open door: the man was holding a heated discussion.

"Predictive my ass!" exclaimed someone else. "Who wrote that crap?"

Connor recognized Evander Garfield and felt the sudden wish to backtrack. Loitering among the cubicles would be impractical, so he considered looking for a restroom and locking himself in a stall. The matter, however, was quickly settled by Yglesias's reply: "*The Economist*."

Connor had just read the piece, which was based on self-reported answers from college graduates, and knew exactly what was wrong with its claims that extrasomy was a better predictor of academic success than social background, ethnicity, or high-school origin.

Emboldened, he walked into the room. "They make the typical mistake of the extrasomic," he declared, "in assuming that performance derives from ability."

"Well, well," exclaimed Yglesias, stepping forth, and Garfield had no choice but to shake hands as well, although he looked like someone interrupted by a child while engaged in adult conversation.

I missed you too, thought Connor, quickly resuming. "Just like well-fed students outperform the malnourished, extrasomics are helped by their health, which is undeserved. Plus, the author unduly rates general aptitude over concrete skills. Any large undertaking needs armies of experts, not a clique of conceited generalists."

"You don't say," Garfield condescended. "And where, um, would your expertise lie?"

Connor felt his ears burn.

"He can argue his points convincingly," said a voice of authority. "The two of you might learn something if you weren't always second-guessing each other." Wade's perennial impatience peered from under his amused expression, and it was Garfield's turn to feel embarrassed. "Connor, my man, welcome aboard. Graciano, I believe you were looking for an opinion analyst?"

He then turned to Garfield. "I need you in Detroit with me; we leave in twenty." And just as he'd shown up, Wade was gone.

Connor's first assignment was to confute the editorial. Yglesias had him work with a drafter from the Rapid Response staff, who helped to translate his self-righteous indignation into the appropriate blend of propaganda and ideology.

At first Connor was aghast at having to work with someone from Garfield's team, but the output was a resounding success and earned overnight respect for Connor as word got around that another old-timer was back, meaning someone from the senate campaign days. It also silenced Garfield and redoubled the scorn each harbored for the other. What is more, the drafter in question led to his rebirth.

Her name was Summer, but she came to him like spring comes to winter. "I'm Connor," he had said when they met. "I know," she had replied, and it made him feel special that she *knew*, like a groupie knows the name of a backup vocalist, or a diehard Yankees fan knows who played right field in the third game of the previous season.

Summer belonged to the outward-facing machinery that spoke for Wade but saw little of him, whereas Connor was part of the hallowed inner circle. Her gaze held earnest admiration for a member of the team that had 'discovered' Wade; someone whose private counsel had perhaps been sought by the candidate himself.

He helped himself to her with abandon, and she responded with tenderness and wit—a balm for his loneliness, an ideal sounding board for the ruminations of a man who hadn't known how sorely he needed someone in whom to confide. The brief sketch that she drew of her life was enviably bland. Born in their dear Chicago, the only child of loving parents, a community-college graduate, she had done a stint in advertising until the wish to fight injustice led her to join Wade's movement. Her stable character was an effective counterweight to Connor's brooding mood, and if campaigning made him feel alive again, it was Summer who made him enjoy the fact.

***

If a heart attack were imminent, read the communiqué, in whose hands would people rather find themselves? In those of an average cardiologist or in those of the world's foremost architect? And who would a defendant rather have for an attorney: an average lawyer or the nation's best violinist? If specialization was essential in the private sphere, it was all the more so in the public one. The structure of modern economies rested on large-scale projects involving a country's health and education systems, its information networks, its infrastructure and technology. All those undertakings—urban planning, crop management, national security—required vast numbers of professionals from countless disciplines whose mastery entailed no special genius or flair, but many years of rigorous training. No great endeavor could rely on the work of a mere handful of individuals, however gifted. An oversized intellect could, in fact, hamper collaboration and become a liability.

Whatever advantage intelligence might confer didn't guarantee an employee's effectiveness on the job. Instruction was paramount, and the denial of adequate opportunities was both a waste of the nation's manpower and a cruel continuance of the exclusion of the many in favor of the few. Witness the enhancement of Ukrainian athletes, which had shown that engineered muscles led to more problems than benefits, as prowess in one dimension diminished capabilities in others, to the point of compromising long-term health. But above all, the number of genes in a person's makeup—extrasomic or not—fell woefully short of specifying a full complement of brain proteins, let alone the connections between neurons. Mental skills were both emergenic, arising from the concerted effect of many genes, and epigenetic, or modulated by non-genetic influences on gene expression.

So any attempt to 'engineer the mind' was at best an empty promise and at worst a dangerous pursuit. If anything could be concluded it was that intelligence, like physical strength, should be kept within the bounds of health, where balance was paramount. Germline engineering should be regulated; extrasomy banned if procured outside the nation's borders; federal aid should ensure that Americans benefited from developments that earned a seal of approval and were available to all. That was Wade's pledge to voters.

***

A reclusive guest had ordered food from the top floor of Dubai's best hotel. The service elevator let out two uniformed employees, one pushing a dinner trolley, the other carrying a tray. They slowly made their way towards the door of a large suite, outside which stood a guard with a menacing, if bored, expression. Another man, presumably a guest—keycard in hand, wearing a white thobe and kufi—caught up with the staff, who stood courteously aside to let him by. He uttered quick thanks and walked on, soon passing in front of the guard, whose eyes were back on the waiters.

At this point his other hand emerged from the thobe and sprayed a jet of gas into the guard's face. The man instinctively covered his eyes; he coughed twice, tried to lunge forward, and toppled senseless, just in time for his attacker to hold the fall, lower him gently to the ground, hook his arms under the other's armpits, and drag him away to the fire exit. The uniformed employees resumed their progress and rang the guestroom bell. "Room service!"

The door opened. "Good evening," said the first waiter as he pushed the trolley in deferentially, followed closely by his colleague. The principal, watching television on a sofa, didn't acknowledge their arrival. The second waiter turned to the guard and offered the bill. "If you please," he requested.

As the guard inspected the item, the man behind the trolley reached under a steel dish cover for a gun, and fired a dart into the guard's back. For good measure, the other waiter brought the tray edge-first onto the guard's head, knocking him out. The commotion made the man on the sofa jump up in alarm, to find a gun pointed at his face.

"Omar Al Faisal," said the waiter, no longer obsequious, "you are under arrest for funding terrorist activities."

The FBI was informed within hours, just ahead of the media. President Reynolds sent a message of appreciation to his Middle Eastern counterpart, and the arrest was broadcast as a major blow to the fundamentalist regime of the detainee's father. The secretary of state signed a formal request for extradition. "The government of the former Emirates," she added publicly, "a progressive state and no friend of Al Faisal, will no doubt be happy to settle the issue quickly."

Around the same time, news of the arrest reached the headquarters of Ibrahim Al Faisal. His aides were apprehensive of his reaction, but he took it with composure. He quietly dismissed them and devoted the night to prayer. At dawn he took some paper, wrote two separate notes, signed them and—in an unusual gesture—pricked a finger to let a drop of blood fall onto each sheet and pressed his thumb to it under the surprised look of a lieutenant. "Just in case," he said, "there's any doubt it's me."

He placed the first note in an envelope, sealed it, and gave his instructions. "By tomorrow, to the Chinese ambassador in Dubai."

To the bearer of the second note he said: "For our U.S. contact."

VERSATILITY

> A human being should be able to change a diaper, plan an invasion, butcher a hog, conn a ship, design a building, write a sonnet, balance accounts, build a wall, set a bone, comfort the dying, take orders, give orders, cooperate, act alone, solve equations, analyze a new problem, pitch manure, program a computer, cook a tasty meal, fight efficiently, die gallantly. Specialization is for insects.
>
> —ROBERT A. HEINLEIN, *Time Enough for Love*

The first thing Valerie did was to make it clear to Jerry Springer that his future hinged on avoiding even the slightest indiscretion. A reminder of Taylor's illness drove the point home: others might be closer to the operation, but, as far as he knew, Valerie could be heir to this company.

She next called on someone who had tried to approach Bruce Taylor in vain for years.

Brent Foyle, managing partner of the New York office of Blake & Whitney, was ten minutes early, which was uncharacteristic of him. At fifty-eight and close to stepping down from his post, he felt like a naughty schoolboy, meeting alone in a downtown private club with a young woman he knew would take his breath away. He wasn't disappointed, even if somewhat taken aback by her complete lack of interest in his studied attempts at chitchat. She was civil enough—charming, even—and for a moment, to judge from the praise that she showered on his practice, Foyle thought that she might be looking for a job as an associate. But when he tried to inquire about her professional aspirations she proved him wrong. "The reason we're here," she said, smiling in a way that didn't so much put him in his place as remind him of his station, "is that one of our companies needs urgent restructuring."

She placed a document in front of him, prepared with Springer the previous evening. Foyle's years of training took over: focusing on the chance to generate a major account, he pored over the charts.

Valerie outlined TensoChem's situation. "If nothing is done," she concluded, "the business will belong to our creditors before the year is over. And for various reasons, my father won't throw any more cash at it."

Foyle looked up. "Is there agreement among shareholders —within the family, I mean?"

"None."

"I see. And Adam Schultz—?"

"Doesn't know about this. Nor does my father, by the way."

Foyle's eyebrows arched up.

"You know my father's attitude to consulting."

He had to grin. "Well, you have a point. But if neither he nor Schultz is in on this, how can we even—?"

"My father doesn't know I'm speaking with *you*, but he fully agrees with my handling the matter. What I need, within five weeks, is to find out if the business is viable. I need cash-flow projections and scenarios. If there's a way to turn this around, I will need your help to convince Hidei Nomura."

Foyle was familiar with Nomura, and nodded. "A blitz study, eh?"

"You can have our Financial Planning Director Jerry Springer on a full-time basis. He has all the data you need. It will be a sprint from beginning to end, but I know you've done it before."

"You do?"

"I spoke with Sunita Chatterjee. We went to Cambridge together."

Sunita was one of his new associates; Valerie's mention of her came as a brusque reminder to Foyle of their age difference, for Sunita was as a mere child in the practice—though one who had just opened the door to a major business opportunity, which was more than could be said of some of Foyle's partners.

He cleared his throat. "I don't suppose you spoke of financial arrangements?"

"She said I would get a quote from you, but gave me a ballpark of your fees. I can pay you half a million up front and half a million when we're done. That's all I can afford at this point."

Foyle rubbed an eyelid. The figure was very close to what he would have asked. Besides, he would have been willing to work at a discount for a shot at the jewel in the crown: the Taylor Labs account.

"It will be a pleasure to help you," he said.

They held biweekly meetings. In the first she met the team doing the work: Senior Manager Lucas Owens and two associates, neither of them much older than Valerie. Springer confirmed that they were working at breakneck speed, straight through the weekends and well into the night. Their initial findings looked promising, so she called Nomura's assistant to set up an appointment. After the second progress review, she knew they had ammunition enough to present a case for a turnaround. Foyle, as expected, had driven the team to shine, and they had also identified improvement areas in the company's international business, which Valerie had assumed to have no future. As things stood, there was only one hurdle left to overcome.

Valerie went to her father again. He was growing older by the day, losing weight and strength in his hands; Valerie felt his skin waxy against hers. Taylor still dressed up every morning and showed up to board meetings, where he laughed and joked as if life couldn't be any sweeter, rather like a bird who puts on a show of health until the point where it settles down, feathers puffed up, never to rise again.

Four years since his diagnosis, Taylor hadn't quite reached that stage, but had only months left to live. He devoted his flagging strength to the upkeep of his image and to coaching his son for the task that would fall all too soon on his shoulders. More than ever, he recognized his former self in Julian—the drive, the flair for spotting a good deal, the leadership skills. But he also realized that his son would find himself at the helm of an empire a decade earlier in life than Bruce had been when he became master of his own destiny.

His study was warm, but Valerie found him dressed in a cardigan, shuffling in slippers between the bookshelves and a low coffee table on which someone had placed a few shipping boxes.

"Decided to pack?" she asked rhetorically.

He turned away from the task and looked up at her with delight. "Summer is here, so I'm returning to Exebridge for good. I don't plan to end my days in New York: it's full of ... youthful energy."

A hundred phrases of empty comfort came to Valerie, but she shrugged them off. "Maybe I'll spend the summer in Devon."

Her father's eyes brightened. "That would be wonderful."

"In the meantime I have good news about TensoChem. But you must hear me through."

Taylor took his accustomed place at the end of a sofa and waited for her to speak. "If," she began, "I provide you with convincing evidence that TensoChem can be made profitable within a year, and get Nomura's buy-in, would you be willing to buy out Neil and Graham?"

An amused frown appeared on Taylor's face. This was the sort of thing he would have done in his youth; it was his own blood talking, and it sent a shiver of joy down his body. "If TensoChem could be made half as profitable as it used to be, I would make your cousins believe it wasn't worth a cent, buy them out and sell the whole thing for a profit. But they would know if it were salvageable, idiots as they are."

"You overestimate them," said Valerie. "All they care about is milking the operation to finance their Formula-1 team. They've left the day-to-day entirely to Schultz, who caters to them and misses the trees for the forest in the process."

"You mean the forest for the—"

"No: when I say something I mean it."

"You know," Taylor sighed, holding his palm two feet above the floor, "you were this big when you first snapped at me like that. You'd think I'd know better by now."

"Or that *I* would," she said contritely. "Anyway, I asked Nomura for a meeting. He expects us on Tuesday and I told him you would come; he thinks this is all your idea. Remember our deal," she added as Taylor's eyes opened wide in alarm.

"But you haven't told me what you've found. You were supposed to let me know. I spoke with Jerry and he said—"

"Leave Jerry alone; he's hardly slept for the last few weeks. And no, I wasn't supposed to consult you: that's not what we said. You must either play along or let the company go."

Taylor ran his hands through his thinning hair. What had crept into his daughter? This sudden enthusiasm of hers was atypical. Could she finally have come to her senses? He had given up on her years ago as far as business was concerned, and while setting aside enough to let her live idly if she wanted, he was leaving the bulk of his capital to Julian. Taylor doted on his enterprise with more consideration than he had ever shown for a living organism. Indeed, he regarded it as another child—one more fragile than its flesh-and-blood siblings; one that couldn't fend for its own.

To appoint the best steward for his business was in his eyes the most important decision a man of his stature could face, and he firmly believed he had made the right choice. Oh well, if Valerie wanted to play CEO for once, he would indulge her. She could then go back to her quaint ideas and queer friends.

"Suppose I say yes," he said. "Do we take Schultz along? I don't suppose you plan to invite the family?"

"Of course not. As for Schultz, if you agree with our findings and decide to buy the family out, you'll want to fire him."

"Well I'll be damned, Valerie, I think I'm starting to like this. All right, let's play ball."

When they showed up in Nomura's anteroom, Brent Foyle and the team were already there. Foyle was at his charming best, but Taylor glanced warily at his daughter and back at the consultants. Valerie had anticipated some awkwardness and quickly intervened. "Dad, you know Brent Foyle, from Blake & Whitney. They have been kind enough to help us put together a presentation for Mr. Nomura."

Taylor quickly regained his composure. "I see," he said, looking at Foyle, "that someone finally had the sense to hire you." None but Valerie read the irony behind the statement.

Nomura saved them from embarrassment by appearing promptly. He invited them to a meeting room and engaged in small talk. Foyle chimed in with witticisms, and soon the room was suffused with the old-boy atmosphere that the men needed to feel at ease. Nomura's head analyst joined them a few minutes later.

Valerie studied their behavior, looking for a chance to get down to business, wishing to prevent Foyle from spilling the beans about the role she had been playing. When the key individuals were recovering from a good laugh, she jumped in.

"Mr. Nomura, we are grateful for this time to share our thoughts about TensoChem. I must confess that even a month ago I thought bankruptcy was unavoidable." Springer took a swill of mineral water from the glass before him. "Since then," Valerie went on, "and not without considerable help," she acknowledged those around her, "I have come to realize that the business is not only viable, but can fully repay its short-term loans within two years—plus interest." Taylor grew pale, but all he could rally up was a raspy cough, for Valerie had moved on.

"TensoChem's difficulties arise not from market circumstances, as you may have been led to believe, but from poor management. Our conclusions are supported by the most rigorous analysis possible, given the time constraints." This served as cue for the consultants, who, for the next fifty minutes, took turns sharing their findings.

Over half of the company's customer accounts were eating into the profits generated by the rest. Since the costs of sales and logistics were unrelated to order size, small clients were disproportionately onerous. There was also great variance in profits among the sectors being served. Textile accounts, for one, could be dropped, and the business would benefit. The food-processing and leather-processing sectors, in contrast, were gold mines, but a lack of proper incentives had prevented their exploitation. And virtually all products were subject to discounts, even among customers of the same sector, and the sales force has little incentive to increase margins for unprofitable accounts.

Recommendations included transferring every low-profit account to resellers; reviewing 160 non-contributing products to identify exceptions worth preserving, with the aim of purging the rest; concentrating the sales-growth effort on food, cosmetics, and pharma; and seeking to reduce discounts in high-volume, low-margin products through a better sales incentive program. Three manufacturing plants, unequal in age and efficiency, would have excess capacity with the new, smaller product line. The sale of the oldest would generate cash flow to pay suppliers and allow TensoChem to reduce production and supply-chain personnel.

Foyle took over from Owens to summarize the benefits that could be expected. He presented debt-payoff scenarios realistic enough to convince everyone that a truce from the creditors, in the form of a debt rollover, was worth pursuing. Foyle knew the Japanese investor and played to his audience, reading the look of satisfaction that gradually drew itself on the man's face.

Taylor felt like when he had made his first million by betting, at the risk of his father's wrath, every dollar on a venture that he knew would succeed, but which he dared not discuss because, while not strictly illegal, it verged on the unethical. He now put on his best poker face, but deep inside was astounded and oblivious of his ailment. In short, he hadn't felt better in decades.

"I am pleased by your findings," said Nomura, with characteristic restraint. He then looked at Taylor. "I can't help noticing, however, the absence of the rest of your Board. How should I interpret this fact?"

Taylor sprang to life like a tiger surveying its first meal in weeks. "There will be a buyout," he said, as if it had been obvious all along. "Schultz will be gone, since these findings won't be acted upon unless we switch to new management. But that means a shakedown in the Board, which will only happen if you agree with our proposals." The inclusive pronoun wasn't lost on Valerie.

Aboard the lift after the meeting, Taylor thanked Foyle, patted Springer on the shoulder, and agreed to a plan being drafted, this time with Nomura on their side. He followed his daughter into the car in high spirits and, as the driver shut the door behind them, Valerie saw his eyes glisten, and Taylor leaned to give her a hug as strong as his health allowed.

***

Their last meeting with Nomura, a month before Taylor's death, was hosted by Brent Foyle. Their arrival at Blake & Whitney caught

Foyle on the phone, so he wasn't in the sky lobby to greet them. Valerie was revved up for the discussion ahead, but the two minutes they spent in the reception imbued her spirit with a sudden sense of wellbeing and a hint of something she couldn't quite place. It was a paradoxical sensation, at once soothing and arousing. She inhaled deeply, pleasurably. She had been looking idly at the receptionist, but her eyes now roved towards the hallway that led to the consultant offices, then to the empty seats in the waiting room behind her, and to the messenger who had arrived moments before and was waiting to deliver a package. A consultant walked out from the offices and brushed past them. Valerie's gaze followed him to the glass doors of the lobby and beyond, coming to rest at last on the person who already stood in the vestibule, oblivious to their presence. Her gasp was so quiet that nobody noticed.

PART THREE: WILL

INFERENCE

There are three scales of intelligence, one which understands by itself, a second which understands what is shown it by others, and a third which understands neither by itself nor on the showing of others—the first of which is most excellent, the second good, but the third worthless.

—NICCOLO MACHIAVELLI, *The Prince*

When it comes to bureaucratic traditions, none exceeds the Middle Kingdom's. What some countries see as a waste of public funds, China has wielded as a grand instrument to accomplish the noblest and vilest deeds since the days of imperial rule. It was therefore telling that the relay had involved so few people. The note was delivered by the ambassador himself to the chief of staff, who spoke briefly with the president before contacting the Ministry of State Security. There, a unit known as the Second or 'Foreign' Bureau, responsible for most of China's clandestine work abroad, sprang into action.

At roughly the same time one of the country's top generals received a call at home. Yingjun Chen, Vice-Chairman of the Central Military Commission, was used to presiding over the meetings he attended. The exception, of course, was when the president was there. Those were usually formal occasions—pageants where everything was rehearsed beforehand. But sometimes the president, who had been the chairman of the same commission in the days of the old communist regime, called Chen to his presence without warning. When such summons came at dinnertime, as they did that evening, it meant bad news, so when he reported to the presidential headquarters his expectations were low. The Head of the Foreign Bureau, Yong Jiahua, was already there.

Although the room held chairs to spare, Jiahua and President Ziyang were both standing and had obviously been conversing for some time. After the usual greetings the president instructed Jiahua to brief Chen.

"A threat was delivered to us yesterday, penned in Arabic by Ibrahim Al Faisal. Here is the translation." Jiahua handed a small notebook to Chen, who read the text slowly, turned pale, moved to the nearest chair, sat down uninvited, and read the text again. Finally he looked up at Ziyang, became aware of his impropriety and rose again.

"Do you think it's true?" asked the president.

Chen knew that the same question had likely been posed to Jiahua, and regretted arriving too late to hear the answer. This made it difficult to provide a cautious reply without sounding incompetent. There was no skirting around the issue; all he could do was speak his mind.

"The birth of the child is true," he said. "That's what triggered the civil war that set up Al Faisal as dictator. It also tipped us off to Cao Xin Pei's activities. Code Seagull is based on the premise that the Beta complement was successfully engineered. The program's purpose since General Feng's time was to locate the children endowed with the full Prometheus module."

"Suppose this child—what's his name?"

"Hassan."

"Suppose this Hassan were indeed alive. What would that mean for us?"

Chen drew in a sigh. "As far as we know, several dozen women visited Cao's facility. Of those, maybe half were treated after Al Faisal's visit to Indonesia. But his accomplice Jianguo Zhang spoke with an Indian scientist … I forget his name, a few weeks before Al Faisal's trip to the island. This makes the child perhaps the first to bear a viable Beta complement, albeit a pilot version involving *only* the Beta. General Feng was convinced that all subsequent fertilizations, maybe thirty altogether, involved the full module. Those are Seagull's targets. But if a functional Beta were to fall into American hands, it would allow them to put together the entire module, since the Alpha is known."

"Meaning what, general?" said an impatient Ziyang.

Chen lowered his head. "In General Feng's words, they would inherit the earth."

The president turned to Jiahua. "So, we agree that Al Faisal can make good on his threat. Why haven't we heard about the child before? Why didn't Feng ever mention him?"

"The child was presumed dead," said Jiahua. "When civil war erupted his family was wiped out. His father, Crown Prince Nessim, was killed in the first strike; the king was deposed and executed soon after. The official version of the mother's death was suicide, although the rebels may have covered a murder. The baby was never found, but everyone thought he had died with his mother."

"Was it a cover-up, then?"

Jiahua was hesitant. Speculation is what he was paid to do, but it always made him nervous to spar with the president. "I don't think so," he said. "Everyone assumed that the king's succession had been extinguished."

"Then why didn't Al Faisal have the boy killed upon learning of his existence?"

"Perhaps he planned to, but discovered that he was living in the United States, which complicates things."

Ziyang grunted. "That hasn't stopped him before. Would he share this information with his son?"

"He has held Omar in confidence before."

"Mr. President," interjected Chen, "even if we could get to Al Faisal before word of this got around, the note's wording is significant. He doesn't threaten to *send* word of the boy's identity to the Americans. What he says is that the information will *inevitably* reach the U.S. government unless Omar returns safely home. I take it to mean that others would speak up if Al Faisal were to have, say, an accident."

"But why," Ziyang insisted, "would Al Faisal share something so sensitive with others? It's an invitation for blackmail."

"Well, if the boy's identity was a recent discovery, then someone—an underling or spy—must have relayed the news to Al Faisal. At least one more person must know."

"Let's assume you're right. What are our options? We don't have enough clout with Dubai to force their hand. Not with an official extradition request from the Americans."

"Maybe not," conceded Jiahua, "but all we need to do is buy time, stall the process. That requires negotiating convincingly with both Dubai and Washington."

President Ziyang nodded as he began weighing alternatives.

"Pardon for asking, Mr. President," said Chen, "but if we were somehow able to have the prisoner delivered to us, would you be willing to meet Al Faisal's request?"

"To send him home, you mean? Sure—in exchange for the Beta carrier."

"Of course," assented Chen.

"It would raise eyebrows if we let him go," cautioned Jiahua.

"If we had the Beta," said Chen, "that would be of minor concern."

"You know what would be good?" remarked Ziyang. "For you to locate the module carrier before this whole thing blows up."

This was followed by awkward silence, which Jiahua broke. "There is one possibility. If the prisoner is being kept in isolation, he will know nothing of this threat. And if he's aware of Hassan's existence, we may use it to our advantage."

"That means gaining access to Omar," said Chen. "As you said, he's locked up."

"Leave that to me," said Ziyang, and the other two exchanged glances. "Who would you send?"

"We have strong operatives on the ground," said Jiahua, "but I would send Quxun Zhu, who speaks fluent Arabic."

Ziyang pondered the suggestion. "We can't risk anything slipping by. I want someone familiar with Code Seagull and able to extract information without force."

"Only one person fits that profile," said Chen. "Colonel Lin Mei Hsieh."

"That woman?" scoffed Jiahua. "She was Feng's protégée."

"As was I, you seem to forget," said President Ziyang.

Jiahua blushed. "Of course, I didn't mean—"

"No, of course you didn't," said Ziyang quickly, allowing Jiahua to save face. "But you will agree that she's the person most familiar with this issue."

"Y—yes, certainly." Jiahua was trapped.

"Good," said Ziyang, turning to Chen. "Get her going immediately." Then back to Jiahua: "You can send your choice along with her: we want the best." Ziyang thus accomplished his main goal in the discussion, namely for the task force to be loyal neither to Chen nor to Jiahua.

***

"Mr. President? Secretary Esquivel is here."

"Let her in," said Reynolds, and the Secretary of State was ushered into the Oval Office.

"Alicia," he greeted her warmly, 'have a seat." He took his place at an angle from her and grabbed a bowl from the table to his left. "Candy?" he asked. "No? Good for you; I've become addicted." He popped one into his mouth and placed them back.

"Even the Lebanese," he said, "are okay with Al Faisal being tried in the U.S. So, what's with Ziyang? Why is he so interested, all of a sudden?"

"I don't know," admitted Esquivel, "but Ambassador Zhu told me this morning that China is willing to negotiate his extradition *under the best of terms*—his words. It means they are inviting us to suggest conditions for backing down."

"Which only makes me more reluctant to give in."

"What does Evans think?"

"As National Security Advisor he likes to err on the side of caution, so he wants us to stand firm. The question is, can we come up with an alternative that, without being reckless, is at least politically, um—"

"Advantageous?"

The president nodded.

"Mr. President," Esquivel said cautiously, "we can delay this by a day or two, at most. The media are all over us. I assume you've heard Wade—"

"Wade is a demagogue and an ass! I've got better things to do than to listen to what he says. What I need to know, Alicia, is whether we are—whether we *should* be—willing to call China's bluff. I know it's always hidden agendas with them, but Christ, there's got to be something we're missing! Ziyang knows how much it would hurt me if we don't bring Al Faisal to trial. Why would he risk an international conflict over this?"

Esquivel cleared her throat. "To find out how much the Chinese really care, we could ask for something big enough that, if they were to grant it, would bolster your image far more than backing down on this issue could ever hurt you."

"I'm listening."

"The opposition constantly harps on how crippling our debt with China has become."

Reynolds grunted. "We can't ask them to shave off debt unilaterally. They would know we aren't being serious, plus there are things even Ziyang cannot accomplish without support."

"No, of course not. But how about asking them to halve the interest rates? Ziyang holds China's financial authorities on a short leash. Of course, the political cost for him would be higher than anything we've discussed so far, but…"

"Do you think it has a chance of flying?"

"At least it will buy time. And on the off chance the Al Faisal affair is as important as they've made it up to be, we'd know for sure."

"Then let's give it a try. In the meantime we must unearth what's really at the root of this mess."

"I agree."

Reynolds was quiet for a moment, then pressed a call button. "Yes, Mr. President?"

"Call General McGrath," he said. "Tell him I need to see him ASAP."

***

Colonel Hsieh emerged from the building where Omar Al Faisal was being held, flanked by a local high-ranking officer and two military police. She walked at a brisk pace across the sunlit courtyard to the waiting vehicle, forcing an irate Quxun Zhu to keep up. Zhu muttered one last protest quickly in Mandarin. "Why did you cut the interview short?"

"Tell you on the plane," snapped Hsieh. She pressed on, smiling at their escort. Zhu had no choice but to follow, fuming beneath his dignified bearing. Fifty feet away, atop the wall of the compound, a cricket rubbed its legs together, one of its eyes swiveling like a chameleon's, surveying the departing officers.

When the aircraft door shut behind them, Zhu erupted, "Al Faisal had just begun speaking!"

"You clearly weren't listening," said Hsieh, inviting Zhu to the seat opposite hers.

"I was busy translating for you," he retorted with the same ironic tone. "But you wouldn't press him for details. Instead you said we were wasting our time!"

"I said it because we'd heard all we needed, but I couldn't explain because our escort spoke Mandarin."

Zhu was beginning to blush. "What did Al Faisal reply," Hsieh pressed on, "when you told him about Prince Nessim's child?"

"He taunted us. He said Nessim got what he deserved for asking his wife to bring into the world another abomination in the eyes of God. Those were his exact words."

"And what does that tell us?"

"That he hates extrasomics, which everyone knows. He was ready to spit on our faces the instant he saw us."

"See? You didn't do your homework. What did Ibrahim Al Faisal always decry, even before denouncing extrasomy? What did he hate about his uncle? What was the supposed insult to Allah? Not extrasomy, but cloning. 'Another' abomination means another clone. We know what the boy looks like: the living image of a deposed king."

Though Zhu managed to keep it shut, Hsieh could visualize the man's jaw dropping. Still he protested. "If you suspected that, why not corroborate?"

"Because," Hsieh concluded patronizingly. "When prying into someone's game, you never reveal your own."

With Zhu properly abashed, she enjoyed a quiet flight back to Beijing.

***

Vance Havelock was still in bed when the call came in.

"Sorry to disturb you at this hour, sir, but a piece of intelligence just came in: there's been a development in the Al Faisal case. Yes, it came through the CIA. I am aware of that, but General McGrath himself said to wake you up. Well, sir, I think you will want to see for yourself."

Director of National Intelligence Norbert McGrath had been close to Henry Lasker before the latter's retirement, and his shoulder straps boasted four stars to Lasker's one, so an hour later Havelock sat facing Larissa Kane. "Okay," he said, "I'm listening."

"President Reynolds received a request from China to drop Al Faisal's extradition process and agree to his being sent to China instead. The stated reason is that Al Faisal's government has been lending financial support to the latest wave of Uyghur unrest, and that Omar Al Faisal is personally responsible. They want to make an example of him—or so they say."

"Why come to us until now?" he asked.

Kane made no apologies. "We needed to confirm our suspicions."

"Which were?"

"Twofold. First, Al Faisal never had anything to do with Urumqi, which is why we had never heard about it; and second, the Chinese started working on the Dubai administration a full week before making their request to us."

"And the president's reaction?"

"Cautious. He knows that stepping down would mean bad press—being accused of giving in to China on yet another issue. But he would agree if the Chinese proved accommodating."

"Are they pressuring Dubai?"

"Coaxing is more like it. They want Al Faisal to be allowed to escape, and fall into their hands. In exchange, China would eliminate the clan's patriarch. The only reason Dubai didn't agree is they know we're watching. This was sent yesterday." Kane touched a button and the blank wall to their left lit up. The image showed two Chinese officials leaving a government compound in Dubai, escorted by a local high-ranking officer.

"This is where Omar Al Faisal is being held. A Chinese delegation was allowed to enter the compound. We can only guess what the exchange was about, but it's a fair guess that they met with him."

Havelock gazed at the image, his mind still processing the previous information. Suddenly he squinted.

Not that he needed to, for the picture was good. The Chinese were a man and a woman. The woman's body was hidden by her colleague's, but her features were distinct. Without taking his eyes off the image, Havelock rose from his seat and skirted the conference table until he stood a few inches from the wall.

"Son of a bitch," he muttered.

"One of our analysts recognized her. That's why McGrath had you pulled out of bed."

Havelock turned to look at Kane, his drowsiness gone. He then stared back at the image, engrossed. Only once had he seen a picture of Colonel Lin Mei Hsieh, an older image of a younger woman. Havelock remembered that the accompanying intelligence had cost a man his life.

COUNSEL

> Any attempt to understand or explain within the framework of classical physics the physical effects of consciousness is irrational, because the classical approximation eliminates the effect one is trying to study.
>
> —HENRY STAPP, *Mindful Universe*

Around General McGrath's table, Vance Havelock now found himself across from Larissa Kane and Eric Ressler. "Normally," said McGrath to no one in particular, "you all get to work in separate buckets. But I just spoke with the president and he has upgraded this to the highest priority, because the shit is barely—and I do mean barely—an inch from the fan. That means any information on this case is to be shared with all in this room, but with no one else. Understood? Now, here's what we've got: on the one hand an assassination ordered by Omar Al Faisal; on the other a biotech operation that the Chinese will risk anything short of war to keep hidden. What links the two?" The general looked around the room.

Havelock spoke up. "A man called Xin Pei Cao."

Kane nodded. "His operation was funded by wealthy customers; Nessim Al Faisal was the last we know by name. When Cao was busted, the Chinese launched an obscure operation that initially suggested bioweapons…"

She glanced at Havelock, who expounded. "But it wasn't. Their aim is to locate any offspring of Cao's pre-implantation treatment."

"Locals?" asked Ressler.

"The women came from all over, but no records were found in Cao's belongings. That's why China set up a hunt."

McGrath turned to Ressler. "When did you learn of Al Faisal's role in Karam's death?"

"Two months after the event."

"And how soon after that did we share the intelligence?"

"Immediately," said Kane. "But it was Mossad that tipped us off, so someone knew already."

"That was two years ago," said McGrath. "But China never made, nor encouraged, any effort to capture Al Faisal's until now. Correct?"

Everyone nodded.

"So, here's what I'm thinking. What if they don't want justice at all, but merely to prevent Al Faisal from falling into someone else's hands?"

"Would you mind," Havelock asked, "my looking at your report on the Karam case?"

She clicked on her pad and slid it over to Havelock. Two minutes went by. Kane stood up, refilled her coffee and returned to the table; Ressler chewed on his fingernails; McGrath stepped out to take a call.

"Tell me," said Havelock at length, "about the man called Zamalek. Are we sure of his identity?"

"We have no DNA," said Ressler, "but a body found the day after the murder is consistent with his age and build. The sliced-off fingertips make it even likelier."

"And the woman?"

"Her name is Fatima Shadid," said Kane. "Also from Al Faisal's circle—the father's, not Omar's. President Reynolds recognized her from the video stills. She was serving drinks at the reception, so we assume that she was involved, but her trail runs cold."

"So, for all we know she could still be in the U.S.?"

"Yes," said Ressler, "though it's doubtful. We suspect she's the one who took care of Zamalek."

"Why?"

"She was the deadlier to the two. There were … stories."

"Such as?" Havelock insisted.

Ressler wasn't one to hesitate much, but he let Kane explain. "There was this man—not your average punk, but a hardcore terrorist. He tried to have his way with her. She cut off his balls and stuffed them in his mouth, leaving him hogtied for his associates to find."

"Okay, I get the picture. Does she strike you as suicidal?"

"She'd have the guts," said Ressler, "but the motive? I mean, the deed was done already."

"Yes, but it had yet to work its effect. Did you post her photo?"

"With all our sources," said Kane. "That's how we learned her name."

"I mean the police."

Ressler shook his head.

"Might be worth a try, don't you think?"

Kane objected. "Then we'd have to explain—"

"Actually," interrupted Ressler, "we can list her as an unknown murder suspect; no details. Her face means nothing to local law enforcers."

Havelock looked at Kane, who sipped her coffee once, then again, allowing silence to stand in for acquiescence.

***

Valerie Taylor rang the doorbell and glanced at her watch. It had taken her longer than expected to reach Boston, and it was already dinnertime. Any misgivings, however, were dispelled by Tony's effusive welcome.

"How long has it been?" he asked as they hugged. "Two years?"

"Almost three. How's Albert?"

"Splendid, just splendid—here, let me take your coat—probably asleep somewhere in Bavaria. He gave a talk this morning and will spend the weekend sightseeing."

Tony Steinberg led her to a cozy study in the house he shared with his partner. Albert Massey held the lead in seniority, but Tony was by far the wealthier, so Massey had moved in with him after accepting the job at MIT. Valerie enjoyed Albert's company, but had been glad to learn that Tony would be alone. After catch-up talk they headed for the kitchen, where he tossed a salad and grilled porterhouse steaks. They reminisced over dinner, and evening found them back in the study, sitting on cushions before a gas fireplace, a mug of coffee in Valerie's hands as Tony rummaged through what was left of a box of chocolates.

"I've been meaning to ask you," Valerie said, feeling the moment was as appropriate as it ever would be. "I trust you'll forgive my prying, but if what I've heard is well founded, then—"

"Gosh, Valerie! That's how I must have looked when I told you I was gay."

Chastised, she began afresh. "We were born during the heyday of offshore babies, and my parents traveled to Asia to conceive me in a semi-clandestine facility. The legality is irrelevant, but my mother said they had followed your parent's lead."

"Oh!" Tony was visibly relieved. "I assumed you didn't know, like a child kept ignorant of its adoption, so I did the polite thing and never mentioned it."

"You're not far off the mark. My parents didn't tell me, and I never cared to ask—until last week. But my father is dead and my mother doesn't have the answers I want."

"I see… This calls for a drink. A drop of brandy, perhaps? At least some port, then." He poured two glasses and returned to the hearth. "In your cells, as in mine," he began, "there are genes related to discoveries over a hundred years old. And I don't mean germline engineering, but physics—specifically, the fact that you can detect an object without communicating with it."

"You're talking about interaction-free measurement."

Tony nodded. "Best known for its application to computing, where it allows the indirect exclusion of wrong solutions to provide the right answer before an algorithm is run. But the principle goes deeper. Quantum interrogation, as it was first called, was conceived not as a computing method but as a way of telling if hidden objects exist or not. Let's say you are trapped in a room with two doors: behind one is a bomb set to explode if you touch the doorknob; behind the other is a safe exit. In the world of classical physics, the best you can do is to toss a coin and pray for luck. But armed with a suitable quantum interrogation device, you can find out which door conceals the bomb. This has been experimentally verified, but the experiments were carried out with beam-splitters and photon detectors in contrived setups that didn't involve explosives. The process only works if the question is posed correctly, which means setting up things so that all alternatives are simultaneously explored. This in turn can only be achieved if whatever is doing the exploration (a photon, for example) is in an undetermined state, just like the qubits of a computer. Here, let me show you." Tony fetched a pad from a nearby table and browsed through it until he found the sketch he wanted. He gave it to Valerie.

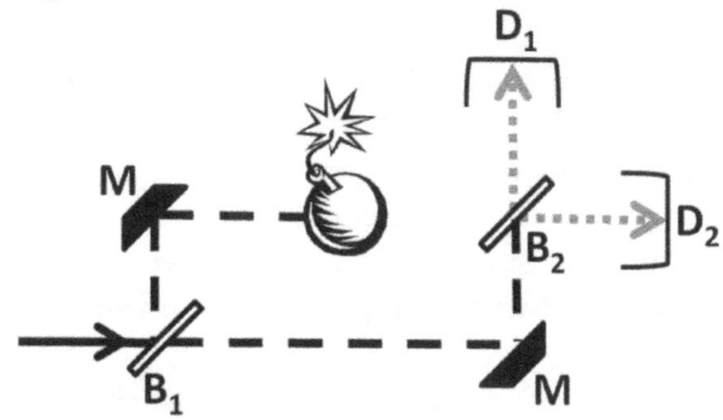

"Mirrors are marked by M, detectors by D, and beam splitters by B. Now suppose," he said, "a photon from a source on the left is sent through the first splitter, giving it a fifty-percent chance of being deflected up instead of straight ahead. The physical state of the photon is undetermined, so it takes each route with equal probability. If it takes the upper path, it detonates the bomb, but there's an equal chance that it will take the lower road, reaching the second beam splitter unharmed. There, it once again goes through a parting of ways."

"Okay, I remember: if there's no bomb, then interference makes all photons strike D_2. So D_1 can only register a strike if there is a bomb but the photon hasn't set it off."

"Exactly, and that happens only when a photon first veers right and then left, which is half (again) of half the time, or 25%—pretty bad odds for anyone to bet their life on. But more complex setups involving repeated runs around the circuit increase the odds to over 99% and still detect the bomb without setting it off. If that sounds too good to be true, it is because no real door is that sensitive. You can in principle get around the problem by using photomultipliers to turn the blip of a single photon into a large signal that actually opens the door. But the setup needs to be exquisitely precise."

"So," said Valerie, "it's impossible to wrangle your way out of real trap with a quantum interrogation device."

"Not impossible, just impractical. The apparatus needs to be crafted to leave quantum coherence undisturbed. That's why this has been applied to computing but not to booby traps. When these ideas arose, they created a rift among cognitive scientists: one group thought that mental decisions were quantum-mechanical."

"Which proved to be the case, did it not?"

"Yes, but there's more. Others had been studying evidence pointing to the odd conclusion that minds react to events *before* they occur. This was long held to be crackpot science, but quantum interrogation hinted at how it might occur."

"But brains don't come equipped with beam splitters..."

"No, but the idea is that mental decisions are equivalent to a photon being split, but instead of exploding bombs you have whatever results from a poor decision. Proponents were careful to say that this didn't amount to clairvoyance, in the sense of knowing when an earthquake will strike or whose sister will be next to marry. It was more like being able to decide in the absence of clues, yet better than random choice would allow."

"And what did their rivals say?"

"They argued that precognitive skills were too great an advantage for evolution to have ignored. But a Dutch group proposed that it hadn't developed because brains hadn't evolved enough to handle it, just like complex language never evolved in birds despite their excellent diction. Both groups chased an imagined holy grail: in the U.S. it was called the Prometheus module. The first camp argued for a latent, rudimentary skill in animals that could be exploited. And some people, even some animals, were found to be prone to prescience, so the genetics behind it became a focus of study. This led to what is known as the Beta complement of the module, engineered in mice but never in primates, thanks to the Milan moratorium. The second camp began by recognizing that brains and sensory organs often evolve in parallel, like a tag team. Animals weren't suddenly born with a pair of eyes, but grew them over millions of years, from simple patches of light-sensitive skin that produced a sensation more like touch than like sight. And brains were just as primitive: modern vision involves an eyeball, a retina and an optic nerve, plus a visual cortex to make sense of the signals. But the cortex has also evolved, so research tried to identify the brain processes needed to decipher the output of quantum interrogation, or the equivalent of a parrot deciphering sentences."

"That's a tall order!"

"Well then congratulations, my dear, because someone called Zhang engineered what is known as the Alpha complement, which *was* viable in humans. The Chinese declared the findings state property, but thousands of Chinese children our age and younger carry the Alpha complement. My parents learned that someone was raising funds by selling the Alpha for huge sums, so they traveled to have the procedure done. Then my father spoke to yours and that was that."

"I have the Alpha complement?"

"We both do."

"And what good has it done?"

"Besides making you smarter than anyone you know?"

"If true, that could be due to a host of factors."

"Your mind isn't fortuitous: it's designed."

"But we lack half the module!"

"Well, imagine again a world of darkness, where every creature navigates by sonar, like bats in a cave. If someone were to turn the lights on, even the best sonar would be no match for a pair of eyes, but only if someone *already* had eyes in their head. The Alpha by itself amounts to a visual cortex but no eyes."

"And the Beta complement?"

"The opposite. But there aren't people walking around with it, so it's hard to say. Damage to the visual cortex makes people effectively blind. They are unaware of light or movement, but if you throw a ball at them and yell *catch,* they will often succeed. It's called blindsight. The team working on the Beta was betting on something like that—go figure."

"But the regulations … what would the full module allow people to do?"

"No idea. It's supposed to open the door to a new plane of awareness, but we won't grow a pair of antennae or something."

"Then how can you be sure that your skills—or mine—are even related to it?"

"Because there are specific things we can measure. Do you have a New Music account?"

"The website?"

"Which ladder do you use—spatial or analytical?"

"Analytical. The other gets me nowhere."

"Nor me. That proves that we share the same complement. What level have you reached?"

"I don't see what—"

"Come one, what level?"

"Four."

"See? Only one in a million reach the fourth level. Just like old college tests had verbal and quant sections, the two ladders in NM correspond to the complements of the module. I'm sure the website admin keeps track of the scores."

"But the website is Chinese."

"Precisely. They already had something like it years ago, minus the rewards." Tony walked to an old escritoire, lifted the central flap and from a pigeonhole pulled out an object that he handed to Valerie. "It no longer works, but a score of 100 on this was like a score of 4 in NM."

Valerie froze. She had seen this before: a small rectangular gadget with rudimentary controls and the characters α/β inscribed in one corner. The memory of an afternoon in Exebridge played back in her mind. She remembered her scores, and those earned before hers.

"What did the second score measure?" she asked hoarsely.

"Why—the Beta complement, of course. Any score above 80 suggested its presence; 100 was a guarantee. At least that's the way it was designed: I don't think anybody ever tested above 30."

Valerie felt dizzy. She reached out with a hand for the tabletop and found reassurance in its coolness. "Suppose," she said, "that the research program *had* worked. Say a boy had the Beta. Would he be recognizable?"

"A baby boy?"

"Well, a man now."

Tony shrugged. "Who knows, I suppose if the person were male, then he, uh…"

When laughter overcame him, it was pure and candid, like when they were children. Tony held his midriff with glee, and though

Valerie failed to see what was funny, she smiled at his innocent humor.

"Oh, it's just that—ha, ha—it's just that, well—ho, ho … okay, okay." He took a breath and wiped away a tear. "Look, I don't know how it would operate in humans, but when the Beta was developed, they wanted to foster interbreeding among the mice used for testing, so they hooked up a pheromone-producing cluster in the Beta, and the Alpha to its receptor. Sure, it made the mice breed selectively, but I doubt the mechanism was ever reverted. That's why I was laughing, because one thing's for sure: if you were to run into a man carrying the Beta complement, you would be one horny little girl."

As he started to giggle anew, Valerie turned to stare at the fire, wondering if it would hide the glow in her features.

THRALL

Man is a credulous animal, and must believe *something*; in the absence of good grounds for belief, he will be satisfied with bad ones.

—BERTRAND RUSSELL, *Unpopular Essays*

The size of the crowd made Connor's skin tingle. He had attended many rallies with Wade and even helped to organize some for the senate campaign, but this was on a different scale. The media said half a million, but an abstract number is no match for the sight of a swarming, vibrant mass of people. He wavered at the back of the stage, hesitant to step closer to the security circle around the space reserved for the candidate, caught between shyness and the self-importance that comes from rubbing shoulders with power. With the roving eyes of cameras on him, Connor did his best to appear busy, fiddling with the pin on his lapel as if it needed adjusting. He then gazed with affected composure at the giant screens across the park, and waited.

Naming the party hadn't been easy, for Wade had been as adamant in his wish to use the word *America* as he had been prescient in his conviction that it would strike a chord with the people. The most appealing names (American National Party, All American Party, America First Party, American Freedom Party, American People's Party, American Patriot Party, Make America Great, etc.) had long ago been adopted—usurped, as Wade would say—by other groups, many of them defunct and forgotten. In the end, *America Wins / America for Wade* was the slogan that stuck, and on all the caps, banners, armbands and pins that peppered the crowd, the bright-red ***AW*** monogram floated over a star-spangled background. (Elsewhere, T-shirts could already be found with the legend *America Weeps*, in the same font.)

The campaign manager's speech was brief, its purpose to focus attention and build impetus. Using adjectives like *proud* and *happy*, he extolled the crowd for their loyalty to a cause that had spread beyond the confines of partisanship to become a national movement. He made flattering comparisons of Wade with the gathered multitude, highlighting their shared patriotism and selflessness. Then, with special thanks to those who had driven from across the country to be present that day, he praised the populace for its unflagging devotion and, as if no better reward could be granted, he ceremoniously introduced "Aamon Spencer Wade, next President of the United States". The throng erupted in a gargantuan ovation: no pop-music star, no religious leader —certainly no politician—had ever commanded such enthusiasm. Waves of fervent support bellowed from the streets. Then a hush fell over the city as Wade began to speak.

"My fellow Americans…" The words were tired, but tone is what counts for a true believer's ears. In short outbursts, as scant in syllables as they were rich in gesture, he spoke of the strength and significance of their movement. He addressed in turn the young, the old, the farmers, the miners, the members of the military, single mothers and factory workers, expressing sympathy for their hardship and showering uplifting words on all. He outlined his vision for America to retake control of the world's economy, just as it stood—and who could doubt it—at the apex of civilization. It would be once more a nation of justice, not of privilege; of confidence, not of doubt; of discipline, not of laxness. He spoke of courage, sacrifice, and triumph. Where others made promises he made demands, and even then was interrupted by cheering, which he fueled with every tirade.

He then turned to the theme of 'the people'.

America, he said, belonged to descendants of immigrants, but had never tolerated foreign interference. "If the extrasomic," he said, "insist on making our people the stewards of foreign interests, they shall be made responsible for whatever misfortunes befall us. We will not bleed alone. As senator for Illinois I successfully pushed to allow private organizations—this party included—to ban individuals with auxiliary chromosomes. If elected to the White House, I will bring another bill before Congress, to preclude such individuals from holding public office." Another roar of enthusiasm was heard, and Connor was transported by the speech, sharing in the crowd's rapture. This was, he felt certain, the moment they had all been longing for. No more capricious governments. Here, at last, was a true leader: someone worth fighting with and fighting for.

Few battle cries are more effective than righteous anger, and Wade knew how to wield it. "Let us not fool ourselves into thinking," he harangued, "that germline enhancement is a benign phenomenon, or just another form of medical therapy. Hard-working Americans may, with some effort, afford plastic surgery, but our chromosomes we are born with. Now, luck is one thing; but I ask you: is it fair for someone to be taller, stronger, better looking, simply because their parents were richer than ours?" The crowd hummed angrily. "Is it fair for someone to be offered discounts because they have an extra chromosome and the rest of us don't? This is a nation whose foundations were laid on principles of equality, in the eyes of God and in the eyes of the law. Let us protect those principles. I want to live in a country where every man, woman and child has access to the same opportunities; where germline enhancements are available to the same extent for all.

"The extrasomic, a mere two percent of U.S. population, control our financial institutions and our corporations. Is that coincidental? Of course not. They help each other; they favor their kind. No more, I say—no more! As senator I made it illegal to purchase genetic modules abroad. As president, you will help me to ban all germline enhancements not sanctioned by the government and offered by our public health system.

"My critics—all of which, not surprisingly, hail from the cosmeticized camp—my critics point to the lack of public funds for such efforts. 'Where will the money come from?' they ask, glossing over the reason for this financial burden. Do you know, my fellow citizens, *why* the government is short on money? It is the interest we pay to countries like China, which has (again, not by chance) the highest concentration of artificial chromosomes in the world; to countries that experiment on human subjects and, having secured the patents, sell them to the rest of the world. Time to put our foot down and say: this, has, got, to, stop!"

He went on, town after town, and Connor followed, feeling the glow of Wade's power like a magic cloak on his back, making people address him as Mr. Dashaw when pecking for crumbs of the political cake. It made him feel more deserving of the estival season, and of the girl bearing its name. He became less guarded around Summer, more critical of others and especially of Garfield; less anxious that her allegiance to him might prevail over their unspoken trust for each other. Because they worked well together: Wade supplied the doctrine, Connor the examples, Summer the words. The candidate was best in attack mode, and his medium was the stage; defense was left to his team. And while Connor and Summer were hardly the only ones on task, they still had their hands full.

"Wade's personal life," read one posting, "is largely a blank. Unattached and seemingly indifferent to romance, he is said to lead a celibate existence. A grand total of two women can be traced to his youth, and both declined to be interviewed. Religious he is not. Born into an overtly Baptist family, Wade never went to church before this campaign. His friends are few and of recent making. He prefers to surround himself with supporters, among which he does all the talking. Indeed, apart from politics and a passion for discrediting his rivals, he indulges in very little of what normally lends warmth and dignity to human life. Partial towards oratory, he famously shuns debates, and on the sole occasion he held one (moderated by an admirer) he made not a single mention of taxes, jobs, or economic policy, using all his allotted time to inveigh against others. What does he believe in? What does he read? (*Does* he?) His speeches are rousing, but merely berate the administration and the views of other contenders. He makes no constructive proposals, and vows only to curtail privilege."

Connor never failed to be outraged. "They're at it again, lambasting Wade."

"The media?" asked Summer.

He smacked his lips with contempt. "Some rich bastard; the media just lends itself."

"Oh, baby," she cooed, "you must try harder. Blaming the rich is old hat, you know? Don't give me that look; what I mean is it won't impress Wade."

"But it's clear who these people are."

"Yes, but have you got anything on them, besides their dislike for us?"

"There must be dirt somewhere," protested Connor. "It's not the establishment they are defending, but Reynolds. And he favors them in return. Why?"

"Well, you let me know when you find out. In the meantime, shouldn't we draft an answer to this piece?"

They did, and a solid defense of Wade went out the next morning. But the critics were relentless, with a fresh attack for every rebuttal.

"Wade is unafraid," said the next editorial, "to contradict himself when it suits his tirades, most alarmingly as regards education. An outspoken advocate of school improvements, he is dismissive of higher learning. What lies behind this conflicting stance? Is personal history to blame? Wade's table talk at the Harvey Foundation event revealed him as frankly uncultured. He once expressed open regret at having been unable to attend medical school, and endorses teaching programs for the disadvantaged. Yet in the same breath he scorns the Ivy League, all schools for the gifted, the teachers who staff them (which he calls interlopers) and every institution on which our nation forged its competitive edge. He conflates privilege of wealth with extrasomy, as if the latter were bad by association. And there lies the nub of his political views, ever since he joined the Senate. Brushing aside the fact that most extrasomics in America are under age and therefore unable to vote, Wade is viciously critical of anything that smacks of germline intervention, on which he blames all the ills of the world.

"Well, the so-called interlopers have taken the hint. Foreign applications for faculty roles have already halved versus last year, in line with the drop in international students. Not long ago this would have been chilling news, and any slander like Wade's would have met with jeering. But angry discourse falls on ready ears these days, for the underprivileged now make up the bulk of the electorate. It is hardly in doubt that Aamon Wade resonates with the majority, but one is left to wonder what good can come from a political platform based on resentment against intellectuals. To this correspondent, whose roots are Cambodian, it is frighteningly familiar."

"It figures," said Connor. "The guy is Asian."

"Ethnicity doesn't mean he was born there."

"Whatever, the mindset is the same: it makes our effort seem futile."

"The campaign?!" exclaimed Summer.

"Our role in it—the drudgery. I want to be making history, not stuck in a back office."

"Lots of history is made in back offices."

"Fine, then I want to *feel* like we're making history."

Summer played with her hair. "And what would that be like?"

"I don't know—more action, scandals, intrigue, brinksmanship."

"Sounds like a bad flick series."

"At least flicks deal with issues decisively, not by dancing around them."

"That's because viewers expect every episode to be packed with thrills. If that's how it went down in real life, every law enforcer would resign or end up in a psych ward."

"Yeah, I guess so… But we live under this illusion—don't we—that someone's in charge; that governments, even bad ones, are managed by people who know what they're doing. Then you see how campaigns are run and it makes you wonder…"

She looked oddly at him. "This isn't about work, is it?"

"Never mind."

"Your dad?"

Connor had told her that his father was doing time for killing a man who had abused Stacey. He had glossed over the sordid context, for even as he grew close to Summer there were things he couldn't own up to.

"My sister's finally in rehab," he admitted. "It seems to have worked—as far as rehabs go—but she has nowhere to stay. Her lease was voided and, well, that's it, really." Encumbered by worries, he hadn't had time to decide whether to expect validation or judgment.

"What if you let her use your place? You're on the road so often..."

"And when I'm not? My studio is too small to share."

"You could stay with me." The suggestion was invitingly offhand, but it caught Connor off guard.

"You would do that for me?"

"Who says it's for you?" she teased.

That was what he liked about Summer: her non-judgmental nature; that and her gentleness. "You know, Stacey practically supported me back when—back when dad…" It was his first good cry since his father had been put away.

"Come here," she said soothingly. "You have a good heart; I can feel it. And I bet Stacey does, too."

A deal was struck: Stacey would use his apartment and receive half his paycheck. Political campaigns being all about pitching in, it was nowhere near what an official would call decent pay, but it was enough. In return, Stacey promised to use her time and Connor's money to look for a more lawful, if less munificent, source of income. The other half went towards groceries, which Connor provided for Summer, whose many skills extended to the kitchen. Her small house had a proper dining table, not stools around a counter. The living room had a sofa and a good setup for media viewing. A fish tank, always bubbling, held a pair of angelfish and three mollies. Summer explained that mealtimes reminded her to feed the fish, and after Connor moved in she religiously asked him to drop a pinch of dry flakes in the tank every evening (morning feedings, just as strictly, were hers alone).

"No offense," he said once, "but aren't they boring pets?"

Summer was unfazed. "They liven up the space. Some people have the TV turned on all day; I like fish."

Well, there was no arguing with that.

***

It wasn't Dominic, after all, who left Cassie. Ethan had been wrong on that count. It was her gradual disenchantment that led to the breakup, and not because Pyle had lost any wit or charm, or grown inadequate in bed, or pulled rank on her, or overstepped the bounds of professional decorum in the presence of colleagues. He was guilty of something subtler.

Cassie, at first merely surprised by Pyle's preference for the subway over taxis, was soon rattled by his taste for takeout over proper dining, then embarrassed when he matched housewarming gifts to the recipient's status, and at last offended when he casually alluded to the ticket price for the only concert to which he ever treated her—all part of the endless train of small privations and self-denial that misers, mistaking vice for virtue, call prudence. She wrote it off as a character flaw, missing the general irony of a broken world where people are forced to embrace money-making for the sake of comfort, only to find it eroded by those who embrace discomfort for the sake of money-making.

Although she felt she would sooner die than make a clean breast of it, she considered making up an excuse to visit her parents in California, and letting Ethan know she'd be there. If she didn't, it was because she couldn't conceive how to procure his forgiveness without an actual apology.

Much sooner did the occasion arise to meet an investment banker called Matthias Kiebler, a man as greedy as Pyle but far more of a sybarite. And it was with something close to relief that Pyle learned about it, because while he hadn't quite sated his lust for Cassie, he was self-aware enough to sense that he would soon be hankering after some sexual variety.

One further episode in Cassie's life is perhaps worth relating (spoiler alert). Several years later, four months pregnant and living comfortably in Manhattan—a round accomplishment in her book, which held no room for something as mawkish as bliss—she attended a celebration of the sort enjoyed by Kiebler, namely the closing of a deal that entailed a hefty bonus for himself. Having helped a multinational called Taylor Labs to float a billion's worth of non-voting shares, Kiebler treated his senior team members to dinner at a superb Soho restaurant.

The two VPs and their significant others were good talkers and even better drinkers, so the Château Margaux that Kiebler ordered was drained empty before the main course arrived. The furthest thing from his mind being the tab, Kiebler asked for a second bottle, and they were all tipsy by the time he produced a pad with a recording of the day's market proceedings, which included a short speech from the company's chairman to a jubilant crowd of stockbrokers, analysts and reporters.

"Julian Taylor," he pointed out on the screen to Cassie, "richest man in New York as of today—although the family prodigy is said to be his sister. That's her at the far end: talk about brains *and* beauty," he winked at one of the VPs.

"Next to her is the bastard she married; and there's yours truly, as you can tell from—Cassie, what's wrong? Not the wine, I'm sure. Do you want to lie down? She's expecting, you know," he added for the sake of the rest, who quickly switched from polite concern to polite well-wishing.

But, if the tale be even remotely in the telling, then happy endings are no guarantee of happiness; nor indeed of endings.

SURPRISE

My own suspicion is that the universe is not only queerer than we suppose, but queerer than we *can* suppose.

—J. B. S. HALDANE, *Possible Worlds and Other Papers*

First things first.

Ethan spent days soaking in the acid bath of melancholy that leads to unfinished meals, bad-movie marathons, insomnia, oversleep, neglected stubbles, strewn socks, beds unmade, and the cursing of the world at large and one's lot in particular. Then one Saturday morning the fog cleared from the bay, to be replaced by the sunny skies and blustery air that can bewilder first-time visitors to San Francisco. Whether his self-pity had been depleted or the realization had dawned on him that he'd been through worse and survived, the fact remains that Ethan decided to shower, preen, clean up his apartment, and head out for breakfast. Upon returning he spent the afternoon weighing his options and exploring job vacancies online. On Sunday he went for an early bike ride, and towards noon began wondering whether to cook something or order lunch online. To ease the decision he fixed himself a gin and tonic, garnished with a rind of lime and a sprig of rosemary, lightly singed. He was three sips into it and sitting at his desk when the bell rang—not the chime from the ground-floor entrance, which was usually ajar, but the upstairs buzzer to his apartment.

Ethan had come to detest surprises, which life seemed to dole out with perverse humor, so he was under the spell of mild annoyance when he absent-mindedly pulled open the door to learn that life dispenses joy as irreverently as it steals it. Two feet from him, as fresh and haunting as on the day they had first met, stood that angel and demon from his childhood, Valerie Taylor.

Ethan, forged by grim experience into a very different creature from the boy who idled the summers away in Devon, allowed himself a brazen stare and made no effort to conceal the sigh that welled up in his chest as he broke into the most astonished of smiles. Time froze into a crystal, which he was in no hurry to disturb, so it was Valerie who spoke first, with a soft blush that Ethan had never had the joy of witnessing. "I apologize … for showing up like this. But the thought of calling or writing felt even more awkward." As she talked she kept glancing over his shoulder as if to check whether he had company. This gave him reason enough to dispel her doubts. Stepping forth, he reached for the back of her neck and, as if helping himself to the drink on his desk, he kissed her greedily.

"And I apologize," he said as they both recovered, "for taking so long to return this. But now you must either step in and stay, or leave and never return, so that I can at least pretend I was dreaming."

***

Standing on the threshold of Graciano Yglesias's office, Connor placed a hand on the doorjamb. "Time to call it a day," he said, looking the part of a devoted but tired collaborator.

Yglesias gave a start, like someone caught watching porn. "Turning in?" he asked, his composure quickly regained.

"Yes. Need anything?"

"No, no, I'll be following soon. See you tomorrow."

Connor walked past a meeting room and through the open floor plan where the analysts worked. It was past eight o'clock and, with Wade out of town, everyone had left; except for Yglesias, Connor was the last person on the floor. Someone had switched off the hallway lights and Connor made his way by the light of the elevator lobby at the far end. He brought his badge up to the sensor and the magnetic lock let him out. Riding down to the garage, he recalled the rumor of a second parking level, from which Wade's caravan could come and go unnoticed. There was no button for that floor.

He walked to his car and reached for the door; it didn't unlock. Connor swore aloud, remembering he'd left the key on his desk, and grudgingly began retracing his steps.

Someone's evening was going worse than his own, for the first thing he heard back on the office floor was Yglesias cursing. Connor assumed him to be on the phone, so he furtively walked to his cubicle to fetch the key. As he rounded the workspace again, Yglesias said: "We have to tell him."

"He can't afford distractions right now," argued someone else, and Connor flinched. Wasn't Garfield supposed to be on tour with Wade?

"It will blow up in our face!"

"Calm down and think," said Garfield.

"Pull up the picture again." There was a pause. "Doesn't look like a terrorist; what's his name?"

"Ethan Karahan."

"I can't read Arabic. How do you know it's from Al Faisal?"

"I recognize the handwriting, and he smudged it—but keep it low." His voice was already so soft that Connor barely made out the words.

"Everyone's gone," said Yglesias loudly, and Connor remembered he wasn't supposed to be there. He was about to leave again when Garfield's figure cast a shadow on the corridor. Connor stepped through the nearest door and found himself inside a dark meeting room, holding his breath.

"Just call Ahmed, okay?" warned Yglesias as they walked past the doorway.

"I'm on it."

When Summer asked what had kept him so long, he made something up and slept fitfully. The next day he kept an eye on Yglesias but saw nothing unusual. On Saturday, Summer returned from a morning workout to find Connor engrossed in a game of solitaire. He reached over his shoulder for her hand, held it to his cheek and let go. Summer walked to the bedroom, kicked off her shoes, stopped by the kitchen for a cold drink, and returned to Connor. "Lunch?" she suggested.

"Uh-huh," he said without looking up.

She looked at the screen on his lap. Connor had few cards left in the stock pile; it appeared he would lose the game soon. He always played the hardest version, with four suits, and usually lost.

"You've been obsessing over that," she remarked, and offered him some soda. He took a sip, handed it back, and shifted a card from one column to next.

"There are better games, you know. Have you tried New Music? It's—"

"No!" snapped Connor, looking up at last. "That's a Chinese scam."

"Meh."

"Yglesias has it on good authority. The site is government-sponsored; it taps into users' brainwaves."

"Many games are brainwave-based. Besides, what would it do—send you subliminals to buy Chinese products? We buy enough already."

"No that, but something perverse for sure. You know that high scorers get job offers in Shanghai?"

"Wouldn't a subversive site be outlawed?"

"By the current administration? They're in bed together."

"Now *that* doesn't make any sense."

Connor shrugged, gave her lips a smooch and tossed the pad aside. "I'm starving."

Summer studied him. "You always change the subject when you're hiding something."

He started to deny it but stopped himself midsentence.

"Well?" she urged.

"It's Garfield," he admitted.

"Ugh. What about him?"

"I overheard him talking with Yglesias on Thursday."

"When you were late?"

He nodded. "They thought I was gone. Garfield said someone called Al Faisal had written about a terrorist or something—I think."

Summer's expression changed. "You *think*? Connor, this isn't funny."

"I know it's not."

"What else did he say?"

"That Wade shouldn't be distracted from the campaign, so better not to tell him."

"Did anyone see you?"

"No, I told you: they thought I'd left—the office was empty. Yglesias promised to call a guy called Ahmed. And they were looking at a picture of someone that Yglesias said didn't look like a terrorist, so I assume it's the person they were talking about."

"Ahmed?"

"No, some other guy."

"Did you see the picture?"

Connor shook his head. "What if Wade is in danger?"

"Don't start speculating."

"Who do you think this Ahmed is?"

"Connor, leave it alone. If they think the threat is real they'll tell Wade, or the Secret Service. Stay out of it."

"You don't think they'll hush it up?"

"No. And don't even *think* of bringing it up with Yglesias."

Connor felt he was treading thin ice. Did Summer know something he didn't? Might she even report his indiscretion to Garfield?

"Yeah," he said, "you're probably right."

"Look, when's the fundraiser?"

"Still two weeks to go: when we return from California."

"If anything serious is going on, we will know by then, don't you think?"

"I guess. But Garfield…"

"I know you don't like him."

"But *he's* the one who hates me."

"You think he has time for you? He's running the campaign!"

"He sure tried to talk Wade out of hiring me—the second time around."

"You never told me that. On what grounds?"

"Graciano doesn't know; or won't say. But give me a minute alone with Garfield, and I'll—"

"You stay away from Garfield."

"I'm not afraid of him," said Connor defiantly.

"Then do it for me."

"For you, I'd do anything."

She looked hurt. "You're just saying that."

"No, I mean it."

"Then promise me something: if I'm ever hurt, or suddenly–"

"Why? Who's trying to hurt you?"

"Nobody, just listen! If I'm run over by a bus or something, promise me you'll take the fish with their food mix back to the pet store."

"The fish?! Who gives a shit about—?"

"See?" she pouted. "It should be enough that *I* care."

Connor laughed, disarmed. "All right, cross my heart."

***

With Ethan out of a job and Valerie having no use for one, they ended holed-up in Ethan's place, discovering each other like old flames making up for wasted years. In the time it takes for a rose to bloom they melded into each other and were swallowed by the experience. Slowly at first, then in torrents, they shared the story of their lives.

As the days went by, Ethan found it amusing to see an assistant show up every morning with items that Valerie had requested on her phone. The woman brought groceries; bottles of wine that Ethan thought he'd never taste; new clothes for Valerie, who never asked if he liked the arrangement but carried on with such grace that he didn't think of suggesting otherwise. They once drove to Carmel, and Ethan, slow to catch on to the habit of being chauffeured, insisted on driving. Valerie's complete disregard for the Porsche he'd bought–she carelessly slammed the door shut and turned her attention to the vanity mirror–was a greater compliment than any admiration he'd received from other passengers. In the afternoons he played the piano for her, and sunsets caught them sitting on the terrace, gazing at the ocean.

"Did you ever," she asked one evening, "in all these years, think about that time at Exebridge?" Valerie's voice died away with the last words; Ethan could sense the effort behind them, which he found oddly reassuring.

"If you hadn't shown up at my door," he said, "that stolen kiss in the garden would be the high point of my career."

She smiled bashfully and they stared into the distance. Minutes passed.

"The sea is calming," she said, "even when it storms."

"I had to move to California to find that out. We never lived on the shore in England, and New York beaches make the British coast seem tropical."

"Yes, there's cold and there's frigid. But, where in the world would you live, given a choice?"

"Um ... somewhere warm."

"Warmer than California?"

"Warmer than San Francisco; and drier. Have you been to Sedona?"

"It's lovely, but I'd miss the sea."

"Australia?" he ventured.

"Funny—such an obvious choice. I've never visited."

"Ah, but you must! What about south of here?"

Memories of yachts and scuba gear crossed her mind. Valerie knew she'd enjoy sharing the starlight with him. "Baja is beautiful. Been there?"

"No. We should go there."

For the first time in her life she felt insecure, and it didn't take her long to understand what was happening. But it still came as a surprise, because her friends didn't fall in love: they had relationships.

"Have you enjoyed America? I mean before your mother—" She caught herself, expecting him to tense up, but he didn't.

"Before she died?" he asked.

"Yes."

"New York was like a blur. You know what they say about missing something only when you lose it. But the best was graduate school; to learn like never before, or since. Was that your experience, too?"

"I loved what I did at Cambridge, but I also felt lonely. Of my childhood friends, Natasha never cared to study anything, and others looked down on her for it, but she's the most genuine of the lot—my anchor to the real world, whatever that means. Another was Tony Steinberg, poles apart from Natasha. He specialized in cognitive science and lives in Massachusetts. He's gay; married to a neurologist called Albert Massey."

"I've heard of Massey. Cool stuff."

"Most of my acquaintances were from Tony's group. We took some electives together."

"In cognitive science?"

She shook her head. "I was reading for a degree in philosophy, and it was suggested that I study set theory. I then took topology for fun."

"Well, it's a relief to hear it was fun."

"Why?"

"Let's just say I've got into trouble for sharing the beauty of certain concepts with people."

"Then you'll appreciate an anecdote from a friend of mine. You must know Sunita Chatterjee from B&W."

"We shared some offsite trainings. I didn't know you were friends."

"She gave me your address."

Ethan laughed. "I never imagined I'd owe her so much."

"Anyway, she was once asked what her profession was. Having said she was an actuary, someone then asked in which movies she had starred."

Ethan grinned wryly.

"But what," Valerie pressed on, "were you trying to explain?"

"When?"

"The thing that landed you in trouble."

"Oh, it was about our sense of self, or why we feel like independent beings. Take a finger caught under a falling hammer: it triggers a sensation we call pain. And while we know that our brain does the sensing, it is the finger, not the brain, we feel like nursing—which is just as well, since that's where the bruise will develop. But habit blinds us to a paradox."

"That the pain and its perception occur in different places?"

"In different realms, even. If the world were devoid of sensation except through fingertips, and fingers lacked a mechanical link to the brain but were still able to send out sensations—say, as radio signals—then the brain, unable to feel pain save at fingertips, and unaware of itself as signal processor, would see fingers as independent entities. The pain felt by one wouldn't be shared by the rest, so even if they fed into the same brain, each finger might behave autonomously. In our world, the flesh that connects fingers to brains is held to forestall such illusions. But does it? What we call awareness becomes manifest as a multitude of independent selves. Yet those selves may just be informing an interpreter, itself devoid of selfhood but exceeding awareness in complexity just like a brain exceeds the complexity of pain signals. What if the ultimate engine of existence merely avails itself of awareness but confines it to parts of itself?"

"God as the unaware creator? That's crazy enough to be worth taking seriously."

More time went by, and as she basked in the silence of his company, a question brewed in Ethan's heart.

"Valerie?"

"Hmm."

"You came back into my life so unexpectedly; if lightning were to strike me dead—"

"Don't," she said, holding a finger to his lips in a reflex gesture made before she realized that, this time, the words were fitting and the mood was right.

He held her hand: "I can't help it. I have felt so lost at times that I need to know if you're playing for keeps. Have I found my way home?"

She straddled his lap and grasped his head. "Like you have no idea," she said, and smothered him with kisses.

***

Connor dropped the subject with Summer, and shared nothing with Yglesias, as she feared he might.

His plans had changed.

When he found time to himself he went online and queried the name he'd heard, but wasn't sure of the spelling. He tried 'Ethan Karahan', which produced no results. Could it be Kharahan? Maybe Qarahan? Karahaan? Charahan?

Damn…

He abandoned the task and went out for lunch. The dishes at *Mi Cocina* had always proved inspiring when he struggled to compose one of his diatribes. He almost ordered tortilla soup but on the spur of the moment said: "I'll have the chicken fajitas, please."

The phonetics stuck in his mind. Fah-hee-tas, he rehearsed silently; always a *j* in Spanish when you'd expect an *h*. That reminded him of something he'd read once: Lo-lee-ta, it began, but he couldn't remember the rest—something about the tongue.

But wait! An *h* for a *j,* or the other way around? He pulled out his phone, keyed in *Ethan Karajan,* and presto, several entries appeared from Caltech and Blake & Whitney. Even better, they seemed to refer to the same person. He had never been genuinely proud of himself, but there's always a first time. He tried the social networks and found no pictures (a shame) but did find an unambiguous statement: *based in San Francisco.*

"To deliver documents?" asked Summer when he said Yglesias had asked him to stay an extra day in California. "Why doesn't he send a scan?"

"I didn't ask." He was a poor liar, but it worked.

"No, of course you couldn't," she agreed. Wade had his quirks, and this was the least of them.

Saturday morning found him sitting in a rental car on El Camino del Mar, where he had parked around daybreak. Nice place, he'd repeated to himself a dozen times, trying to stay awake after the rush of adrenalin had abated. The sun was up; the light good; the zoom on his phone set to max. He had taken some snapshots already: of a jogger, a woman and her dog, a delivery crew, a fancy car that drove by.

He fought off boredom with loud music pumped through a headset, so even with the window down he didn't hear the car door shut a few yards away, nor did he notice the picture taken of his face by the smartly dressed man that strolled down the sidewalk next to him, phone held casually at one side, then again held in front as if looking up something—a man with a much longer history of keeping an eye on others.

Roughly around nine, the door he was watching opened to let out an old man on an errand. Disappointed, he took a picture anyway. Ten minutes later the door opened again.

Gosh, the girl was stunning!

But Connor didn't lose sight of his target. One, two, three snapshots he took of the couple as they strode to the car that he'd missed earlier. They boarded, the driver put two carry-on pieces in the trunk, and they left.

A day's work done, Connor drove to the airport and was home by evening, with no one the wiser.

***

At the FBI, while they waited, Ressler and Kane discussed the coming election. He knew where Kane stood on the issue, so Ressler didn't bother walking on eggshells.

"Why are democracies so easily seduced by radicals?" he griped.

Kane looked askance at him. "Are you just venting?"

"No, I'd really like to know."

"Well, there's a good thesis I read once, a thousand pages of it."

"Did it have an executive summary?"

Kane gestured as if to say, if you will.

"People," she confided, "don't support what someone says, but *why* it is said. When they are led, by means foul or fair, to believe they've been cheated—that what is rightfully theirs has been squandered, stolen, or diminished by others—they fall for promises of restitution. Only if they happen to be close enough to bureaucracy, or perceptive enough to see through it, do they realize that administrations are weaker than they seem; that the financial and political hurdles are too numerous for drastic change; that social behavior, not that of its officials, is to blame for a nation's problems. The bulk of an electorate believes that governments are, or should be, able to impose their will. And they mistake sobriety for weakness or, what is worse, for self-interest. Of old they would clamor for a fearless king. Today, what they long for is dictatorship. They forget that dictators impose themselves not just when required but at every opportunity. And by the time a nation is wrecked, it's too late."

Ressler didn't like the thesis. It made the drives and motives of mankind ring desperately hollow, more suggestive of taxonomy than of politics. (*This self-aware organism, unique for its ability to make the world less unfair, acts instead like the creatures it belittles, constantly vying for sex and dominance.*) But he could readily picture half his family behaving like that, despised by the other half.

"Ah, here we go," said Kane, as Emilio Balderas arrived with Lou Hayes in tow.

"Check this out," Balderas declared without preamble, "Lou here gets a call from the coroner—the *retired* coroner—of the eighty-first Brooklyn precinct, who says he remembers Jane Doe, but claims she was a victim, not a perp. Now, the good man is in his dotage and has seen a fair number of bodies—right?—so who can say how reliable his memory is. But we look at the precinct records and, sure enough, a female gunshot victim was taken to the medical examiner two days after the Lebanese reception." Balderas laid a post-mortem picture on the table. The features matched Fatima Shadid's.

Kane was perplexed. "The woman was offed, too?"

"That's what I thought, until Lou started asking questions—just doing his job, you know," he smiled at his colleague.

"The shooting," explained Hayes, "involved two women. Same medical examiner, same lab tests, everything. The first had her face blown to bits, so no ID was possible; the body was never claimed. This was the second," he pointed at the photograph. "Name was Nadia Karajan, a long-time Brooklyn resident, not someone just arrived from Cairo. What's more, the ages don't match, because Shadid was supposed to be younger. The police report begins with a call for help from this woman," Hayes again pointed at the table, "saying she's killed an intruder. Her son is heard arriving while she's on the phone, which means there were no witnesses to the shooting. Another call is then made by him, and dispatch keeps him on the line until the police arrive, by which point the woman is dead."

"Who is her son?" asked Ressler.

"Ethan Karajan: British immigrant, early twenties, clean file. He lives in San Francisco."

"Wait—so is Karajan the woman's married name?"

"Unknown father; the last name's hers."

"Interesting," said Ressler. "Let's track the guy, but don't get him spooked."

"Yeah, that's what Havelock said."

"Where *is* Havelock?" asked Kane.

"In the Pentagon," Balderas answered, "double-checking something, because the story gets better. The bodies were long gone, but coroners always keep DNA from murder cases, so we asked for samples and checked the file for previous matches, because we thought we'd found our killer but now we had our doubts. There was no match on either woman, so Jane Doe was still Jane Doe. But Havelock," here Balderas looked at Kane significantly, as if gauging her reaction to what he would say next, "Havelock wanted to know if their DNAs had been matched against *each other*. Turns out they hadn't, so the lab ran the test—"

"Don't tell me they're related," ventured Ressler, incredulous.

Balderas grinned like someone sharing a joke. "Same person."

"I don't get it. Tampering?"

"No, their blood was processed separately by different technicians at different times; seals unbroken."

"But that," said Kane, who was just as stunned as Ressler, "only happens with twins, or…"

"Exactly," said Balderas. "Two people, different ages, same DNA—but Havelock is pinging me. Is that thing working?" he asked Ressler, who turned on the device in question. Balderas entered a code on his phone and Vance Havelock appeared seated at the table, his shape blending awfully with Kane's. "Sorry, wrong seat," she said, and they laughed as she scooted over.

"We see you clearly now, colonel."

"I can confirm they were clones," Havelock began. "And the police had it right: the victim was the older one. The blood proves it. The victim's is clean; the other has traces of Karam's virus. She's the killer."

"Thank you, colonel," said Ressler. "This certainly narrows down the scope of our investigation, even if it leads to new questions. Only thing intrigues me. You had a hunch about this development, did you not? Would you mind shedding some light for the rest of us here?"

***

When Valerie told her mother about her rediscovery of Ethan and its pleasant sequel, Odette couldn't help but wish them well. While she had never met the young man, nor was fully aware of the context behind their shared history, her experience in love (and its absence) had taught her how rare it is to find a soulmate when social milieu and individual temperament stand in the way. Odette offered to host them in France, so they dutifully flew over, allowing the mother to validate her daughter's taste in men.

Informing Julian was a different story. Valerie called him with the excuse of asking for the family yacht for a trip to Baja California, but also to preclude any gossip. The siblings had been on cool terms with each other since their father's death, when Taylor, while leaving a billion more of his net worth to Julian, had allotted a slight majority of the empire's voting shares to Valerie, a decision deemed no less sagacious by the board (in public) than its new chairman judged idiotic (in private), furious at his sister's having preyed on the old man's frailty to sway his dying wishes in her favor. Julian's outlook on life had matured since Devon, but he still found no reason to hold back from qualifying the romance as *une liaison absurde*. "He's after your money can't you see," he reproved, though in the end agreed to lend the cruiser.

PERFIDY

Man is the Only Animal that Blushes. Or needs to.

—MARK TWAIN, *Following the Equator*

Around mid-morning the lobby was quiet. The receptionist, lamb-faced, gazed at the man who walked up to the desk. "Special Agent Louis Hayes," he said, flashing his badge.

She didn't blink.

"I need information about a former employee."

"Karajan?" she inquired, turning her attention back to her computer screen as if the question were rhetorical.

"What?" asked Hayes, like someone whose trousers have dropped to the floor.

"Oh, I'm sorry. I thought this was about Ethan Karajan."

"Has someone asked about him?" Hayes felt increasingly foolish with every question.

"Um, twice. Two weeks ago a delivery service asked for his address, then last Tuesday—no, Wednesday—the police came, and—"

"Hold on," interrupted Hayes, pointing at a camera globe on the ceiling. "How many days of footage do you keep?"

This time the girl did blink. "Uh, I'm not sure… Shall I call security?"

"If you don't mind." Hayes sounded crushed.

***

It promised to be a swell evening. The event would begin in the ballroom at seven, and the Secret Service was already manning the elevators when a message from Graciano Yglesias requested all participating staff to convene for prepping. No waiters were present, but forty glasses with small amounts of wine sat on the conference table. Mindless of protocol, some people had begun sipping.

Connor looked excited as he drew Summer aside, whispering, "is Garfield on his way?"

"I think so. Why?"

"Nothing, I had a chat with Graciano."

She looked alarmed.

"About the wine," he added mysteriously before turning to greet someone.

When Garfield appeared Yglesias shut the door. "Okay everyone, listen up. Let's begin with a toast. Everyone have a glass?" Most didn't, so he waited for all to equip themselves.

"To *America Wins*. Bottoms up!" Glasses were drained. "You too," he prodded Garfield, and looked pointedly at Connor while the other complied. "All done? Good. Now let me explain what we're doing here."

"Keep an eye on Garfield," said Connor. Summer replied with another worried look.

An hour earlier, Connor had been the first person in the room with Yglesias, who had handed him a glass. "This is what we'll serve upstairs," he had said. "Can you help me pour?"

"It's excellent," said Connor, and began the task.

"A great vintage," agreed his boss. "Now, it has come to our attention that in spite of every precaution, the government—or someone working for it—has infiltrated our lines."

Connor stopped pouring.

"We have a mole in our headquarters," said Yglesias. "An informant. What's more, an extrasomic."

"But the blood tests," said Connor, "isn't that what—?"

"Oh, you and I are above suspicion. Why do you think we're having this conversation? Keep going, we need a taste in every glass." Yglesias moved to the next row of glasses as he spoke. "When the campaign scaled up, we were forced to accept medical records. With our staff ballooning, we didn't have the bandwidth to run the test in house—at least that's what Garfield said. And at the time, I concurred."

"Garfield," echoed Connor. Then he suddenly said: "I know you're close, but would you vouch for him?"

"For Garfield?" Yglesias sounded genuinely surprised. "Why shouldn't I? He has more at stake in this than anyone."

"He's also best positioned to make it fail."

"Hmm, that's an odd thought..." Yglesias set the bottle on the table and placed his hands on his hips. "But if I suspected his motives, how would I catch him?"

Connor hadn't the faintest idea. "You could mandate a retest," he suggested, determined to say something.

"Then Garfield could walk out of the building and I'd have no proof, nor any way of knowing who was behind the infiltration."

"Right."

Yglesias now retrieved his glass and swirled the wine. "But, here's another way." He took a sip and swallowed with significance.

Connor looked at him, then at the liquid he'd been drinking.

"The wine we just had," Yglesias explained to the gathered staff, "is not just smooth or complex or expensive—though it's all of that. It will allow us to play a game of 'gotcha' with the lobbyists this evening. Because while our rules forbid extrasomics from joining our party or even entering this building, I am sad to say that corporate interests have weaseled their way into our ranks with a deceitful, disgraceful, extrasomic spy," he spat out.

The room became awfully quiet.

"The good news," Yglesias continued, "is that extrasomy can be flushed out. And I do mean flushed, because the presence of extrasomes in a person's cells" (here he again raised his glass, now empty, as if for another toast) "reacts in the space of five minutes—quite harmlessly—to an odorless chemical in this wine, by bringing color to the cheeks of impostors."

People looked down at their glass. A few placed it back on the table. Murmurs went around the room. And Connor scrutinized Garfield, who was in turn fixed on Yglesias with an unmistakable expression of *you've got to be kidding me!*

But Yglesias didn't return Garfield's gaze, for he was looking in Connor's direction.

No, not at him, precisely, but—

"Ms. O'Keefe! You seem to be feeling unwell this evening."

"I'm fine," Summer answered, tremulous.

She turned to Connor for confirmation, but his stare was already locked on her, horrified. Her cheekbones, nose and ears showed well-demarcated areas of pigmentation, like a raspberry pregnancy mask. She looked about, frightened, then touched a hand to her face. "Oh God," she whispered. Space formed around her as others distanced themselves. Yglesias now looked at Connor.

Summer made for the door and people moved out of her way.

Garfield, however, caught her by the arm. "My team, my responsibility," he declared with the emotion of a cadaver. "I will see her out."

Connor looked on helplessly as others looked away, embarrassed. She turned back only once. *The fish*, he read from her lips, adding a final touch to a surreal scene.

Connor turned to Yglesias. "I—I don't—I never—" he babbled.

"I know," Yglesias said drily. "Make no fuss and stay here until the function is over and I have a word with Wade. I'll post a guard outside." He then looked around at the thirty-odd people who were staring wide-eyed at the scene. Yglesias took his time, eyeing them all in turn. In the end he nodded and allowed himself a grim smile. "This hasn't been our finest day, but I'm glad that everyone else here is loyal and true. Thank you for that. Let's keep it up—and not a word about this, even to one another. Although," he smiled bleakly, "you can safely enjoy the wine. Let's go: time to head upstairs."

Alone in the room, Connor slunk off to a corner and, over the three longest hours of his life, refrained from turning to the only substance at hand—an otherwise perfectly good merlot—to keep his wits about him. At ten, the door opened to let Wade in, followed by Yglesias. As the senator's Old-Testament figure approached, Connor tried to read the man's expression, a task as futile now as ever. Would he be fired on the spot? Shown out of the building like Summer?

The hand that landed on Connor's shoulder suggested otherwise.

"She had us all fooled," said Wade. "I told Garfield you could hardly be involved. But given the circumstances, well, you understand. Let this be a lesson for the future: the enemy is everywhere; we cannot let our guard down."

Connor nodded. At least he wasn't being kicked out.

What followed was less encouraging. "I doubt she will dare to contact you, but you'll have an escort assigned just in case. Keep a low profile, stick to your work, and don't speak with anyone until after the election. Can I trust you with that?"

"Yes sir."

He was on probation, then—so much for forgiveness. And Yglesias added insult to injury by sharing the details of the arrangement, for the appointed guard wasn't Secret-Service grade, but one of Garfield's goons; a gorilla of a man known simply as Noah.

"You were staying at her house?" asked Yglesias.

Connor hung his head.

"You can't return there. Do you have a place of your own?"

"My sister is using it."

Yglesias nodded. "That's probably just as well; it could be bugged. Valenzuela will supply an apartment."

"What about my … stuff?"

Yglesias grimaced. "How fast can you collect it?"

"Fifteen minutes."

"We'll scout her place; Noah can drive you tomorrow if the coast is clear."

When they arrived before noon the next day the street was quiet. Someone was parked across from Summer's house and gave them an all-clear sign. "Fifteen minutes," said Noah and Connor stepped out.

It soon became clear that she hadn't returned: the bed was unmade and the kitchen was in the state he'd left it. He crammed his belongings into a duffel bag and returned to the foyer. The house felt eerily quiet; the only movement came from the bubbling aquarium.

The fish.

He felt sudden fury well up inside him. "I'll take care of the fish alright," he muttered, stepping forward.

He kicked the tank hard with the outer edge of his heel. The glass shattered, letting the water out through a half-moon gash. Two liquid inches remained, barely enough for the mollies. The angelfish were less fortunate: both flopped helplessly on the floor.

He had never seen a fish gasp for oxygen, and as their tiny gills pulsated his rage turned to remorse. He reached down, picked them up by their tails and dropped them into what was left of water. He fetched a plastic container from the kitchen, set it next to the glass and tilted the tank's contents, fish and all, into it. He sealed the top and retrieved the food tin from the shelf.

Noah was surprised to see him carry back to the car what looked like a ration of soup. "Is that what we came for?" he asked.

Connor begged him to drive to the pet store, where he learned he had to pay for the fish to be taken off his hands. This made his blood boil again, and it gave him sudden pleasure that Summer might, after all, think he'd killed them. As he handed the food over, something jiggled inside the tin—a paper with a phone number in Summer's handwriting.

He nearly tossed it away, but on second thought stuffed it into his jacket.

***

Ressler called it progress. At least now they had a proper manhunt to conduct, something they were used to. Balderas was less sanguine, voicing his frustration at being third in what was now an open race. He had posted lookouts outside Karajan's address, but there had been no sightings. He was also worried that his source in Wade's team had been unusually silent. But things were indeed coming together: a week's worth of camera footage (all they had) yielded a good view of the police impersonators. They were both in their thirties, with Mediterranean looks and a professional demeanor. National Security was duly notified and the video was given to the imaging team.

The Feds had braced for a long wait, so they were doubly thrilled when news came in the next morning that one of the faces was on Homeland Security's no-fly list.

At General McGrath's request they convened with Colonel Havelock in the Pentagon.

Well before the general's arrival, Larissa Kane confirmed the unsub's identity as an Al Faisal partisan. "Which is both good and bad," she added. "Their boldness suggests they had no time to waste, so the trail is hot. But it also denotes confidence. I'd be surprised if these two are still in the country."

"Why would they leave?" asked Ressler.

"If they're gone," interjected Balderas before Kane could reply, "they won't be using their real names." He glanced dejectedly at Hayes, who had been busy online during the conversation.

The young agent felt everyone's eyes on him and looked up. "I was looking for Karajan on the TSA system. He's made little effort to hide: went to France for two weeks, flying commercial, then on a private jet to Baja California."

"Private jet!" exclaimed Ressler. "What is he—a drug lord?"

"If we found him this quickly," Kane said, "then so can Al Faisal. We've been given a break but need to move soon."

This ignited an argument over agency jurisdiction, and over who should take the next flight out to Mexico, which was Kane's natural space. Ressler and Havelock opposed bringing foreign-stationed officers into the fray, but Kane reminded them how little they knew of what they were up against and argued for using local eyes and ears in case Al Faisal was still ahead.

Havelock agreed, but privately worried that they'd heard nothing of the Chinese, or from them. "Something doesn't add up," he said. "If Karajan is related to killers who worked for Al Faisal, then why are they after him?"

"Treason, betrayal, rogue behavior—take your pick," volunteered Kane.

"When was he naturalized?" asked Havelock.

"Four years ago," said Balderas.

"That's too recent," said Havelock, his eyes still on Balderas, "to gain the trust of someone like Al Faisal. You know I'm a fan of the Bureau's checks, but have you checked Karajan's background?"

"It's squeaky clean."

"He could be Al Faisal's quarry," suggested Havelock. "But hunted men keep a low profile."

"Maybe he doesn't know he's being tracked," said Kane. "But I agree we're missing something."

At this point McGrath arrived. Informed of their findings, he sided with Kane, but was frank about his concerns. "This is no routine engagement, Larissa. I am familiar with your field work, but you have a family now, so I'm asking you straight: are you up to doing this yourself?"

She nodded.

"Very well, then, you will lead the task. But things can get ugly down there, and diplomatic channels are out of the question. I'm sending Havelock with you."

"I want in," griped Ressler.

"Of course you do, but we can't have a delegation. I will allow one of yours."

Balderas and Hayes started to speak over each other; Ressler raised a hand and they shut up. He studied them quickly: the experienced, slightly overweight father of two; the eager, fit, unattached young man.

"Lou will go," he said.

DISTRESS

For I had yet to learn that happiness can neither be achieved nor held by endeavour.

—GAVIN MAXWELL, *Ring of Bright Water*

It began smoothly enough. The yacht picked them up at San Felipe and they sailed south, stopping at places Valerie remembered fondly, swimming with whales, catching Humboldt squid at night, enjoying local food in small fishing ports. The weather was spectacular. After several days along the Bay of Angels they crossed the gulf to Tiburón island, where they were surprised to spot foxes and sheep. Their best dives were off Loreto's harbor, behind Carmen island, where the waters hold vast amounts of sea life.

But idylls take their name from the not-so-pleasant events they lie next to, and as they neared the tip of the peninsula Ethan began to feel sick. He first took his malaise for disagreement with a dish of crustaceans, but when gastric symptoms didn't show up and other, recognizable ones did, he began worrying in earnest. This was not the sudden onslaught of the strangeness he had experienced before, but a slow-onset variant of the feeling. He hid it from Valerie for as long as he could, but by the time they moored at Cabo San Lucas, shortly after dawn, Ethan's misery was obvious.

"Shall I fetch a doctor?" she asked.

Ethan looked at her helplessly. "Won't do any good. Remember I told you about a … sensation I get sometimes? I thought it was gone, but it's back, like a ghost that's caught up with me."

"Can you describe it for me?"

"It's like a nagging sense of something being wrong."

"Wrong with you?"

"Wrong with the world."

"Like a gut feeling?"

"Except that gut feelings are about something, and this is devoid of an object. Imagine reality progressing along its accustomed track, then unexpectedly jumping into the wrong groove."

"No source, then?"

"No. It's maddeningly unspecific. But it had always hit like a thunderbolt and now it crept up slowly, as if making up its mind to strike. Now it grows stronger by the hour."

"Why didn't you tell me this before?"

"I had to make sure that it had nothing to do with—" His expression was piteous, all self-confidence gone.

"With me? With us?"

"I was afraid for your sake; afraid that my presence was putting you in danger."

"And if that were so, would you be able to tell?"

"I thought I might. I considered leaving—making up some excuse to leave you alone for a while. It wouldn't be first time that a mental change of plans relieved the feeling. Except this time it didn't. I thought of us both returning to San Francisco, but that didn't help either."

"Does the feeling change with your state of mind, then?"

"Not with its state, but sometimes it changes with my resolve."

This prompted Valerie to bring up something she had long wanted to share with Ethan but had never found a moment ripe enough for. And that was how the matter that had lain unspoken between them was finally addressed. She told Ethan about her conversation with Tony, about the Prometheus module and the Beta complement.

"Do you think," she asked, "this could explain your experience?"

Ethan was fidgety, confused, feeling ill. What she said made sense, but he didn't trust himself enough for interoceptive judgments. "I thought I wasn't extrasomic," he said.

"Did Nadia ever hint that you were?"

"I honestly don't think she knew."

Valerie looked steadily at him. "There's a way to find out."

"Sure, genetic profiling."

"No, I mean to find out right now. Do you have a New Music account?"

He shook his head. “I once thought of signing up—” Ethan suddenly recalled something.

“What is it?”

“The strangeness: I felt it before opening the account that time, so I didn’t follow through.”

“And does it hit you again now if you think about playing the game?”

“No, but then I’m feeling it regardless.”

“Hold on,” she said, and fetched a laptop and a headset. Valerie sat next to him and logged on. “Now,” she said, handing both to Ethan, “try it.”

He put the headset on, read the instructions and tried to focus. He felt no better and no worse.

“The username says ‘Valerietaylor123’. Does it think I’m you?”

“The account is mine, but the system is brainwave-driven. That’s the whole point.”

Ethan took the headset off. Was it wise to use her account? He considered postponing the exercise, but felt no relief.

“What’s wrong?” asked Valerie. He shook his head and put the visor back on. He was given an option: spatial or analytical ladder? A help menu showed some examples; one look made it clear that spatial was the way to go.

He started playing. The scenarios were trivial, and gave him access to songs he’d never heard before. He removed the headset to report his progress and the music stopped. Valerie informed him he would have to start over. “That’s why you can’t play for someone else,” she explained.

He restarted and breezed through the first, second, and third levels. He read the messages from the system aloud to Valerie, who pressed his arm encouragingly. The fourth level was more interesting; ten minutes passed; he wasn’t sure she was still there until her hand reassured him.

The fifth level at last brought a challenge: directionless paths, timelines that turned back on themselves but were different at every go. He failed, tried again, and succeeded. His new score was displayed: 127.

Ethan expected congratulations and new music options, but instead the view in his headset turned blue, as in a system crash, except that instead of gibberish the message said: *This is not part of NM. Your location is known. On a different device, log into highbetascore.com/ with your username after the slash.*

He read the text aloud and was startled when Valerie tore off the VR from his face. "That was stupid of me," she said, with a worry on her face that was different from the sympathy shown so far.

For Ethan, however, the reprieve was unmistakable. He suddenly felt better. She was glad to hear that but remained unconvinced. "Suppose we went ashore for a walk. Do you feel it worsening?"

He concentrated. "No."

"Then let's go. Keep talking to me; I'll try to think of something."

They ambled down the pier, Valerie supporting him like she would an old man. Iannis, her bodyguard, followed them at a distance, within sight but out of earshot.

Ethan described for Valerie every episode he remembered of the strangeness, including the darkest one before Nadia's death. Valerie struggled to find a common thread. They entered the yacht club and washed down some freshly-baked *conchas* with weak coffee before strolling on.

They crossed the marina gateway, and that was when Ethan abruptly tightened his grip. "It's here," he gasped. "Whatever is going to happen is happening now."

Valerie could only stare at him, spooked. "What do I do?" She felt Ethan tremble as he weighed his options like a man with a gun pointed at his face.

"Don't follow me," he growled and ran along the wharf away from her.

Iannis sensed that something was amiss and began trotting towards Valerie, in no great haste, for he could see no danger.

A windowless van screeched to a halt next to Ethan. The side door slid open and two men dashed out. Ethan avoided a collision as they skirted around him; by the time he realized their intent he was surrounded.

He reacted when one grabbed at his shoulder. Leaning into the tug he shot out a foot at the second assailant, but as the man fell back on the pavement Ethan received a crushing blow to his neck, and his legs buckled. He struck out blindly towards the blow, then felt a jab in his side and a burning sensation. On his knees, dizzy from the wallop, he caught the wrist that held the needle and landed a punch. The man fell back; Ethan staggered to his feet but was pushed down by the first aggressor. He tried to wriggle free but felt his strength fading. Straining to turn around he caught sight of a third man emerging from the driver's seat, and as he wondered why they all looked Chinese he lost consciousness.

They carried him to the dock by the arms and legs. At the end of a pontoon someone triggered a powerboat ignition and studied them urgently. Valerie cried for help and waved frantically, but Iannis held her back.

"No," he insisted as she struggled, "they are armed."

The men had reached the boat.

"Then *you* do something!" she screeched, pushing an elbow into his chest. Iannis scoped the group and Valerie was about to yell again when a different cry sounded out from the far end of the marina.

Two coastguard officers were sprinting towards the waterfront, followed by three Americans in civilian clothes, all carrying handguns. "Alto! Policía!" bellowed the man leading the chase.

The Chinese dumped Ethan into the craft and jumped aboard. The pilot reached between the seats for an automatic rifle and sprayed a burst. The Mexican in the lead collapsed on the dock, his gun clattering on the boardwalk to plunge into the harbor. The others took cover—behind a sailboat, next to a dumpster or, in Havelock's case, behind a squat mooring-post, which left his body half-exposed. Hayes returned fire but his shots went wide.

The powerboat veered for a channel between the yachts and made its way to sea. Havelock sat up, rested his arm on the bollard and fired a single, careful shot. One man on the boat slumped forward, but was pushed overboard, allowing the craft to gain speed. Havelock fired again and missed. The boat had slipped out of range.

"This way!" called the second coastguard officer, dashing to a patrol boat moored on the same dock as Valerie's yacht. Havelock followed, with Hayes and Kane close behind. In the runaway boat one of Ethan's captors requested instructions. He then stooped for a medical kit and drew blood from Ethan's neck.

"Now what?" he yelled into the phone, and tucked the vial into his jacket.

They were all heading for open sea. The coastguard officer snarled orders into a receiver.

"Reinforcements?" asked Kane.

The Mexican nodded, then jerked his head at the horizon. "No land ahead," he yelled into the wind. "They won't get far."

Havelock studied the craft they were trailing. It was of military make and easily able to outrun its pursuers; but the seas were choppy, allowing the patrol boat to sit lower in the water and slowly gain on the lighter craft, which risked tipping over if it went any faster. He glanced back at the receding land, and saw a larger vessel sluggishly leaving port. By the time it caught up, the show would be over one way or another. They were now a hundred yards from the Chinese, and his worries shifted away from the absence of providential rescue to the immediacy of resumed bullet sprays, when a very different sight drew his attention back over the bow.

The sea in front had swollen up to part, Moses-like, above the waves. "Holy mother of God," he muttered appropriately, as a dark shape took form, shedding white saltwater from its flanks to rise ten feet above the surface, crowned by an even taller tower. The boats instinctively eased on the throttle.

"No!" shouted Kane. "It's now or we lose them." Reluctantly, the pilot accelerated again. "Try to ram them," she instructed, and as the Mexican veered to intercept, Kane took aim and fired.

She hit the Chinese pilot in the head and the speedboat began drifting. The leader shrieked into the mouthpiece, then barked an order. His accomplice grabbed the gun and began firing while the other jumped overboard and swam for the submarine. Hayes, sitting fore and left, took a round in the face and toppled overboard. Havelock and Kane ducked behind their seats while the pilot crouched as low as his robust physique allowed.

The boats were now twenty yards apart. "Jump before we hit," yelled Havelock, and plunged into the waves. Too late, the Asian tried to pull the dead pilot from his seat, but the patrol boat rammed them starboard side, breaking the man's neck with the impact and flipping the two boats over.

Bodies were flung out to sea. Havelock covered the distance in a few strokes and dived under the flotsam. He emerged dragging Karajan by the chin. In the dead-engine silence, a helicopter could be heard drawing near. A hatch opened on the submarine and an armed seaman appeared, followed by a female officer.

The coastguard boat floated upside down between Havelock and the submarine. He hung onto the broken hull, keeping Karajan's head above water. Slowly, he inched his way until he could peer out behind the broken stern. He recognized Lin Mei Hsieh on the sub's deck. Divers met the Chinese swimmer, stuck a regulator in his mouth and took him under.

Kane was still trying to reach the patrol boat. A few strokes ahead swam the coastguard pilot. Hsieh addressed the seaman, who shouldered his rifle. A pop came from the Mexican's head and his body floated face down in the water. Kane took a quick breath and dived.

The helicopter was now upon them; Hsieh wheeled around and disappeared belowdecks, followed by the seaman. Havelock felt the wind from the rotor on his face as the submarine submerged. He waved and a rescuer was lowered on a winch. The man reached the water and swam towards him with a harness and a life vest. Still some feet away, he tossed the gear and pointed at Ethan. Havelock wasn't one to rush to judgments, but the rescuer didn't look Mexican.

"U.S intelligence," he shouted as he slipped his arms into the vest.

Once buoyant, he strapped Karajan's body into the harness. "Ready," he signaled with a thumbs-up. The rescuer clipped his harness to Ethan's and they were hoisted aloft. Havelock waited for them to be helped aboard. Then another face peered out of the chopper and Havelock waved again, but was greeted by the barrel of a rifle pointed down at him.

He slipped his arms out of the vest and sank below the spray. His arms clawed desperately at the sea, but the drag of his clothes held him barely two feet beneath the surface. As he stared into the depths a swirl next to his ear was followed by the bubbly trail of a projectile tearing its way into the abyss. He was trying a second breaststroke when he felt a kick in the back as a bullet cut through his body and into the ocean, leaving a bright-red trail that felt warm against his chest.

His lower body went limp and he floated back to the surface, face down in the swells. A wave pushed him against the overturned boat, and an odd indifference came over him. He recalled accounts of men who had been shot—some had reported blinding pain; others none at all. The next shot would finish the job; he pictured sharks claiming his body.

Then he was sinking. The upturned boat rose above his head and moved on top of his head, as if to swallow him. He broke through the surface again, into a twilit air-pocket under the hull, surrounded by debris and upside-down seats. Larissa Kane held him by the collar. He tried to smile but water sloshed into his mouth and he coughed up foamy blood. Kane raised a finger to her ear. "They've left," she said encouragingly.

Havelock listened through labored breathing. The whine of the rotor was weakening. Presently they heard a boat engine, and Kane prepared to head back out. Havelock shook his head but lacked the strength to avoid being pulled under. Water rushed up his nostrils and he thought he would choke, but within seconds the sun shone on his face. The coastguard lowered a dinghy for them, and Havelock wondered if he might actually make it. Like someone dozing while watching a movie, he passed out.

RECOURSE

Prove to me that you're divine: change my water into wine.

—TIM RICE, *Jesus Christ Superstar*

For someone used to a sheltered existence, the experience of raw, primal fear is like the opening of a portal to hell. It can happen by accident, as when a surgeon learns that a patient has died from a needle mislaid inside a closed incision; or when a policeman realizes that the shadowy figure he has just shot was a child; or when a mother sees her baby's stroller plunge in front of a commuter train because her back was turned (an event captured at least once on video). The feelings unleashed make all previous sensations—anger, love, jealousy, desire, joy, frustration, the pain of broken bones—seem like nothing against the stomach cramps, the palpitations, the yearning to crawl out of one's skin and unwind the clock to undo the unendurable, the need to erase the awful emotional freight that suffocates the soul.

So it is with stranger abduction, which submerges victim and bereaved in a pool of agony, where they must remain for the duration. Valerie wished the world to put on a show on a par with her distress: police, cavalry, marine troops—nothing would have seemed excessive.

In contrast, the bureaucratic visit from the local authorities, for whom her life-altering event was something they would rather put behind before lunchtime (they promised to open an 'investigation') all contributed to the otherworldly aura of the situation. She shut herself in the master suite of the yacht and sat on the edge of the bed, shaking.

Even there she wasn't left to her thoughts for long.

Should they leave port? enquired the skipper. Did she want her jet flown in from California?

"We're staying put," she answered curtly.

Though she hardly knew what benefit it might bring, she felt the need to be alone, so when another knock came a few minutes later she pulled the door open with impatience: "What!"

It was Iannis, looking contrite.

"This may be unrelated," he explained, "but some days before embarking I spotted someone on the street, scoping out your—uh—Ethan's place."

"What?! Why didn't you tell me?"

"Because it wasn't the first time something like that happened. I assumed a paparazzo was trying to get a shot, so I took a picture of him instead."

Valerie wiped an angry tear off her cheek. "And?"

"I sent them to a friend who runs pictures through the system, and I just got this back." He produced a phone with the image of a young man sitting in a car in San Francisco. A caption had been added over it, with the name Connor Dashaw and a Chicago address.

"Give me that." She grabbed the device and locked herself in again, suddenly grieving for her father. He would have been the one to call at that moment. Not the sick, worried person he became in the end but the strong, confident presence from her childhood, the man who reminded her so much of—

"Julian!" she cried into the phone.

"Valerie, what's wrong?"

"It's Ethan," she sobbed.

"My god… What has he done?"

"Nothing—he was abducted."

"Come on! In Mexico?"

"Yes. Some men took him out to sea, but then a helicopter—"

"Whoa! Where are you? Are you safe?"

"Yes, yes, I'm fine. It's him they were after, not me."

"Of course not. You're the one they'll want money from."

"Julian, you're not listening! This *isn't* a ransom thing."

"Says who?"

She went through the morning's events, from their walk along the pier up to the picture just received from Iannis.

"All right," he said in a calmer tone, "how can I help?" His voice was so much like his father's that she could almost picture the old man on the other end.

"You can call your friends in the Bureau."

There was a pause.

"My friends?" Julian had quickly become less placating. "Surely you don't mean Clarence Leigh, *the* Director of *the* FBI?"

"Yeah, whomever."

"*Mais tu rigoles, Valérie!?* What am I supposed to say—that my sister's fiancé has been kidnapped in Los Cabos, so will he please mobilize every federal agent to find him?"

"Yes! Why wouldn't you do me that simple favor?"

"Oh, Valerie…"

"I see," she said drily, as her misery overcame her impatience. "Let me speak in a language you'll understand. Here's the deal: you contact the Feds, or take whatever action leads to Ethan's safe return, and I will sign away, not just the one percent you need to control Taylor Labs, but half of my entire stake in the company. That's two billion dollars, Julian."

His voice, when he answered, was raspy and reluctant. "Listen, you're obviously not yourself right now. Why don't you fly over to New York, where we can—"

"No!" she yelled. "You either take my offer now and keep your end of the bargain, or never speak to me for the rest of your fucking life."

The pause was longer, and for a moment she thought he'd hung up on her. Had she empathized with the narrow range of feelings that ruled his heart, she would have sensed a blend of pity, for a sister beside herself with anguish, and envy, of being able to love someone—anyone—more than all the money in the world.

"I'll do it," he said.

Years later, as an old man, he would wonder why this, the greatest triumph of his career, had always tasted like defeat.

The exchange provided an outlet for Valerie's pain, but did little to assuage it. She was soon lying back on the bed, her upper teeth carving marks into her lip as she confronted the slow torture that lay ahead. She would now have to call her mother, before Julian did. As she meditated on this, Valerie realized that it was her grandfather she missed most. The old Frenchman would have found a way to comfort her, if only by pulling out something from his pocket; maybe a wasp that fed on spiders…

She bolted upright. On the table outside her cabin lay the headset as they had left it that morning.

When she logged onto the website, several numbers appeared. They were coordinates, followed by words. *This is your location. If we know it, so does NM. Can you talk?*

"It's too late," Valerie typed feverishly. "His name is Ethan Karajan. He was taken at gunpoint an hour ago by professionals. Flown somewhere inland. Now what?"

The page took a while to react. She cried again at the thought that they had signed off. But eventually another question appeared.

Did you see who took him?

"I thought I had, but 2 groups were involved. One snatched Ethan from the other." Like dogs fighting over food, she thought. The act of putting it in words underscored its hopelessness.

The next message made her forget to breathe.

Any Asians?

Valerie fought the urge to see if anyone was watching over her shoulder. "How do you know? Who are you?"

Another pause, which felt like ages. She inhaled the lungful she had skipped.

Because that's what I meant to warn about. I am male, younger than Ethan, Prometheus carrier. Are you related? A carrier, too?

A carrier—was this a disease?

"Only Alpha," she typed.

And Ethan?

"Only Beta." She couldn't believe what she was writing, let alone that someone understood it, but she rested her elbows on the table and her cheeks on her knuckles in anticipation.

Did he carry a phone?

Of course: they wanted his location.

Valerie leaned back, her mind racing. Twice she made for the keyboard, only to pull back. The third time she spelled out her answer: "How can I take you on faith?" She paused before hitting send, and added: "Can I ask you something, as assurance that you are what you profess to be?"

Like a Turing test?

"Something like that."

Go ahead.

Valerie had never felt ill at ease with her abilities, much less been disgusted by her hands, which now felt cold and sweaty. How to reveal an impostor? Technical questions wouldn't help, nor would knowledge of known paradigms reveal anything. She wanted something hard enough to stump anyone, yet broad enough to elicit an unrehearsed answer.

Right…

"With as little jargon as possible, explain free will (or explain it away)."

Five seconds went by. Valerie placed her hands on her knees and squeezed tightly, bouncing her legs on the balls of her feet. Maybe she had assumed too much about her interlocutor.

Ten seconds. She felt her hopes crumble.

Slowly, in one-sentence bursts, the reply appeared.

The term was coined before humans could understand it. Freedom refers not to the absence of obstacles, nor does will refer to desire. It describes a choice that is neither random nor entirely determined by the state of the world (the chooser included) prior to the choice itself. Long after the notion was intuited, humans lacked the ability to understand how causal chains can be formed that are not continuations of existing chains. The missing concept, and the only jargon I will use, is causal-order superposition. If A is the state of the world (including its agents) before a choice C, and D is the state after it, then causal-order superposition allows the existence of agents such that C begins a new causal chain not fully determined by A, yet nonrandom. This happens when C is an irreducible event, meaning it cannot be decomposed into a more granular sequence of events that are ordered in time, like A and D can be. The choice C involves a set (not a sequence) of non-ordered interactions whose effect is different from what any sequential decomposition of C would produce, even allowing for feedback.

Valerie's agitation decreased. If this was the real thing, then there was a chance of seeing Ethan alive again.

"All right," she typed, "you have my attention. Yes, he did carry a phone, now probably soaked in saltwater. What else do you need?"

***

Connor understood the depth of his disgrace when Wade announced that his running mate would be Graciano Yglesias. That was the ticket for which Connor had worked so hard. So when Yglesias began handing other people new tasks that should have rightly fallen on Connor to perform, it became clear that he had been sidelined. Colleagues no longer shared gossip; messages to him dwindled. His one consolation was that Garfield had been humiliated as much, if not more, than he had.

You don't know the first thing about Garfield.

Summer's words rang in his head like a bad song that defies forgetting. The truth was he also hadn't known the first thing about Summer. Yglesias had never told him how he had learned about the existence of a mole in their team, nor how he had come to suspect her. Several times Connor had taken out Summer's note with the phone number, just to stare at it. He looked it up online without success, drawing a blank even from those websites that promised, in exchange for a fee, to reveal the number's owner. He wondered what he might say if he called and she picked up. Would he let his true feelings ring out—*how could you!*—or would he just tell her to go to hell?

He didn't dare to call from inside his current apartment, for if Yglesias thought Summer's house was bugged, then didn't it stand to reason that a party-owned loft surely was? Calls from campaign headquarters, however, were routed through encrypted wi-fi, as an excuse to block external devices. Perhaps Wade's paranoia could be turned to his advantage.

Early one morning from a bathroom stall, he dialed the number. The result was disappointing: a recorded voice (not Summer's) said his call had been noted, and the line went dead.

He flushed the note down the toilet.

***

At first, as anticipated, Julian got no further than the Director's assistant, who politely took his message. More of a shock was for the call to be returned within the hour. It was, Julian felt certain, a sign that he had filled his father's shoes and become an icon in his own right. Clarence Leigh wasn't just willing to help but offered to send an officer over immediately. And not just a badge-wielding punk, either, but a member of the Bureau's senior staff: a man called Eric Ressler, who arrived that very afternoon and listened with grave interest to Julian's account of his childhood and of Valerie's, of his misgivings regarding Ethan's sudden reappearance, and of the pair's trips to France and Mexico. Would Julian mind if they called his sister on the spot? He didn't mind at all, so they made the call and, having spoken with Valerie, Ressler devoted even more time to her security escort Iannis.

Dour but not uncivil, he reminded Julian less of a nosy detective ascertaining guilt than of a battle-scarred platoon commander planning a strike. So impressed was he with the proceedings, that he made a note to make a sizeable donation to the FBI as soon as time allowed. Assuming, of course, that things panned out favorably.

DISCORD

Politics, as a practice, whatever its professions, had always been the systematic organization of hatreds.
—HENRY ADAMS, *The Life of Henry Adams*

Connor emerged from the mall and walked among the parked cars, picking out fries from a paper bag. Noah had followed him to the food court as usual, but now he was nowhere in sight. As Connor began wondering why, a voice said 'FBI' and he was strong-armed into a limo with tinted windows.

One man sat next to him, facing rear, while the second shut the door behind them, leaned against the car and helped himself to Connor's lunch.

A third, seated across, held up a badge. "Eric Ressler, National Security Branch. This is Special Agent Balderas."

The man called Balderas was already rummaging through Connor's pockets, and produced a wallet and phone, which he handed over to Ressler while running a wand over Connor's body. "He's clean," he pronounced.

"You have the wrong person. My name is Connor Dashaw. I work for Senator Wade."

"We know," said Ressler. "What's the password?" he asked.

"Beg your pardon?"

"Your password," replied the officer, holding Connor's phone up for him to see.

In no position to negotiate, Connor spelled out the six digits of his birth date, and Ressler began browsing.

"Maybe I can help, if you tell me what—"

Ressler motioned for silence and kept scrolling. When he found what he was after, he showed it to Balderas, who now spoke.

"We can, as they say, do this the easy way; or we can do it the hard way." His expression was wooden. Connor guessed that Balderas had few friends and little wish to make new ones. "The easy way is for you to tell us what you've done with Karajan. The hard way, well, you wouldn't like it."

Connor began panicking. "I—I don't understand."

Ressler showed him the picture of Karajan outside his San Francisco address, and Connor felt the world crashing down on him.

"Oh," he said, "I took that a few weeks back. I don't know him, I swear. It's just that he—I heard that—"

"Heard what?" asked Balderas.

"That he was a terrorist." Connor became suddenly defiant. "Why don't you ask Summer?"

Balderas grabbed him savagely by the jacket. "Is this your idea of a joke?" he sputtered. Connor was suddenly a frightened doe. "Answer me, you fucking prick!" Balderas raged, shaking him. Connor shut his eyes, expecting a rain of blows.

Ressler, good cop, reached out for his colleague's shoulder. "Emilio," he said, "he doesn't know."

Balderas looked sideways at Ressler, then dubiously back at Connor. "He's the one who called," explained Ressler, holding the phone up for Balderas to see the call log.

Reluctantly, Balderas released his grip, pulled out his own phone, looked up something hurriedly and held the device up to Connor's face. "That's what was left of her when we found her. There was cement in her lungs."

Connor took one look and jerked his head aside. He put his mouth in the crook of his elbow and heaved; a trace of bile trickled down his sleeve, followed by a half-chewed potato wedge.

Several shallow breaths later, having wiped his mouth on the same sleeve, he protested: "It—it can't be. There's a mistake. It can't be her."

"Want to see the rest?" volunteered Balderas.

Connor shook his head and let his face fall into his hands. "Oh, God!" he moaned softly.

"Now," said Ressler, businesslike, "about Karajan."

Connor looked spent. "Evander Garfield," he said. "I overheard him mention Karajan. I always suspected Garfield, but Wade would have never believed me. That's why I told Summer."

"With whom was Garfield speaking?"

"I don't know. I was in another office and couldn't see him."

The partition behind Connor slid down. Next to the driver (another thick neck with a crew-cut and shades) he was surprised to see a debonair young man wearing an expensive blazer, a red-on-white striped shirt, cufflinks, a button-down collar, and, yes, a pair of shades, but unlike the pilot sunglasses worn by the driver, these green-tinted tortoiseshells belonged in a Sunday brunch in the Hamptons.

Connor sensed the barge-in was unwelcome, but allowed. He half expected a handshake, but the man only brought his hand to rest on the leather divider. The face, vaguely familiar, was impossible to place out of context.

"The man you helped to abduct," said the aristocrat, "is engaged to my sister and has never hurt anyone in his life."

"I believe," he went on, "that you didn't plan any of this; that things have gone sideways, as it were; that you wish it would all go away. Am I right?"

Unsure, Connor thought it best to nod.

"Well, perhaps you *can* make it go away. If you don't know Ethan's whereabouts, then lead us to those who do. If you've done nothing wrong, then we will go after those responsible and back to our lives."

"That's easy for you to say," Connor demurred. "You don't have a care in the world."

The man looked at Ressler with an acid smile. "See? It's about money."

Connor shook his head. "It's not," he protested weakly.

"And yet you brought it up," said the man, "so it stands between us. What if it didn't? What would it take, to use your expression, for you to have not a care in the world, and be a trifle more sensible?"

Connor thought of an absurd figure. "I don't know, ten million."

He assumed they would laugh, but the young man nodded. "If you had ten million, would your actions be less clouded by emotions?"

"Who says they're clouded? Maybe you're the ones who have it all wrong."

"Fuck you," said Balderas.

The aristocrat raised a calming hand. "Fair enough; let me rephrase the question. If you had ten million, do you think your actions would be, um, no more misguided than mine?"

Connor shrugged, nervously. "Money corrupts."

"Come, come, we both know that's a rehearsed answer." A hand reached inside the blazer. "But let's find out. May I have the routing number for your bank account?"

Connor looked warily at Ressler, which he perceived to be the most senior of the group. "If this is a trick, it won't work."

"No trick," the patrician persisted, "merely an attempt to shake your deep-seated convictions. Account number, please."

Connor's mind raced. If they were feds, then why not follow due process? Why hold him in a car instead of taking him downtown? Maybe they didn't have as strong a case as they claimed. But if they were gangsters, then he was as good as dead anyway. He tried to stall again. "How do I know this isn't a sham, to make me talk?"

This time the young man did laugh. "Well, in case you haven't noticed, I *am* trying to make you talk. But the money's real, and if what you said is true—if this, um, Garfield is the one behind it—then you have nothing to worry about, right?" The patrician turned to Ressler, who assented with the barest trace of a nod.

Connor struggled fiercely with himself. "And you will let me go?" he asked.

"That depends," said Ressler, "on whether you tell us what you know instead of dodging the question."

Where was the catch? If he took a bribe, he might be accused of something—anything—with the money as evidence. For years he had shared an account with Stacey, opened to help with his tuition—the same that he had later used to pay for her rehab. He said the number aloud, feeling a pang of guilt at embroiling her, of all people.

"Done," said the man, showing him a deposit notification. "Fifteen million, which leaves you ten after taxes, because if you don't declare this, our friends here will pay you another visit, in far less civil terms than today's."

"I pray," grumbled Balderas, "that you know what you're doing."

"Of course I do," said the other, still addressing Connor. "You see, here's how this works: if you lie to us, report this conversation to anyone, or do anything to get Ethan hurt, I will hand over to the FBI, not fifteen, but a hundred million to make sure that, Wade president or not, you never see the outside of a prison cell again. Are we clear?"

If it hadn't been, the catch was now plain to Connor.

"Done with your lunch?" asked Noah. "Geez, you look like shit."

"Where were you?" demanded Connor with unusual impatience, holding a crumpled bag like an unwelcome gift than had been foisted upon him.

"None of your business," said the other, looking again at the number on his phone, from the girl who had flirted with him for the last twenty minutes. They drove in silence to the office and, for once, Connor was grateful for the sullenness of his escort.

Along the way their phones began chirping, and by the time they arrived the last thing on anyone's mind was Noah's whereabouts or Connor's appearance. To be fair, nobody looked quite the same after the bombshell hit the news that Evander Garfield had just been arrested.

More information surfaced, bite-sized, and Connor's blood pressure rose and fell several times in a matter of minutes.

The charge was murder.

No, it was terrorism.

But there *was* murder involved, of which Garfield was held as accessory.

It had all taken place years earlier.

Whose murder? Connor was brave enough to ask.

A Lebanese head of state, someone explained.

Oh, said Connor, as if this made the act a misdemeanor.

No, of course, he clarified, that's awful. How like the government to pull such a stunt at this juncture.

That's brinksmanship for you, he reflected, chiding himself on the truth of Summer's macabre wisdom.

His feverish mind eventually turned to the bank account and his parvenu wealth. The deposit in question, which he still believed would disappear at any moment, listed one Julian Taylor as the source.

A full minute passed before the name, the face, the memory of the diners at Elixir—the supermodel, the snotty Asian girl and their male companions—all coalesced into an image of betrayal that tore through his self-respect like a chainsaw.

***

SHOW HOST: Welcome back to *The Political Scene*. We will now take questions from the audience. Christine, from Omaha, asks how a candidate can remain on the ballot with a terrorist as campaign manager. Well, Christine, let's remember that accusations are no proof of guilt. But [turning to his left] I will defer to someone in a better position to reply.

WADE SUPPORTER: Garfield is the one being investigated, not Wade. And guilt by association is what the current administration is betting on, since they stand to lose the election and are grasping at straws. This ridiculous side-show aims to distract the electorate from the wrongs being done to our nation. How do we know that Karam wasn't murdered by the Lebanese after he flew home? He was under secret service protection in D.C. If they did a poor job, then why not question former President Garcia?

SHOW HOST: Thank you. We now have Travis, from Fort Lauderdale, who is concerned about all the ships arriving in port every day, and asks if we should trust Homeland Security's assurance that the Shanghai videos are doctored? I believe he refers to the videos showing Westerners collapsing while the Asians around them are unaffected. How [turning to his right] should we respond to such concerns?

WADE DETRACTOR: Of course the videos are fake. Have any flights from Asia been suspended? No. Has Chinatown been quarantined, in San Francisco or New York? No. Has anyone stopped eating noodles or lychees imported from Hong Kong? No. The only video we can trust is the one showing a taxi driver in Memphis—a third-generation Vietnamese—rescued from angry mob by the police. Now *that* is outrageous; not the fake videos on Wade's media.

WADE SUPPORTER [interrupting]: Anything can be faked, you know—videos, faces, voices.

SHOW HOST: No speaking out of turn, please.

WADE DETRACTOR [resuming]: It is irresponsible to support a man with nothing to offer the world but belligerence when one of his closest confidants is not only suspected, but has been *formally charged* with terrorism. Yes, I'm as angry about my paycheck compared to that of certain individuals. And yes, I do believe there are things rotten in the system, but I don't go around blaming foreign genes when those who wish me harm are just as made-in-America as I am.

HOST: Okay, let's hold that thought, because it leads naturally to our next question. Roberto, from Houston, asks how to explain the countrywide rift we are facing. Perhaps [turning to someone on remote split-screen] our Washington expert can shed some light.

POLITICAL ANALYST: Crooked politicians have always existed, but we were long immune to them because we relied on institutions, whether regulatory or academic, for facts. Then along came what was meant to be the layman's liberator—the internet—and it instead became the layman's curse. Because by making everyone's words equally easy to share, trust in institutions declined and an ancient human instinct took over: the evolutionary-driven desire to be a part of something, which makes people persistently favor groups they've been assigned to, even when the only link between group members is membership itself.

WADE SUPPORTER [dismissively]: People know when lies are peddled as truths.

***

In the meantime, Connor waited for the other shoe to drop, because even in his panic on the day of the interrogation, he had managed to withhold one key fact from the FBI, namely that Yglesias had received the news of Al Faisal's message with no hint of surprise. So, if Yglesias was incriminated, which looked increasingly likely, it would spell the end of the campaign and of Wade's reputation.

Perhaps, too, it would ruin what was left of Connor's life. It was as if his wishes had been granted by an evil genie, coming to pass in a sick, scrambled way. Having envisaged pain defeated by shrewdness, leading to glory and thence to love, Connor had instead witnessed love defeated by shrewdness, leading to abashment and thence to pain. His self-involvement prevented him from seeing that the major scandal unfolding before everyone's eyes had drawn attention away from his minor dishonor. Yglesias began giving work to him again, and even Wade deigned to greet Connor aloud when their paths crossed one morning.

All of which didn't make the wait any less excruciating, because secrets in the hands of some people are like liquor in the hands of a drunkard, or casino tokens in the hands of a gambler. Possessed of a major piece of information, he was caught between a growing itch to unburden himself of it and the inability to confide in a soul. He drew George Valenzuela aside. "All I need," he urged, "is five minutes with Wade. Can you get me five minutes?"

"Uh, this isn't a good time. Why don't you go through Yglesias?"

"I don't trust Yglesias. Not with this."

"Aw, man…" Valenzuela wasn't buying it.

"Look," he insisted, "just tell him I have some info—something that will grab Reynolds by the balls and protect Yglesias at the same time. Can you do that?"

Valenzuela eyed him dubiously. "Why does Yglesias need protection?"

"Just tell him, okay?"

AGENCY

> Too many hypotheses and systems of thought in philosophy and elsewhere are based on the bizarre view that we, at this point in history, are in possession of the basic forms of understanding needed to comprehend absolutely anything.
>
> —THOMAS NAGEL, *The View from Nowhere*

Ten miles north of Cabo San Lucas, along the peninsula's western rim, an unpaved road led from the coast into the arid hills, then partway up the incline of a shallow gully. Yellow shrubs, organ-pipe cacti, dwarf mesquite trees and lechuguilla plants provided scant shelter to lizards, rodents, birds, and the odd scorpion or two. In a dusty glade at the end of the road stood the safe house, plain and somber, built of cinder blocks and adobe tiles. Its front door was shut, but the overcast sky made the heat bearable. An open window and its rear-facing twin provided natural ventilation. The warm breeze, bearing a hint of rain, had all but effaced the tire tracks that ran up to the building. Squatting beside a boundary wall, an old dog took a difficult crap.

Two men, automatic weapons in hand, stood guard outside the house. Wearing loose, long-sleeved cotton shirts, they were evidently used to standing for hours under the sun. Their tanned skin, taut muscles, and faces darkened by well-groomed stubbles would have made a casual observer take them for minions of some local drug baron—had their beards been less thick and their eyes more indigenous. The dog would have noted that they smelled more of lamb and za'atar than of beans and tortillas.

Three hundred yards away, Larissa Kane adjusted her long-range viewer. "Can you take them?" she asked.

"That's not the issue," replied the sniper. "But even if we nail them both at once, the open window will alert anyone inside."

"Well," said Kane, reaching into a rucksack, "bioweapons may well be a cottage industry these days, but we still have the upper hand in one field." She pulled out a metal case and, releasing the catches, revealed several dragonflies, their wings folded, embedded in foam rubber. She held one up for all to see. "Good old high-tech," she pronounced.

She placed the metal insect on the ground and fished out a control pad and a visor. The task-force around her (five men in gear, including two snipers) surveyed the proceedings with interest. "Looks too small to carry much wallop," observed one dubiously.

"It's a dazzler," said Kane. "We don't want the hostage hurt. Is the audio on?" They all confirmed. "All right, eyes on your targets." The insect came to life and buzzed over their heads.

Kane viewed the scene from behind the dragonfly's eyes as it hovered, circled, and took off in the direction of the house. "On my word," she said, and the snipers touched their triggers.

One target presently turned his head in the direction of the open window, as if following a sound.

"Fire!"

Sharp reports were followed by a flash from within the house. The snipers reloaded, but it proved unnecessary: the sentries had fallen like rag dolls.

"Two down," cried someone.

"Move in," instructed Kane behind her visor. "They're blind as bats."

The snipers switched to assault weapons and the men trotted off while Kane continued: "I will talk you—shit! I've been shot down." She tore the visor off and fetched another drone, which overtook the crew as they neared the house.

***

One consequence of Garfield's arrest, and of the shift in team priorities, was that rules and procedures were somewhat relaxed. Noah still babysat Connor but was less punctilious about it; the car that parked at night outside his apartment was now missing.

But this new state of affairs worried him in a different way. He couldn't get rid of the image of Summer's corpse, and it had become increasingly clear to him that if anyone in Garfield's circle had murdered her, it had to be Noah. Because while he was convinced that Garfield was a devil to the core, Connor couldn't picture that man's thin frame handling his own dirty work. Noah, on the other hand, had strength enough to strangle anyone barehanded, and was always packing: Connor had seen the holster when Noah's jacket flapped open. He had a recurring nightmare where Yglesias discovered Taylor's bribe and Noah took Connor to the secret parking floor to shoot him in the head.

He was in no danger as long as they were in public, but the evening rides back to the apartment suddenly took on a sinister tint. Connor made it a point not to walk in front of Noah and, now that September had brought cooler weather, he took to wearing the same baggy jacket every day, leaving it casually lying around in the car for Noah's groping hands to become used to its presence; comfortable with its harmlessness.

And one night, at an hour when Connor felt sure that Stacey would be out, he called a cab and went to his old place. There, from a safe in his closet, he pulled out a revolver, not unlike his father had done years before, bullets snug inside the barrel, unaware that they had a fated rendezvous with flesh.

The gun fit easily in his jacket, which showed no sign of the added weight. Before leaving the apartment he left a note under Stacey's pillow: *The money is legal. Don't touch it. Love, Connor.*

The next day he was called upstairs. "Man," said Valenzuela, "whatever you claim to have, Wade wants you here right away."

***

Headache. Nausea. Ethan opened his eyes. The room around him was artificially lit. Straight ahead he could see the blackness of night through an open window. He lay on his back on a soft surface. A bed? More of a cot. His right arm felt numb and cramped. He moved it and heard the rattle of the chain that cuffed his wrist to the bedrail. He tried to prop himself up and his stomach churned. Rolling onto his shackled side until his face protruded from the mattress into space, he breathed deeply and the nausea subsided. He heard unintelligible voices of several men, speaking with the same inflections that Nadia's killer had used. One of them approached; Ethan tried to look up at the man's face, and passed out again.

Daylight. The sickness was gone, but his head still throbbed. His wrist, now free, was sore where the handcuff had bitten into his flesh. He tried to nurse it but found that they had merely switched the cuff to his left arm, this time wrapping the wrist in cloth under the metal band.

His free arm had a bruise in the crook of the elbow. Two puncture marks showed that someone had clumsily drawn blood and missed the vein the first time.

There were voices again; Ethan turned his head to the sound. Two men wearing crocheted taquiyahs sat at a table, studying a laptop screen. Hearing the chain rattle, the leader glanced over his shoulder at Ethan and typed something. The other man gazed at him in turn; they seemed to be reporting on his condition. More words were exchanged.

The leader stood up and walked over, speaking. Ethan stared at him mutely. The man phrased a question, its meaning lost on Ethan. Then he uttered a long string of words. This tirade was directed at his associate, who opened his eyes wide, then laughed.

The leader gestured at Ethan, as if proving a point, and spoke dismissively. Ethan caught the gist of the expression and shook his head. "No," he said, "I have no idea what you're saying."

The man looked at him, bemused. In broken English he addressed Ethan: "I said we slit your throat and you … no reaction. You not speak Arabic?"

"Wh—why should I?" Ethan asked, startled by the raspiness of his own voice.

The man hissed a chuckle, glanced at his accomplice and shook his head.

"You thirsty?" he asked Ethan. He nodded. His throat felt like dust, but his head was clearing up.

They gave him some water.

"They say we kill you," said the man, "if you are not Hassan."

That name again. Who were these men? Where were the Asians?

"Which Hassan?" he asked.

"*You* don't know?" The men looked at each other and Ethan felt a new stab of the strangeness.

"I—" he began, eager to deny any knowledge, not only of Hassan but of the whole situation. The thought, however, had the effect of making the strangeness intensify, and he struggled for words to make it go away.

The man picked up a large knife and approached him. "Are you, or not—Hassan?" It was an ultimatum.

The answer burst out from Ethan. "I am Hassan."

The man pondered the reply. *Yes*, he appeared to say with his eyes, we knew that from your face. But he still wasn't satisfied. "How," he challenged, formulating his next question with the knife, "do we know this is truth?"

Ethan felt he was being dragged somewhere he didn't belong, forced to stick to an imposture. How to keep lying, now that he'd begun? Countless answers ran through his mind. Only one of them promised to chase the strangeness away.

"I can prove it. There's a website, but you have to log in."

The men glanced at each other and held a quick debate. The leader eventually put the knife away and picked up a rifle, which he kept aimed at Ethan, allowing the other to unchain him from the cot and cuff his wrists before him. He was led to the table where the laptop lay open and the leader stood behind as Ethan sat on the chair. "Go," he said, prodding him with the muzzle.

Ethan reached awkwardly for the keyboard and slowly typed highbetascore.com/valerietaylor123 into the browser window, feeling the strangeness decrease with every keystroke.

The page displayed the word *Downloading*, and a progress tracker. Seconds went by and the leader shifted impatiently. Then an abstract holograph projected from the screen, and they were all surprised to see it begin to morph, to the sound of soft but arresting music.

It was unlike anything he had ever heard, but drew him in at once. With no recognizable style, the sound was strangely suggestive, like a long-forgotten melody heard again in midlife, reviving the intensity of youth, blending mysterious tunes that were impossible to hum but which carried the soul along, drug-like, making the listener feel like the hero of a story, when planets align and power shines through in a soothing way. The image came to Ethan of a cat purring.

As for the men beside him, those wretches whose lives had been stripped of melody by religious stricture, who believed themselves to be mountain lions but lived more like mountain goats, for them it was like for a young man watching a woman disrobe. The music swallowed them whole, as the morphing shape whispered in a tongue only Ethan could understand. It folded upon itself time and again, like a Shepard tone grown into a symphony, suggesting that the strangeness—that hideous feeling that always preceded disaster—held a hidden, benign purpose.

The shape twisted, gyrating in a space that wasn't there, beckoning Ethan to follow. He tried to resist it and the vertigo quickly assailed him. But it was seductive this time, inviting him to relax, teaching him to feel his way inside his mind, to explore the sensation that had always terrified him, to peer into…

Future states of mind?

They were many, far more than he could glimpse at once; one for every course of action open to him. Not all equally at hand, some were more distant than others; murkier, not visually but in a sense that was almost tactile. Clear scenarios branched out into hazier ones, which faded further into mental fog. The bifurcations were always of two flavors: enticing or repellent. The ocean of options became an unfolding map, and he slowly understood that the shape and the sound were but crutches; that the branching future was his own, the visions his choices, the flavors what he would experience in each case.

To wait a bit more seemed enticing; to stand up and run felt repellent. To speak out was bad. To let the music play its course was good. To let things happen, good; to force their hand, bad; to observe, bad; to listen, good. This last option now became clearer. Startling sounds were good. Looking at the source was bad. Shutting his eyes was good. Other options, all other branches: bad, bad, bad…

The music was interrupted by a buzz behind them: a sound like a hummingbird. Ethan drew in a breath and felt the urge to turn around, but the strangeness disallowed it. Shut eyes tight!

Brightness lit the inside of his eyelids like a camera flash.

His captors cried out in pain. In a reflex gesture, Ethan also brought his hands up, but the flash was gone, leaving only a ghostly trace in his retina. The music had stopped and so had the strangeness.

He went ahead and looked. One man moaned, hands pressed tight to his eyes. The other, in helpless fury, turned in the direction of the buzzing and fired his weapon blindly at the sound. His aim was true and the buzzing stopped.

Something clattered on the ground as Ethan's eyes fell on the open window—not the one through which the drone had flown, but the one beyond the table. He reached it in two strides and leapt through, head first.

He took a tumble on the dirt outside, rolling over unhurt. The first thing he saw was a yellow dog, its leg raised in the act of scratching. Ethan didn't see it as the people-chasing sort, so he scrambled to his feet and dashed into the shrubs, leaving the compound as fast as a handcuffed man can run.

A dirt path sloped down towards the coast. It was an obvious escape route, so he instead turned uphill and away from the trail. He reached a large outcrop and scurried around it, taking cover under an overhang, which was not far from the house but providing enough shelter to keep him invisible from the air. He heard distant shouts as his captors were nabbed—by whom or on whose orders he had no idea. As far as he knew it might be the Asians again, so he stayed put.

Three hours he stayed in the brush, attentive. He once heard the buzz of another drone, which drove him to flatten his shape against the rock to avoid being spotted. Then silence.

Towards dusk he ventured out.

Moving further away from the house, he carefully picked his way down the hillside. As darkness descended he crossed the lower portion of the dirt path and again stood still, listening. Only crickets could be heard. He avoided the path and trudged on.

By moonlight he reached a paved highway and began walking south, guided by road signs, which were regularly lit by headlights. Ethan tried to stay out of their glare, walking outside the shoulder, his back to traffic. He held his hands to his nape, fingers intertwined so that, from a distance, the handcuff strands looked like bracelets. His shirt dirty and untucked, he hoped to pass for someone that people would instinctively avoid. Only once, when red-and-blue strobes announced an approaching patrol, he headed back into the scrub, crouching low until the lights disappeared.

He walked all night along Mexico's Route 19, his throat parched, his body warmed by the steady exertion. He reached the city limits of Cabo San Lucas at four in the morning; the marina towards dawn. Iannis was the one who spotted his shape stumbling along the quay.

But Valerie reached him first. Sleepless, disheveled, and bursting with relief, she ran to catch Ethan as he collapsed on the pier.

DISABUSAL

> It is not true that suffering ennobles the character; happiness does that sometimes, but suffering, for the most part, makes men petty and vindictive.
>
> —W. SOMERSET MAUGHAM, *The Moon and Sixpence*

Everyone, at some point in their life, holds the most important conversation they will ever have: a marriage vow, an interview, an angry altercation, a business deal, a confession. How soon do they grasp the relevance of this exchange? As it unfolds? Years later? Never?

Goethe's Faust famously underestimated the weight of his chat with Mephistopheles, even when the pact was made explicit. How to judge, then, those who fall prey to implicit, unwritten terms?

Wade was dry and noncommittal when Connor walked in. That aside, the senator was his usual, inscrutable self.

"What is this I hear," he asked, "about Reynolds and Yglesias?"

"Well," Connor began, "I used to work at this restaurant."

He explained what he had recently uncovered, after sifting through hundreds of shareholder names, matching holdings to companies to people, to eventually hit on the incriminating link that he knew must exist.

While President Reynolds maintained that his business assets were held by a blind-trust company, the trustee was a man called Orson Haggart, who controlled 51% of an insurer called Segufarma, of which the biotech giant Taylor Labs held the remaining share. The financial deal and the trust setup, moreover, dated back eight years.

"So," Connor concluded, "Reynolds invested in Taylor Labs before taking office, when it was still a British firm. All his talk of protecting national interests is hogwash."

"Well," said Wade, stroking his chin. "That's a most interesting finding. If you are right, then we have Reynolds cornered. You've done a good job. Now, where does Yglesias fit into all of this?"

It's now or never, thought Connor.

"Has Yglesias spoken with you," he asked, "about whatever Garfield is being accused of?"

Connor had practiced this question, or variants of it, many times in front of the mirror, ever since becoming dimly aware that he might, after all, be working for a monster. Yglesias clearly had something to hide, for neither he nor Wade had spoken in Garfield's defense, except to attack his accusers. Nobody, not even the accused, had said 'wait a minute, you have it all backwards: I'm the aggrieved party here'.

What Connor wished to ascertain was the extent of Wade's involvement. He wanted a reaction: defensiveness, which would spell guilt; or a show of surprise—even if insincere—which would invite further probing. Wade might call for Yglesias and confront them both; or he might ring for Noah… He almost wished for the latter, if only for the certainty it would bring.

But where Connor's mirror practice spanned all of twenty minutes, the candidate's could be measured in years.

"Of course he has!" Wade replied. "His help is essential in this, as in everything. But," he declared, fixing Connor with a stare that pinned him like a fly to the wall, "you came here not for the sake of Yglesias, but to tell me something—something you think I don't know."

Where was the man's anger? Where was his fear? Connor saw neither. Wade had turned the tables on him, but there was still no sense of alarm, of indignation, of loss of nerve. It suddenly struck him that this was his first one-on-one with Wade; their first *tête-à-tête*.

"Did Yglesias," he asked, "mention the message that Garfield received, from a man called Al Faisal?"

Wade brushed the question aside with one of his own, not as someone changing the subject but as someone who knows the follow-up to be germane: "Why do you think I have such a sway on people?"

Because, thought Connor, you don't ask what people think: you know it already and spell it out for them.

"Because you give them hope," he said instead.

"No!" Wade thundered like the bass of an organ. "That's poppycock for the media to repeat. I connect with people because I know their feelings, because I know what drives them to do what they do; to wish what they wish. I even know why *you* came to me today, with doubt in your heart. I know that after that woman's betrayal you suspect double-crossing from anyone: from Yglesias, from Valenzuela, even from me. But look into your soul, Connor, for the answer. What led you to me? What made you join this movement in the first place?"

"The wrongs I have suffered," Connor said viscerally, and felt an abrupt pang of shame.

"Exactly," said Wade, and his endorsement washed away Connor's guilt. "I dare to say what the masses believe but lack the courage to articulate. I give voice to their hatred, to their disgust with success and meritocracy."

"So, Al Faisal—"

"Never speak that name again. Not here; not to anyone."

Wade picked up the phone and asked his assistant to find Yglesias. "What you uncovered," he continued, replacing the handset, "won't exonerate Garfield, but will get us an executive order to stall the inquiry until the election, by which time it will be too late."

"And, the truth…?"

"Connor my man, you have yet much to learn. Lying is universal; what counts is how lies are used. Great power accrues to those who don't fear lies but exploit them; because people may *ask* for the truth, but will only believe what makes sense to them. Evidence of their stupidity just makes them dig their heels in: shown that Galileo was right, they disbelieved Darwin; shown that evolution was true, they doubted climate change; and today, knowing they should have protected nature, they still question the damage it can wreak."

The phone on the desk rang. "Graciano," said Wade, "the time has come. We must release the scourge."

"And will this," Connor asked, pointing at the phone, "get us ahead of extrasomics?"

"Oh, yes," Wade gleamed impishly. "Their downfall shall be our gain."

***

From a hospital bed in Virginia, head propped up by a pillow, Vance Havelock gazed listlessly at the screen on the wall. Live broadcast showed a teeming crowd on the National Mall, gathered for Aamon Wade to speak from the steps of the Capitol. The stage was still empty, but the candidate would show up at any moment. Havelock muted the audio and looked out the window at the scattered clouds.

Earlier that day an aide had informed him of General Lasker's passing. The old man had died peacefully in his sleep, and Havelock realized that he envied his mentor, who had never lived to experience the sorry, bedridden condition that had greeted Havelock on awakening as a maimed officer whose career has been stymied by wounds received in a botched operation. He could feel nothing from his waist down and, to judge from the guarded replies of his surgeons, would never walk again. Soon enough he would be forced to sit through counseling, a prospect worse than the debriefing he had already undergone.

The sound of the opening door disturbed his self-pity.

Into the room walked a young woman, the sight of which made him feel that he had seen nothing but replicas of beauty all his life. A uniformed major, her long hair pinned up under a beret, shut the door and approached the foot of his bed. "Colonel Havelock?" she enquired.

Her fresh voice was a welcome change from the staff's formality. He could tell she wasn't used to rank, but the uniform suited her admirably. She had an offhanded, reassuring poise, and the way she looked at him, her gaze neither anxious nor threatening, took him back to a time when his daughter, now a grown woman, had picked up a sparrow chick that had fallen from its nest.

"You'd make one hell of a soldier," he said.

"I doubt that," she said. "But I fooled the officer at the desk."

"I bet you did," he grinned, finding it soothing after days of bitterness. "What brings you to a cripple's bedside, if not to finish him off?"

"A wish to help."

"Oh, it's too late for that." He pointed at the muted screen, where Wade had just appeared. "They adore him. And he will lead us all to hell."

The young woman picked up the remote from the bedcovers. "Do you mind?" she said, and turned the volume on.

"Extrasomics," Wade was saying, "have planted poisonous seeds in our midst. They think the seeds will sprout and infiltrate the government and our industry, like they have done elsewhere. Well, we have a surprise for them. The time has come to fight fire with fire!"

Cheering rose. Wade let it ripple through the crowd, then quelled it with a raised hand. "The poison they have sown is called the extrasome, which is present in their cells, not ours. And not just *any* extrasome, but one whose foreign signature is as clear as the iron-hot marks with which cattle were branded in the past. And that, my fellow Americans, will be their undoing. Word has reached me," he proclaimed, even in his delirium using words that cast blame away from his person, "that two days ago, a blessed scourge made its way into the water supply of the greatest cities of the world. And of this one, too," he added sardonically.

"Blessed, I say, for it is harmless to those of us whose cells are untarnished. Harmless even to those, God forgive them, who have chosen the path of extrasomy but whose genes were forged in this country."

The multitude was now silent, heeding his words with an interest that verged on disquiet.

"But to those whose cells hold the seeds of the enemy, whose extrasomes belong to that vain species that carries alien biology in its being—to them it shall be lethal, and even now is reaping what none but themselves have sown; so that never again shall they be able to harm our people!" His eyes bulged and his neck veins stood out in relief.

This was his moment of triumph; his apotheosis.

The media showed individuals looking at one other with doubt. Some examined their canteens with concern. A subdued hum arose, followed by a harsher murmur. Flanks of the throng fanned out, people peeling off in slow waves of selfish concern from what was no longer a loyal swarm but—belatedly, ashamedly—a disillusioned rabble. Then someone in the stands uttered his displeasure. Booing blended in with the muttering. Cameras captured uncomprehending faces on the podium; the smile of Yglesias frozen as he ineffectually tried to keep his composure.

"What!" cried Wade. "Where are you going? Boo yourselves." A few stalwart partisans cheered on. "Yes!" he urged, "that's the spirit. Let those motherfuckers leave if they want. Let them run to their children, if they are still alive," he taunted, leering diabolically. "Let them—"

But from Wade's team someone had stepped forth. Footage later revealed the gun, but live action is too quick for live commentary. Four shots rang out, followed by two more in a deeper timbre (thirty-eights and nine-millimeter, as it transpired). Cameras panned out, then zoomed in: an agent lay dead on the ground, as did Wade. Service members bore down on the man who had killed the assassin, whose body was in turn buried under a dogpile tackle.

"What the hell just happened?" asked Havelock, dumbfounded.

"Why! Wade just poured out his heart to the nation," said the young woman.

"Yes I can see that, but did you have anything to do with it?"

"How could I? I'm here with you."

"Someone you know, then?"

"You mean people with a certain genotype. That sounds rather like Wade's pigeonholing."

"So, it's true that you're running the show."

"Does it look like we're trying to run anything?"

Havelock pointed at the screen. "Tell me you didn't make him say what he said."

"People's thoughts can't be dictated. Ideas don't come in cartridges that can be inserted through the ear."

"Then what—how did—?"

"Have you ever been so drunk that you said things you shouldn't have?"

"Sure, but alcohol produces slurring, incoherence. Wade was lucid."

"Alcohol removes some inhibitions, but dream states are far more effective. Have you ever done something in a dream that you would never do while awake—no matter how drunk?"

"Is that what he did?"

"We just uncorked what was ready to gush forth, making sure that Wade didn't give a damn who was hearing."

Havelock looked at the havoc replaying on the screen. "There are easier ways to bring someone down."

"Oh, killing is easy. Any idiot can fly an airplane into a building, as was amply demonstrated back in 2001. To land a broken one safely, now that takes skill."

"Won't people die, then?"

"No. The virus is real, but it's been neutralized."

"And what about justice?"

"You mean retribution."

"Call it what you want."

"Comeuppance has nothing to do with this. If your hand is gangrenous and you can't prevent rot from spreading, you chop it off. Does that gladden you? No. Does it hurt? Probably more than the rot ever did."

"So," Havelock looked disappointed, "that was it?"

"Minutes ago you were disgusted by Wade's rising to power unchecked; now you seem underwhelmed that he won't."

"I'm not. I just thought it would take more to bring him down."

"What did you expect—a showdown?"

"No… Well, maybe."

"As a soldier, you know that stealth often works better than force."

"Yes, but this doesn't taste like victory. It lacks … oomph."

"Would it be more true to form if we'd shown up riding on dragons?"

This wrenched a grin from Havelock. "A friend once told me not to expect that. But it leaves too much unexplained."

"Like what?"

"The Prometheus module: what is it? Where is it? Those henchmen drew blood from Karajan, and he doesn't even *have* an auxiliary chromosome."

She smiled. "Won't the Chinese be disappointed…"

"So this," he indicated his legs, "was all for nothing?"

"Don't jump to conclusions. Genes are easy to spot in an extrasome."

"But that's where the Alpha is."

"The Alpha wasn't meant to be hidden. I hope your colleagues didn't throw that blood sample away."

"Why?"

"Because it has everything you need. The Beta is a microRNA strand, active only in neurons, sperm, and blood cells." From a pocket of her uniform, she pulled out a memory chip, which she placed on the dresser, beyond his reach. "This shows its location and spells it out fully. Add it to any fertilized egg with the Alpha, and you'll have the full module."

His tone became guarded again. "Why are you telling me this?"

"Because I know that I'm not endearing to you, not because of who I am but because of *what* I am. Some people, colonel, think the same of you, and for the same reason. But you embody what's best about this country: you do a thankless job and you do it well."

"That's flattering, honey, but if you've read my chart you know that henceforth I will be lucky to use the toilet without assistance. My hero days are over."

"The second reason for my visit," she said, "is this." She produced a loaded syringe and removed the protective cap.

"To put me down like a dog?"

Her head shook reprovingly. "And this chat we just had, when I could have slipped in while you were half-dead? But I'll do nothing without your permission." She pointed at his drip bottle with the needle. "May I?"

"Heck, it's not like I have much to lose."

Gray liquid coursed down the catheter hose. As she dropped the syringe in the hazardous-waste bin, he suddenly asked: "Is there an afterlife?"

She looked at him quizzically. "Where's that coming from?"

"Just answer me, if you can."

"In plain terms, the answer is no."

"And in terms … not so plain?"

"There was, and there will be."

"What kind of answer is that?"

"It has to do with time and with causality. The structure of time is non-orientable. Eternal life doesn't imply an infinite hereafter, just as it doesn't imply an infinite heretofore: life always happens for the first time."

"So, our sense of awareness—"

"Is like a drop in the ocean."

"A drop…" repeated Havelock, and dropped into the abyss.

***

He heard the distant sound of a siren, moving closer, stopping as if it had reached somewhere, maybe a hospital.

Havelock was suddenly awake.

The room was empty, the window dark, the TV off; the red digits on the nightstand clock said 9:00 pm.

He looked at the dresser. The surface was bare. He instinctively tried to get out of bed, and a wave of pain brought him crashing down on the mattress. Lying sideways, he groaned as blinding stabs traveled down his hip. Flexing the knee lessened the pain a bit. Cautiously, he let himself roll back on the bed until he was face up again. He then reached for the call button.

"Colonel!" exclaimed the resident, surprised. "How are you feeling?"

"It hurts," said Havelock between puffs, his eyes glistening with tears. The officer approached his side. "Where?"

"My hip—everything!"

"I'll spice up your cocktail—wait, did you do that?" He was pointing at Havelock's bent knee, a mound under the sheet. Havelock winced impatiently. "It gets worse if I stretch it. What can you give me?"

"Hold on." The resident grabbed his phone. "Dr. Carlyle," he said, "you'd better come up to Colonel Havelock's room. No sir, good news." Ending the call, he turned to the patient, grinning broadly.

Asshole, thought Havelock, before it struck him that the pain was cause for celebration.

***

"Maybe a nurse put it in a drawer," Havelock said. "How long was I out?"

"Uh, about two days. You had us worried." The surgeon held up a memory stick. "Is this what you want?"

"Yes." Havelock took his pad and plugged the chip in. He browsed through the contents while the physician kept pressing and probing his legs and abdomen.

"Major," Havelock said at length, "I am mailing you two files, and I need a favor. Shut the door first, will you?" The surgeon obliged, making a mental note that Havelock had addressed him by rank.

"Were you briefed about my case?" asked Havelock. "And I don't mean the injuries."

"It's strictly need-to-know."

"Well, there's no time for formalities; this place will be crawling with Pentagon staff very soon. I am sending you two classified files. The first, called Nerve, contains instructions for some sort of nano-bot involved in spinal regeneration. I need you to see if any are still in my bloodstream."

"What makes you think—?"

"I'll explain later; believe me it will be worth your while. The second, called Toxin, describes a virus antigen. I need it checked against blood samples from anyone admitted complaining about the doomsday bug that Wade was describing."

Of the third file, which he had already forwarded to his team in Nevada, Havelock said nothing. It contained blueprints of the Prometheus module, with workarounds to the issues that had stumped researchers everywhere.

PURPOSE

> Aristotle's great insight was that teleological explanations, in order to be complete, must terminate with something which is an end in itself.
>
> —JULIAN BAGGINI, *What's It All About?*

Heartstrings are more readily tugged by tragedy that strikes the very young, but misfortune may well be crueler on the elderly, for the character-forming lessons that disasters are said to hold are worthless to a life that is ending.

Three bolts were drawn in programmed sequence, and the penitentiary released a broken man into the Illinois winter. His possessions amounted to a phone with a small cash credit, a cheap pair of overalls, the sneakers and watch he had worn the day of his arrest, and a winter jacket a size too large for his frame. Like thousands of paroled convicts for as long as anyone could remember, Ron Dashaw shuffled out slowly, almost reluctantly, the atmosphere feeling colder on his skin than the prison yard's air.

Weeks earlier, the news of Connor's death had sent him straight to the infirmary and very nearly to the grave. Word spreads quickly in prison, and everyone from the warden down had expressed their sympathies. Fellow inmates not normally known for their civility had shown him every consideration. But, reminded of their own fears, they had also begun shunning him. His parole hearing, as crowded as Eleanor Rigby's burial, took place without incident, and Ron was placed under twenty-four-hour surveillance, the system's aim being merely to get him through his sentence alive and nourished enough to walk out of jail on two feet. That goal achieved, the doors shut him out with as little ceremony as they had once shut him in.

Two police cars were parked outside the perimeter. Behind them a delivery truck and a bright-red sedan sat by idly. No pedestrians were in sight. He knew that a bus stop was just down the road, but his parole officer's suggestions regarding work and shelter had been disheartening, so he zipped his jacket up to his chin and, thrusting his hands in its pockets, began to walk, squinting from the sun and the biting wind, trying to recall if he had been told this was Wednesday, or maybe Thursday.

The red car's door opened as he neared the curb and a stylish blonde emerged from the driver's seat, wearing shades and a navy-blue overcoat. She could be visiting some rich inmate, because the jailhouse was the only building in sight and she clearly was no officer's wife. Ron scanned her like a dying man might look at a fresh rose bouquet, out of the dim recollection of a once-pleasant sensation.

When it became apparent that their paths would cross, an unconscious awareness of his aspect made Ron veer away to avoid embarrassment. Vexingly, she stood in his way, forcing him to sidestep and mutter a clumsy apology.

"Dad," she said.

He stopped, unable to reconcile the voice with the speaker. Stacey removed her sunglasses. "They said you'd be discharged today." She attempted a smile, but the sight of him prevented it from blooming.

Ron blinked, straining his eyes.

"Sweetie?" he asked.

She took a step closer and Ron extended a hand, not daring to stroke her cheek but touching her coat lapel instead. He stole a glance at the parked car, then back at her outfit, with astonishment and concern.

"It's okay," she said. "I'll explain later. Let's go." And she guided him gently to the vehicle.

To say that Ron died a happy man would be a stretch. But he lived long enough to meet his grandchildren, and expired in conditions far more comfortable than he had ever foreseen. Neither he nor Stacey ever worked again.

***

This time they met over a glass of bourbon and a shared sense of guilt. Kane had led Hayes to Mexico, but Ressler had ordered him there, and each felt solely responsible. So they spoke of other things; of what everyone else was talking about.

"The Chinese sure made short work of Al Faisal," said Ressler.

Kane silently agreed. "What do you make," she asked, "of Reynolds's sudden elevation from villain to role model?"

Ressler snorted. "You know what? I've come to think that people love being duped. Hell, they don't even mind *knowing* they're being duped. But what they will never, ever forgive is being *told* they're being duped."

"I guess it's fortunate that both gunmen were Wade loyalists. And," she ventured, "I learned that you were familiar with Dashaw."

"I won't ask who said so," said Ressler. "But yes, we nearly booked him the day Garfield was arraigned. Turns out McGrath had already talked the Director out of it."

"A good call, some would say."

"That depends. Now the guy's being hailed as a savior."

"Ironic, how heroes are made."

Ressler shook his head. "Don't read too much into it. Dashaw was just a misguided kid; I doubt he was trying to make history."

"So, what happens now?"

"Garfield and Yglesias rot in jail. The guard has agreed to testify, avoiding the death penalty for O'Keefe's murder."

"And how does that sit with you?"

"Like hell. But the call wasn't mine to make."

***

"It's beautiful," agreed Ethan, as the hydroplane drifted across the glassy surface to the dock.

The lodge, built of brushbox hardwood and stone, sat on a cliff east of Darwin, not far from Kakadu National Park. Valerie showed him the deck, the rushing stream, the hot tubs, and the boat house. A four-person staff was out to welcome them.

Ethan had yet to get used to these little rites but was glad to find the table set, the cellar stocked, and the beds made. Still, he wondered at the size of the construction, which seemed excessive for its manifest purpose.

"How many bedrooms?" he asked.

"Just four," she replied."

"Then why—?" he began.

"That's my surprise," she said, leading him to the far end of the living room. She walked to a large paneled door and flung it open. Ethan followed her across to be greeted by a familiar scent, as the reason for the bulk behind the façade became apparent. The entire contents of Exebridge Hall's library had been shipped from England and lovingly arranged in the most beautiful suite of rooms that Ethan had ever seen.

"Now you'll never get me out of here," he said.

Later that evening, safe and snug beside him, Valerie studied his profile. "I'm glad the lab confirmed the results. I can't say I wasn't worried."

"Well, don't be. The feds said that since I'm not extrasomic, nobody will chase me."

"But they never explained why someone *did,* earlier."

"They said it was probably the NM website that triggered it."

"Yes, but your birthplace remains unknown, as does Nadia's background. It's not like them to close a case like that, without digging deeper."

"Did you really want more digging?"

Valerie shook her head. "I just wanted to be sure I wouldn't lose you."

"Lose me! Why?"

"Given all that was happening, I was afraid that you'd be claimed by—oh, I don't know—a higher destiny."

Ethan huffed dismissively.

"Why not? You could have turned out to be a prince or something."

"Yeah, right."

And they laughed together at the silliness of the idea.

Printed in the USA
CPSIA information can be obtained
at www.ICGtesting.com
LVHW050255110324
774083LV00001B/119

9 780578 446295